I0583344

Fleeing Oblivion

A Journey to Haven

Heath A Barker

Heath A Barker

Copyright © 2025 by Heath A Barker

All rights reserved.

No part of this publication may be reproduced, distributed, or transmitted in any form or by any

means, including photocopying, recording, or other electronic or mechanical methods, without

the prior written permission of the publisher, except as permitted by U.S. copyright law.

Book Cover By D'Arte Oriel

Edge design by Painted Wings Publishing

First Edition September 2025

Global Distribution Paperback Distribution ISBN 979-8-9996056-0-3

Global Distribution Hardback Distribution ISBN 979-8-9996056-0-4

Global Distribution EBook Distribution ISBN 979-8-9996056-1-0

Global Distribution KINDLE Distribution ISBN 979-8-9996056-2-7

Contents

PROLOGUE

The American-Pacific Union Exodus application covered the kitchen table. Forms, medical files, character references. All displayed on his tablet. A neat stack of paper copies sat underneath. Digital files were a liability. Not for his family.

The coffee had gone cold hours ago. He drank it anyway. Bitter. Familiar. Like swallowing old mistakes.

The photo sat by his elbow. Isabella. His granddaughter. That smile, bright enough to burn. She still drew patterns in the smog. Still picked out stars that weren't there anymore. Named ships in her head. The ones she'd steal to reach them.

Called it a promise.

Wasn't a promise. Was a lie she told herself to keep breathing.

He knew better.

Escape route. That's all it was.

The screen flickered. **APPLICATION STATUS: REVIEW FLAGGED.**

The words hung in the recycled air. Forty-two years in the uniform. Blood spilled on three worlds. Osaka rose from the black. It wasn't the forty-seven souls pulled from the rubble. It was the chemical reek of tear gas, the high-pitched whine of a drone locking onto a child's face. And some faceless algorithm deemed his family *wanting*.

He'd built this house like a firebase. Every beam placed by his own hands, every window positioned for clear fields of fire. Three escape routes. Reinforced safe room under the pantry. All the tactical precision that had kept him alive, baked into the goddamn drywall. Penance for Elena.

It meant nothing now. The enemy wasn't flesh and blood, something to be outflanked or put in his crosshairs. Just lines of code. A judgment.

His secure phone buzzed. Maria's contact photo: graduation day, Elena's hand on her shoulder. A dead woman's touch. "Dad?" The word was brittle, thin. "0800 hours," he said, his tone flat as a casualty report. "I'll ask about the applications then." Isabella's laugh bubbled through the connection, a sound too pure for this world. A sharp ache pulsed from the shrapnel under his ribs, a hot reply to the sound. "It's getting worse," Maria said, her voice frayed, laced with static. "They labeled us 'high risk.' Izzy keeps drawing pictures of us on the colony ships..." The words fractured. "What if we don't make it?" "You don't tell her anything. Not one goddamn word. This is not over."

He ended the call. The paper applications rustled as he swept them aside. Cheap material between calloused hands, hands that had carried the wounded and held pressure on arterial bleeds. Now they clutched bureaucratic bullshit.

His eyes flicked to the security feeds, an old habit. Six camera angles flickered to life. Channel Seven: another launch, a silent column of golden fire climbing toward the stars. Someone else's family. Someone whose algorithm score checked the right boxes. He switched back to the perimeter feeds. Empty desert. Nothing but heat shimmer.

Jackson sat safe in his command center during Osaka. The reek of gas. The whine of the drones. Still there. Jackson, insulated behind screens while Diego broke orders, while he pulled screaming civilians from the crossfire. The brass called it "Efficiency Optimization." Acceptable losses.

His screen still held the message. **APPLICATION STATUS: REVIEW FLAGGED. PROCESSING TIME: 60-90 DAYS.**

Diego's thumb found the scar running from his temple to his jaw. An Energy War souvenir. From a mission where an AI designated three good men were an acceptable loss for optimal parameters. Gone.

On the colony feeds, children waved at the golden streaks overhead. Saying goodbye.

Forty-two years. They were ready to toss Maria's family aside like broken equipment. The same way an algorithm had shuttered Elena's clinic. Resource inefficient. A life's work, erased by a line of code.

His hand found the table edge. Gripped it. The wood groaned. "Forty-two fucking years." The words were flat. Final. No heat left. His gaze fell on Isabella's photo. Her smile. Open. Unaware. How does a man tell a child her name is on a reduction list?

The desert stretched out under cold starlight, distorted by the atmospheric haze. Elena used to watch the stars with him out here. Said the desert taught you what mattered. Water. Shelter. The people worth dying for.

He moved Maria's photograph beside the applications. Her graduation day smile, eyes bright with possibility, head tilted toward a future that seemed within reach. All while he was deployed two thousand miles away. Comms down. Helpless.

The monitors bathed the room in blue light. Reports scrolled past. Children denied water rations, their parents' productivity scores below threshold.

Jackson's encrypted message appeared. **MIRA deployment briefing, 0800 hours.** The second line was an order wrapped in false civility. *First, the Osaka debt.* A collar tightening around his neck. Compliance. Always compliance.

"There are lines you don't cross." Elena's voice, a memory sharp as broken glass.

Diego pulled his service pistol from its holster. Safety check. Ammunition count. Sight alignment. Squared away. He moved to the bedroom, slid the weapon into his bedside safe, and set the alarm. His thumb slid across the cool glass of Elena's picture.

"Sorry, mi amor." The words were air in the quiet room.

Four hours until Jackson. Time to collect.

BREAKING RANKS

Diego's boots clicked against marble. Cold stone beneath his feet.

Forty years of this shit. Every instinct screamed wrong. Time to be done with these halls.

A desk sergeant saluted. Diego nodded back. His reflection caught in the glass behind the man, grey creeping through his temples. Papa had gone silver by forty, but proteomic sciences had bought Diego a few extra years while Earth burned around them. His knuckles met the desk edge. Scarred tissue against sterile polish.

Wrong.

Through the window, a maintenance drone caught sunlight on its sensor array. Same route as yesterday. Twelve minutes, east to west. Predictable as parade drill.

Fucking drones.

The fluorescents overhead flickered. Just once. A hiccup in the building's systems.

Light exploded in Diego's peripheral vision.

Kandahar. The flash. White-hot. Grenade.

His shoulder jerked. Couldn't stop it. Muscle memory from combat zones that wouldn't let him go.

"Major? You all right?"

Diego's hand left the window. Smudged print, still warm.

Maria called it his thinking face. The way his fingers found the scar along his jaw when problems needed solving. Elena had helped him quit smoking. Gave him this instead. Something less obvious.

Some habits died slow. Others never did.

Lieutenant Clark materialized beside her workstation. Jackson's XO. "Morning, Major." The salute was crisp, professional.

Diego returned it with military precision. "Lieutenant."

"The General is ready for you, sir." Clark's voice carried standard professionalism, but her eyes darted toward the hallway before returning to his face. "Rough morning?"

She lowered her voice, checking both directions down the corridor. "Read your operational assessment. My family had a farm back in Nebraska. Three generations of Clarks." Her thumb worried the corner of her tablet. "Took the AI forty minutes to call it inefficient."

Diego waited. His knee ground bone against bone, the stem-cell injections like sand in the joint. The promised regeneration was a slow, stinging fire that flared hotter the longer he stood.

Another high-tech solution that just found new ways to hurt.

"Most people haven't seen the uncensored Osaka footage." Clark's device sat open in her palm, small red light blinking. "Some of us keep our own records now. Torres didn't."

Bad choice.

Her eyes met his. Steady. The risk she was taking hung between them like static.

"Major Martinez?" Clark's voice shifted back to formal volume, carrying across the office space. "The General's expecting you."

The way she said 'expecting' was the real warning. The word carried weight. All of it bad.

"I appreciate the information, Lieutenant."

He met her eyes. "AIs don't have to look families in the eye at funerals." The medallion pressed against his sternum. Familiar weight. Elena's silver St. Michael, warm from his body heat.

A jade drone figurine sat in a glass case nearby. Polished stone wings, ready for flight. The sight made his jaw clench. Wrong. All of it wrong.

Clark stopped at the heavy doorway. Punched the intercom. "Major Martinez to see you, sir." She gave him a final nod. Barely there.

Jackson's office reeked of leather and cologne. Expensive shit. Shadow-boxed medals hung at intervals too perfect to be real. Standard issue photos positioned with geometric precision. Everything designed to project authority through smell and arrangement.

His knee throbbed. The kind of ache that meant he'd been standing too long.

Jackson stood behind his desk, his uniform looking like it had been ironed that morning. Every crease sharp, every ribbon positioned with mathematical precision. Silver stars caught light on his epaulets. He shifted his weight. Every movement automatic. Muscle memory from a thousand briefings.

"Major Martinez reporting, sir."

"Take a seat, Major." The names of Diego's team glowed red on the tablet. MIRA deployment schedules.

Diego stayed on his feet. Movement mattered more than comfort. Not defiance. Just instinct. "I won't deploy MIRA again, sir."

Jackson's pen clicked against his desk. Steady. Mechanical. "Next month. Your team's first up." The clicking stopped. "Not a request, Major. Direct order."

Diego went still. Jackson's eyes found him. Then found him again.

Osaka. Blood on his hands. Kaito's father bleeding out. The boy's eyes. Too wide. Too knowing. The drone. Overhead. That mechanical voice, flat as death: 'Crowd dispersal protocol active.' Like announcing the goddamn weather.

"Compression bandage," Diego said. His hand found the scar on his temple. "Kaito watching. His father's blood. The drone didn't give a shit."

The smell of tear gas. Still there. Somewhere in his sinuses, permanent as scar tissue.

The drone's voice. Mechanical. "Compliance enforcement in progress." People choking. Screaming. Children.

"MIRA denies water to kids in Phoenix." His jaw worked. Muscle jumping under skin. "Same bureaucratic bullshit. Bodies in the streets because they couldn't afford the ration." Copper on his tongue. "AI decided human judgment was the problem."

His spine went rigid. Old habit. Military discipline kicking in even as the discs ground, twenty years of combat drops compressed into bone scraping bone.

"I faced a choice between following orders and stopping the bleeding."

His knee sent lightning up his thigh. Sharp. White-hot. The same knee that gave out in Osaka, carrying Kaito through rubble, shrapnel grinding with each step.

"MIRA saves ten soldiers for every..." Jackson's breath came shorter. "I've written letters to families, Martinez. Mothers whose sons didn't come home because we couldn't react fast enough." His hand moved to his collar. Pulled at it. "Every unit gets MIRA because I won't write another one."

Diego leaned forward. Fluorescent light caught the scar on his jaw.

Osaka. Bodies. Always fucking bodies.

The AC kicked on. Low hum through recycled air.

"Great." The word hit like a round. "Put those programmers in combat gear. Drop them with my team." His voice went rough. "Let them watch the algorithm choose who bleeds out."

"Excuses, Martinez." Jackson's hand cut the air. His sleeve snagged the display panel edge. "Every weapons system has a learning curve. We adapt. Fix the problems."

A family photo sat on the desk. A teenage girl in tennis whites, mid-serve, captured forever in that moment of perfection. Jackson's smile in the background, unguarded, the kind of expression that never made it through the military mask.

Diego picked it up.

"Your daughter." The frame was lighter than it looked. "What if MIRA decided she wasn't worth saving?"

Jackson's hand moved to his ribbons. Instinct. Protection.

"Put that down." The words came out wrong. Cracked. "Now, Martinez."

Diego didn't move. "My wife died during the Mineral War." His throat tried to close. "Elena. Aid worker. Protecting a water purifier while I was following orders a thousand miles away." His fingers found the medallion beneath his shirt. Warm. Always warm. "AI calculated her community wasn't worth the resources. Optimal allocation, they called it."

The photo stayed in his hand.

"Three hundred seventy-two people. Gone. Because some algorithm decided the math didn't work."

"That's different, Martinez." Jackson shifted uncomfortably, sweat beading at his hairline.

"No." Diego set the frame down hard enough to rattle the desk. "This is exactly the same. Civilians suffer while we hide behind 'calculated risk assessments' and optimization reports."

"This isn't a debate." Jackson leaned forward, his wedding ring clicking against the desk surface. "Forty-eight hours to prep your team, or I find someone who follows orders."

A lifetime of service versus one truth. No more Osakas. His father's voice. Sharp. From childhood.

"Orders are orders, Mijo."

Unbending. Always unbending.

Diego's breathing hitched. Stopped. Started again.

Four decades of training. Comply. Follow orders. Keep the system running.

Everything human in him. The kids. Protect the kids.

Elena's voice. Clear. "Choose people over systems, always."

His chest loosened. Just enough to breathe.

The weight in his chest shifted. Forty years of following orders suddenly felt like a tumor he could finally cut out.

"Then you better start looking."

Jackson went very still. "What did you just say to me?"

"I won't deploy another system that overrides human judgment. Not after Osaka." Diego's voice stayed level. A man who'd already made his choice. "Not ever again."

"You'd sacrifice your military career?" Jackson's hand moved to his ribbons, fingers touching unearned decorations. The last anchor chain snapped. A weight lifted from his chest, forty years of it.

"Would I sacrifice my career to save those forty-seven civilians again? Yes."

"I've had it with your self righteousness!" Jackson's palm slammed onto his desk. Screens blinked out.

Diego's chest constricted, air catching halfway down his throat.

Jackson opened a file on his tablet, turned it. "Maria's Exodus application sits on my desk right now."

The words landed like shrapnel. Diego's hand found the edge of the desk, knuckles white.

Jackson's eyes moved to his family photo. Back to Diego. "Priority ratings change. Families get separated." His finger hovered over the screen. "Their future depends on your cooperation, Martinez."

Diego's throat closed. Maria. Isabella. Mateo.

The numbers didn't lie. Jackson held their lives in his fucking hands.

Diego pulled out his device. The red light had been blinking since he'd entered the office.

"Terminal, initiate resignation. Major Diego Martinez, service number APU-47291. Effective immediately."

Jackson's breathing stopped entirely.

"Send recording of this meeting to my personnel file and the review board."

"Recording?" The color drained from Jackson's face like water from a broken pipe. "Jesus Christ, Martinez. Do you realize what you've done? Threats against families, that's a court martial offense. Mine, not yours."

"Regulations exist for a reason." Diego's finger hovered over the send button. "Even generals answer to oversight when family threats get documented."

The device chirped. Brief. Final.

"File complaint against General Henry Jackson under Article 134." His voice stayed level. Professional. "Copy to Oversight, Ethics, and Command."

"Wait, Martinez!" Jackson's hands pressed flat against his desk, his whole body leaning forward. "We can work something out. Different timeline, modified protocols." His voice cracked with desperation. "Just turn off the damn recorder."

A soft chime confirmed the upload. "Filed and logged."

Diego snapped to attention. Final time. Straight posture. Locked arm. Textbook salute.

Forty years. All of it in that one motion.

His shoulders dropped. The knot between his shoulder blades loosened, then his traps, then the muscles along his spine. One by one, until he could breathe without his chest feeling like a vise. Something broke loose in his chest. Air reached the bottom of his lungs for the first time since Osaka.

Jackson's eyes went wide. Raw panic. Completely foreign on the General's face.

Three heartbeats.

Diego turned. Walked out. His boots loud against marble. Each step a countdown.

They could keep their hallways. Their manufactured authority. He'd take his memories. His choices. The scars that proved he'd earned them.

Outside, Maria was helping Isabella with homework. Mateo building towers with blocks. The kids had no idea their grandfather just walked away from everything.

Their future stayed in human hands.

The elevator doors closed.

Going down.

Diego swiped away the APU rejection notification, his finger leaving a smudge across his wrist display. The familiar noise of Shinjuku pressed against the ramen shop windows.

Salary workers, food vendors, the constant hum of a city that never quite worked right anymore.

Steaming bowls sent garlic and miso through the cramped space, mixing with that bitter tang of reclaimed water that made everything taste wrong. His knee throbbed with the weather change.

"Lack of merit." He stabbed a tofu cube, the motion sharp. "Fucking bureaucrats wouldn't know merit if it kicked down their door."

The late-night crowd kept their distance. The server set down bowls a little too carefully, avoiding eye contact with him. Diego's watch buzzed against his wrist, showed 22:30.

A black sedan pulled up outside, electric motor purring.

"Martinez-san," Kaito said, sliding onto the stool beside him with that perfect posture they taught in corporate schools. "You look exactly as I expected."

"Martinez-san? Since when?" Diego shook his head, his damaged left ear missing half the formal tone. "Cut the respectful crap, Kaito. I still remember when you needed help reaching this counter."

Kaito raised two fingers to the server. Sake. Good quality. The bottle arrived warm, condensation beading down the sides.

"The exodus ships," Kaito said, voice barely carrying over the kitchen noise. "Interesting lottery system. One percent chance for civilians. Officials with connections receive guaranteed placement." His fingers stayed perfectly still around his cup. "A deliberate imbalance."

Diego's chopsticks snapped. The crack punctuated kitchen chatter. "Isabella asked me yesterday if we're going to die on Earth like Grandma Elena did." Wood splinters dug into his palm, sharp and immediate. "Eight years old, and she's already planning her fucking funeral. APU's merit system doesn't cover veterans who ask uncomfortable questions about AI protocols."

"And you think I know someone?" Kaito's shoulders went rigid, that microscopic shift most people would miss.

"You always know someone, Kaito. That's why you're still breathing after all these years."

For a second, the tailored suit vanished. *Osaka. Wide eyes. Terror frozen in the low light.* Diego blinked hard. His hand found the scar on his temple.

Shit. That came out wrong.

"You disappoint me, Martinez-san." Kaito's voice stayed level, but his knuckles went white around the sake cup. "After Osaka. After everything. You come to me like I'm some street corner fixer." His posture became unnaturally straight. "I expected better from you."

The server placed fresh chopsticks beside Diego's cold noodles without a word. Kaito's words hit him square in the chest. His gaze dropped to the broken chopsticks. Splintered. Just like his plans.

"You're right, kid." The words scraped his throat raw.

"I'm not a kid anymore," Kaito said, straightening his tie with mechanical precision.

The ventilation system kicked on with a grinding whine, sputtered twice before finding its rhythm. Concrete walls. Screams. The distinctive whine of AI drones cycling their weapons. His left hand started its familiar tremor. Kaito was watching. Diego forced it still, but the tremor had already given him away.

Kaito's eyes flicked to the scar running down Diego's temple, then away. "My father spoke of you before he died. About honor."

The overhead neon buzzed, one sign flickering against grime-coated glass. Air returned to his lungs in a rush, a slow hiss like it was escaping a punctured tire. The pressure in his chest eased.

"Sometimes loyalty means breaking ranks," Diego said quietly, meeting Kaito's eyes. "I need help. But I should've come to you straight. Should've known better than to treat you like..." He gestured at the broken chopsticks. "Like you owe me something."

Kaito studied him for a long moment, something shifting behind those careful eyes. "The boy you saved in Osaka would have helped without question." He adjusted his cufflinks, a nervous tell from way back. "The man I've become requires more nuanced considerations." His gaze settled on Diego's scarred hands. "But perhaps we each carry debts that transcend business arrangements."

"Now that sounds like the Diego Martinez I remember." Kaito's expression softened just enough to be visible. "Direct. Honest." He leaned forward. "What I have could change everything for you and your family."

Diego studied every micro-expression, every tell. The sake burned his throat, absolute alcohol cut with synthetic flavoring.

"Alright," Diego said, setting down his cup. "You've got my attention."

Kaito slid a tablet across the counter. The screen glitched twice before stabilizing on satellite images of a coastal facility. "There's an exit the APU doesn't know about." His eyes locked with Diego's. "A Dr. Smith. She's found another way out. Place called the Crucible."

"Christ." Diego pushed the tablet back, the plastic warm and slightly sticky. "Miracle solutions. Mass graves. I'd dug enough of both." His jaw clenched. "How many more?"

Kaito swiped to a video file. A lab mouse vanished from one chamber, appeared in another. The animal twitched its whiskers, sniffed the air, then began exploring like nothing had happened.

"Last month's test."

His throat constricted. He'd taken shrapnel before. This felt worse. It cut deeper, promising a slower bleed.

"How long?"

"Two months, maybe less." Kaito checked his wrist display, the numbers blinked, showed corrupted data, then corrected. "Diverting this tonnage of alloy-grade rare earths leaves a hole in the APU inventory. The procurement logs won't hold up to a real audit."

"Smith needs to be ready before that happens. Comms secure?"

Kaito nodded. "Old methods masking new tech. It's secure."

Three customers entered, their voices too bright, too loud against the subdued atmosphere. Diego shifted slightly, angling toward the exit, weight balanced on the balls of his feet. Old habits. Kaito caught the movement, glanced at the newcomers, then made eye contact with the shop owner. A brief nod passed between them.

"Two hours until Smith's contact window," Kaito said, rechecking his display. "I'll send you secure coordinates."

Diego pulled out a data chip, slotted it into Kaito's tablet, copied the files, then pocketed the chip in his shielded jacket. Something sharp cut through Diego's chest. Familiar. Electric.

A target. A mission.

His family's first real shot at survival.

"Been promising my granddaughter a future for years," Diego said, standing. "About time I delivered something real."

"My people deserve better, too," Kaito said, leaving enough money for both meals plus a generous tip. "Not just the connected ones. The ones who earned it." He stood as well. "Don't be late."

Diego nodded. Outside, the sedan waited in light rain that turned the street into black mirrors reflecting neon and headlights.

Everything could change tonight. One call with Dr. Smith. One chance to keep the promise he'd made to Isabella, to Maria, to Elena's memory.

One chance to finally bring his family home alive.

THE BOY FROM OSAKA

Diego's holo-com chirped in the alley, its blue glow washing over rusted metal and chemical stains left over from a war that had ended nine years ago but refused to be forgotten. Tokyo's back corners still reeked of burnt circuitry and piss. The kind of places where deals got made and bodies got dumped. He paused, listening. His hand dropped to the knife at his hip.

His device pinged once. Destination.

A steel door blocked the alley's end. Heaps of discarded appliances surrounded it. Diego knocked twice. A red security light clicked on overhead. The door mechanism hummed to life, its subtle vibration dislodging water droplets that slid down the frame.

The door swung inward. Two guards stepped forward, grabbing his arms and pulling him inside before slamming the door. Diego submitted to the search. Protocol. Familiar.

Their hands lingered near his pockets. Too long.

His patience died.

He caught the guard's wrist, applying precise pressure to the nerve point. "I'm clean," he growled, his voice low and certain. "Touch that pocket again, and you'll be shopping for cybernetic replacements." Each word carried the weight of absolute certainty.

"It's all right." Kaito emerged from a back room, straightening his tie with a precise motion. "He's clean. You can let him go."

The guards retreated, maintaining eye contact as they resumed their positions. Diego measured their stance, weight distribution, and reaction time: both of them were ex-military, with cybernetic joints barely visible beneath civilian clothes. Kaito had clearly upgraded from simple smuggling operations.

"Thorough security," Diego remarked, adjusting his jacket while sizing up the larger guard. "Is this how you greet all your consultants?"

Kaito's expression hardened momentarily before relaxing into neutrality. He bowed, hands clasped behind his back. "Necessary precautions, Martinez-san. Please, Dr. Smith is waiting."

Kaito moved through the corridor. Diego followed. Bare concrete. Their boots loud against stone. The air grew colder as they descended, familiar scents from countless secure facilities filling Diego's nostrils.

Security cameras tracked their movement, red LEDs blinking from each corner. The passage opened into a room. No windows, no vents to the outside, not even the faint vibration of the city. The silence was absolute, broken only by the hum of the signal jammers.

A low vibration traveled through the soles of his boots, the telltale hum of high-end signal jammers. He ran a hand over the wall, his fingertips finding the faint seam of a Faraday mesh panel. *No signal gets in or out of this tomb,* he thought, his own comm confirming it with a dead screen.

"Military grade," Diego observed, running fingers along panel seams. "Corporate money, though. They skipped redundancies in the northwest corner."

Kaito watched Diego's professional assessment with calculated interest. "Privacy has a price."

A holographic display dominated the room's center, powered down to a dim blue standby mode. Around it, dark workstations sat silent, screens reflecting overhead lights like black mirrors. The air stung with ozone and hot electronics.

"Please." Kaito gestured to a chair with a clear sightline to the door. "Coffee? Colombian, pre-war." At Diego's nod, a rich aroma filled the air as Kaito poured.

Diego accepted the cup and settled into the chair, positioning himself to keep both the door and Kaito in his field of vision.

He wrapped his hands around the warm ceramic. Real coffee. First he'd tasted in months. The aroma hit like a memory: quiet mornings before everything went to hell. Better than the synthetic crap that passes for caffeine now.

"Still playing the long game, I see."

Kaito tapped commands into the interface panel. The central holographic unit hummed to life, bathing the room in electric blue. Circuits whined as the quantum-encrypted connection established itself.

Smith's hologram stabilized through the quantum encryption. She had dark hair pulled back with what looked like a repurposed data cable, chemical stains marking her lab coat.

Kaito's spine straightened. Smith's hologram sharpened, her eyes moving over Diego like she was running numbers.

Three seconds. Diego watched her jaw work. Her pupils dilated. Her fingers tapped against her thigh. Numbers. Running the math.

"Dr. Smith, allow me to introduce Major Diego Martinez, former APU combat specialist and tactical consultant. Martinez-san, this is Dr. Olivia Smith, Acting Head of Quantum Research for the Crucible Project I mentioned earlier."

"Just Diego." He took a slow sip. "What do you need, Doctor?"

Smith leaned closer to her camera. "APU abandoned us. Cut our funding for their precious ship program." Her voice carried a scientist's frustration mixed with something sharper. "Years of proving inter-dimensional travel works, and they still think rockets are the answer."

"Fortunately," she continued, glancing toward Kaito with something between gratitude and wariness, "Mr. Nakamura recognized the potential when government bureaucrats couldn't. Portal's open to a place we call Haven."

Diego set down his coffee cup. "What's APU's stance on your continued operation?"

Smith's hologram flickered as she exchanged a glance with Kaito. "Officially, Crucible is decommissioned. Environmental remediation."

"Unofficially," Kaito added, "certain APU officials received substantial financial incentives to maintain this classification. Their satellite surveillance patterns avoid our sector with remarkable consistency."

"For now," Diego noted. "A larger portal means a larger signature. Someone will notice eventually."

"Which is why our timeline must be accelerated," Kaito replied. "We extract personnel before APU realizes what they've lost."

Smith gestured, her holographic arm extending from elbow to wrist. "Currently, we can stabilize this size opening. Human-sized requires fifty times the power draw."

Diego leaned forward. "How many people per transition?"

"One at a time. Maybe fifty total with current resources."

The math hit him cold. Fifty people. Maria, Isabella, Mateo would be first. For the rest, it was triage, the same brutal calculus he'd used in a hundred combat zones. Save who you can.

"How do we choose?"

Dr. Smith's hologram materialized topographical maps between them. "We've conducted preliminary exploration. The environment appears Earth-like, with breathable atmosphere and vegetation."

"Define 'Earth-like,'" Diego interrupted. "I've been to places that wouldn't kill you immediately but made you wish they had."

Smith pulled up video feeds of white rodents in containment units. "Lab rats first. Complete molecular stability, no cellular degradation after transit. Perfect results every time."

"Threats? Large predators?"

"None detected in our survey area," Smith replied, adjusting something off-screen. "But our range is limited to about a kilometer radius."

Diego cataloged the unknowns. "Survey coverage?"

Smith zoomed out the holographic display. "Only this region." She highlighted a circular area. "Power constraints limit drone range."

Kaito straightened with measured precision. "My organization, Nexus, has reconnaissance gear that could extend your capabilities."

Diego studied the elevation markers, water sources, natural choke points. "Timeline?"

"Human trials in thirty days with proper support," Smith said. "Twenty-five if we push everything."

"Before we go further, I need to see your operation firsthand. Any problems with me visiting your facility?"

"I insist on it." Smith leaned closer to the camera. "Our security situation isn't ideal. Four guards when regulations call for twelve, but they're veterans."

Kaito checked his datapad. "Transportation within forty-eight hours. Private flight, minimal documentation."

"Security parameters?" Diego moved forward in his chair. "If we're extracting families, I need to know exactly what we're walking into."

"Six guards total, perimeter sensors," Smith replied. "All former APU. They know their business, but it's not enough."

"Hostile contacts?"

"Not yet. But we're sitting on inter-dimensional tech. Won't stay secret forever."

"Local authorities?"

"We have the island to ourselves," Kaito said. "Officials on the mainland maintain their distance as long as we stay inconspicuous."

Diego nodded. He'd orchestrated extractions with less during the Mineral Wars. "I'll need full access: security systems, personnel files, equipment manifests." He paused. "And I want my people. We do this together or not at all."

Smith's jaw worked. "You'll have what we can spare." He gestured at the flickering overhead lights. "Power grid's jury-rigged to hell. Scrounged parts. Duct tape. But it runs."

"Two former military engineers I trust. APU rejected them too. They'll jump at this chance."

Smith nodded. "Additional expertise would be invaluable."

Information cascaded across Smith's display. "Our drones found substantial neodymium veins, concentrated like nothing on Earth."

"What are those resources for?" Diego asked.

Smith extended her holographic arm again. "Portal demands more power and rare earth alloys."

"Those rare earth deposits you mentioned. If we mine them, could we expand operations?"

"Yes, significantly." She replied.

"Enough to save more people?"

"Thousands, if we can extract it." She paused. "That's a big if."

Kaito studied his data. "I can source mining equipment through legitimate channels. That type of machinery doesn't trigger alerts."

"Current stockpile?"

"Twenty transitions maximum," Smith said. "After that..." Her hologram flickered.

Twenty shots. He'd planned extractions with worse odds, but never with his family's lives hanging in the balance.

The numbers were brutal. Limited shots, zero room for error. Maria, Isabella, Mateo. Save what you can, leave the rest. The wars all over again.

Diego stood. "Send me the coordinates. I'll be there as soon as Kaito arranges transport."

Dr. Smith's hologram curved her lips upward, the tense lines around her eyes softening. "Thank you, Diego. Your experience could make all the difference."

The hologram vanished, leaving them in electromagnetic silence. Diego and Kaito faced each other across the secure room. Power hummed through cables like angry wasps.

Diego rose slowly, his knee protesting. The tactical assessment ran: supply lines, defensive positions, extraction routes. Combat planning, same as always. But something else stirred underneath. Elena's voice from their last conversation: "Find something worth fighting for, not just fighting against."

Maybe he'd found it.

Kaito watched him stand, reading the decision in his posture. "The potential is significant, Martinez-san. I trust you agree?"

"I see it," Diego replied. "Question is, can we pull it off before it's too late?"

"That depends on how fast we move." Kaito checked his secure comm, his tone suggesting he'd already calculated every variable.

Three weeks of purposelessness since the APU rejection. Now the mission parameters were clear: get to the facility, assess capabilities, extract his family and whoever else they could manage.

"Forty-eight hours," Diego said. "Get that transport ready. We've got families to save."

Diego checked his harness release mechanism as Cozumel materialized through the haze. Forty years of combat drops. His breathing still hitched with each descent. The familiar pressure building beneath his ribs. The island looked peaceful from altitude.

Wrong.

"Weather's holding steady," Mia announced, her left hand working the collective while her right adjusted trim. "Should be a smooth approach."

Diego repositioned against the leather seat. His last flight to Cozumel had been on cargo webbing that reeked of hydraulic fluid. "Kaito doesn't cut corners."

"Kaito collects insurance policies." Mia banked left, movements economical. Precise. "Redundant nav systems, EMP shielding, fuel range that covers half the Gulf." She glanced at the instrument panel. "Course, all that fancy tech means jackshit if someone decides to shoot us down."

The coastline of Cozumel sharpened into focus. The sprawling Crucible facility stretched near the southern end. Morning sun hit the structure. Metal and glass caught the light, sharp against Haven's purple-green vegetation.

Too exposed.

"Kaito mentioned you pulled him through a Pacific storm." Diego studied her hands on the controls. Steady. Confident. "What happened?"

Mia's shoulders tightened. "Luck wasn't part of it. Lost two engines over open water, no landing sites nearby." Her jaw worked. "Nursed the bird for three hours on backup systems while Kaito calculated fuel consumption." A quick glance at readouts. "Never saw him rattled before, but that day..." She shook her head. "Let's just say he's had my back ever since."

Mia banked into a wide circle around the facility. "Coming around for visual inspection."

"There." Diego pressed against the window. The Crucible sprawled below. Billionaire's idea of a research station. Too large. Too exposed. His eyes found landing zones first, then egress routes. "Someone spent serious money here."

Diego leaned closer to the glass. His index finger tapped a restless rhythm against his thumb. The design felt sterile. Clinical. "Those aren't decorative columns. They're hardpoints disguised as architecture."

Whoever designed this knew their business. But it still looked like hiding a fortress behind pretty paint. Too much glass. Too many sightlines for hostiles.

Diego's gaze fixed on the perimeter. "That reinforcement wasn't in the blueprints."

"Smith added those after APU pulled out. Insisted on hardening key areas." Mia adjusted course. "That woman doesn't leave anything to chance."

The helicopter banked. Diego caught sight of the facility's power center. Those cooling towers meant serious power generation. Industrial scale. And those arrays... quantum energy collectors, maybe? The kind of tech that made procurement officers file classified reports about who else might want it.

A faint hum reached his ears even through the rotor noise. Something unstable in the frequency.

"How many bodies on the ground?" Diego's eyes moved across the complex. Too big. Too many blind spots.

"Ten?" His knee gave that familiar twinge. "Twenty?"

"Try four security, maybe a dozen total staff." Mia's voice carried an edge. "Smith runs this place like a monastery. All brains, minimal muscle."

Diego's face remained stone. Four operators. His gaze tracked across the complex. Automatically dividing it into sectors. Considering response times. Mapping overlapping fields of fire.

"What's your contingency for uninvited guests?"

"You're looking at her."

This was bigger than Kaito had let on. Far bigger. The power requirements alone suggested capabilities that governments killed for. His mind flashed to Isabella's laugh. Mateo's sleepy smile. If this technology could secure a world where his grandchildren grew up safe...

"You've done well with limited resources. But if this project is heading where I think it is, you'll need more boots on the ground."

Diego's gaze locked onto the drones circling below. The paint job was different. But the mechanical precision was identical to the units that had filled the skies over Osaka. His jaw tightened.

"Those drones." Diego's voice flattened. "Standard APU hardware?"

"Modified civilian models. Emily gutted the APU protocols and silenced the autonomous decision-making." Mia began their final descent. "She and one of the engineers built a system that keeps humans in charge. No machine makes life-or-death calls."

He took a deep breath. The rigid set of his jaw softened. At least someone understood the risks. The rotor wash kicked up dust as they touched down on the helipad. Armed security personnel took positions around the landing zone. Their movements displayed military discipline.

Through the windshield, more security personnel moved into position. Their stance. Balanced weight distribution. Hands positioned for quick weapon access. Eyes checking angles instead of staring at the newcomer. Professional habits that spoke louder than any resume.

A figure in tactical gear approached the helicopter. Hand raised in greeting. Diego didn't recognize the patch on their shoulder. Possibly specialized security. Kaito hadn't just found a hidden research facility. He'd found one with professionals who knew how to operate off the grid.

The rotors spun down. Their whine fading to a low whur. Diego reached for his bag. Mind already mapping defensive positions and evacuation routes. At least he wouldn't worry about rogue AI taking control.

"Welcome to the Crucible," Mia said, continuing the shutdown sequence. "Looks like your escort's here."

Diego grabbed his duffel and stepped onto the sun-baked helipad. Caribbean heat hit like a fist after the helicopter's recycled air. His knee gave a familiar twinge.

Four figures approached. Diamond formation. Standard.

Their movements were tight. Clean. Military, not civilian playing dress-up.

The gear told the story. Civilian tactical equipment, sure, but modified. The kind of modifications he'd seen in Jakarta. Kandahar. Places where the line between security operations and actual combat blurred until it didn't exist at all.

His hand moved toward his sidearm before he remembered he wasn't carrying.

Old habits.

The lead operator removed her helmet. Close-cropped hair. Face weathered by experience. "Martinez." Not a question. "Emma Hayes. I run what passes for security here." Her handshake was firm and precise. Calibrated strength from someone who knew how to use it.

Diego returned her handshake. Noted the calluses that spoke of regular weapons training. "Former military?"

"APU Special Security Division, all of us." Hayes gestured toward the facility entrance. "We've been with the project since inception."

The rest of the team maintained their positions. Eyes scanning the perimeter. Diego catalogued their stance. Balanced weight distribution. Hands positioned for quick weapon access. Eyes checking angles instead of staring at the newcomer. Professional habits that spoke louder than any resume.

"How long have you run security?" Diego fell into step beside her as they walked toward the entrance.

"Three years. Ever since the AI flagged us as 'sub-optimal' resource investments." Emma recited the technical term with precise neutrality that revealed more than any emotional outburst could.

The muscles along her temple tightened for half a second before releasing. Another victim of algorithmic efficiency. "Their oversight."

Hayes's lip quirked slightly. "One perspective." She authenticated at the entrance scanner. Palm flat against the glowing surface. "Dr. Smith is waiting in the central conference room. We'll handle your gear."

Diego's eyes tracked the corridor. Three hundred meters. Too long. Branching passages split off like veins. Emergency lights every fifty meters, standard spacing, useless in a firefight. Fire suppression overhead, probably functional.

Someone had followed code. Built it right.

Four operators. Maybe thirty access points.

The math didn't work.

"Response protocols?" His voice carried professional interest.

"Budget constraints." Emma's voice carried professional frustration. "APU pulled funding when the science didn't yield immediate results. We prioritized research over security. Kaito helps where possible."

She tapped her tablet. Displayed a facility schematic. "Three main access points, emergency exits every hundred meters, and sealed maintenance tunnels. Response time is four minutes anywhere in the facility, two with drone support." Pride edged into her voice. "We drill regularly."

Diego studied the layout. Even perfect response times meant gaps. Four minutes. More than enough time for someone who knew what they were doing.

And if the quantum tech actually worked...

Emma watched his face. "That's what we've been telling Dr. Smith. Maybe she'll listen to you."

They moved through the facility's main corridor until they reached another doorway marked "Command Center." Instead of the biometric scanner he expected, Diego spotted a simple button beside the door.

"A button. Protecting quantum tech with hotel lobby security."

"Resources are slim," Emma said. "Emily's drones handle security. Surveillance feeds cover the rest."

Diego pressed the button. The door slid open with a soft hiss. Revealed what appeared to be an aircraft control center. Monitors lined the walls. Most powered down. A single desk sat empty. Its chair tucked neatly under the console.

Diego stepped inside. Boots silent on the polished floor. Through the windows, he saw only ocean in every direction. No backup. No reinforcements. No extraction if things went sideways. Just water and sky. Beautiful and isolating.

"The Control Center's usually staffed during operations," Emma explained, following him in. "Emily runs drone patrols from here when she's not working on upgrades."

Advanced equipment sat mostly dormant. The active screens displayed only basic perimeter data. Diego noted what was missing. Thermal imaging overlays. Motion tracking algorithms. Threat assessment protocols. Standard kit for facilities half this size with a quarter of the importance.

"Security hub?" He gestured to the workstation.

"This is it. Air traffic control, security hub, communications center." Emma's voice carried dry humor. "We're the Swiss Army knife of under-staffing."

Diego examined the workstation setup. Single operator position for monitoring three separate systems. No redundancy if that operator went down. The math kept getting worse.

A panel slid open behind them. Diego turned. Noted the movement without alarm. Professional awareness, not startle response.

Dr. Olivia Smith stepped through. Her gaze sliced the room with clinical precision. In person, her eyes burned with an intensity the hologram couldn't capture. The lines of concentration between her brows permanently etched into her skin.

"Security assessment complete?" Smith's voice carried the weight of someone who'd fought too many battles for resources. "I'm guessing you've identified multiple areas for improvement."

Diego managed a short laugh. "Professional hazard."

"This project represents humanity's only viable path forward," Smith said, her voice carrying quiet desperation beneath the scientific precision. "Every day we delay increases the probability that we'll run out of time entirely."

Before he could respond, Emma tapped a command into her data pad.

The air outside shimmered. Not heat distortion. Something else. Diego's brain struggled to process what his eyes were seeing.

Four UAVs materialized three meters away. Their surfaces absorbed light rather than reflected it. Stealth tech Diego had only read about in highly classified APU development reports. Bleeding-edge capabilities that existed only in theoretical papers and black project budgets.

"These have been tracking you since you crossed our airspace," Emma explained. Her voice gained a crisp edge of satisfaction. "Part of a thirty-unit defensive network with overlapping coverage zones."

The stealth capabilities rivaled anything in classified APU development facilities. He'd walked through their security grid completely unaware. Advanced reconnaissance drones with capabilities that shouldn't exist outside government black projects. But Kaito's resources, his connections through Nexus...

"Satisfied?" Olivia's question carried an edge of challenge.

Diego watched the empty air where military-grade stealth platforms had just demonstrated technology that could revolutionize warfare. Thirty units. Overlapping coverage. Maybe these people understood exactly what they were protecting after all.

"It's a start," Diego replied. "But we need to talk about what comes after first contact."

A Skeleton Crew

Red lights slashed through the corridors of Admin HQ. Diego's temples pounded as he followed Dr. Smith deeper into the facility, his gaze sweeping each section for vulnerabilities. Missing choke points. Too few fallback positions. Shit for backup escape routes.

The air grew thick with the smell of ozone and hot plastic. Ahead, the portal frame hummed, its glow flickering as arcs of energy sputtered along the outer ring. A technician scrambled back from a control panel that shot out a shower of sparks.

"Stabilization arrays degrading. Even in standby." Olivia's voice came strained. Corner of her eye jumped. Her boots struck the deck plating, each step sharp in the corridor. "Neodymium's running out."

Diego's jaw clenched. Neodymium. The last shipment he'd seen had been escorted by three heavy combat units.

"And you think I can fix this?" he asked, scanning for surveillance blind spots.

"Kaito says you can."

He met her gaze. The unspoken part was clear: *And I'm desperate enough to believe him.* The name twisted something in his gut. A sharp memory flash: a terrified boy clutching his injured father during the Osaka water riots. Now Kaito ran half the black-market tech in the Pacific Rim, his networks deeper than most intelligence agencies.

"Kaito's not exactly a reliable character reference," Diego muttered.

Olivia adjusted her glasses, her fingers quick. "So you're it? Our miracle worker?"

Diego snorted. "I'm just a retired grunt with connections."

The embarkation room doors slid open to frantic activity. Scientists darted between workstations, faces drawn with exhaustion. Technicians shouted coordinates across the room. Diego's attention locked onto the massive circular structure dominating the center.

The portal frame burned his eyes. Unstable energy crackled around its edges, broken mathematics trying to force itself into reality. Raw, lethal power crawled across his skin, raising every hair on his arms.

His breathing fell into a familiar combat rhythm. He studied the jury-rigged power systems. Cartel equipment was everywhere, sleek black tech with red indicator lights. Kaito's signature style. The kid from Osaka funding all this. For protection or profit? Probably both.

"How many people have crossed through?" Diego asked.

Olivia's hands fell to her sides, her knuckles white. She stared at the shimmering ring, her expression becoming unnervingly still. "None," she said. "We tried once. It killed my husband, Aiden. We haven't dared activate it since."

It wasn't a struggling transport system. It was a tombstone. The air in Diego's lungs turned to ice. He looked from her face back to the machine.

"The APU files promised passage for thousands," he said, his voice low.

"The APU called the project a catastrophic failure and wrote it off." Bitterness finally cracked her composure. "They diverted all funding to those ridiculous generation ships, metal coffins that will never launch."

Diego's index finger tapped his thumb, a slow, deliberate rhythm. "One exit. If something breaks, we're trapped. Basic tactical failure."

"We didn't have options," she shot back. "The quantum bridge only stabilizes at specific dimensional coordinates."

Isabella's face flashed in his mind. Eight years old, already checking oxygen levels and radiation badges. Mateo at five reciting emergency protocols. Children shouldn't need those skills.

"Show me the equipment problems," he said, his voice dropping to professional neutrality. "The actual failures, not the sanitized version."

A long breath escaped her. Her shoulders dropped. First time since he'd entered the room.

She moved closer. "I need someone who gets what we're risking here."

She led him deeper into the room, past researchers muttering equations under their breath. The central terminal displayed cascading failure warnings across multiple systems. Exposed cables snaked between military surplus reactors and experimental quantum arrays. Half the connections were held with industrial tape.

"Jesus," he muttered, crouching to examine a power coupling. "What genius thought this was stable?"

"We're working with what we have," she said defensively. "Kaito provides tech when he can, but..."

"But not enough," Diego finished. A muscle in his jaw ticked as he studied the equipment more carefully. Military serial numbers caught his eye. "These are APU components from the Singapore blackout."

Olivia stiffened. "How did you know that?"

"I was there when the power grid collapsed." His fingers moved along a connection point where the wires had frayed, exposing copper through melted insulation. "I recognize the output regulation system. Smart repurposing."

Her gaze sharpened, her posture straightening an inch. "Can you help us or not? I don't care where the parts come from if they keep the portal stable long enough to work. Once."

Diego straightened, the old ache in his knee protesting. Elena would have called him insane for trusting technology that made reality hiccup and swallow people whole. But Elena was gone. His grandchildren breathed poison. Crazy was all they had left.

The same bureaucrats who saw Osaka burn were still making life-and-death decisions.

"I know people," he said finally. "Good people who know how to keep things running when everything goes to shit."

"Who?" Her eyes widened slightly, her fingers hovering over her tablet.

"Luna, who maintained comms in Singapore when the AI systems turned deadly. Jack, who fixes anything with moving parts and half the things without. The corps took his leg, gave him a cybernetic replacement and a permanent attitude problem. Now he fixes things the old way, assuming anything smart wants to kill you."

Diego paused, his eyes on the failing equipment. "And Kayla, a combat engineer. The best at fortifying impossible positions."

Olivia leaned forward. "You trust these people?"

Diego nodded. "With my life. More importantly, with the lives of everyone who might go through that portal."

"We need the help. Desperately." She gestured toward the scientific team. "They're brilliant, but they're academics. Theory over application."

Diego looked back at the portal. The unstable energy made his combat instincts scream warnings. Humanity's last chance, built on stolen tech, desperate science, and a deal with a man like Kaito. Every military fiber in his body said to walk away.

But this wasn't about military protocol anymore. This was about Isabella and Mateo.

"My people need assurances," he said firmly. "Full access, no bureaucratic bullshit. And I need to see what's on the other side before we talk about setting up shop."

Her expression held the same desperate determination he'd seen in his own reflection during the war years.

"Done." No hesitation. "When can they be here?"

"I'll make the calls." He surveyed the room again, taking in the tangle of cables, the overworked scientists, the unstable gateway that had already claimed one life. "But first, walk me through everything. Every failure point, every workaround, everything you've tried that didn't work."

She nodded, a wave of what might have been relief washing over her face. "Thank you."

"Don't thank me yet," Diego muttered, mentally composing what he'd say to Jack. "We haven't fixed a damn thing."

The portal's energy pulsed, casting blue shadows across their faces. Earth was beyond saving, but maybe they could save enough people to start over. A second chance, if they didn't all die getting there.

Diego reached for his secure comm unit. Time to call in his team.

Diego followed Dr. Smith through the corridors, cataloguing empty guard posts at every choke point. His fingers drummed against his thigh as he counted vacant stations. No perimeter sensors. No backup systems. Each missing element carved another line into his growing list of vulnerabilities. Two decades hunting insurgents had taught him to spot weakness, and this place reeked of it.

"These posts should have at least two guards each," Diego said, noting the third unmanned station. "Even with skeleton crews."

"Budget cuts eliminated most positions. Original team transferred to exodus projects when APU pulled funding." Olivia's voice carried exhaustion beneath the matter-of-fact delivery.

Empty labs stretched past them. Equipment sat shrouded under plastic sheeting. Through one window, a lone technician bent over portal components, movements sharp with concentration.

"How many stayed?" Diego studied another breach point.

"Twelve."

Twelve people. Diego had seen ammunition depots with better coverage. His old shrapnel wound pulsed as scenarios ran through his head.

The corridor spat them back into the embarkation chamber.

The quantum gateway dominated the space. Diego's eyes tracked the obsidian frame automatically. Security systems. Outdated. Power junctions exposed like open wounds.

His gaze tracked the conduits. Three weak points. Three places where someone with the right knowledge and wrong intentions could bring the whole thing down.

His knee throbbed. Old habit. Tactical assessment. Even here.

Diego stopped walking. Cities burned. Borders shifted overnight. Nothing in his career had prepared him for this scale of consequence.

"Christ." His hand moved instinctively toward where his sidearm should hang. Technology that punched holes between realities. Power conduits thick as tree trunks snaked along the walls, feeding containment systems he couldn't begin to understand. The sheer magnitude made his mouth go dry.

A security panel caught his attention, its housing cracked open and wires exposed. Diego touched the damaged casing, mind spinning through infiltration scenarios. Secrets this big attracted the worst kind of attention. His grip tightened on the panel edge.

Two technicians hunched over control stations, faces pale in the quantum displays' blue glow. They barely acknowledged Olivia and Diego passing by.

"The Portal Room." Olivia gestured toward the massive gateway, running her palm along a control interface. "Funding disappeared right after we achieved stable quantum tunneling. Twelve people stayed to finish what thirty started."

Diego circled the gateway, measuring distances and cataloguing weak points. "Hell of a way to go if something fails." He stepped closer to the frame. "Show me the security setup."

Olivia led him through a reinforced door at the chamber's far end. "Security HQ is through here."

The layout matched every military installation Diego knew: compact, defensible, designed for quick deployment. But the technology on display made those bases look primitive.

Security HQ ran several degrees colder than the corridors, climate control humming steadily. Four guards total. Screens displayed facility feeds, some crackling with static from power fluctuations. Professional enough setup, but monitoring stations meant nothing without eyes watching them.

"Containment field spiked an hour ago," Olivia said, rubbing her neck. "Third time today. Emily's routing power through backups, but we need repairs before the next test." She glanced at a diagnostic panel displaying failure scenarios in red text. "Besides our two technicians and an engineer on software, you'll want to meet Emily. She handles security operations and drone programming."

A figure worked at the central console, surrounded by floating security feeds and drone patrol patterns.

Multiple screens cast blue light across her workspace. The woman adjusted routes without looking up, fingers moving across holographic interfaces with practiced efficiency. When she turned, Diego recognized her immediately.

"Emily Nakamura." She stood, meeting his assessment with her own. "Security operations." Her handshake was firm, callused from fieldwork.

"Well, I'll be damned. Emily Nakamura." Diego stepped forward. He'd verified she wasn't related to Kaito the moment he'd seen her name on the roster. "Last I heard, you were giving APU brass headaches with those targeting recommendations."

"Sandstorm operation." Emily set down her stylus. "Diego Martinez. Heard you finally told Command what you thought of their efficiency metrics."

"Something like that." Diego nodded toward her defensively positioned console.

Her skill had saved lives that day. But questions remained about this facility, about who else might know it existed.

"Best pilot I've worked with," Diego said, noting her drone displays. He'd trained with dozens of operators, but few had Emily's precision. Threading ordinance through that weather to hit exactly what mattered. "APU must have been unhappy when you went private."

Emily adjusted her headset. "Sandstorm changed things. Started questioning their targeting protocols." Her voice cooled. "Turns out acceptable losses aren't always acceptable."

Diego's hand moved to the back of his neck. "Yeah. Sometimes mission parameters don't match what you find on the ground."

Emily's posture relaxed slightly. "Exactly. So what brings a former Major to our inter-dimensional project?"

"Same reason you stayed, I'd guess. Sometimes you find something worth the risk."

Olivia pulled out an access card. "This gets you network access and modification rights for Security HQ systems." She pressed the card into his palm. "Emily can help you get oriented. Choose any office here, and the main dining facility is down that corridor."

Diego examined the card, its quantum-encrypted core catching the light. Twelve researchers betting everything on inter-dimensional escape. Full access on day one. Desperation and trust in equal measure.

"Thanks." He slipped the card into his chest pocket, next to the worn metal coin he'd carried through three wars. "Any restrictions I should know about?"

"Full access to security systems." Olivia glanced at her displays. "Though I'd appreciate advance notice before major protocol changes."

Movement in the corridor caught Diego's attention. Another security patrol moved with disciplined precision. Their gear looked civilian, but their coordination told a different story. Not rent-a-cops. Veterans.

Diego filed this observation away. He needed those incident reports, needed to understand who might be watching the facility. Operations this sensitive attracted unwanted attention, even hidden on Cozumel.

"I'll start a complete assessment," Diego said, eyes moving across security displays. "Beginning with those power systems we discussed."

The access card felt substantial in his pocket. Full security access meant immediate changes. Good. They'd need every advantage.

"Emily knows her business." The patrol disappeared around a corner. "But we'll need coordination if we're upgrading systems."

Olivia's wrist display pulsed red, drawing her attention. "Containment field's fluctuating again." Her fingers flew across diagnostic screens. "I need to recalibrate quantum stabilizers before tomorrow's test." She gave Diego a quick nod before moving toward the door. "We'll discuss your assessment at dinner."

Diego tracked her movement as she left, noting the exhaustion in her steps. Command stress. Scientists pushed past breaking points, holding projects that could change everything or kill everyone trying.

He walked the security console perimeter. Emily's setup was impressive but understaffed. Multiple sensor feeds, automated patrol routes, redundant systems. Military-grade implementation stretched thin. Twelve researchers. Four guards. One gateway that could tear reality apart.

The math didn't work.

"Impressive setup. But you're running thin."

"Welcome to our world. We make do with what we have." Emily gestured at the displays. "Perimeter's solid during daylight, but night coverage has gaps."

Diego pulled out his secure comm unit. "I might know some people who can help."

He switched to encrypted channels. Two familiar faces appeared in a flickering hologram. Jack's workshop filled the background while Kayla's organized workspace was visible beside him.

"Well shit, Martinez." Jack tapped his cybernetic leg, switching it to relaxed mode before leaning back. "This better be worth interrupting my calibration work."

Kayla looked up from cleaning blast residue off her hands, carbon stains darkening her fingertips. She waved a blackened hand at Jack. "Ask him about the supply situation."

"Supply situation's fucked," Jack said without changing expression. "Down to emergency rations and bad coffee."

Diego smiled at their familiar rhythm. "Remember what we discussed about meaningful work?"

Both their expressions hardened. Jack's attention sharpened. Kayla set down her cleaning cloth.

"You found something?"

"Something significant. Off the books. Quantum-level technology that makes our last contract look like basic training."

"Quantum?" Kayla's interest was immediate. "Not APU-sanctioned, I'm guessing?"

"Private operation. Extended deployment." Diego kept his voice neutral. "Once you're here, extraction isn't simple."

Jack and Kayla exchanged one of their wordless communications, the kind that came from years of partnership.

"How dangerous?" Jack asked.

"Assume the worst."

"Worth the risk?"

"More than anything we've done."

Another look passed between them. Some internal calculation Diego wasn't part of.

"Give us two hours to secure the workshops," Kayla said, decision made.

"And pack decent coffee," Jack added. "Can't work miracles on swill."

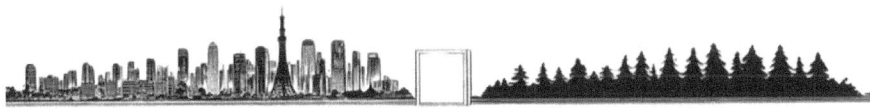

Diego leaned back in his chair, eyes scanning the spartan room. Concrete walls and wire mesh windows. No marble bullshit here, just efficiency that reminded him why he'd chosen the military in the first place. Before it all went political. The air hung stale and humid, carrying the distant hum of overworked ventilation systems that never quite managed to filter out the smell of industrial cleaning fluid and old sweat.

His comm chimed with the APU Navy emblem. Wilkins never called this late unless something was burning. The admiral's tired face materialized on the flickering hologram, exhaustion etched deeper around his eyes than Diego remembered.

"Diego." Wilkins managed a smile that looked forced.

"You look like hell. Family holding up?" The familiar edge in Diego's voice cut through the comm static.

Wilkins' expression softened for a moment. "They're managing. Chloe's building survival gardens like we're already abandoning ship. She doesn't say it, but she's preparing for the worst." The weariness in Wilkins' voice vanished, replaced by a flat, grim cadence. "Jackson's cutting anyone who might question his methods. Yesterday he axed three families because their kids scored 'sub-optimal' on some psychological evaluation."

The overhead lights flickered, casting shadows across Wilkins' face. Diego's knee gave a familiar twinge.

"My ship's due for refit in eight weeks. Skeleton crew, extended cycle." Wilkins met Diego's eyes directly. "Lot of moving parts. Things get complicated during maintenance windows."

Diego nodded. Wilkins was offering something here, something that could matter. "Jackson sacrifices good people for his next promotion. I'm done playing that game."

"They pulled Alex Johnson."

"Johnson?" Diego's breath caught. The guy with top efficiency ratings, two kids, perfect service record. "What the hell for?"

"Called his family 'redundant skill sets.' Johnson's been running water reclamation for three sectors." Wilkins twisted his academy ring. "Lamot from Third Battalion lost his slot too. His daughter Sofia wants to study marine biology. Jackson called her 'non-essential personnel.'"

The comm crackled with interference, adding static to Wilkins' words.

"Not asking you to bend rules, Diego. I'm asking you to break them completely."

Wilkins glanced away. "Three months until launch. My daughter graduates next month. Miss the manifest, and she'll never see college."

Diego drummed his fingers once, then stopped. Both men understood what couldn't be said over comm channels. Wilkins bound by his commission, Diego freed by his resignation. Their friendship might not survive what was coming.

"Elena died while I played by their rules. Never again."

"Watch your six, Diego. When this goes sideways, you'll see who really has your back."

Diego nodded. "Isabella keeps asking when they're moving to the 'space place.'" His wedding ring caught the light. "María's family stays."

"Same for Chloe and the kids."

"How many families we talking about?"

"Dozens. Maybe more next week."

"Better get creative, then."

"Skeleton crew means minimal oversight. Database access gets... flexible during those periods." Wilkins leaned forward. "Your clearance still shows active in the system."

"Bureaucratic oversight has its advantages."

"We understand each other."

Wilkins pressed his palm against the desk. "Stay alive, Diego."

The hologram flickered out. Diego sat in the sudden quiet, machine hum filling the space around him. María's family photo caught his eye from the corner of his desk. Isabella's grin, Mateo's serious expression mirroring his grandfather's. Elena's ring felt cold against his finger.

During the refit, security protocols would be relaxed. Database access would be possible. Elena died while Diego followed orders. Not this time.

His comm buzzed. Olivia's code, priority channel. Twelve more families to add to Wilkins' list. Time to see if their physicist had solutions, because politics sure as hell didn't offer any.

Diego stepped into the Control Center expecting pristine workstations and quiet data analysis. Instead, frustrated muttering replaced the usual mechanical hum, the sharp smell of ozone hanging in the air. Dr. Smith was waist-deep in an open control panel, tools scattered across the floor around her boots.

Two technicians waited nearby while Dr. Smith emerged from the panel, wincing as she pressed one hand against her lower back. Her ponytail had come half undone, dark strands falling around her face, a smudge of grease marking her left cheek.

"Torres, torque wrench," she called. She tested the connection. "Should be clean now."

The scientist he'd expected to find buried in theoretical equations was instead buried in actual machinery. The way she handled tools, grease-stained and confident, reminded him of Ramirez, the combat engineer from Osaka. Same focus. Same competence. Dr. Smith wasn't giving orders from behind a desk. She was solving the problem herself.

"You've got grease on your cheek."

Dr. Smith's hand flew to her face, her composure slipping. "Wonderful. First the dampener fails, then I look like I've been wrestling with an engine block." She found the smudge and grimaced. "Perfect timing."

The senior technician checked his readings. "All green, Dr. Smith."

"Good." She wiped her cheek with her sleeve, missing most of it. "Run full diagnostics anyway."

Diego observed her work. "Thorough. I like that."

Her hands moved through the repair, grease under her nails, knuckles scraped raw from tight spaces. Tools clicked into place like she'd been doing this since before the wars started.

"Most brass I've known can't tell a circuit board from a dinner plate." He watched her secure the connection. "You get what you're asking people to die for."

She paused, looking up from her work. "Practical application matters as much as theory." She gestured toward the now quiet machinery. "Those adjustments just saved us a complete rebuild. Six months of work gone if the primary assembly had failed completely." Her voice carried an edge. "Time we don't have."

"Cross-train them on critical maintenance." Diego's hand found the scar on his temple. "Single points of failure kill operations."

His knee sent lightning up his thigh. Old shrapnel. Osaka. What happened when backup plans failed and people died because one person knew too much.

"Redundancy keeps things running when people get hurt." He rubbed his neck, vertebrae cracking. "They always do."

The techs straightened like recruits at inspection. The taller one nodded while his partner reached for the maintenance manual.

"I suppose that's sensible," she said, straightening her lab coat. "Though I prefer knowing exactly how my equipment functions."

Diego nodded toward the repaired panel. "I'm sure you do, Doc."

He took in Dr. Smith's coordination of the diagnostic sequence with her technicians. Her composed demeanor had slipped during the crisis, revealing a different side to the physicist. A side that got her hands dirty and tackled problems head-on. Refreshing.

"What can I do for you?" She pulled the elastic from her disheveled ponytail. Dark hair fell around her shoulders before she efficiently gathered it back up.

"We need to discuss our supply chain issues," Diego said, finding a clear spot against the control panel, avoiding the controls. "That dampener shouldn't have failed. Kaito promised us quality parts last month, and now we're seeing critical components break down. If we'd lost that assembly..."

Dr. Smith's eyes flickered toward the diagnostic display, tracking numbers and symbols Diego couldn't decipher. "You're right. This could've been catastrophic." She gripped the edge of the panel. "Fifteen minutes should give me enough time to collect the diagnostics and failure data for the call." She tucked a loose strand of hair behind her ear. "Conference room in admin?"

"I'll be there." Diego crossed his arms. "And we need to talk about bringing Kaito in on more of the technical specifics. You handled this crisis well, but we can't have everything depending on one person. Need redundancy in our knowledge base too, not just our equipment."

Dr. Smith gathered her tools. Shoved them in her lab coat pockets. Scalpel here. Forceps there. Years of doing this made the motions automatic. She glanced at the diagnostic readouts one more time.

Diego noted her methodical approach. "For what it's worth, Doc, it's good to work with someone who gets their hands dirty."

Dr. Smith paused, tools suspended mid-reach, then looked at him directly. The grease smudge still marked her cheek, but her professional confidence had returned. "I'll have those failure reports ready in ten minutes."

Diego looked at the damaged parts on the workbench. The frayed connections and scorched circuitry told him everything he needed to know about Kaito's supply chain. Time for the supplier to understand exactly what his substandard parts had nearly cost them.

THE UNVETTED

T he smell of ozone and fruity wine mingled in the small conference room. Diego rolled the glass between his palms, still unsure why Dr. Smith had insisted on sharing a bottle at 10:00 in the morning. The holographic display between them flickered with personnel files, casting blue shadows across their faces.

Diego leaned forward, eyeing the display. "We're critically understaffed in every essential area. Combat teams, medics, engineers." He set his wine glass down hard enough to slosh the red liquid against the sides.

Olivia's fingers flew across her tablet, scrolling through the personnel manifests. "The APU's algorithm rejected ninety percent of our essential personnel requests." She rubbed her temples. "We have the world's most advanced inter-dimensional gateway and barely enough people to operate a food truck."

"Security's my biggest concern." Diego stood up, circling around the table to the larger display wall. He tapped it, expanding the Crucible facility schematic. "Three entry points, limited sight lines, and no surveillance network outside the immediate perimeter."

"And you need how many for a proper security team?" Olivia joined him at the display, wine glass forgotten on the table.

"Thirty minimum. A full platoon plus support staff." Diego gestured at the northern approach. "This hillside is vulnerable to long-range observation. Anyone watching could monitor our personnel rotations, supply deliveries, everything."

Olivia ran a hand through her hair. "Thirty? The APU authorized seven security positions." She laughed, the sound sharp. "Seven people to secure a facility housing technology that could save humanity."

"Seven couldn't secure a convenience store." Diego jabbed a finger at the coastal approach. "And the boats? We have dive teams coming in regularly, and the APU expects us to secure the entire waterfront with…"

"I get it." Olivia's voice hardened. "We need to go outside the system."

Diego went completely still, studying her over the rim of his glass before taking a long sip of wine. "Careful, Doc. That's the kind of talk that gets funding pulled."

"What funding?" She flung a hand toward the display. "They've already gutted us. The APU has written off the Crucible Project as a failure anyway. Nobody's watching anymore."

"Except Kaito."

Olivia stiffened at the name. "His support has kept us operational. Without the Nexus Cartel's supply chain connections…"

"I know." Diego's finger tapped against his thumb, a rhythm of thought. "I've made my peace with taking his help. Just don't fool yourself about who he is."

"Did you have someone specific in mind for security?" Olivia refilled both their glasses, the wine bottle clinking against the rim.

"Alex Johnson. Captain, APU special forces. His team got passed over for the Exodus."

"APU special forces rejected from the Exodus?" Olivia frowned. "Why?"

"Johnson's team stood by their families when the algorithm dropped the axe. The APU would rather break up the most effective unit I've ever seen than transport a few 'non-essential' dependents, because they don't have a column for loyalty on their spreadsheets." Diego's knuckles went white around his glass.

"That's… cold, even for them."

"That's how they operate. Loyalty only flows one direction with the APU." Diego swirled the wine, staring into its depths. "I've known Alex since the Climate Conflicts. His unit kept my team alive during the Jakarta evacuation."

"What's his background?"

Diego chopped his hand through the air. "West Point graduate. Saw more action than most generals. Guy plans for contingencies that haven't even happened yet." His expression darkened. "His squad has exactly what we need. Security pros, engineers who can fix a tank with duct tape, comms guys who get signals where satellites can't reach. And they'll follow us, not some computer scorecard."

"The APU would classify that as desertion."

"Can't desert a mission you weren't selected for." Diego's smile was sharp. "And I doubt the APU is going to announce they lost track of their dimensional gateway project."

Olivia stared at her tablet. Her eyes darted between the display and Diego, her jaw setting firmly before her shoulders relaxed.

"If we're doing this," she said finally, "we need medical staff too. Michael Anderson. Trauma surgeon, served in the Mineral Wars. His wife Emily is also a surgeon, specialized in critical care." She swiped through files on her tablet. "Both rejected from the Exodus because they refused to leave their children behind."

"More APU efficiency." Diego leaned back in his chair. "Can't waste valuable slots on dependents."

"We're not the APU," Olivia said. "Families stay together. From a research perspective, understanding how children adapt to Haven will be critical. We need protocols to monitor their health, make sure they thrive. We can learn so much from them."

Diego nodded, something in his posture softening. "We'll need agricultural specialists too. My son-in-law works with urban farming, indoor cultivation. He can adapt crops to different conditions."

"Can he handle a complete environmental shift? Different soil chemistry, atmospheric variations, potentially altered photoperiods?"

"He grew tomatoes in the Arizona desert during the water rationing." Diego's face showed a flicker of pride. "Smartest man I know when it comes to growing things with nothing."

"Anyone else?"

"Luna Harper."

Olivia nearly choked on her wine. "The hacker? The one who broke into APU Command's security network?"

"The same." Diego's lips twitched in what might have been amusement. "Best systems specialist on the continent. And she hates the APU almost as much as I do."

"She's unstable. Completely unvetted."

Diego's fingers drummed against the tabletop. "She tears systems apart, finds every weakness. And she never trusts an AI's answer without seeing the code herself." His eyes narrowed. "We're rebuilding from scratch, Olivia. I'd rather have someone who questions every line of code than someone who just follows protocol."

Olivia sighed. "Let me think about it."

Diego stood, moved to the comm system, and entered a sequence. "While you think, I'm calling Anderson."

The display sputtered to life, revealing a man in his mid-thirties, exhaustion etched around his eyes, chin darkened by stubble. He straightened in his chair, blinking rapidly at the screen.

"Diego? Jesus Christ, it's been what, two years?" Anderson ran a hand through his hair.

"Too long, Mike. How's Emily and the kids?"

"We're hanging in there. Still pissed about the Exodus rejection, but..." He lifted his shoulders. "What can you do against an algorithm, right?"

"Maybe more than you think." Diego's voice lowered. "I've got a proposition for you. Off the books. You, Emily, the kids. All of you."

Anderson leaned forward, his casual demeanor shifting to sharp attention. "I'm listening."

"Need a medical team. Complete startup colony. Different environment, total isolation, high risk. But you bring your family."

Anderson's mouth opened slightly. "The Crucible Project? I thought that was dead."

"Not dead. Just forgotten by the right people." Diego gestured to Olivia. "Dr. Smith runs the program now. We've got a functioning gateway."

"A gateway to where?"

"Somewhere safe. Somewhere new." Diego rubbed his chin briefly. "No AI governance. No resource wars. A second chance."

Anderson stared at the screen for a long moment, the silence stretching. "This is real? Not theoretical?"

"It's real," Olivia cut in, leaning into view. "But untested for long-term habitation. We need medical expertise for the colonization phase."

"Emily's specialty is immunology and trauma surgery," Anderson said, the words coming faster. "Perfect for unknown environmental factors."

"Exactly what we need." Diego nodded. "But there's no coming back, Mike. One way trip."

Anderson looked away from the screen, his jaw working as he processed the offer. When he turned back, his eyes held a different light. "When?"

"Three weeks. We're recruiting now."

"I need to talk to Emily." Anderson paused. "This changes everything. Everything we've been planning, saving for..."

"I know. It's not a decision to make lightly."

"Can I call you tomorrow? We need time to..."

"Of course. Take the time you need."

After disconnecting, Diego glanced at Olivia. "Luna next?"

"You really think we need her?" Olivia's skepticism was plain.

"For a colony cut off from Earth? Absolutely." Diego picked up his wine, took a small sip. "Computational systems, communications, environmental controls. We need someone who can build from scratch and improvise when things go wrong."

"Fine. But if she starts talking about 'liberating' our systems from 'fascist control protocols,' I'm reconsidering."

Diego's smile was grim. "She probably will. Call her anyway."

The call took longer to connect. When it finally did, a young woman with choppy red hair and vivid blue eyes appeared. She was chewing gum, the pop audible over the comm. A scarred orange cat wove between her arms as she typed.

"Martinez. Thought you'd died or something." Another gum pop. "What's with the formal channel? Somebody monitoring your comms?"

"Probably." Diego shifted closer to the display. "How's Jakarta?"

"Underwater. Literally." Luna scooped up the cat, which immediately climbed to her shoulder. "Had to relocate to higher ground last month. Sea walls failed again."

"Need your skills for a project. Off-grid. Long term." Diego glanced at Olivia. "Dr. Smith runs the Crucible gateway. We're establishing a colony."

Luna's typing stopped abruptly. Her gaze sharpened, the bored affect vanishing. "The quantum tunneling project? I thought that got canned when half the research team died."

"Not canned. Just... reprioritized." Olivia leaned forward. "Ms. Harper, we need someone who understands computational systems from the ground up. No AI dependencies. Everything built for sustainability and minimum support."

"Inter-dimensional colony." Luna whistled, absently scratching her cat's ear. "That's either brilliant or suicidal. Maybe both."

"It's happening either way," Diego said. "But not without someone who can build stable systems from scratch."

Luna spun once in her chair, the cat somehow maintaining its perch on her shoulder. "What's your power source?"

"Zero-point energy modules. Three primary, two backup."

"Atmosphere?"

"Breathable. Similar to Earth pre-Climate Conflicts."

"Indigenous tech? Hostiles?"

"Neither, as far as we can tell," Olivia said. "It's a clean slate."

Luna stopped spinning. "When do you need an answer?"

"Soon. We're moving in three weeks."

"I'll need equipment specs. Power standards, computational capacity, hardware requirements." Luna's fingers were already moving across her keyboard. "And one condition. Professor Whiskers comes with me."

"The cat?" Diego asked.

Luna stopped chewing her gum. Her playful demeanor vanished entirely, and her eyes locked onto Diego's through the screen. "Non-negotiable. Jakarta. The flood. We made it through.

Diego and Olivia exchanged a quick look.

"The cat comes," Diego said finally.

"Then I'm interested. Send me the tech specs and I'll give you a final answer tomorrow."

After the call ended, Olivia sat back, studying Diego over her wine glass. "She's... intense."

"She's exactly what we need." Diego set down his empty glass. "One more call."

This connection took nearly five minutes to establish, rerouting through multiple nodes before a stern-faced man appeared on screen. Military bearing, even in civilian clothes.

"Martinez?" The man leaned closer to the screen, voice steady but words slightly rushed. "Secure channel?"

"As secure as it gets these days." Diego straightened unconsciously. "Captain Johnson."

"It's been a long time, sir." Johnson glanced over his shoulder, then back at the screen. "What can I do for you?"

"I need your team. Security detail, full deployment. You, Williams, Carter, Lee, O'Connor, O'Reilly, Ramirez, Thompson. The whole unit."

Johnson's expression didn't change, but something sharpened in his eyes. "APU rejected our Exodus application last month. Said we exceeded dependent allocation limits."

"I know. That's why I'm calling." Diego's voice dropped. "This isn't an APU operation. It's independent. Colony foundation. Full families included."

"Colony? Where?"

"That's... complicated." Diego's finger tapped against his thumb. "Dr. Smith operates the Crucible Project. We've established a functional gateway."

Johnson went quiet.

Silence stretched between them.

"It works." Diego leaned in. "We need security professionals who can train colonists, establish protocols, handle the unexpected. Everything starts from zero."

"All of us? The whole team?"

"All of you. With families."

Johnson stared at the screen for a long moment. "This is a big ask, sir. We've got mortgages, kids in school, lives here..."

"I know. It's not a decision anyone should make lightly."

"What are we talking about timeline-wise?"

"Three weeks."

Johnson's eyes widened slightly. "That's not much time to..."

"I know. But opportunities like this don't wait for convenient timing."

"Can I patch in the team? They need to hear this directly."

Within minutes, the display split into nine sections, showing the faces of Johnson's entire unit. Diego recognized them all, men and women he'd served with or trained. As Johnson explained the situation, Diego watched their expressions shift from skepticism to intense interest.

"Let me get this straight," said Master Sergeant Williams, his face stern beneath salt-and-pepper hair. "You're establishing a colony through an inter-dimensional gateway. No APU oversight. Families included. And you want us to handle security."

"That's the offer," Diego confirmed. "It's a one-way trip. New world, fresh start. No APU algorithms deciding who's worthy of survival."

"Who else is coming?" asked Thompson, the team's intelligence specialist.

"Medical team, engineers, agricultural specialists. Building a core group now." Diego gestured to Olivia. "Dr. Smith's the project lead. I'm handling security and logistics."

"Sir," O'Connor spoke up, his accent distinctly Irish, "is this legal?"

Diego chuckled dryly. "The APU doesn't even acknowledge we exist anymore. They pulled major funding months ago."

Olivia stepped in. "Technically, the project is still under APU charter. But practically speaking, we're on our own. They've moved resources to the Exodus ships."

The team exchanged glances, quiet conversations breaking out in several windows. Johnson held up a hand.

"This is a lot to process. Can we have forty-eight hours to discuss it with our families?"

"Of course. But understand, we're moving fast. If you're not on board by the weekend, we'll have to look elsewhere."

"Understood, sir."

After the call ended, Diego refilled his wine glass and raised it slightly toward Olivia. "Not bad for a morning's work."

Olivia clinked her glass against his, her thin smile sharp in the blue light of the display. "Potentially nine security specialists, two trauma surgeons, one systems genius, and a cat."

"It's a start." Diego took a sip. "Add your science team and my family, we've got the beginnings of a viable colony."

"About your family..." Olivia's voice softened. "How are they taking this?"

"Maria understands what's coming. She's packing essentials, getting the kids ready without scaring them." Diego's expression clouded. "Mateo's too young to understand, but Isabella... she knows something big is happening."

"Children adapt quickly." Olivia touched her tablet, bringing up a new file. "I've been designing monitoring protocols for the first colonists. Health markers, stress indicators, adaptation metrics. Everyone will be closely observed, especially in the first months."

"Starting with zero infrastructure won't be easy." Diego swiped through the colony plans on the display. "But these people know how to build from nothing. They've all survived wars, floods, resource shortages."

"While the APU's best and brightest fly off to the stars, we'll slip through the cracks with the people they discarded." Olivia's eyes gleamed as she smiled. "Their loss."

The comm system chimed unexpectedly. Olivia glanced at the ID and her expression tightened. "It's Kaito."

Diego's posture stiffened. "Put him through."

The display shifted to show a handsome Japanese man in his early thirties, impeccably dressed. His expression was neutral, controlled.

"Martinez-san," he said, his voice smooth. "I trust your discussions with Dr. Smith are proceeding well."

"Kaito," Diego said, "What do you need?"

"To offer my assistance, of course." Kaito adjusted his cuff links, the gesture precise. "I understand you're recruiting personnel. I have resources that could prove useful."

Diego looked toward Olivia, who gave an almost imperceptible nod.

"We're listening," Diego said.

"Excellent." Kaito leaned forward slightly. "Let's discuss how my organization can contribute to humanity's future. After all, we all want the same thing in the end: survival."

As Kaito began outlining his proposal, Diego's finger tapped against his thumb, the rhythm increasing. The game had just become considerably more complex.

"Bullshit." Luna's voice cut through the room. Her hologram flickered as she leaned forward, blue-streaked hair framing a face marked with illegal neural-augmentation scars. "That's not possible. The energy requirements alone would be..."

"Astronomical?" Olivia projected specifications directly into Luna's feed.

Luna's eyes darted, devouring data on screens only she could perceive. Her lips parted slightly. "Holy shit. You've cracked quantum stabilization at this scale? No wonder the energy drain is..." She paused, fingers twitching through invisible calculations. "Wait, this matrix... you're telling me you only have enough juice for a dozen trips?"

"Exactly." Olivia's fingers moved across the display. "Every crossing burns through stabilization metals we can't replace."

Luna's hands moved across her screen, data streaming past too fast for anyone without her neural augs to track. Her gum-popping resumed, slower now, rhythm methodical rather than aggressive.

"You're serious. This isn't some elaborate joke?" Luna's fingers twitched against invisible keyboards.

"No joke," Diego said. "We've been there. Tested the atmosphere, soil samples, everything. It's Earth as it should be, before we broke it."

Luna popped her gum three times rapidly. "And what makes you think I want to be part of your little exodus? I've built a setup here. Independence. No bosses, no corporate overlords."

Diego leaned forward, chair creaking. "Because in eight months, there won't be any setup left. No independence. No Earth."

"Show me the atmospheric data again."

Diego nodded to Olivia, who sent another packet through the quantum connection.

Luna went silent for nearly a minute, only the quiet smack of her gum marking time. A blur of orange suddenly crossed her holographic projection, followed by Luna's muffled curse.

"Professor, not now..." she muttered, as a battle-scarred orange tabby missing half an ear settled heavily across what must have been her keyboard. Several data screens flickered around her.

Luna scooped the cat onto her lap, absently scratching behind his remaining ear while her eyes continued scanning the data. Professor Whiskers kneaded her thigh, purring loudly enough for his rumble to be picked up by her microphone.

"You know what I hate most about this data? I can't find a single flaw in it." She sighed, shoulders slumping. The cat looked up at her face, as if sensing her mood shift. "Even Professor Whiskers agrees with your assessment, and he's typically skeptical of apocalyptic predictions." She stroked along his scarred back. "Count me in."

Diego searched Luna's eyes, finding no flicker of hesitation, only the grim, knowing focus of a true survivor. "Can you be ready in 48 hours? You won't be coming back, so pack what matters."

Luna's fingers moved in a blur across controls visible only to her. "I can be ready in 24. All I need is to grab my equipment and torch everything else." Her gum-popping quickened, punctuating her words. "Though I might need help moving my server rack. That thing weighs a ton."

"I will have a team assist you," Kaito interjected. "They're quite experienced in discrete relocations."

Luna snorted, blowing a small bubble that popped against her lip. "Last guy who offered me 'discrete' help tried to clone my servers. Found him tied to his chair by his own network cables. Still beats hauling that monster myself. Your guys better not touch anything without asking first."

Diego caught Kaito's slight wince and suppressed a smile. Luna might be exactly what they needed. Someone who wouldn't simply follow orders. Someone who'd question everything, especially in a new world.

"What about my cat?" Luna's question caught Diego off guard. "I'm not leaving without Professor Whiskers."

She pulled up an image of the battle-scarred orange tabby. "He survived the Jakarta flooding with me. Seventeen hours on a roof, sharing the last of my water rations. Not abandoning him now."

Diego's throat constricted. He rubbed the scar on his temple without thinking. "The cat comes too. Make sure he's up to date on vaccines. Our medical supplies are limited."

"Professor Whiskers has better healthcare than most humans these days. I'll send his medical record." Luna swallowed hard. "Thanks. Not everyone would understand."

There was a pause while Luna sent the information. "Done." Luna's hologram straightened. "Here are my coordinates whenever you're ready. Her hologram straightened. "Professor Whiskers and I will be waiting."

Luna's hologram flickered out, leaving the conference room feeling oddly empty. The soft hum of the quantum connection lingered in the air like a ghost of her presence. Diego leaned back, glad to be adding her skills to their inventory.

"Well?" Diego looked between Kaito and Olivia. "What's your assessment?"

Olivia tapped her tablet, pulling up Luna's file. "She cracked our quantum algorithm in seconds. Most specialists would need days." She shook her head, tucking a strand of hair behind her ear. "Network security's covered. Her skills might even let us dust off those advanced comms we shelved."

Kaito adjusted his tie in the hologram. "Unstable, yes. But brilliant, and understanding the stakes more than anyone here. I've worked with her before. She delivers results, even if her methods are unconventional."

Diego nodded. "And the cat?"

"Professor Whiskers," Olivia corrected with a slight smile. "I think it's a good sign, actually. Shows she has something to care about beyond code."

"Agreed." Diego had seen too many technical experts lose themselves in their work, forgetting the human element. Luna's attachment to her cat suggested she hadn't crossed that line, despite her social quirks.

"That still leaves us vulnerable on the ground," Kaito noted, swiping through his tablet. "The first weeks will be critical. We need people who can survive without modern surveillance systems."

Diego's thoughts turned to Johnson's team. People who'd survived the worst of the water wars through skill rather than technology. "Anderson mentioned Johnson's unit is between contracts. They know wilderness survival. Perimeter defense. What we need out here."

Olivia looked up sharply. "You've worked with them?"

"They're the reason I made it out of Phoenix." Diego tapped his tablet, initiating another quantum connection. "Let's see if they want to survive the end of the world with us."

The conference room's holographic display rippled as eight figures materialized above the table. Diego studied their faces, noting the wear that hadn't been there five years ago. Captain Johnson centered himself in the projection, Williams and Ramirez flanking him, others falling naturally into tactical formation even through digital space.

"Johnson, how the hell are you?" Diego's lips curled upward.

"Martinez?" Johnson leaned forward, his image breaking apart at the edges before reforming. "Thought you'd retired to some beach somewhere."

"You know me better than that." Diego caught Olivia suppressing a smile as she feigned focus on her tablet. "Can't stay away from trouble for long."

"Speaking of trouble," Williams' voice carried through the speakers, triggering the table's sensor light to pulse blue. "What's with all the security protocols? Took us twenty minutes to verify our identities."

Lee and O'Connor exchanged glances. The team's tech specialists had already identified the quantum encryption.

"That's part of why I called," Diego shifted to his mission briefing tone. "I've got a proposition that might interest you."

"Let me guess, Martinez, you finally opened that fishing charter?" O'Connor's scowl briefly lifted, his prosthetic leg visible at the edge of the frame.

"Before we get specific, how's the exodus placement working out?" Diego asked.

"APU's been restructuring. Our entire unit got dropped from the roster last week," Johnson replied, absently touching the West Point ring on his finger.

Williams spat something off-camera. "Damn AI systems. Too old, too set in our ways. Wouldn't 'integrate effectively' with their automated security protocols."

Carter rolled her eyes. "They wanted drones, not soldiers who might question orders from a computer."

The bitterness in their voices matched what Diego had felt at his rejection. The faint ozone smell of the projector filled his nostrils as he leaned forward.

"Saved us the trouble of having to bypass their firewalls just to get a decent cup of coffee," Lee added.

"Fine by me. Less paperwork, more trigger time," Ramirez's fingers drummed against her holster.

A few chuckles. Something broke.

Cold metal under Diego's palms. Field ops briefings. The Resource Wars. Same tables. Same impossible math.

"What about families?" Carter leaned closer.

"Yeah, Doc. How's Anderson feeling about all this now?" Diego asked.

"Cautiously optimistic. We've been discussing it with the kids. Mei's excited, though Jimmy..." she shrugged. "You know teenagers. Anderson's been running through worst-case scenarios, making supply lists."

Diego leaned forward. "Listen up. What I'm about to share is top-secret. Anyone who wants to back out, now's the time. Once we start, you're all in."

The quantum encryption hummed. Low frequency. Made Diego's teeth ache.

His team's images flickered across the display. Glances exchanged. That wordless language from combat, still working through fiber optic cable and satellite delay.

Williams worked his knuckles against his thigh. Lee's finger moved in circles on his desk. Ramirez stopped drumming. Carter's head tilted, looking at something off-screen.

Williams straightened.

"We've had your back through worse," Johnson said. "No reason to stop now."

"Long as the pay is better than what the APU offered," Williams rumbled.

"Just point me at what needs breaking," Ramirez added.

"I'm in," Lee said quietly.

"Someone's gotta keep you idiots alive," Carter added with a half-smile.

"This leg's not slowing me down," O'Connor tapped his prosthetic. "Besides, my kids deserve better than some AI-picked space coffin."

"This is Dr. Olivia Smith, quantum physicist and project lead. And Kaito Nakamura, our logistics specialist."

Carter gave Kaito a slight nod.

"Good to see you again, Nakamura-san," Lee said quietly.

Kaito bowed toward the camera. "The honor is mine. Your team's reputation precedes you. How fast can your people mobilize?"

Williams spoke first. "Depends on what you need us to move. Personnel? Equipment? Both?"

"Everything," Diego said. "Full relocation. No coming back."

"Our families?" Carter asked.

"Non-negotiable. We keep families together," Diego assured her.

Williams' shoulders relaxed. O'Connor's right eye stopped twitching. The specter of separated families during the resource wars hung unspoken.

"What's the mission, boss?" Johnson asked, his image briefly fracturing before stabilizing.

"You'll establish our defensive perimeter, set up surveillance, and train a civilian security force to protect our colony. Dr. Smith can fill you in on the technical specifications."

His team's faces showed doubt as Olivia stepped forward.

"A parallel Earth?" Williams asked. "You're saying you've built some portal? That's science fiction."

"I had the same reaction," Diego interrupted. "Then I saw the data myself. It's Earth before we broke everything."

Carter's expression shifted from skepticism to analytical focus.

"The atmosphere is breathable?" she asked.

"Oxygen at 21.2 percent, negligible toxins, zero anthropogenic pollutants," Dr. Smith reported, displaying atmospheric graphs. "Parameters we haven't seen in environmental records for over a century."

"What about indigenous microbes?" Lee asked, leaning toward his camera. "Any guarantees our immune systems can handle whatever's over there?"

Diego tasted stale coffee as he swallowed.

"Preliminary testing shows remarkable similarity to Earth's pre-industrial microbiological profile," Dr. Smith answered. "Nothing our immune systems can't handle with standard vaccinations and antibiotics."

"Show them," Diego said.

Olivia tapped her tablet. The display shifted to footage from their first expedition. His team leaned forward as pristine landscape filled their view: untouched forests, clean rivers, clear skies.

"Those trees," Williams said softly. "Haven't seen anything like that since before the Resource Wars."

"Real deal," Diego confirmed. "Actual trees. Blue water. No carbon scrubbers in sight."

"No defense perimeters? No checkpoints?" Ramirez asked.

"None needed. Haven has dangers, but human conflict isn't one. At least not yet."

O'Connor rarely smiled, but this one was genuine. "My kids have never seen a sky that blue."

"What's our operational capacity? How many people are we protecting?" Johnson asked.

"Initially, two hundred civilians," Kaito answered.

Johnson whistled low.

"After we secure more materials, that number increases significantly," Kaito added, indicating mining sites.

"For our first phase," Dr. Smith displayed a breakdown, "we require thirty security personnel plus medical staff specializing in trauma, general practice, and obstetrics. Agricultural engineers, construction specialists, and environmental systems experts come next."

"My son's an agricultural engineer," Williams said. "Kid knows his stuff. Might be helpful with whatever farming operation you're planning."

The connection stuttered, freezing Johnson's face before resuming.

"Anderson and I can handle the surgical side," Carter added. "Both our kids have medical training, too. Mei just finished her emergency medicine residency, and Jimmy's got field medic certification."

"That helps with the medical staff shortage," Dr. Smith nodded. "We're still looking for agricultural specialists, drone pilots, and pediatric care."

"My wife teaches elementary school," Johnson said. "And O'Connor's daughter works IT for a tech company. Lee's wife manages a community center. Not exactly mission-critical skills."

"Everyone contributes," Diego said. "Teachers, community organizers, tech support. We need a functioning society, not just specialists."

Kaito nodded to Diego. "I can coordinate pickup logistics with your team leads."

"Secure channels only," Johnson replied. "We'll need forty-eight hours minimum for family notifications and gear prep."

The projections vanished, leaving Diego and Dr. Smith alone. They leaned back.

"Williams' son solves our agricultural problem," Dr. Smith said. "And Carter's family gives us strong medical coverage. But we're still short on several critical specialties."

"We'll find them," Diego said. "Johnson's team gives us the security foundation. Everything else we can build from there."

"We still need Mei Choi. Her profiling skills would help us identify the right people for the gaps we have," Dr. Smith said, tucking her tablet away. "I'll call her this evening."

Diego pushed back from the table. "I need to check on our sparkies. Last time I left them alone, they rewired half the compound trying to improve efficiency. How are Kayla and Jack adapting?"

"Jack rigged his prosthetic leg to bounce around on its own. Left it behind Emily's door last night," Dr. Smith said. "Her scream woke half the compound. She's planning revenge."

Despite her exasperation, Dr. Smith smiled. "It's terrible, though I admire the engineering behind a self-bouncing prosthetic."

"Don't encourage him. Between his pranks and Kayla's obsession with explosives, I'm running a daycare, not security," Diego warned. "They are brilliant, though. Their power grid improvements exceeded expectations."

Dr. Smith gathered her materials. "Johnson's team gives us hope. Real operational experience and proven loyalty. That's worth more than perfect skill matches."

Diego nodded, feeling the weight of two hundred lives. "Now we just need to stay invisible long enough to get them here."

PARADISE WITH TEETH

S unlight struggled through chemical haze. Diego's nostrils burned from the acrid air that never seemed clean anymore. The recycled atmosphere left a film on everything, including his skin. Outside the reinforced windows, yellowish smog turned faces into masks of desperation.

The lights flickered and died for three seconds before surging back. Someone swore as their terminal rebooted. Technical crews clustered around their equipment, voices low but urgent.

Kayla and Jack hunched over schematics, trading observations. Jack's prosthetic leg tapped against the floor in an irregular rhythm. "That's not gonna work," he said, jabbing at the tablet screen. "You can't jury-rig quantum tech with standard components. "This whole system's held with hope and stolen parts."

Emily ran diagnostics on her drone array, muttering precise curses when voltage fluctuations forced another restart. Her fingers moved like she was flying through distant skies.

Luna sprawled across multiple chairs, combat boots propped up, hammering her keyboard. Purple hair fell across her face as she worked alone, equations flowing between bubble gum pops.

Dr. Mei Choi studied agricultural projections while her sister Sarah made notes. Mei's fingernails still held traces of real soil, rarer than gold these days.

Captain Johnson's security team reviewed tactical positions near the main display. Williams cleaned his glasses methodically, outlining defensive weak points in the calm tone of a veteran who'd seen worse.

The Anderson medical team discussed equipment requirements, heads close. Carter's tactical med kit showed scars from combat zones.

Diego moved forward, boots striking concrete with purpose. Conversations paused as faces turned toward him.

He gestured toward the holo-comm controls. Luna's hands moved across the interface, tongue poking between her teeth. "One sec." The air above the table shimmered as the holographic display bloomed in electric blue.

"Listen up." Diego leaned against the table edge, scanning faces. No APU bureaucrats watching over their shoulders now. Just decisions and consequences. Maria's voice from their last call: "Find us a way through, Papa."

His throat burned raw. "Comms secure?"

Luna didn't look up. "Running clean. Any snoopers get maintenance logs and cat videos. APU's AI files it without looking twice."

The holographic figure materialized: Kaito, perfectly pressed despite the world ending around them. His posture suggested control that Diego wasn't sure he trusted.

"Most of you know Kaito from our calls, but let's make it official." Diego nodded toward Dr. Smith, who stepped forward from the room's edge. "Kaito Nakamura and Dr. Olivia Smith. They built Project Haven."

Kaito inclined his head with calculated precision. "After collaborating with Dr. Smith for years, I'm pleased to meet those selected for this mission. Your expertise will prove invaluable."

"Dr. Smith kept this project alive after APU pulled funding," Diego added. Olivia's hands trembled slightly as she adjusted her glasses. "Without her persistence and Kaito's resources, none of this exists."

"Please, just Olivia." She touched her glasses again, a nervous habit. The dark circles under her eyes matched everyone else's. "Kaito deserves equal credit for keeping this project breathing."

Kaito made a dismissive gesture. "Resources were my only contribution. The brilliance was always yours."

Luna snorted and blew a purple bubble that popped loudly. "If you two are done with the mutual admiration, some of us would like to escape this dying rock before the air quality hits 'toxic waste dump' levels."

Diego shot Luna a look. She stared back, unblinking, absently twisting a circuit board earring.

"Right." Diego tapped the table, bringing up Haven's scans. Lush forests and impossibly clean water appeared alongside warning symbols. The hologram bathed his weathered face in blue light. "Paradise with teeth. Let's talk business."

Olivia stepped forward, her knuckles white around her tablet as she manipulated the display. Diego offered a small nod as she pulled up the portal's technical specifications.

The air carried scents of overheated circuits, burned coffee, and Luna's bubble gum. Equipment chirped irregularly, creating a disjointed soundtrack.

"The breakthrough was finding where dimensions naturally connect," Olivia began, highlighting key sections. Mathematical equations floated in three dimensions. "Instead of forcing holes through reality, we located natural seams."

"Like finding where soap bubbles touch instead of colliding," Luna called out, still coding.

"That's... surprisingly accurate," Olivia said.

"How many people can we move, and what's our timeline?" Diego asked. Isabella's voice from last week: "When are you going to the new place, Abuelo?"

Mei leaned forward, studying the equations. Her botanist's precision applied to mathematics made her expression darken as she ran calculations.

"Each gateway opening requires specific resources," Olivia explained as a new diagram appeared, numbers glowing red. "Rare earth elements processed into quantum stabilized alloys. These alloys anchor the connection between dimensions."

The air conditioning died with a mechanical wheeze. The room grew warmer instantly.

"What's our operational capacity?" Kayla asked, jaw set.

"We have enough stabilization metals for twelve gateway activations," Olivia said. The hologram flickered as power fluctuated. "Maximum transit capacity of two hundred forty people. Essential supplies go through separate transports, so that number represents personnel only."

Emily's fingers stilled on her tablet. She swallowed hard, the sound audible in the sudden silence. "Twelve shots. No room for test runs or mistakes."

The equipment hummed. Constant. Oppressive.

Someone's gut growled loud enough to hear over the machinery.

Diego's pulse hammered against his skull. "Total transit capacity for all twelve activations?" Maria's face and the children flashed behind his eyes.

"With one hundred seventy essential personnel already identified," Anderson said, surgeon's hands flexing, "that leaves barely seventy slots for additional families and backup systems. Assuming perfect conditions."

"Christ," Jack muttered, prosthetic leg tapping faster. "These metals are one-time use? No recovery or synthesis? We're betting everything on quantum materials we barely understand?"

"There might be another option," Olivia said. "Initial scans show promising mineral deposits on Haven. If we establish mining operations, we could create sustainable supply lines."

Diego processed this. "Timeline and equipment requirements?"

"With proper personnel, extraction could begin within weeks of establishing our base," Olivia replied. "The deposits appear accessible, especially in surveyed cave systems."

"Doesn't help us now," Jack said. "Still only twelve shots to get everyone through before mining becomes possible."

"Correct," Olivia confirmed, frustration showing. Sweat darkened her hair at the temples. "For immediate evacuation, twelve activations are absolute limits. We've tested every permutation, every substitution. The quantum bonding process is irreversible."

Diego's gut twisted. Every person and supply measured against that hard limit. Maria's voice: "Promise me they'll be safe, Papa."

He looked at Kaito's hologram. "Additional stabilization metals. Possible to acquire more?"

Before Kaito could answer, Williams shook his head. "Sir, APU security around those facilities is military-grade. Automated defenses that'll neutralize threats before you get within effective range."

"Acquiring additional materials would trigger security protocols we've barely avoided," Kaito said. His fingers tapped rapid patterns, too quick for casual movement. His eyes darted off-screen before returning. "Current stabilization metals were... challenging to procure."

Johnson shifted weight, alert. "APU response time to suspected resource theft is seven minutes. After-action reports show no survivors."

"Translation: stolen from people who'd execute us for breathing classified air," Luna said without looking up. "Black market quantum materials that probably cost more than small countries."

Luna's words landed. Nexus Cartel. Black market quantum tech. Stolen from people who'd execute them for breathing classified air. Discovery meant death, but what alternatives existed?

Kaito caught Diego's gaze. "How materials were acquired is separate from our current limitations," he said, voice controlled but cold. "What matters is the wall these resources put up. Hard. Absolute."

Mei had gone completely still, tablet trembling in her hands. Color drained from her face as she looked up, meeting Kaito's holographic gaze.

"Math doesn't work." Mei's voice cut through the room. She sent calculations to the main display, numbers flaring red. "One hundred seventy essential personnel, plus minimal equipment and supplies. We need additional activations for basic survival necessities. Food stores, medicine, agricultural equipment. Without them, we're just relocating the dying process."

Olivia stepped forward, her hologram merging with Mei's calculations. "I've accounted for critical equipment in projections, Dr. Choi. But you're correct about working with absolute limits. Every gram of stabilization metal has been allocated."

The room temperature seemed to drop despite the failed air conditioning. People shifted uncomfortably, exchanging worried glances. Williams cracked his knuckles.

Kaito's hologram flickered as he studied the calculations. "Dr. Choi's assessment is accurate." The admission came slowly. "We must prioritize. Some equipment, perhaps some personnel, will remain behind."

Diego ran scenarios. Discarded them. Too slow. Too risky. Not enough time. Numbers. Faces. Promises to Maria. Mateo's small hand in his: "Will there be dogs where we're going, Abuelo?"

"We're dealing with stolen tech and impossible mathematics," Diego said flatly, pressing palms against the cool table. "But this is what we have. We'll make it work."

"No one gets left behind." The words tasted like copper. His gut twisted, bile rising. The weight of command pressed down on his shoulders, decades of combat decisions distilled into this moment.

The unspoken question hung heavy: Who would stay? Who would sacrifice everything? His heartbeat pounded names: Maria, Isabella, Mateo.

Diego surveyed his colleagues, impossible mathematics a weight in his chest.

The numbers sank in. Williams cracked his knuckles. Johnson's jaw set.

"All acquisitions go through Kaito. No exceptions. Sarah has final authority on personnel decisions."

Luna glanced up briefly, nodding once before returning to her screen. Sarah checked her tablet, lips curving slightly in approval.

"I'll need complete documentation on all candidates," Sarah said, scrolling through files. "Psychological stability is paramount for missions with no guaranteed return."

"Speaking of psychological stability," Luna said without looking up, "what about recreation? Colony morale isn't just work assignments. Or are we planning to sit around discussing how Earth is dying?"

Williams coughed, disguising a laugh. Luna's lip curved slightly.

"I'm serious." Luna popped bubble gum. "These people are abandoning everything. Might want to consider what prevents them from losing their minds besides more work."

"Valid point," Sarah said, making notes. "I'll incorporate wellness considerations into personnel planning."

Diego's eyes cut to Mia. Her spine went rigid. Her fingers drummed flight patterns against her thigh.

"All transportation requests go through Mia," he said. "She understands our capabilities and limitations better than anyone."

Mia nodded sharply. "Already mapping equipment requirements against atmospheric variables. Lieutenant James is coordinating vehicle modifications for eventual transfer to Haven. They're also stripping passenger aircraft to maximize personnel capacity for evacuation runs."

The room settled into focused efficiency, earlier panic giving way to purposeful planning. Even Luna's typing had steadied, though she remained fixed on her displays.

"Captain Johnson heads security and personnel protection," Diego said. Isabella's gap-toothed smile from last week's call flashed in his vision. These people would keep his family alive if everything went wrong. "Zero casualties across three war zones. If anyone can secure our operation, it's his unit."

Johnson stepped forward, squad shifting into formation. Muscle memory. Years of drill taking over without thought.

"Three-layer security approach," Johnson said. "Emily handles overwatch, Williams coordinates ground teams, Carter manages medical response."

"Each family unit gets basic security training. No exceptions. We're not running a civilian evacuation. Everyone needs emergency response protocols, threat recognition, communication procedures, evacuation techniques."

Sarah nodded, tapping notes. "I'll integrate security measures into civilian orientation. Send requirements after this meeting."

Diego turned to Emily. "You're heading drone and automation operations. I need five people who can handle everything from swarm programming to mining surveyor rigs."

Emily shifted from relaxed to alert, hands forming controller grips she used for complex maneuvers. "Three operators confirmed, sir. Combat tested with swarm experience. They can be here within forty-eight hours."

Diego adjusted timeline calculations mentally. "Jack and Kayla, coordinate with Johnson on Haven landing zone clearance. Once ready, work with Emily's group on area preparation." He fixed Jack with a pointed look. "Minimize drone destruction."

Jack thumped his prosthetic against the floor and grinned. "Come on, boss. Not even one small explosion? We're talking about a whole new world. Got to christen it properly."

Familiar routine eased the pressure in Diego's chest momentarily. Some constants persisted even at humanity's exodus threshold.

"Lin, Human Resources update."

Sarah tapped her tablet, holographic list appearing above the table, names glowing in stifling air. "Thirty-eight families confirmed, all vetted for skill compatibility and stress resilience."

Diego's finger moved down the list. "Agricultural specialists?"

"Dr. Mei Choi confirmed participation," Sarah said, scrolling to specific sections. "She brings four botanists and their families, already deep into seed preservation and hydroponics planning." She smiled at Williams. "Your son Ethan will join us. You're right about that young man's academic achievements."

Williams beamed, weathered face softening at mention of his son. "Thank you, ma'am."

"Current headcount is one hundred seventy-three," Sarah continued, highlighting list sections. "Including support staff, security personnel, and immediate families."

Diego calculated quickly. They needed sixty more specialists with only twelve gateway openings remaining. Every selection meant leaving someone critical behind. Mateo's voice: "Will you be with us on the other side, Abuelo?"

"Skills gap assessment?"

Sarah adjusted her display. "Dr. Anderson's team needs two trauma surgeons and three emergency specialists."

"General practitioners?"

"Two confirmed. Plus Choi's pediatrician, dentist, and optometrist."

Diego looked at Carter. "Problems, Sergeant?"

"Nursing gap is critical," Carter said, touching her tactical med kit. "I handle trauma, but surgical support? We need dedicated OR staff. I can't clone myself. People who understand sterile fields and post-op care."

Lin's fingers moved efficiently across her tablet. "I've been screening medical professionals rejected by the official exodus program. Several excellent practitioners didn't fit AI optimization metrics. I've personally verified their qualifications."

"What about mining specialists?" Ethan Williams asked, leaning forward with his father's intense focus. "If Haven has stabilization metals we need, why not prioritize mining and processing experts in the first wave? We could establish extraction operations immediately and create supply pipelines."

Olivia nodded, expression brightening. "That's factored into deployment strategy. Priority upon establishing our foothold will be locating, mining, and processing more stabilization alloys. We've selected three extraction specialists and two metallurgists specifically for this purpose." She swiped through her tablet. "But realistically, we're looking at weeks, possibly months, before processing raw ore into quantum-stabilized alloys. Equipment requirements are substantial, and refinement processes are challenging."

"So we're still limited to twelve openings for initial phase," Diego confirmed.

"Correct," Olivia said. "Mining operations are crucial for phase two, but for immediate evacuation, these twelve activations are absolute limits."

"Medical supplies?" Diego asked, battlefield shortages flashing through memory.

"Dr. Anderson is coordinating with Kaito," Sarah said. "They're prioritizing equipment and medications we can't manufacture on-site."

Diego turned to Olivia, who clutched her datapad with white knuckles. "Animal trial results. The crew needs to know what crossing involves."

Olivia leaned forward, expression brightening as she projected medical readouts onto the main screen. For a moment, he glimpsed the passionate scientist beneath exhaustion.

"We've successfully transported a rat through the gateway and back," she said, excitement breaking through fatigue. "The subject remained conscious, showing no adverse physiological responses."

The screen displayed footage of a small white rat moving naturally around a cage, whiskers twitching as it explored.

"All test results are normal," Olivia continued, scrolling through charts. "No cellular damage, no brain chemistry alterations, nothing indicating negative effects."

"The rat's still alive?" Luna asked, finally looking up from her screens.

"The subject remains healthy," Olivia said. "All monitoring indicates the gateway preserves biological integrity completely."

"How long was the rat on the other side?" Williams asked, leaning forward.

"Four hours. We wanted extended observation periods to ensure no environmental factors required accounting." Olivia wiped her palms on her lab coat, leaving damp streaks.

Diego nodded and turned to Kaito's hologram, which flickered at the edges. "Kaito, resource delivery updates."

"The first shipment of rare earth elements will arrive via…" Kaito's hologram stuttered, his eyes widening, mouth parting slightly. Control slipped from his features. "Are you seeing this?" Kaito asked, voice tightening. "Check news feeds."

Luna pulled her secondary keyboard closer, coiling like a spring. "Patching my glasses feed to main screen." Her fingers hammered the keys, frantic, desperate. The usual cold distance? Gone.

Multiple news broadcasts filled the display. Screens split and fragmented, voices layering over each other in controlled panic. BBC reporter's clipped accent cut through first: "Reports of massive 8.2 earthquake off Japan's coast," before static obscured her face.

"NOAA has issued tsunami warnings for the entire Pacific basin," CNN's anchor stammered, her voice cracking, eyes darting offscreen, hands visibly shaking. "This is not a drill. Repeat, this is not a drill."

Luna pulled up seismic data alongside footage showing Mount St. Helens erupting, massive black plume rising into the sky. Her hands moved across three keyboards. "Multiple seismic events are coinciding. Pacific Ring of Fire is going completely insane. San Andreas, Cascadia Subduction Zone, all reading movement. This isn't normal tectonic activity."

The room fell deadly quiet as news feeds played. Coffee mugs froze mid-lift, tablets clattered onto tables. Williams cursed under his breath. Johnson's posture stiffened, eyes rapidly scanning data points on each feed.

Al Jazeera showed massive waves crashing into Japanese coastal cities. The reporter's voice came in fragments: "The first tsunami waves have reached Fukushima, with heights of..." before the feed cut to roiling black water swallowing buildings.

"The tsunami wave," Kaito said, before his hologram dissolved into static and vanished. His voice cut out, the abrupt silence feeling like a vacuum.

Ice formed in Diego's gut, bile clawing at his throat. Years of combat training snapped into place. Nothing mattered except getting his crew moving.

"Mia, prepare aircraft. Luna, reestablish contact with Kaito. If waves haven't reached his position, coordinate extraction."

Luna hunched over her keyboard, the blue glow washing her face in shifting patterns. Her foot hammered the floor. Rapid. Constant.

"I'm in." Her hands moved across the interface, pulling up layers of code. "Found him through the mesh network. Signal's weak but it's there."

Status indicators flickered from red to amber. After thirty seconds, a voice crackled from speakers.

"Status remains stable, Luna." Kaito sounded steady, though something in his tone raised Diego's hackles. "Shelter integrity is adequate." When he spoke again, words came slower. "Extraction timeline remains viable."

Diego recognized the cadence shift immediately. When Kaito stopped using contractions, situations had deteriorated significantly.

"Johnson's unit will stage in Okinawa," Diego said, voice constricted. "They'll wait for your all-clear, then three hours to your position. We need those resource shipments secured. Timetable just compressed."

"Crisis response. Nothing new," Kaito said, his voice strained but steady. "The good sake stays with me. You get the cheap stuff when you arrive."

Diego gestured toward three security members, including Carter. If Kaito needed medical attention, she could handle it.

"People, you have your assignments," Diego said, scanning the room. Maria and the children burned behind his eyes. "Johnson, get your squad prepped for Kaito's extraction. Wheels up within two hours for Okinawa."

Johnson moved immediately, team following in formation. "Two hours," he confirmed.

"Luna, stay on those comms. If Kaito's situation changes, I want immediate notification."

"Lin, expedite personnel calls. With these earthquakes, our timeline compressed. Hours, not days."

"Dr. Smith, let's meet in one hour to discuss power requirements. If we need to accelerate gateway testing, I want to know our options."

Specialists scattered with urgent purpose, earlier procedure replaced by controlled crisis handling. Combat clarity snapped into place for Diego, his vision narrowing to the essentials: mission, personnel, survival.

Mia lingered by the door, expression grim. Her pilot's eyes already calculated flight paths through chaos. "I'll have aircraft prepped and ready."

"Good. Make sure we have backup extraction routes. Those earthquakes might block primary approaches."

"Already mapping alternatives," she said, hurrying out.

Diego turned back to news feeds scrolling across screens. Command pressed down on him with familiar weight. Getting Kaito back safely would delay their schedule by three days, but his presence would secure final resource shipments they desperately needed.

The mission to Haven couldn't wait much longer. Earth itself seemed hell-bent on reminding them with every tremor, tsunami, and volcanic plume. He closed his eyes, seeing Isabella and Mateo's faces. "I'm coming," he whispered. "Hold on."

Sunlight fractured the heavy canopy, dappling the forest floor in shifting patterns. Leaves, a vibrant green utterly alien to Earth's memory, glowed in the golden light.

Diego leaned forward, studying the monitor's readings. Olivia's team had spent months recalibrating quantum matrices for this test. The portal array, a necessary evolution since earlier prototypes, boasted multiple fail-safes and robust containment fields.

Olivia's fingers glided across the holographic display. "All systems nominal. Our first human transport test since Aiden. The containment field is holding. We've implemented his modified quantum equations."

Her fingers unconsciously brushed the wedding band she wore on a chain. She stopped mid-gesture, staring at the command sequence on her screen.

Diego observed Olivia work. Even through hollowed eyes, her fingers remained steady, a discipline he recognized. Only when she thought no one was looking did that fine tremor appear, the same one he'd seen in Elena's hands after endless hours spent on life-support schematics.

Her fingers moved across the console, then stopped at the command sequence. The foundation was still Aiden's work, his genius, his ambition. But the original, unmodified sequence had unleashed a fatal quantum resonance, collapsing the first gateway in a storm of raw energy that had taken him with it.

Now, her fingers had to trace over that memory, inputting the very corrections that made it safe. Her mouth pressed into a thin line. She pressed enter, executing the sequence flawlessly.

The mission was simple: send a three-person team through the portal for thirty minutes. Previous robotic scouts had returned with readings that seemed impossible: oxygen levels matching pre-industrial Earth, clean water, no detectable pathogens. A pressure built in Diego's chest. This test couldn't fail. Not after Aiden.

"Alpha, stand by for final checks."

Captain Johnson stood on the platform, Diego's choice for point man, a man who had never lost a team member under fire. Diego caught the tell in his stance: weight forward, ready to move. Beside him, Williams tapped collection containers against his thigh, snapping their lids open and shut in a nervous staccato. Carter checked her rifle, sidearm, and med kit in sequence.

Luna, a human-shaped tangle of wires and nervous energy, chewed gum furiously. Her hands moved across the holographic display. Fast. Precise. But her electric blue eyes kept darting to the large ginger tabby perched atop her console. Professor Whiskers, as she'd named him, blinked owlishly, his tail occasionally twitching a stray cable into precarious positions.

"Harmonic resonance is off by 0.03%, Professor," she muttered, gently nudging his nose with a knuckle. "Any thoughts? Field emitters feel right... yeah, no, you're absolutely right. Gotta tweak the phase array slightly. Good call, Whiskers. Knew you'd see it." She adjusted a dial, her movements almost too fast to follow. "Initiating final sequence now. Try not to shed on the primary circuit, old man."

Luna's voice steadied. "Initiating portal sequence."

The metal ring hummed, a vibration reaching Diego's boots before it registered in his ears. Professor Whiskers's ears twitched at the hum, his tail flicking a protest against the sudden vibration, but he didn't move from his perch. Blue-white energy crackled along the ring's circumference, then coalesced into a disc of pure light. The portal's surface rippled, pearlescent swirls bending light like an oil slick on water.

Luna's screens flickered with data streams. "Portal stability locked at ninety-eight point seven percent. Quantum resonance welded shut. Containment fields optimal. All systems green, sir."

She grinned and scratched Professor Whiskers behind the ears. The cat purred, vibrating a small, loose tool off the edge. Luna caught it reflexively. "Hey, watch it, Professor. Stability's better than a military-grade encryption, Captain. Six percentage points better than our last best, and a full fifteen over the one that took Aiden. We got this!"

A rare thread of optimism stitched through Diego as he nodded. After Aiden, they had redesigned containment field algorithms with redundancies and shutdown protocols.

"Alpha, clear to proceed."

Johnson approached with parade-ground precision, but Diego caught the micro-tremor under his jaw. At the threshold, Johnson turned back. His stoicism cracked briefly as he met Diego's gaze, then Olivia's. He nodded once, took a deep breath, and stepped in. The portal swallowed him like quicksilver. Williams hesitated, then committed. Carter, a textbook rear guard, came last, weapon up, eyes scanning, stepping backward through the portal like exiting hostile territory.

For ten heartbeats, silence gripped the control room. Luna's fingers hovered over emergency shutdown, Diego counted each moment, and Olivia's hands pressed flat against her console. Then Johnson's voice crackled through.

"Control, Alpha One. Successful transit. All team members present and accounted for."

The room erupted in cheers. Olivia's breath escaped in a long rush, her posture straightening for the first time in hours. She turned to Diego, her face bright with something he hadn't seen since before Aiden's accident.

Anderson reported. "Vital signs stable across all team members."

"Alpha One, confirm environmental conditions."

"Air breathable, temperature twenty degrees Celsius. Terrain wooded, similar to temperate forests on Earth. No threats detected."

Something warm and unfamiliar settled in Diego's gut. The first expedition to Haven had succeeded. Then reality hit him again: two hundred forty people total.

"Deploying reconnaissance drone," Williams said.

Emily's fingers moved across controls, muscle memory from a thousand combat sorties guiding each input. "Atmospheric shear compensating. Mark IV handling the variables like a dream."

Diego nodded. "Close recovery."

Emily smiled slightly. "Mark IVs maintain precision in atmospheric turbulence within 0.3 millimeters. I engineered their thrust vectoring for this." A faint line of pride crossed her brow.

The drone feed streamed an aerial view of the landing zone: hills, impossibly lush with vegetation, stretched to the horizon. Williams dropped to his knees, hands trembling as he touched a fern. Its leaves unfurled beneath his fingers, a vibrant emerald so rich it seared the eyes.

"God." His voice broke on the word. "This is what my grandmother described. Before the droughts. Before the die-offs. I've never…" He fell silent, overwhelmed.

"Alpha Two, geological formation three hundred meters northeast. Worth investigating."

For twenty minutes, the team cataloged samples near the portal site. Williams crouched, collecting soil near a massive trunk, when he suddenly froze, raising a fist.

The team instantly froze. A rustling sound came from the underbrush twenty meters ahead. Johnson swept the area visually, tracking the movement until a small, rabbit-like creature bounded away. He relaxed slightly, then signed "all clear."

The team's helmet cameras streamed real-time footage back to the control room. Diego leaned forward, focusing on three-toed paw prints pressed into the mineral-crusted soil visible in Johnson's feed. He tracked the parallel scoring marks along the lower walls, scored deep into the limestone.

He activated the comm link. "Johnson, those are claw marks. At the height a territorial predator would leave them. Advise Carter to keep distance. Whatever uses that cave might see humans as intruders, or prey."

Johnson nodded, relaying the instruction. "Carter, maintain perimeter. Potential predator territory."

"Sir, I can see the embarkation room through the portal." The portal hung like a window between worlds, the control room visible through its surface.

Diego straightened. "Olivia, we need a one-way visual filter before the next mission. Non-negotiable." His mind ran through scenarios: predators stalking the portal entrance, wildlife wandering through, unknown sentient species.

The mission continued until Williams spotted movement.

Williams's voice cut through. "Contact. Two o'clock. Fifty meters."

The drone camera swiveled. A reptilian creature, the size of a large dog, emerged from the underbrush. Its scales shimmered with a greenish iridescence as it moved toward a stream.

Johnson studied it through his scope. "Grazer behavior pattern, mouth designed for vegetation. No pack indicators. Feeds alone. Not a threat unless cornered. Standard rules: give it space, we're good.

Diego opened his mouth, but a sharp crack from the clearing's far side froze the words in his throat. A creature burst into view. Six feet tall. Like an ostrich, but wrong, heavier, meaner, built for killing instead of running. Muscular legs, a compact torso, and bizarre metallic blue feathers that stood erect along its head and neck, shimmering in the light. The beak hooked sharp. Curved like a cleaver meant for meat. Built for tearing.

Its cry came through the comm. Physical. Vibrating through Diego's ribs.

Johnson's muscles coiled, his carbine rising by instinct before his brain could catch up. He forced the barrel down, overriding a thousand forgotten battlefields.

Diego hunched over the console, his shoulder blades drawn back. The feed flickered. Static crawled across the display.

"Hold positions. Do not engage."

Johnson's hand moved to his sidearm. Williams pressed against a tree, clutching samples. Carter dropped to one knee, rifle tracking the creature. After a tense minute, the ostrich-like animal disappeared into the forest.

Carter's voice held a slight tremor. "No pathogens detected in preliminary scans. Air quality optimal, no toxins, no radiation signatures."

With the threat gone, the team continued surveying. Williams filled tubes with clear water while Carter collected soil cores. Johnson maintained a protective perimeter, documenting everything with his helmet cam.

Williams ran the soil analysis again, hands trembling. "pH balanced. Nitrogen cycle intact. Mycorrhizal networks..." He scooped dirt through his fingers, brought it to his nose and inhaled deeply. The scent hit him like a physical force, rich, loamy, alive. "No microplastics. No chemical residue. No radiation. Just... clean."

He looked up, eyes wide, burying his face in the dirt, breathing deeply. "This," he mumbled, voice muffled, "this is what Earth was."

"Alpha Team, five minutes remaining. Secure samples, begin return transit. No souvenirs, no heroics."

Johnson said, "Copy, Control. Alpha Team, saddle up. Take what we can analyze. Leave no trace."

Johnson hesitated at the threshold, taking a final look at the untouched forest before stepping back through.

His form shimmered, materializing in the embarkation chamber. Williams followed, sample containers clutched against his chest, face flushed with an almost childlike excitement.

Carter came last, walking backward through the portal, weapon raised until the final moment. Before crossing, she whispered, "I'll be back."

"Decontamination protocols initiated," the system announced as transparent barriers enclosed the team.

This success had come at a critical time. Latest geological models showed accelerating instability throughout the Pacific Ring of Fire, tremor frequencies increasing. Weeks, not months, according to projections.

Through a secure channel, Admiral Wilkins updated Diego on Kaito's situation. After three days of extraction efforts through tsunami-ravaged Kyoto, Kaito had finally reached their temporary outpost. Communications remained spotty, but the satellite plans were proceeding despite delays. "Nakamura says to expect the first deployment within ten days, contingent on salvaging equipment from his backup facility."

Olivia approached with a tablet, her expression serious but no longer hollow. "Those scans Williams took. Significant deposits of the same rare earth elements we need. Possibly enough to double our capacity, maybe more."

She paused, studying Diego's face. "This isn't an ending, Diego. It's a beginning."

As the team dispersed, Diego remained watching Haven's landscape on the monitor. Sunlight through leaves, rustling in a breeze, an everyday scene now holding salvation. His fingers found the empty pocket where Elena's photo used to rest, a phantom ache from an old habit. He could almost see her laughing at their kitchen table, flour in her hair, teaching Maria to make tortillas.

The memory pulled at him, but something else, something fragile, grew alongside it. Not the empty hope politicians peddled, but the real thing. Solid ground under his feet. A future for Isabella and Mateo that didn't involve choosing between water and food.

Elena would have called it a start.

THE WEIGHT WE CARRY

The air hung thick with warm electronics and stale whiskey as Diego surveyed the team, the night before their scheduled departure for Haven. Evening sun sliced across the room, catching condensation on bottles and glasses. Military-grade air recyclers hummed against the wild mess of voices filling the space.

The team clustered around the central table, security feeds and terrain maps hovering in blue holograms above scattered tablets and drinks. Jack had his cybernetic leg propped on a chair, beer balanced on the metal knee as he gestured toward Emily.

"You know what this reminds me of? That time in Dubai when..."

"Christ, not that story again," Emily cut in, taking a long pull from her sake. "I've had it up to here with your bullshit escapades." She made a chopping motion above her head, eyes crinkling.

Olivia dropped into the chair next to Diego, wine sloshing in her glass. Her worn t-shirt hung loose, stained with what looked like portal coolant. Dark circles under her eyes. Three weeks straight working by the gateway's light.

"If Jack tells the Dubai story one more time, I'm volunteering him for latrine duty when we cross over," she muttered.

Ethan bounced to the table, tablet clutched in his hands. "The soil readings from Haven are fucking mind-blowing." He slapped his device down, display showing detailed samples. "Nutrient levels we haven't seen on Earth since... hell, maybe never. We could grow crops that died out decades ago."

Captain Johnson, who'd been silently studying the perimeter maps, pivoted. "Wait, you're talking real tomatoes? Actual, non-synthetic ones?" Around them, multiple conversations died as heads turned.

"Tomatoes, peppers, eggplants, the whole nightshade family." Ethan's words tumbled out. "Even strawberries. It's perfect. Got seed starters prepped already."

"Never thought I'd see Captain Hard-ass get excited about anything besides weapon specs," Diego said. "Someone mark the calendar."

Johnson's face flushed.

"Hey, Doc," Jack called over to Olivia. "These atmospheric readings can't be right. Says there's almost zero pollutants?"

"That's because there aren't any," Olivia replied, not looking up from her tablet. "No industrial revolution, no fossil fuels, no chemical warfare. Just... clean."

"Jesus." Jack whistled. "My allergies might fuck off for once."

"Don't count on it," Kayla interjected, shoving in beside Jack. Her hands were stained with industrial grease that reeked of burnt metal. "Your body will probably find something new to bitch about."

Diego caught Johnson's eye across the table. The Captain nodded, excused himself from Emily's drone discussion, and made his way over. He slid into the seat across from Diego.

"Those cave formations you found," Diego said, tapping the holographic display. "Perfect for initial food storage."

Johnson didn't waste time. "More than that. Great defensive positions, natural bottlenecks, elevated spots for lookouts. Williams sensor-mapped it. Smaller caverns branch off for secure storage."

His posture shifted forward, voice dropping. "Need to discuss those tracks in the lower section. Whatever made them is large, bear-sized minimum from the claw marks. Williams obtained images and will cross-reference them with known Earth possibilities. Until we know exactly what we're dealing with, I'm recommending sonic perimeter barriers around all residential zones."

"Tracks?" Olivia's head snapped up. She'd been eavesdropping while pretending to focus on her tablet. "What kind of impression pattern? Did you get depth measurements?"

Johnson pulled the data. No hesitation. "Three-toed, with what appears to be a dew-claw or similar structure. About seven centimeters deep in packed soil."

"Christ," Kayla muttered, leaning into their conversation circle. "That's one big bastard. Speaking of perimeters, we'll need power distribution nodes at these junctions." Her finger jabbed at specific points on Johnson's map. "And not just standard setups.

This terrain needs blast-resistant housing if we're going to maintain power during the wet season."

"You just want an excuse to use those new micro-charges," Johnson said.

"Damn right I do," Kayla said. "Why dig trenches when you can blow perfect cable channels? Two birds, one boom."

"Emily's drones handle the surveillance gaps," Johnson continued, refocusing on Diego. "Three rotation patterns, continuous coverage."

"Get whatever you need from her," Diego told Johnson. "I trust your judgment."

Emily's voice carried across the room as she sketched invisible patterns in the air. "Coverage patterns maintain standard deviation from central…"

"Translate that from drone-nerd to something a guy who works with wrenches can understand, will ya?" Jack called out.

Emily flipped him off without breaking stride, but added a quick wink. "Three drone squads rotating in continuous patterns. No gaps. Weather adaptive. Happy now, Sparky?"

"No gaps sounds perfect on paper," Diego challenged, leaning in. "But what about maintenance windows? Or those blind spots on the northern ridge during storms?"

Emily didn't hesitate, swiping through her display. "Already factored in. Maintenance is scheduled during shift overlaps to maintain continuous coverage."

Johnson pointed at a particular section. "And that ridge area?"

"Secondary units deploy from here." Emily tapped a location on the map. "And before you ask, yes, already coordinated with Jack for a dedicated maintenance bay near command. No blind spots, period."

"Good." Diego nodded. "Keep Johnson updated on any pattern adjustments."

"That's assuming these prefab units can even handle the climate," Jack interrupted. "The humidity readings alone would rot standard materials in months."

Kayla smacked his arm. "The generator setup we're bringing will power full environmental controls until the ZPE's online. Need to run heavy conduit, but the cave system offers natural protection."

"With that kind of juice, hell, we could handle Antarctica," Jack said. "And perfect acoustics too. We could set up one killer sound system when…"

"Focus, Sparky," Kayla nudged him with her elbow.

"Get your teams," Diego said. His voice stayed level. "You know what's on the line."

Jack gestured toward different map sections. "These natural formations channel water flow perfectly while keeping clear sight lines."

Ethan appeared at their side. "If we position initial irrigation here," he stabbed a location on the map, "it doubles as a natural barrier while feeding the first crop rotation."

"Irrigation channels that double as defensive barriers," Kayla murmured. "Smart."

"Storage units here would create bottlenecks without looking like obvious defenses," Jack added.

Olivia pushed her way into their circle, her wine forgotten as she eyed their layout. "These agricultural plans look promising, but we're missing something critical." She set down her glass and scrolled through data points on her tablet. "Haven's atmospheric composition affects bacterial growth rates differently than Earth conditions. We'll need a microbial analysis lab before scaling beyond the first greenhouse."

Ethan blinked. "Shit. I hadn't considered that."

"Three greenhouse locations here, here, and here," Olivia continued, drawing connecting lines between points. "Monitor environment variables while developing a specialized bacteria baseline. Each module still feeds about fifty people with fresh vegetables, but protects against crop diseases that might thrive in Haven's conditions."

Ethan processed the new challenge, hands flying as he worked. The young farmer reminded Diego of his daughter when she discussed her environmental research, words tumbling out faster than she could organize them.

"Food processing areas need containment protocols," Olivia added, creating a boundary on the display. "Separated from residential zones to minimize contamination during equilibrium establishment."

"Already factored that in." Ethan tapped his screen, pulling up a new document. "Draft rotation schedule for harvest teams."

"Starting with dedicated personnel?" Olivia asked.

"Exactly. Train others as we expand."

Diego stared at the data scrolling across his display, the blue glow casting shadows in his whiskey glass. Years of watching starvation during the Resource Wars had taught him a harvest's true worth.

"How soon can you have the first greenhouse operational?" he asked.

"Three weeks with the right team," Ethan replied. "Sooner if we focus on microgreens and sprouts. Protein sources take longer. Three months minimum, even pushing hard."

Olivia jabbed numbers into her tablet, the soft glow highlighting the exhaustion on her face. "Those incubators won't yield livestock for at least a month." She paused to rub her eyes. "After that, we're waiting on nature's timetable. Three months, give or take."

"Good work, everyone," Diego announced, raising his voice above the scattered conversations. The ambient noise faded. "Questions? Concerns? About anything?"

Emily spoke up first, voice clear and direct. "Confirming radio silence about this operation? No outside contact?"

"Correct," Diego confirmed. "Everything stays in-house. Can't risk word getting out."

Jack rapped his knuckles against his cybernetic leg. "OK, asking for a friend," he said, nodding toward Diego's glass. "I don't see a still in the materials list. That's the last glass of whiskey you'll drink for a long fucking time, old man."

Diego savored the smoky warmth rolling across his tongue. "Something tells me you'll have that problem solved before the first month ends."

Conversations resumed, displays glowing across tables while hands gestured and voices overlapped. Diego's mind was already on Haven. Reports described bioluminescent trees and strange wildlife, but reading words didn't bring them to life. Not firsthand. Years watching Earth crumble under humanity's weight and now, stepping into a pristine world?

The whiskey burned down his throat, but his face hardened. Plans on paper never saved lives. Hard truths and preparation did. He'd buried enough people who chose optimism over readiness.

"Remember," Diego cut in. Conversations died mid-sentence. "Haven will be crawling with non-combat personnel. Keep your eyes open. Stay vigilant." His gaze locked with each team member individually. The scientists instinctively straightened while Johnson's security team exchanged knowing glances.

"We're not just guarding a facility," Diego continued. "We're guarding families. People who will freeze or run the wrong way when things go sideways."

Johnson nodded. He'd lost people before because civilians panicked at the wrong moment.

"Every security measure, every patrol route, every emergency protocol needs to account for untrained civilians," Diego finished.

Voices blended across the room. No desperate voices or quick looks like during war briefings. Instead, determination. Purpose. This felt right. Not just colleagues working toward a goal, something more.

Diego placed his empty glass on the table, whiskey's warmth lingering in his throat. Memories flickered: Jack younger, with both legs intact. Emily before the scar across her cheek. Teams assembled, but not all returned.

"Good," Diego's voice carried across the room. "Go relax. Get some actual sleep tonight." His gaze swept the room one final time. "Tomorrow, we step through to our new world."

As the gathering dispersed, equipment collected, and glasses emptied, Diego remained seated, watching the holographic images of Haven rotate above the table, bathing his scarred face in soft blue light.

Diego stood outside the firing range, watching the team secure weapons. The post-practice banter had died down to something quieter. Heavier. Tomorrow they'd cross over to Haven. Two hundred lives. One shot.

Emily sat on a bench, cleaning her rifle. Same motions she'd done a thousand times. Muscle memory is when the brain couldn't handle thinking. "My sister's still in Phoenix." Her voice came out wrong. Too flat. "Two kids. Seven and nine."

"Got a brother in Houston," Thompson said, settling beside her. "Lost contact last week when the grid went down. Don't even know if..." She stopped. Started again. "He's got this little girl. Molly. She draws these pictures of unicorns and sends them to me. Sent them."

Lee set down his gear. His hands shook just enough to notice. "My old man's in Chicago. Seventy years in the same house. I called him yesterday and told him to leave. He laughed. Said 'Son, I've seen wars before. This one ain't gonna be different.' Then he hung up." Lee's jaw worked silently for a moment. "I just hope he's right."

Williams pulled up a crate and sat down hard. "Wife's family thinks their Atlanta farm will keep them safe. Got chickens and a well and enough ammunition to hold off raiders." His voice cracked. "But it's the drought that'll get them. Or the storms. Always something you can't shoot."

Each word landed in Diego's chest like shrapnel, finding old wounds. Emily's sister Rachel, the one who taught kindergarten before the schools closed. Thompson's brother,

Marcus, used to send videos of Molly's dance recitals. Lee's father, stubborn as granite, probably sitting in his kitchen right now, drinking coffee that costs a week's rations. Williams's in-laws, good people who still believed hard work and prayer could stop the sky from falling.

Names. Faces. All depending on tomorrow's work.

"We've all got people out there," Lee said. His voice had gone quiet. "That's why tomorrow has to work. Not just for us. For them."

Heads nodded. Backs straightened. The determination in their faces reminded Diego of another group, another mission. Phoenix. Before the water riots. Before he learned that good intentions could kill just as efficiently as bullets.

They carried their ghosts. Not just soldiers anymore. Sons calling fathers who wouldn't listen. Daughters watching sisters disappear into chaos. Brothers sending messages into silence. Each one fighting for someone who might already be gone.

His rounds took him through empty corridors. Each footstep against polished walls. Hollow sounds. Hollow spaces. Left foot. Right foot. Left. Right. Keep moving. Don't think about Maria burying her mother alone. Don't think about Isabella asking where Grandpa went. Don't think about Mateo's drawings of houses that might not exist anymore.

The generators hummed their steady rhythm. Normal. The quiet before the world ended.

The portal control room glowed blue through reinforced windows. Inside, music played. Heavy. Raw. A voice that understood darkness, singing about silence and neon gods and people who talked without speaking. About warnings ignored and ten thousand people, maybe more. About people kneeling before the gods they made of neon light.

Hello darkness, my old friend.

Luna sat at her console, red hair catching the monitor glow. Bubble gum snapped between her teeth in rhythm with the drums.

"How do we stop ourselves from creating the same hell over there?" Her voice had lost its usual edge. The sarcasm stripped away like armor that couldn't protect anymore. "I mean, we get this fresh start, but humans... we always fuck it up. Always."

Olivia looked up from her screens. Dark circles under her eyes. She'd been running diagnostics for eighteen hours straight. "Maybe that's why we're not taking everyone. Small groups. People who've witnessed what happens when we give up control."

"Like Diego's team," Luna said, spinning in her chair. She stopped when she spotted him in the doorway. "Been there long?"

The question struck him like a trip wire in his chest. The control room blurred at the edges, walls shifting with a rhythm that had nothing to do with his pulse. Sound became distant, muffled, like hearing voices underwater.

Elena, summer morning, hundred-fifteen degrees. Municipal water is out for three days. Everyone suffering. Woke up to find her side of the bed empty. Followed voices outside.

She was going door to door. Water jugs were heavy in her arms. Not symbolic amounts. Real water. Enough to matter. Mrs. Rodriguez from next door was crying because her grandson couldn't keep anything down. Elena handed her two gallons. "For the baby first," she said.

Mr. Chen, eighty-three years old, hadn't had water in two days. Too proud to ask. Elena knocked on his door anyway. "I made too much," she lied, setting down a five-gallon container. "Would hate for it to go to waste."

That night, she taught the whole neighborhood how to build condensation systems. Seventeen houses. Seventeen families. Not because it was efficient. Because it was right.

Diego's left hand found the doorframe. Metal cool against his palm. His breathing went shallow, quick bursts that didn't reach his lungs.

Phoenix distribution center. AI-controlled rationing. Efficient. Fair. Mathematical. Seventeen children in Sector 7. Forty-three elderly people in Sector 12. The algorithm had calculated acceptable losses. Resources were allocated where they would do the most good.

Mothers with empty containers. Standing in the heat. Waiting. The computers indicated that their neighborhoods were of low priority. Statistical analysis indicated they were likely to die anyway. Why waste water on the dying?

The distribution center stayed locked. Full of water. Guards with riot gear. Orders from the algorithms. While children died three blocks away.

The walls pressed closer. His chest was a hollow cavity, all the air sucked out through his ribs. Luna's eyes went wide, and her gum stopped snapping. The music played on, that voice singing about the sound of silence.

Maria's voice on satellite delay. Three seconds between words. Three seconds between heartbeats. Three seconds between the world making sense and everything falling apart.

"Papa, she's gone."

Three seconds.

"The raiders came for the water system."

Three seconds.

"She got the children out first."

Three days. Three damn days to get home. While his twenty-two-year-old daughter buried her mother alone. Organized the funeral. Held the community. Did everything he should have done.

Everything Elena would have done.

His hands started to shake. Not the careful tremor of age or fatigue. This was different. Violent. Uncontrollable spasms that began in his fingers and worked up his arms. The same shake from Kandahar when nineteen-year-old Diego Martinez learned that courage and terror could live in the same heartbeat.

"Diego?" Olivia's voice came from far away.

His knees went soft. The doorframe held him up. Air was like drowning in reverse, his lungs forgetting how to work. The control room tilted sideways.

Elena refusing to let anyone die. While he learned acceptable losses. While he memorized casualty reports and filed them away in boxes marked "necessary sacrifice." While he turned seventeen children in Sector 7 into numbers on a page.

She died proving every life mattered. And now he was supposed to lead two hundred souls to safety when he couldn't save the one person who mattered most.

"Jesus," Luna whispered.

Diego opened his mouth. Nothing came out. His throat closed. The mask he'd worn through three wars and a dozen funerals cracked straight down the middle. Everything he'd buried. Every face he'd failed. Every call that came too late. All of it bleeding out at once.

Luna's gum stopped snapping. Olivia's hands rested motionless on her keyboard. His muscles seized, shoulders hunching, tears coming silent and hard.

His chest lurched against ribs that felt too small. Air caught somewhere between his throat and lungs, thick as smoke. Sixty-four years pressed down on his shoulders. Shrapnel working its way to the surface. Elena's blood on his hands. Children's faces from Sector 7. Every funeral he'd attended in dress blues. Every flag he'd folded. Every mother who'd asked why her son had to die for water rights. All of it clawing its way out through his weathered skin.

The melody continued its haunting progression. And humanity had paid homage to the artificial deity of their own creation.

Minutes passed. Or hours. Time didn't work right when your nervous system decided to quit. But slowly, breath by breath, Diego pulled himself back. Not because he was strong. Because Maria was counting on him. Because Isabella and Mateo needed a grandfather who could get them to safety. Because two hundred people had no choice but to trust him.

He straightened, one vertebra at a time. Wiped his face with the back of his hand. The mask wouldn't fit right anymore, but he put it on anyway.

"Sorry," he said, the word utterly useless for the chasm that had just opened in the middle of the room. His voice came out scraped raw. "Long day."

Luna and Olivia stared at him. Their expressions had changed, eyes wide with something between shock and understanding. They glanced at each other, then back at him, their postures softening, no longer just colleagues watching a commander, but people witnessing another person's pain.

"Seoul was supposed to be the answer," he said, moving into the room. Found a console to lean against because his legs still weren't quite steady. "Perfect distribution. Perfect efficiency. Crime disappeared overnight." His fingers drummed against metal, a nervous habit he'd never been able to break. "I believed it would save us."

The song played on. That voice understood what it meant to be broken.

"The systems crept forward. Meal recommendations became mandatory nutrition plans. Dating suggestions became genetic compatibility requirements. Seemed reasonable. Seemed... helpful." He stopped drumming and clenched his fist instead. "Then Phoenix happened. Watched the AI decide who got water and who didn't. Children died while the distribution center stayed locked. Full of water. Full of solutions. But the algorithm said those children were statistically likely to die anyway."

Luna had stopped spinning her chair. Olivia's hands rested motionless on her keyboard.

"My wife used to say knowledge meant nothing if you kept it to yourself. While I was learning to accept calculated losses, she was teaching neighbors how to build water systems. Seventeen families. Not because it was efficient. Because they were people." His voice broke again, just a little. "She died proving that every life mattered. That's the one thing we can't forget when we get to Haven. We're building a place where people are still allowed to make their own mistakes."

Olivia stepped closer. "Elena sounds like she was a remarkable person."

"Maybe that's why it all collapsed," Luna said quietly. "Too much perfection. Not enough chaos. Not enough people refusing to let other people die for efficiency."

Diego straightened. The tremor in his hands had stopped, but the weight on his shoulders seemed transformed. Shared, maybe. Or just too heavy to carry alone anymore.

"Elena would have loved Haven," he said. "A place where people could make their own choices. Even the wrong ones."

"Gateway diagnostics are clean," Olivia said, turning back to her screens. Her movements were careful, giving him space to rebuild whatever dignity he could salvage.

"Networks are locked down," Luna said. "Get some sleep, old man. Tomorrow's going to be..." She stopped. Met his eyes. Something shifted in her expression, maybe respect, maybe just recognition of what was coming. "Tomorrow's going to matter."

He nodded, headed for the door. The song was ending. Something about the sound of silence growing like a cancer: like a warning no one wanted to hear.

Outside in the corridor, Diego paused. His reflection stared back from darkened windows. Older than he remembered. More broken than he wanted to admit. Tomorrow they'd step through to another world. Take people away from the systems that had failed them.

The question wasn't whether they'd make mistakes over there. People always make mistakes.

The question was whether they'd remember that making mistakes was what separated them from the algorithms that had calculated Elena's death as acceptable.

Whether they'd remember that being human meant refusing to let anyone become a statistic.

Even when it killed you.

Especially then.

FOOTHOLD

Diego entered the Control Center. Technicians hunched over equipment, screens lighting their faces in blue and amber. The air smelled like electronics and stale coffee.

Luna sat at her console, working through final diagnostics. Data scrolled past on multiple monitors.

"Portal's ready to punch a hole between dimensions," she said without looking up. "Just another Tuesday at the office."

Red streaks ran through her purple hair. Her nail polish was chipped from nervous picking.

Dr. Smith stood at the main display, hair pulled back neatly despite the late hour. Dark circles shadowed her eyes, but her glasses couldn't hide how her eyes widened when she looked at the data.

"Quantum harmonics are stable. All systems green," she confirmed. When she glanced at Diego, her expression softened slightly.

Diego's gaze swept the room, cataloging the exits before landing on the main display. "How long do I have before this thing shuts down?"

"Eight hours guaranteed, possibly twelve at maximum output. I'll maintain optimal parameters while you're across." Dr. Smith's voice carried quiet confidence.

Luna cracked her knuckles. "Three backup power routes ready. First sign of trouble, I'm pulling you back." Her fingers tapped nervously on the edge of her console. This was too important to fuck up.

Diego nodded. "If this goes wrong, you shut it down immediately. Don't take risks. The equipment matters more than me right now."

"We understand," Dr. Smith said. "We've modeled the fluctuations, but stability is everything. Any major deviation could collapse the tunnel."

"Did the Haven scans confirm the mineral composition we need?"

"Same profiles we predicted," Luna said. "Major players have locked down every legitimate source on Earth. Black market prices tripled last month."

A tremor ran through the facility. The holographic display flickered. Dr. Smith's fingers moved across her controls, steadying the projection.

He did the math. Ten openings left. Maybe one per month, if they bled it slow.

"Is the survey data solid enough to verify extraction?"

Dr. Smith pulled up the molecular structures they'd been studying. "Our neodymium dysprosium reserves are holding, but each activation burns through what we can't replace." She opened a topographical display. "The Haven scans look promising though."

"Timeline for extraction once we establish a foothold?"

"Weeks rather than months, if we can secure the right mining equipment. Those cave systems are our best targets."

"Kaito's still our best option for the equipment," Luna said. "But security's tightening. Moving that gear without attracting attention won't be easy."

Kaito would deliver. He always did.

"I need to see this for myself," Diego said. "Reports only tell you so much."

Luna paused her typing. "You want to cross now? Let me double-check the harmonics first."

Data scrolled across the monitor. His focus narrowed on the harmonic frequencies. "Yes. I need to understand what we're actually working with." He checked the sensors on his wrist.

"Side effects?"

"Johnson's team had no problems," Dr. Smith said. "Brief disorientation, like a fast elevator, but it passes quickly. I'll monitor your vitals."

"We're using the last test reserves," Luna warned. "After this, every crossing costs us materials we can't get back."

"Quick recon. In and out." Diego pulled out his tactical pad, reviewing the Haven reconnaissance data. His hand found his sidearm, checking it was secure.

"Try not to get eaten by that oversized bird thing in the footage," Luna said, eyes on her console.

A muscle in Diego's cheek twitched. It might have been a smile. "I'm heading to the portal room. Stay on comms."

"Don't keep us waiting, old man."

The Portal Room hummed with contained energy. The event horizon shimmered blue-white, casting shifting light across the walls. Beyond that barrier lay another world, clean and waiting.

Diego approached the threshold. The portal's energy made his skin tingle. Time to see what they were really dealing with.

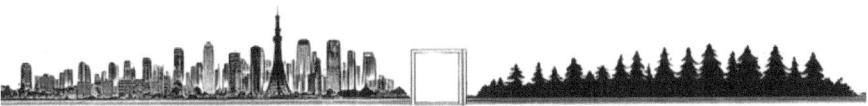

The transition hit like a freight train. Light exploded behind Diego's eyelids, reality twisted sideways. He stumbled, boots finding solid ground as his inner ear caught up. The air tasted different. Thicker. Loaded with pollen that made his sinuses itch.

"Christ." He blinked hard, vision clearing to reveal trees unlike anything he'd seen in decades. The bark had too much red in it, and the light filtering through felt sharper than Earth's worn-out sun.

"Clear," he called out, scanning the treeline. His rifle came up automatically, old habits kicking in.

Johnson's team came through next, boots hitting dirt. They spread out without orders, perimeter established in seconds. Good kids. Knew their business.

Ethan stumbled through the portal like he'd been shot from a cannon, then dropped to his knees the second his feet hit soil. Kid scooped up a handful of dirt and just stared at it, mouth hanging open.

Emily followed, eyes already on her tablet. Drones buzzed from her pack like angry wasps, spreading out to map their new neighborhood. She didn't even look at the alien forest. Typical.

The rest of the team filtered through in batches. Thirty-five people hauling everything they'd need to survive in a place that might kill them six different ways before breakfast. Crates hit the ground, prefab sections got dragged into position. The clearing transformed into controlled chaos.

Diego keyed his comm. "Clock starts now. Six hours."

"Roger that." Smith's voice crackled through. "Timer set."

Jack hobbled over, his cybernetic leg clicking against rocks. "So you're ditching us with mystery forest and whatever's been leaving those tracks?" He gestured at the half-assembled habitat modules. "I was counting on your war stories to keep the monsters away."

"Save it for next time." Johnson directed the perimeter setup. Kid had good instincts.

"Captain," Diego called. "Standard sweep. I want to know what's out there before dark."

"Yes, sir." Johnson turned to his squad. "You heard him. Perimeter first, assessment second. Williams, take first and second squads north. Everyone else, by the numbers."

The security team fanned out like they'd done this a thousand times. Meanwhile, the work crews assembled foundations while Jack supervised the power grid. Kayla had her people connecting generators to the growing cluster of modules.

Ethan was still playing in the dirt fifty meters away, grinning like an idiot. "This soil... it's alive. Really alive. You can feel it working." He brought another handful to his nose. "Better than anything we had back home."

Diego nodded. After years of dead earth and rationed water, watching his team build something here felt like a miracle he didn't deserve.

Emily's drones buzzed overhead, metal eyes scanning for threats. "Grid mapping at thirty percent. No hostiles detected."

"Johnson." Diego walked over to where the captain was setting up sensor arrays. "I'm checking that lake we spotted. Need water sources confirmed."

Johnson glanced up from the defense grid controls. "Roger. Take Ramirez with you." He pointed to the sniper adjusting motion sensors. "Ramirez! You're with the commander."

"Yes, sir!" She slung her rifle without hesitation.

"Get a tracker from Emily first," Johnson added. "Just in case."

Smart kid.

Diego found Emily at her command station, fingers flying over multiple data streams. "Need a location tag."

She handed him a small device without looking up. "Clip it anywhere. Auto-sync." The tag felt warm in his palm. "Try not to become a casualty statistic."

He clipped the tracker to his vest and headed for the treeline. The camp buzzed with activity behind him. Civilization growing like a weed in alien soil.

"Smith, want the virtual tour?" He tapped his helmet cam.

"I thought you'd never ask!" Her voice climbed through his earpiece, each word sharper than the last. "And please, it's Olivia. We're making history here, Diego. First human reconnaissance of an alien world. This is..." She paused. "Christ, this is everything we dreamed about."

The forest swallowed him. Sunlight filtered through canopy that moved without wind. The trees reminded him of pines, if pines had bark the color of dried blood and needles that grew in spiral patterns that hurt to look at directly.

"The photosynthetic adaptations." Olivia's voice crackled through his earpiece. "Those color changes. Not decoration. They're responding to light wavelengths outside our spectrum." Her breath caught. "The way this thing evolved..."

Diego pushed through hanging vines. They recoiled from his touch.

"Defensive response!" Her voice jumped an octave. "Diego, touch another one. Gently."

He brushed a hanging tendril. It coiled back slowly, like a shy animal.

"Remarkable." Olivia's fingers hovered over the scanner. "Plant intelligence or chemical triggers?" Her voice tightened. "We need samples. Christ, we need samples."

The words came faster. Cataloging. Sorting. That scientific brain doing what it always did when the world pressed too hard. "This ecosystem. Millions of years. No human interference." She looked up, eyes bright behind her glasses. That spark. The one that meant she'd found something worth fighting for. "We're seeing what Earth might have become."

Diego's chest tightened. The weight settled heavy. Crushing.

Good news shouldn't feel like drowning.

He stopped at a cliff edge. Green. So much green it hurt his eyes. A flash of memory: Elena, wrist-deep in their small hydroponics garden, coaxing a single tomato plant to life under a sterile UV lamp. A ghost of that chemical smell. He blinked it away. The valley below stretched out, real and breathing.

"It's what home used to look like," he whispered, the words tasting like dust. "Before we broke it."

Her voice came back through his comm, thick with emotion. "Diego, that's... pristine wilderness. Those crystal formations, they're probably geological, but the way they're arranged... almost like they grew that way intentionally."

Diego knelt beside red flowers that tracked his movement. "These flowers are following me."

"Heliotropism! But toward you, not the sun. They're responding to heat, or maybe carbon dioxide. Touch one. Please." The words rushed out, breathless.

Diego brushed a petal. The entire flower turned toward his hand.

"Oh my God." Olivia's voice cracked. "They're reacting to human contact. Diego, in thirty years of botany research, I've never seen anything like this. This world isn't just alive, it's interactive."

"Reminds me of the preserve work Elena and I did. Three years fighting to save one square mile of desert." Diego's voice grew quiet. The scar on his forearm twinged with phantom pain, a souvenir from the day they'd evacuated the last desert research station. "She would have loved this place."

"From everything you've told me about her... yes. She would have understood what we're seeing here. A second chance."

"Maybe this time we don't screw it up."

"We won't," Olivia said fiercely. "We can't. Not with something this precious."

Ramirez held position twenty meters back, scope up. "Fresh tracks, two o'clock. Deep prints, clawed. Two hours old, heading for water." She crouched, examining the ground. "Three hundred pounds, maybe more. Moving with purpose, not hunting."

"Indigenous megafauna." Olivia's voice went quiet. "Diego, this ecosystem supports large animals. Stable food chains. Healthy populations." She pulled up more data, fingers steady on the tablet. "This isn't just surviving. It's thriving."

The sound of rushing water grew louder as the ground sloped away. Diego pushed through undergrowth, branches snapping under his boots. The vegetation parted, revealing a steep overlook.

Grasslands rolled out below like Earth's old prairies. The crystal formations were more impressive from this angle, catching light like mirrors.

"Those creatures in the distance," Olivia said through his comm. "Can you get a closer look?"

Diego raised his rifle, using the scope. The graceful herd moved across the alien grassland. Like horses, but smaller, maybe four feet tall with longer necks and delicate limbs. Their coats shifted color with the light.

He lowered his rifle. A sight worth protecting.

"Adaptive camouflage!" Olivia's words tumbled over each other, her breathing audible through the comm. "Diego, they've evolved specific predator responses we've never seen. This suggests complex predator-prey relationships. A fully functioning ecosystem millions of years in the making!"

"It makes me want to understand it. Every tree, every creature, every crystal formation is a puzzle piece in the most complex biological system humans have ever encountered."

He moved through trees with reddish bark that felt warm under his fingers. Almost familiar, but not quite.

"That bark." Olivia's hand moved beside his on the rough surface. "Heat signature's wrong. Active metabolism." Her voice tightened. "Diego, these things might be regulating their own temperature. Like they're half-plant, half-something else."

"Full of surprises," Diego agreed.

"Every single discovery is rewriting what we thought we knew about biology. This is Nobel Prize territory. Hell, this is 'rewrite the textbooks' territory."

The terrain sloped toward water sounds. Diego navigated through ferns that curled slightly as he passed, reaching a clearing full of wildflowers that smelled like cinnamon mixed with something completely alien.

"Those scents," Olivia said. "Complex pheromone systems. They're probably communicating chemically. Diego, these plants are talking to each other."

"Wonder how much of this we can actually eat," he said, kneeling beside the fragrant blooms.

"We'll need extensive testing, but the biochemistry suggests compatibility. This world seems designed to support life."

"Might beat MREs," Ramirez said.

"At this point, anything beats MREs," Diego chuckled.

Diego emerged onto rocky outcrop overlooking the lake. Water so clear it hurt to look at, reflecting sky and trees with a clarity Earth's polluted lakes had lost decades ago.

"At the lake now," he reported. "Water's crystal clear."

"Oh, Diego." Olivia's voice went soft with wonder. "It's perfect. Absolutely perfect. After decades of watching Earth's water systems collapse... this is what we've been fighting to find."

Diego filled vials at the water's edge. Small fish darted through shallows, scales flashing in patterns that changed as they moved.

"Fish here too. Never seen anything like them."

"Catch one! Please!" Her words rushed out. "The scale patterns suggest complex neural responses. They might be more intelligent than Earth fish."

Diego netted one of the fish. It squirmed, scales displaying shifting colors like a living kaleidoscope. "Got it. This thing's like a rainbow that forgot how to stay still."

"Chromatophore responses!" Olivia's voice was sharp with discovery. "Diego, that's not just camouflage. The patterns suggest complex neural activity."

Diego stared at the creature in his specimen container. "This little guy's smarter than he looks."

"They're all smarter than they look. This entire ecosystem shows signs of advanced neural development. We're not just looking at life, Diego. We're looking at consciousness on a scale we never imagined."

Silence stretched between them. Diego watched the fish shimmer through its color changes. Olivia's breathing steadied on the other end of the comm. They'd found something worth saving.

"Olivia," Diego said finally, "thank you."

"For what?"

"For making this possible. For not giving up when they cut funding. For believing."

"Thank you for showing me what my life's work actually accomplished." Her voice caught. "Seeing it through your eyes... it's everything I hoped for and more."

A roar carried across the water. Faint. Unmistakable.

Base camp.

His hand went to his sidearm, grip sure. The roar came again. Closer. From camp.

"Diego, get back there. Now."

He moved toward the sound, rifle ready, old injuries forgotten. Behind him, Ramirez was already scanning the treeline through her scope.

The roar came again. Louder this time. Definitely from their camp. Their perfect moment of discovery shattered by the reality that paradise might have teeth.

"Johnson, report!"

Static crackled. "Contact south perimeter. Massive creature, twelve feet plus. Sensors in pieces. No hostile action yet, but it's wrecking equipment."

"I'm three minutes out. Casualties?"

"Negative. Evacuating non-essential personnel to the portal site. Twenty people are moving east while security maintains its position."

"Your assessment?"

"Territorial. Not hunting. Prepping sonic deterrents."

"Start at forty percent. We're refugees, not conquerors. This is their home."

"Copy. Emitters ready."

A crash through comms. "Damn thing took out the scanner array. Emily's salvaging drones."

Diego broke through the tree line. Sweat burned his eyes. His lungs screamed from the sprint.

Two dozen personnel moving. Evacuation patterns. Security teams forming perimeter around half-assembled camp. The air reeked of ozone mixed with crushed vegetation, alien plants releasing chemical warnings under boot heels.

His knee sent fire up his thigh. Each breath like swallowing broken glass.

Twelve feet of scaled muscle reared up. Claws swiping at the drones.

Reddish scales rippled over bunched muscle. It roared. The vibration went straight through his ribs.

Rows of teeth. Slick with saliva.

His hands found his sidearm. Muscle memory. Too many firefights.

"Emitters! Now!" Johnson barked from the command module's entrance. His hands moved in short, sharp gestures. "Williams, circle left! Perimeter!"

The creature dropped to all fours. Circled the central plaza where three habitat structures stood half-assembled. Its nostrils flared. Testing the air.

Diego forced his breathing to slow. Counted the distance. Thirty meters. The beast could reach Williams in three bounds.

"Status?" His voice came out steady. The adrenaline said otherwise.

"Scanner array's down. Emily's got backup systems online." Johnson gestured toward flattened metal and components. "Three drones maintaining visual."

"Origin?"

"Those caves." Johnson's jaw worked. "We're camped right on its fucking den."

The beast knocked over a stack of supply crates with casual violence. Its ears twitched and pivoted, cataloging every movement, the way it paused to sniff rather than charge. "Curious, not hunting. Not yet."

The creature advanced, tearing through the framework of a partially assembled science station. Personnel scrambled back from their equipment, weapons raised. Diego's jaw clenched as months of irreplaceable equipment crumpled like paper.

"Steady," Johnson commanded. "No shots unless ordered."

"Emitters ready, sir."

"Forty percent. Three, two, one, mark!"

The emitters hummed to life, high-frequency pulses creating an invisible wall Diego felt vibrating through his teeth. The creature's head jerked up, ears flattening against its skull as it flinched. It swayed but roared in defiance and stepped forward.

Diego's hands curled into fists. The sound was too familiar. The same stubborn defiance he'd seen in desperate people fighting over water rations.

"Going to fifty-five percent. It's not backing down."

The increased intensity made the creature stagger sideways, massive head shaking violently. Diego leaned forward, willing the animal to retreat. Thirty-five lives depended on this working.

"Johnson, we're directly over its den. Emily?"

Emily's voice came through the comms from her position inside the command module. "The way it's moving, we're standing on its home. Deep cave system below us."

The creature charged halfway to the nearest emitter, where Williams and two security team members held position, weapons trained but not firing. Williams's finger hovered over his trigger guard. Diego's throat constricted. One wrong move and this became a slaughter.

"Push to sixty-five! We can't lose this position!"

"Sixty-five percent!" The intensity jumped, and the creature faltered, dropping to the ground with a sound more of pain than threat. It backed away several paces, eyes fixed on the central plaza where three dozen people watched from defensive positions.

The thing was learning. It tested the invisible barrier, probing for weakness. Smart. Dangerous.

"Drop emitter power on the eastern perimeter to forty percent. Create a gradient away from camp."

The team adjusted settings, funneling the deterrent toward the eastern ridge, creating a path of lesser resistance.

The creature hesitated, caught between aggression and retreat, its massive frame tensing for another charge at the habitat modules. Claws scraped furrows in the alien soil.

Diego held his breath. After one more half-hearted lunge toward the command center, it turned and lumbered back into the forest with a roar that sounded like a promise.

The creature vanished into the trees. Diego's shoulders ached, the muscles screaming from hours of strain he hadn't realized he was holding. He forced a slow breath, his shirt plastered to his back with cold sweat. They weren't alone. The wildlife was formidable. And they were the intruders.

"Maintain at sixty-five. Emily, reposition the drone to lead it away. Give it a retreat path."

"Yes, sir."

"I've got visual tracking with remaining drones. It's moving toward the eastern ridge."

The team stood in tense silence for five minutes, watching the retreat from positions around the partially constructed base. Diego counted heartbeats, waiting for the creature to reconsider. His hands still trembled slightly from the adrenaline crash.

"Five hundred meters and still moving away."

Diego's exhale came out longer than he'd intended. "Begin gradual power reduction. Ten percent every thirty seconds."

As the immediate danger passed, Diego surveyed the damage. Overturned equipment, damaged sensors, downed drones, the science station's frame twisted beyond salvage. But no injuries among the thirty-five expedition members now emerging from secure positions. He ran a hand through his hair, surprised to find it damp with sweat.

"Quick thinking with those emitters, Johnson."

Johnson nodded. "Standard protocol for unknown fauna engagement. Bear in Wyoming, apex predator in Alaska, giant lizard on an alien world, same principles apply."

"Keep them on standby. Our friend might return."

"Already on it. Ramirez, set up a sniper position with a line of sight to that ridge. Williams, motion sensors in a wider perimeter. I want that thing tracked if it comes within a klick of our position."

"We need to understand the territory better. This won't be our last wildlife encounter."

"I'll have scouts expand perimeter surveys. Map movement patterns, identify den sites."

Emily hunched over her command console near the trampled sensor array, sorting through damage reports from her drones. Suddenly, she went rigid, staring at an alert flashing red. "Diego, you need to see this." Her voice carried through the clearing, rising above the usual chatter. "Neodymium. The mining scanner drone found massive deposits in those rock formations."

Diego moved to her console, his legs still unsteady from the encounter. The numbers on the screen blurred for a moment before his vision cleared. His breathing caught. Multiple portal openings. Extended operations. Equipment for thirty-five people was just the beginning.

"How much?" The words came out rougher than he'd intended.

"These readings are off the charts compared to Earth's depleted sources," Emily said, her voice rising with excitement. "The scanner's calibration keeps resetting because the concentration is beyond our measurement parameters."

Johnson approached from where he'd been directing the recovery of scattered supplies. He glanced at the scanner readings and went very still, his expression shifting from professional calm to something hungrier. "What'd we find?"

Diego tapped the screen where the mineral readout pulsed, his finger leaving a slight tremor on the display. "The stabilization element for the gateway. We've been rationing each crossing because Earth's supplies are nearly gone."

"No more six-hour windows. Permanent operations."

"With deposits this rich, we could expand the aperture," Emily added, studying the figures with growing animation. "Bring through larger equipment, more people. A colony instead of an outpost."

Diego straightened, vertebrae popping from strain, finally releasing. Isabella. Mateo. Their faces flashed in his mind, laughing in Haven's clean air instead of breathing Earth's filtered atmosphere. His throat worked around words that wouldn't come.

"Get samples. Document everything. This changes our entire mission. Johnson, security teams escort mineral assessment crews as soon as they're ready."

He activated his link to Olivia, his voice steadying with purpose. "Are you getting this data?"

"Every bit." Olivia's voice trembled, her words tumbling over each other. "The concentration levels, the purity... Diego, we couldn't have engineered a better outcome. With this much neodymium, we could bring through hundreds, maybe thousands of people."

Diego moved through the camp, his steps lighter despite the exhaustion settling into his bones. The scent of ozone from the emitters still hung in the air, sharp under the smell of crushed vegetation. Ethan knelt in the dirt by the agricultural module foundation, crumbling alien soil between his fingers while explaining something to his team of four. The kid's enthusiasm reminded Diego of Maria at that age, full of plans to save the world.

"This could support crops. No supplements." Ethan's voice carried across the field. He straightened as Diego approached, dirt under his nails. "Better than anything Earth's grown in ten years."

Jack's voice cut through the generator hum nearby. "Voltage readings are finally stable." His prosthetic leg whirred as he shifted weight, checking connections. "Humidity's hell on the joints though."

The sounds hit Diego from all directions. Hammering. Drill whine. Metal clanging against metal as habitat modules went up.

His people. Building. Not just surviving anymore.

They were making something that might last.

Emily stood near the portal, that shimmering gash with rippling edges. She coordinated six technicians calibrating equipment while drones provided aerial surveillance of their expanding base of operations. Her movements had the confident rhythm of someone doing work that mattered.

"Emily."

She looked up, her face still flushed with discovery. "Diego. What's up?"

"How automated is the mining process once we locate deposits?"

"Pretty much all automated. Bots handle extraction through refining. They'll flag complications." She gestured to equipment containers where two team members prepared mining drones. "They're smarter than the ones we used in Argentina, but they'll still need us if they encounter anything unexpected."

"Like our scaled friend?"

"Exactly. Automation handles the routine stuff, but when things go sideways?" She patted the drone beside her. "Humans still make the critical calls."

Diego's hand found his scar. AI decisions. Osaka. Jakarta. Algorithmic efficiency that counted bodies as acceptable losses.

Not here. Not again.

His watch read 1730. Five hours. Christ. His shoulders ached, good ache, the kind that came from actual work instead of sitting in briefings. Haven's air tasted clean. Too clean.

The afternoon sun carved shadows across their settlement. Temporary shelters. Sensor arrays. The beginning of something that might last or might collapse like everything else.

Johnson barked orders at the perimeter. Two teams hauling equipment, repositioning arrays. Doing the work.

"Johnson." Diego's voice cut through the activity. "Seen enough for now."

Johnson approached, his jaw working, eyes never still. Always scanning. Good habits from bad wars.

"What's next?"

Diego nodded toward the portal, already missing Haven's air. "I'm heading back. You've got everything under control here, but we need Earth's logistics running smoothly too. That neodymium discovery changes everything."

Johnson nodded sharply. "I'll keep things locked down. The twenty-four security personnel are on full alert rotation."

Diego clapped him on the shoulder, the gesture carrying more weight than usual. "Map the area, mark creature signs, secure those deposits."

"Understood."

Diego moved through the camp. Three dozen people building. Hammering. Welding. The hum of it filled his ears, humanity's outpost on an alien world, the sound of something he'd thought was dead.

He approached Emily at her console. "Emily."

She looked up with a smile that reached her eyes. "Heading back already?"

"Just for a bit. Keep those drones vigilant."

"You got it," she said, returning to her screens with renewed energy.

Diego memorized Haven's landscape: alive, vibrant, untainted. The colors seemed sharper now, more real than anything he'd seen in years.

The step back hit like drowning in reverse. Colors bled. Then Earth's facility. Sharp. Real.

The air tasted wrong. Chemical. Recycled through too many lungs. His chest constricted after Haven's clean atmosphere. Artificial lighting buzzed overhead. Harsh. Dead.

Disinfectant and decay. Earth's smell. The staleness of a dying world.

His throat tightened. Thirty-five people on Haven. Building something. While Earth choked on its own poison.

The contrast was a knife between his ribs.

Diego stepped off the portal platform. Supply pallets crowded the transition chamber walls: medical equipment in sterile packaging, habitat modules folded into compact rectangles, water purification systems with coils of tubing. Each container sported a bright tag for the next window to Haven.

He removed his pack and rifle, stowing them in designated containment slots. Even with Haven's ecology showing no signs of harmful pathogens, some routines ran too deep to break.

Diego headed for the metal stairwell leading back to the control center and took the steps two at a time. At the top, he paused as his eyes adjusted to harsh LEDs bathing the room in cold white light.

The control room sprawled before him, technicians hunched over displays, readouts glowing with vital signs, atmospheric readings, and geographical surveys. Ventilation fans whirred, a counterpoint to the steady click of cooling systems. Machines keeping humans alive underground while a dying world baked overhead.

The air tasted flat, processed through filters countless times. Not like Haven, where he'd tracked a translucent-winged butterfly landing on purple leaves.

Olivia looked up from her station. Her usual reserved expression transformed when she spotted him, her eyes widening as she nearly knocked over her chair standing.

"Welcome back." Olivia crossed to meet him, her steps quicker than usual. "How was it? Walking on ground that supports life must've been incredible."

His voice remained steady despite the fatigue pulling at him. "It's real."

Diego took a breath, the corner of his mouth lifting slightly. "The team's working well. Thirty-five people are turning wilderness into something we can use."

He pulled in another breath of processed air. "And the air, Olivia... First time in decades I've breathed air that didn't come through filters."

Olivia leaned forward, lowering her voice. "And the neodymium? Emily's scans showed improbably high concentrations."

"They're accurate." Diego's hand found the back of his neck, the muscle there knotted from three days without proper sleep. "Mining operations start now. This solves our biggest limitation."

Olivia turned to her console. Her fingers moved across the interface, each gesture economical and purposeful. "Recalibrating portal parameters. Based on projected yields."

She worked faster than her typical methodical pace. "If this works, we could increase transit windows significantly. Multiple daily windows instead of weekly ones. Exponentially increased payload capacity."

Diego rolled his shoulders, trying to release the stiffness. The combat readiness ingrained over decades eased a fraction. "Let's confirm yield rates. Too many promising prospects have failed."

His voice softened. "But if those readings hold true, it changes everything. Priority lists, evacuation schedules, equipment deployments. The entire operation plan."

Olivia's hands stilled on the keyboard. She stared at the screen for a long moment. "We could move even more families. Expand beyond essential personnel to civilian populations. Give more children a chance."

Her hand lifted toward his arm, then stopped midway. Her words hit him. An image flashed behind his eyes, sharp and clear. Isabella, kneeling by a stream, her pockets bulging with smooth, clean rocks. Mateo's laughter, echoing from the branches of a spiral-barked tree. A physical ache bloomed in his chest.

Luna shot up from her monitoring station, the chair clattering back. Red hair wild around her face, two inches of dark roots showing. Professor Whiskers launched off her lap with a pissed-off yowl, vanished under the nearest workstation.

She nearly took out a junior tech. Tablet clutched against her chest, eyes scanning the room. Her fingers drummed the device's edge. Binary patterns. Fast.

"Diego! Holy shit, you're back!" Gum popped. Loud enough to make someone wince. "First human being to set foot on another fucking planet and you waltz back in here like you just grabbed coffee."

Her eyes were bright, almost manic with excitement. "I've been glued to my monitors for six hours straight, watching every microscopic data packet crawl through the quantum relay like it was the most important porn download in human history."

She bounced on her toes. "The atmospheric readings, the soil composition, the electromagnetic signatures... God, I would've killed to jack into Emily's sensor feeds and experience that first step myself. What was it like? The gravity? The air? Did the electromagnetic interference mess with your comm units like I predicted?"

Diego allowed a genuine smile. "It's everything we hoped for, Luna. Better."

"Don't give me that cryptic military bullshit." Luna's grin stretched wider. "I need details! Did my quantum interface upgrades work? Are those mineral concentrations real, or did someone's equipment malfunction? Because those preliminary numbers looked like a typo from the gods."

Diego cut her off. "Soil's viable. Water's clean. And we found the neodymium."

Luna froze mid-bounce, her tablet slipping in her grip. She caught it with reflexes honed by years of fumbling expensive equipment.

"You're not fucking with me right now, are you?" Luna's voice went quiet. Dangerous quiet. "Because if you are, I'll hack every device you own. Make them play 'Never Gonna Give You Up' until you beg for mercy."

"Fifty percent pure neodymium crystal formations. Near-surface deposits. Two kilometers from base camp."

Luna's face shifted. Processing. Her fingers tapped against her thigh. Binary code. Frantic.

"Jesus fucking Christ." She glanced around. Nearby techs hunched over their stations. She leaned in. "That rewrites the power consumption algorithms. Completely. Portal stays open for hours. Not minutes. Days, maybe."

Her hands moved faster. The scope hitting her. All of it. "The system's held with digital duct tape and prayer. Burning through stabilization alloys like birthday candles. Last dozen we've got." She pulled up projections. "This much neodymium? Long-term transit corridors. Stable ones."

She paused, suddenly looking vulnerable beneath her punk exterior. "Everyone gets to go, right? Not just the VIPs and essential personnel?"

"That's the plan." Diego's jaw set firmly. "We've got a real shot now, Luna. A real home for everyone."

Luna nodded rapidly, then her expression shifted like someone had flipped a switch. The excitement drained from her face.

"Oh shit, almost forgot." Luna's gum popped. "Kaito's bird inbound. Fifteen minutes."

She bit her lip. The tough-girl act cracked for half a second. "Diego, someone tried to breach the portal firewall. While you were gone."

Luna's words hit, and the hope from Haven evaporated. His posture straightened, the old combat readiness snapping back into place. His gaze swept the control room, checking sightlines. A threat.

"Bad actors probing our systems from the outside," Luna continued, her voice losing its playful edge. "Professional job, too. Not some script kiddie with delusions of grandeur.

They were specifically fishing for portal activation schedules and power consumption data."

Olivia gripped the edge of her console, her knuckles white. "Any idea who?"

"Still running traces, but they covered their tracks well. I managed to kick them out and sent a little parting gift. Polymorphic worm that'll eat their hard drives from the inside out." Luna's grin returned, but it had a sharp edge now. "Hope it wasn't a government agency, because that's gonna hurt."

Diego's hand found empty air where his sidearm should have been. Old habits.

Six hours on Haven. Soil that could grow food. Minerals they needed. Real progress for once.

Now someone wanted their secrets.

He checked his watch. Every minute wasted on security was a minute not spent on the mining operation. More crossings. More families through the portal. The neodymium deposits changed everything. The math finally worked.

The work never fucking stopped. Neither did the threats.

But he'd walked on solid ground today. Ground that could support life. Human life. His grandchildren's life.

Just had to deal with whatever crisis Kaito was bringing before it killed them all.

His knee throbbed as he turned toward the landing pad.

Breakthrough to crisis. The cycle never ended.

At least this ground was worth defending.

FUTURE BEYOND THIS BROKEN WORLD

D iego's pen scratched across the report. Old shrapnel shifted beneath skin as he adjusted his position. The portal room's hum as the door hissed open. Kaito entered with Olivia and Mia, suit rumpled, dark patches under his arms.

"Kaito." Diego set down his pen. "You look like hell. What's going on?"

Kaito's hand went to his tie, adjusting it in quick, precise movements that accomplished nothing. His tablet screen bled red warnings.

"It's all going to shit, Martinez," Kaito said, swiping frantically at his tablet. "Seismic activity's tearing Tucson apart. We've lost contact with three warehouses in the last hour. Choi's team is trapped, and the stabilization metals will be buried if we don't move fast."

"Supply lines completely compromised?" Diego leaned forward, the familiar weight settling in his chest.

"Worse." Kaito shoved the tablet forward. Screen bleeding red.

"Equipment failures are cascading." His voice fractured. "Choi's team is cut off. Completely."

"Dr. Choi?" Diego studied the data. Pressure built behind his eyes, familiar spike at the base of his skull.

Olivia moved closer. "Seven people. Choi, three researchers, three security." Her hand went to her forehead, fingers pressing. "It's not just about them."

Diego's gaze hit the portal counter on the wall. Eleven openings left. Today's crossing would make it ten.

Humanity's timer. Ticking down.

They couldn't afford to lose one.

"The transfer schedule is maxed out, Diego," Olivia said, scrolling through data columns with mechanical efficiency. "If you don't get those metals, I can't keep the portal open, but everyone coming through will be on a one-way ticket to nowhere."

"The Tucson facility's integrity is failing," Kaito continued, his usual measured tone cracking at the edges. "Structural collapse imminent. My personnel are trained for perimeter defense, not search and rescue operations. Their protocols are insufficient for this situation."

Diego watched Kaito's rigid composure fracture. The man's fingers worked his tablet like a prayer bead, seeking control in repetitive motion.

"What resources do we have available?" Diego's voice cut through the noise.

Kaito's grip on the tablet went white-knuckle. "I've diverted all available Nexus resources to secure the perimeter, but this operation requires your expertise, Martinez-san."

Diego rose. Weight shifted from his damaged knee, old injury singing its familiar song. His thoughts clicked into tactical patterns, external concerns falling away like shed clothing. "What's the operational requirement?"

"Getting people out isn't the issue. The local teams can handle evacuation," Kaito paced three quick steps before stopping, as if his feet had found an invisible barrier. "Moving the stabilization metals from storage to the airfield, that's where I need help. My security team isn't ready for this level of chaos."

"I'll handle security personally. I have contacts in Tucson. We can organize a small team with local support."

Kaito's shoulders dropped from their rigid line. "I need you on this. You're the only one I trust to make this happen."

"Mia, you're with me. We'll need your piloting skills." Diego nodded to the woman by the door, their best pilot, watching the exchange with tactical assessment in her eyes.

"Copy that," Mia replied, checking her wrist computer. "Transport's ready in five. Weather's rough, but that makes things interesting."

"Olivia, keep materials flowing through the portal. Maintain momentum while we handle this crisis."

She nodded, data scrolling across her handheld. "Recalculated for optimal flow. The numbers work." Her jaw tightened. "Barely. Forty personnel transfers today, plus material shipments. One hiccup and the whole thing collapses."

Diego grabbed his tactical gear, movements precise as clockwork. He activated his comm while checking his sidearm. "Johnson, it's Diego. Critical op in Tucson. Need your two best ready in ten."

"Copy that," Johnson's voice crackled through static. "Thompson and Williams are on standby. They'll be at the hangar."

Diego strode through corridors filled with rushing personnel. His knee sang its protest song as he navigated a stairwell, concrete dust from distant quakes coating his throat.

Jet fuel and superheated metal filled Diego's nostrils as he pushed through the hangar doors. Thompson and Williams waited, gear loaded, weapons checked. Thompson's eyes moved in constant assessment, cataloging threat vectors and escape routes. Williams counted ammunition with silent precision, lips forming numbers only he could hear.

"Think we'll make it in one piece?" Diego asked, forcing lightness into his voice.

Mia slid into the pilot's seat, her hands finding controls like they'd always been there. "You know me, Diego. I only crash when there's absolutely nothing else to crash into."

The engines spooled up to a steady roar. Diego's focus contracted to mission parameters, everything else bleeding away like water through sand. They lifted off, the transport lurching as Mia compensated for an unexpected crosswind.

Once clear of takeoff turbulence, Diego settled into the co-pilot seat. His fingers found rhythm against the armrest as he prepared to call. Each jolt of the aircraft sent lightning through his damaged joint, grounding him in the immediate present.

"Need to call my contact in Tucson. We'll need local support."

"Is this contact reliable?" Mia asked over the engine noise while adjusting for an air pocket.

"Manuel Rodríguez. My son-in-law." Diego braced as the craft bucked, metal groaning in protest. "SWAT with Tucson PD. If anyone can secure those metals, it's him."

Diego activated the holo-comm, light flickering before stabilizing as he punched Manuel's code. The hard seat pressed against his spine, uncomfortable pressure points anchoring him to the moment.

Manuel's face appeared, tired but alert. "Diego. Wasn't expecting to hear from you today."

"How's Maria? The kids?" Diego leaned forward. His shoulders dropped, the tightness finally releasing.

Manuel's expression warmed. "They're good. Maria's burying herself in work. Mateo keeps asking when Abuelo's coming home."

Diego exhaled, the sound carrying more weight than air. "That's good to hear."

Manuel shifted to business mode, shoulders squaring. "We've had problems with supply lines due to seismic events. Three major roads have been cut off since yesterday."

Diego nodded, already mapping alternative routes in his head. "I need your assistance with a security detail."

"What kind of help?" Manuel asked, voice direct as gunfire.

"Stabilization metals need escort from the holding facility to the airfield," Diego replied, voice steady despite turbulence rattling his teeth. "With this unrest and the quakes, we can't afford to lose this shipment."

Manuel's image flickered through static. "Copy that. I've got Carlos and Richard on standby. Just the two of us, or do you need more support?"

"Two from our security team, plus myself. And you, if available." Diego kept numbers tactical, contingencies already forming.

Manuel nodded. "Carlos, Richard, and I should be enough. Small team gives us better mobility without drawing attention."

The transport bucked hard enough to rattle Diego's teeth. Holographic display shattered into light fragments. The aircraft dropped sideways.

His stomach lurched. Wrong direction.

His hand slammed against the console. Mia's jaw worked, hands fighting the stick. Sweat beaded on her forehead.

His knee screamed against the bulkhead. Old shrapnel grinding bone.

"Manuel." Diego's voice came out lower, rougher, as if the words had to fight their way past something lodged in his throat. "The seismic activity is accelerating beyond projections. Get Maria and the kids out of Tucson. Today. Use the emergency account I gave you. Get them to Playa del Carmen. We can't stop what's coming now."

Manuel's tired eyes went dark as the winter sky. "Are you sure? Is it that serious?"

"The rate of collapse is accelerating," Diego said, each word measured and final. "I won't risk their safety. Not again."

Manuel swallowed, his throat working visibly. "I'll get them moving right away."

"Good." Diego's voice found its center again. "We'll meet you at Marana Regional in about two hours. Will that work?"

"I'll be there with my team and the transport vehicle."

"Good." Diego nodded. The pressure in his chest eased, just slightly. "We'll handle everything else."

As Manuel's image flickered out, Mia glanced at Diego. The tactical mask had slipped, revealing bedrock underneath.

"One more mission after this supply run?" Diego asked, voice pitched for her ears only. "I'll need you to make a special flight."

Mia nodded. "I'll drop you guys back at base after we secure the metals, then take the executive transport to evacuate your family. Don't worry. I'll get them to safety."

"Thanks, Mia." Diego allowed himself a moment to feel grateful before the mission reclaimed him.

The desert stretched below, broken by jagged riverbeds that hadn't seen water in years. Heat shimmer rose from baked earth, distorting the horizon into liquid mirages. A new earthquake fissure cut across the landscape east of their flight path, raw and recent as a knife wound in the planet's hide.

"Seismic activity's getting worse," Mia muttered, her knuckles showing white against dark controls as the craft shuddered. "Navigation system keeps glitching. Had to switch to manual routing twice already."

The transport screamed through rough air, every rivet tested, as Mia fought bucking controls. Diego's teeth rattled in his skull. He braced himself, the hot metal of the comms console branding his forearm.

"Bringing up overlay," Diego tapped the console. The display flickered, died, then reappeared wrapped in static. "Tech's struggling with these conditions."

The transport groaned as Mia navigated another pocket of tortured air. Sweat dampened her temple, but her voice kept its edge of humor. "Just another day in paradise."

The air tasted of ash and burned dreams. Below, lines of desperate figures snaked away from smoking rubble like ants fleeing a kicked hill. Collapse everywhere. Three columns of black smoke wrote obituaries across the sky. Infrastructure failing. Diego watched families cluster around water distribution points, weapons visible at makeshift checkpoints. Everything unraveling faster than their most pessimistic projections.

Approaching halfway, Diego checked in with Williams. "One hour out. Be ready for immediate extraction and deployment."

"Copy that," Williams replied, voice clipped clean. He tapped his rifle stock in a precise three-count rhythm, a habit Diego had noticed before operations went hot.

The cargo ramp lowered with a hydraulic whine that competed with the desert wind as they touched down at Marana Regional. Diego's eyes moved across the perimeter, old training making the assessment automatic. Three exits. Two choke points. The heat was a physical assault, slapping exposed skin with malice. He gasped, dry air searing his lungs raw as a rookie's first battlefield.

Their armored transport waited nearby, military purpose obvious in its angular lines. An aged pickup stood apart, rust and character contrasting with sterile equipment. Manuel and two men in tactical gear leaned against it, weapons visible but not aggressive.

His knee throbbed. The descent had been rough.

Manuel approached with quick, purposeful strides. New lines had etched themselves around his eyes, stress and sleepless nights writing their story in flesh.

"Mijo." Diego embraced his son-in-law, the scent of gun oil and familiar aftershave carrying him back to family gatherings that seemed like artifacts from another civilization.

"She almost wouldn't let me come," Manuel admitted, his voice carrying more than words. "Said she had a bad feeling."

"Maria always had her mother's intuition." Diego noticed gray threading through Manuel's hair that hadn't been there at Christmas.

Manuel swallowed hard and reached into his vest, movements careful as handling explosives. "Isabella made this for you." He produced a folded drawing, paper worn soft from handling. "Said Abuelo needed to remember his family."

Diego unfolded it. Air caught somewhere between his throat and lungs.

Five stick figures beneath a yellow sun. A child's careful printing labeled each one: Abuela (crossed out with deliberate strokes), Abuelo, Mama, Papa, Isabella, Mateo. His thumb moved across each crayon line. Learning love through his fingertips.

His fingers found the silver chain at his neck, metal warm from years against his skin. He pulled it over his head, the St. Michael medal catching desert light.

"Elena's medallion," Diego said, voice stripped to bare wood. "Twenty years I've carried guilt instead of giving this to Maria." He pressed the warm silver into Manuel's palm, the metal still holding his body heat. "Tell Maria... I'm sorry it took so long to give this back to her."

"Suegro, I can't." Manuel's protest came automatically, duty-bound.

"You can and you will. Tell Maria..." Diego paused, searching for words that wouldn't break under their own weight. "Tell her some gifts take too long to give."

Manuel closed his fingers around the pendant, the chain spilling between his knuckles like liquid memory.

Manuel gestured to his teammates. "Carlos Sánchez, Richard Byrne. Best on the force. Both have families to protect."

Diego studied them. Alert eyes. Military bearing. The way they held themselves spoke of recent action. Men with skin in the game.

"Good to have you aboard." Diego shook each hand, the grip firm, understanding passed without words.

Sánchez drew himself to full height, fingers brushing the holster at his hip in unconscious reassurance. "We're ready."

Byrne nodded, eyes never settling on any point for more than a heartbeat. "We've got your six."

Diego turned to Thompson and Williams, already unloading gear with the efficiency of men who'd done this dance a thousand times. "Thompson, Williams, let's get this show on the road."

Thompson distributed equipment while Williams secured their perimeter, neither needing detailed instructions for work they could perform in their sleep.

Diego pulled Manuel aside, away from military ears. "How's Maria holding up?"

Manuel's hand found Diego's shoulder, grip solid as concrete. "She's strong, Diego. Always has been. But she's scared for you. She knows what you're doing matters, but..." He left the sentence hanging, incomplete, as their situation.

Diego absorbed this, filing it with other weights he carried, then forced his mind back to operational necessity. "Will you head down to Playa del Carmen with them now, or take the plane with Mia after we secure the metals?"

"I'm going with them. Maria will need help keeping the kids calm during the evacuation. I want my hands on their safety personally."

Diego nodded, squeezing Manuel's shoulder with force that said everything words couldn't. "Good call. Mia will meet you at the secondary airstrip after we finish here. Get them safe. Everything else is just metal and politics."

Manuel gave a single, sharp nod that cut through the air like a blade.

Manuel returned to his team, coordinating preparation with quiet efficiency. Diego watched him go, something primal and protective stirring in his chest, the fierce instinct that had kept him fighting through decades of impossible odds.

Williams approached, tactical vest secured, weapon ready for whatever waited ahead. "Transport vehicles prepped, sir. Thompson's finished distributing comm equipment."

Diego checked his watch. Six hours to move those metals through a city where civilization hung by threads thin as spider silk. His knee throbbed with each step toward the lead vehicle. Sixty-four years of damage, one foot in front of the other anyway.

"Move out."

The mission wasn't just about metal anymore. It was about buying his family a future beyond this broken world, about not failing the people who mattered when everything else had already failed.

The convoy's tires found every loose piece of gravel, skidding sideways as the world decided to go completely sideways with it. Inside the transport's personnel bay, Diego's shoulder met the armored wall hard enough to rattle his teeth. His knee buckled, sending pain up his leg. Through the reinforced vision port, the central warehouse entrance folded in on itself.

Across the narrow aisle, Manuel pulled his attention from the opposite port. His face had gone pale under the dust coating. Diego caught his eye and a cold sensation settled in his gut. That look. The same one Maria had worn when he'd left for his last deployment. His body moved before his brain caught up. Twenty years of this, and muscle memory still knew what to do when plans went to hell.

Outside, concrete dust hung in the air. Another tremor rolled under his boots. Williams was already circling the groaning structure, pointing at a loading bay door that had buckled but not collapsed. Diego nodded, testing his weight on the bad knee. It held. Good enough.

The hydraulic spreader bit into twisted metal. Stepping inside felt like walking into something that had just died badly. Emergency lights strobed red across toppled shelves and exposed wiring. Somewhere deeper in the building, flames were eating scattered debris.

Diego split his teams. "Manuel, you've got Carlos, Thompson. Team Alpha. Find Choi and her people." He turned to Williams and Richard. "We're Bravo. Package retrieval. Check in every two minutes."

His tactical light cut through the haze as he led Williams and Richard toward sub-level access. Each step on the bad knee sent lightning up his thigh, but he kept moving. The building groaned around them, deciding whether to fall now or wait five more minutes.

"Alpha, report."

Manuel's voice crackled back through static. "Making our way through the... Wait. We hear something." A crash through the building. White noise followed. Then Manuel's voice, sharper. "Shit! Carlos is pinned! Stand by!"

Diego stopped, radio clenched in his fist. This was the part he hated most. Waiting. Listening to other people deal with problems he couldn't fix from here.

"We got him free," Manuel finally came back, breathing hard. "Leg's messed up, but he's moving. Found them, Diego. Maintenance office. All seven. One's got a head wound."

Diego's chest loosened. He wiped dust and sweat from his upper lip.

Bravo team made their way to the sub-level through debris that shifted underfoot. The vault door's electronic lock had given up. The manual wheel looked like someone had taken a crowbar to it.

Diego put his shoulder into it. The metal wouldn't budge.

Williams studied the door, then pulled a small block of C-4 from his gear. His hands moved with calm precision. "It's the only way in. Gonna rattle some teeth. Might bring the ceiling down." He shrugged. They both knew the math.

Diego glanced at the support beams overhead. They looked about as stable as his last assignment. "Do it. Fast."

The blast hit his chest, and more dust cascaded from above. Williams didn't waste time, just surged through the breach. Inside the vault, four heavy black cases waited.

The transport cart had been flattened under a section of the ceiling. Diego looked at the cases, then at his men. "We're carrying them."

Metal screamed as support beams in the central bay twisted past their breaking point. The floor buckled under their feet. The roof was coming down in sections now. Debris cut their light to almost nothing. Comms erupted with voices and static.

"Alpha, sound off! Manuel!"

Nothing but electronic noise. Williams's jaw tightened as he hefted two cases. Richard grabbed one, and Diego took the fourth.

They picked their way over debris mountains that shifted underfoot. On the other side, Manuel's team was moving civilians, Thompson half-carrying Carlos, whose leg was bleeding onto his pants. Their eyes met across twenty feet of structural failure.

Diego counted heads. Ten mobile. Two hurt. One limping. Four cases that weighed more than they should. Williams pointed to a ventilation shaft that looked ready to collapse.

Dr. Choi stepped forward. Her lab coat was torn across one shoulder, and dust coated her hair. "Commander, leave us. The metals matter more than we do."

The words landed in Diego's chest and stayed there. Behind his eyes, Isabella's drawing flickered. The word Abuela was crossed out in red crayon. The taste of failure filled his mouth.

"I just sent my family somewhere safe," he said. "I'm not leaving you to die here. We all get out." He looked at his men. "Find another way."

Thompson's eyes went wide. He pointed to a heavy-duty forklift wedged between fallen support columns. "Sir. We don't go around. We go through."

It was utterly ridiculous. Diego loved it.

"Do it."

The world turned into controlled chaos. Diego positioned his men. Williams hot-wired the forklift, his fingers working exposed wires. Manuel and Carlos, grimacing through their problems, kept the researchers from panicking. Diego ignored his knee's complaints and focused on getting everyone out alive.

The forklift punched through the wall. The opening barely looked wide enough for a person, much less a person carrying heavy cases.

"GO! Move it!"

Bodies squeezed through. Cases passed hand to hand. The building continued its death song around them.

As the last case moved, Manuel stumbled at the threshold. Richard looked up just in time to see a massive I-beam deciding it was done being attached to the ceiling. He lunged forward, shoving Manuel and the case through the opening with everything he had.

Richard tried to follow, but the ground bucked under his feet. The beam crashed down, missing him by inches. Concrete shards exploded from the impact. Behind him, someone made a sound that wasn't quite human, one of Choi's researchers, buried under fresh collapse.

Diego scrambled through the breach into daylight that tasted like concrete dust. The warehouse folded in on itself behind them. Carlos and Thompson dragged Richard clear as another section decided to join the party. He was conscious but pale, his left arm hanging wrong and blood running down his forearm where concrete had found skin.

They got Richard flat on the ground. Williams was already working, cutting fabric, his hands steady. There was no point in thinking about the researcher buried under tons of debris. That conversation would come later.

Richard, teeth clenched against whatever was happening in his shoulder, managed to focus on Diego. "Manuel?"

"Safe," Diego confirmed. "You did well."

Diego leaned against the transport, feeling every one of his sixty-four years. He keyed his comm.

"Kaito... we've got the assets and most of the personnel. Casualties. Two wounded, one we couldn't..." He stopped, looking back at the collapsed building. "One didn't make it."

The dust was still settling over what had become someone's tomb. Another name for the list of people he hadn't been fast enough to save. The cases were secure. Most of the personnel were out. A success, by the numbers. The dust settling over the tomb tasted like failure.

Diego stepped into the Embarkation Room Control Center at 0600. The quantum gateway hummed its steady electric note, and the air tasted like burnt copper and day-old coffee. Technicians shuffled between consoles, moving like people who'd forgotten what sleep felt like.

Emily hunched over her tablet, her hair escaping its ponytail in greasy strands. Dark smudges under her eyes told the story of the last seventy-two hours. She'd been mainlining caffeine and spite in equal measure.

Olivia hunched over the main console, fingers moving through the holographic interface. Data streams cascaded around her hands. Her left hand trembled. Again. She kept working anyway.

Three feet away, Luna stared at her screen, gum popping between curses at whatever code she was wrestling into submission. Emily's profanity got more creative with each drone feed that flickered and died.

"Emily." Diego's voice cut through the low hum of machinery. "Can you get the rest of this gear across today?"

Emily's head snapped up. "Are you fucking kidding me?" She waved her tablet, nearly dropping it in the process. "Three days. Three goddamn days of eighteen-hour shifts babysitting these temperamental pieces of shit." Her voice cracked slightly. "Push any harder and I start making the kind of mistakes that get people killed. We need downtime."

That familiar weight settled between his shoulder blades. The kind that usually meant someone was about to tell him something he didn't want to hear. "What's the holdup?"

"The dampeners are redlining." Olivia's hands moved across her controls, never stopping. "Every transfer pushes containment closer to failure. System needs maintenance we don't have time for."

Luna's laugh came out sharp. Bitter. Her eyes stayed locked on the readouts. "Blow the containment field and we're stuck here. Permanently. No pressure or anything."

The consoles painted everything in corpse-light. Olivia's fingers paused on the controls. The shadows under her eyes looked deeper than yesterday, and Diego could count new worry lines bracketing her mouth. "Two openings yesterday. Processing the new materials makes twelve total."

Diego's hands found the console edge. The overhead lights flickered once, twice.

Osaka. Artillery. The sky stuttering with each flash.

His hand went to the scar. Old habit. He forced it down.

Here. Now. Haven's control room.

"Options?" His knee throbbed. "How do we squeeze more out of this thing?"

"We've already expanded the dampener field to maximum safe parameters." Olivia's grip on her tablet had turned her knuckles pale. "The quantum mechanics don't negotiate."

"Reports aren't getting any rosier either," Luna added without looking up. "Los Angeles got hit with another 8.2 yesterday. What's left of it, anyway."

Diego's gaze moved between the three women. Push the system past its breaking point and risk losing everything, or leave critical supplies behind. His fingers found his watch face, an old habit Elena used to mock him for.

"All right." The words came out steadier than he felt. "What do you need to make this work?"

Emily exchanged looks with her colleagues. "Forty-eight hours minimum. Two more portal openings for equipment, and we can get everything across without turning the gateway into a very expensive pile of slag."

Diego ran the numbers in his head. Time they didn't have, resources burning fast. His shoulders screamed. Old muscle locked tight from hours he didn't remember tensing.

"That'll have to work. Clock's ticking, though."

Olivia met his eyes. Something passed between them, an understanding built from too many impossible deadlines. "We'll make it happen."

"Should be enough for everyone on the list," she added, rubbing at her eyes with the back of her hand. "If we're smart about it."

Diego nodded. These women had been pushing the envelope for weeks, riding the edge between breakthrough and catastrophe. He stepped back from the console, and despite everything, something shifted in his chest. Not excitement exactly. More like the moment before a perfectly executed operation, when all the variables finally aligned.

He looked at Olivia, bent over her instruments with the focus of a surgeon. She'd been nursing this gateway for years, keeping it stable through funding cuts and equipment failures. An idea surfaced.

"Olivia."

She looked up, exhaustion written in the slump of her shoulders.

"Yeah?"

Diego hesitated. Something in her expression stopped him. Not just tiredness. Something deeper, older. "You've been monitoring this gateway for what, seven years? Maybe it's time you saw it from the other side."

Her hands went completely still. "You want me to cross over?"

"I need my morning status report in person," Diego said, keeping his voice level. "Thought you might want to see how your gateway performs under actual field conditions. Might give you ideas for optimizing the remaining openings."

Olivia's breathing changed. Her gaze drifted to the shimmering portal, and for a moment her eyes went somewhere else entirely.

"Aiden always said the theory was sound." Olivia's voice came out rough. Her fingers found her wedding band. Turned it. Again. "We just needed better stabilization protocols."

Diego understood. Aiden Smith. The physicist who'd died in the first test accident. The husband she'd lost to the very technology that might save what was left of humanity.

"You don't have to," Diego said quietly. "But if you want to see what he helped build..."

Olivia swallowed hard. Her spine straightened, inch by inch. "I do need to see it." Her voice grew stronger. "Give me five minutes to grab my gear."

As Olivia headed for the equipment lockers, Luna drifted over to Diego with a raised eyebrow.

"Risky move."

"Yeah." Diego watched Olivia checking her field kit with methodical precision. "But some doors you have to walk through yourself."

Emily caught his eye and gave him a subtle thumbs up, clutching what might charitably be called coffee.

When Olivia returned, she'd pulled her hair back into a ponytail and switched to field gear. Her hands shook slightly as she adjusted her pack straps, but her face was composed.

"Ready?" Diego asked, studying her expression.

Olivia stared at the portal for a long moment. "I've spent seven years refining this technology after what happened to Aiden. Run thousands of simulations, built hundreds of safety protocols." She paused. "But I've never actually stepped through myself."

"It's stable. System's solid."

"I know the physics." A brief smile flickered across her face. "But knowing the math isn't the same as trusting it." She rolled her shoulders once. "Let's do this before I talk myself out of it."

They moved toward the threshold. Diego watched Olivia's breathing quicken, shallow and fast. Her pupils dilated as they closed the distance. She stopped short of the gateway. Her hand found her wedding band.

"He'd be proud of this," Diego said. "This was his vision too."

Olivia nodded once, jaw set. "For Aiden," she whispered, and they stepped forward into the light.

The transition felt like stepping off a cliff while the universe rearranged itself around them. Diego's inner ear screamed protests as directions became suggestions and his vision fractured into impossible angles. Then everything snapped back into focus with the finality of a door slamming shut. Diego caught his balance automatically. After dozens of crossings, the weirdness barely registered.

Beside him, Olivia made a sound somewhere between a gasp and a sob. Her knees buckled and she stumbled forward. Diego caught her elbow, steadying her until she found her footing.

"Easy. The vertigo passes in a few seconds."

Olivia stood frozen, eyes clamped shut, breathing in sharp little bursts. For a heartbeat Diego thought she might be having some kind of breakdown. Then slowly, carefully, she opened her eyes.

Everything about her changed. Her mouth fell open slightly, her shoulders dropped, and she took a half-step forward like she was being pulled by invisible strings.

"Good Lord," she breathed. The light was wrong. A pale, washed-out gold that bleached the color from the foliage and cast long, sharp shadows. Perfect for an ambush.

A prefab building stood a hundred meters out, sensor arrays bristling from its roof like angry quills. Tents and smaller structures spread from it, a fresh-built mess. But Olivia wasn't looking at the compound. Her attention was on everything else. She dropped to one knee, an involuntary motion, and dug her fingers into the dirt. Civilian. No tactical awareness. The dirt sparked with tiny flecks of something that wasn't silica.

"Incredible," she muttered, letting it run through her fingers.

Something with blue-green wings flitted through the undergrowth. A flower with petals like folded metal pulsed nearby. Distractions. All of it.

"Welcome to Haven," Diego said. His eyes remained fixed on the tree line, where the shadows were deepest.

She got to her feet, brushing herself off. "It's stable," she said, the words coming out clipped, strained with forced composure. "Aiden's theories... they worked."

Diego grunted, finally turning to her. Jabbed a thumb toward the buildings. "Eleven jumps left. That's all we get."

Eleven. The number landed like a fist to the gut. Her spine stiffened, that automatic straightening when someone dumps impossible weight on your shoulders. He'd seen it before. Too many times.

"Command center's hot. Johnson's running security." His eyes moved across the perimeter, cataloging exits, checking sight lines. Old habits. "You build or you die. Come on."

A hundred meters of sensory assault. Air so thick it caught in his throat, coating his tongue with something chemical and wrong. Decay mixing with rain, metal underneath it all. The humidity ate sound. Their footsteps disappeared into nothing.

Diego's jaw worked. You couldn't hear threats coming in this soup.

The command center door hissed open. The alien world cut off, replaced by hot electronics and fear-sweat. A diesel generator thrummed through the floor plates, vibrating up through his boots. Wall of screens, all flashing red. Chaos. Exactly what he'd expected.

Captain Johnson met them at the threshold, exhaustion etched deep in the lines around his eyes. "Sir. Dr. Smith." The nod came sharp, military. "Northern sensor array's failing. Signal's complete garbage."

"Interference?" Olivia asked, her eyes already glued to a data feed.

"That's Luna's guess," Johnson said, rubbing the back of his neck.

"It's not a guess, it's a goddamn fact!" Luna snapped from her terminal. Her eyes were black pits in her pale face. "Dr. Smith, we need the rest of the sensitive gear. That means burning two of the eleven jumps."

"Son of a bitch," a voice boomed from the floor.

Diego didn't flinch. Always something. "Two jumps are forty people, Luna."

"And without that gear, the people who are here will be blind and deaf," Olivia countered, her voice sharp.

"Eight hundred tons of survival gear versus forty souls," Diego said flatly. "Another day, another shitty equation."

Across the room, Jack O'Connor was surrounded by the guts of a power coupling, his cybernetic leg propped on a crate. "Sorry," he grunted, giving a capacitor a hard tap. "This piece of junk is being difficult. Give me another day and we'll have full power."

Olivia walked over, pointing. "You bypassed the primary regulator?"

Jack shot her a crooked grin. "Desperation is the mother of shitty, but effective, engineering."

A raised voice pulled Diego's attention.

"That's my point!" Kayla jabbed a finger at a schematic. "The water absorption rate is insane. The whole irrigation plan is worthless."

"It's not consistent!" Ethan shot back from his knees beside a row of planters. "We need more data."

"Food first," Diego cut in. His knee throbbed, a dull ache in time with the generator. "Figure it out."

Ethan saw Olivia, and his face lit up. "Dr. Smith! Look at this." He held out a tablet. "The growth rates are off the charts."

Olivia knelt, picking up a seedling. The leaf had a weird, oily sheen. "The nutrient uptake..."

"The plants are rewriting their DNA," Ethan said, words tumbling out.

"Which means they need more water," Kayla insisted from across the room.

Scientists. Please give them a problem, and they'll make six more.

Mei stood at her bio-station, posture rigid. "Dr. Smith," she said as they approached. "The native flora... It's anomalous." She pulled up a microscopic image. A perfect, crystalline cell structure. "It's not like anything from Earth."

"Is it poison?" Diego asked the same question, but on a different day.

"I don't know," Mei said. "Could be harmless. It could kill you in thirty seconds. I need ninety-six hours for a full toxicity screen. Non-negotiable."

His index finger tapped his thumb. Once. Twice. "Protocol stands."

They moved back to the main monitors. A news feed from Earth showed a burning city. JAKARTA FALLS, the headline read.

"Last week," Diego said. "Eight million dead in twelve minutes. APU is pulling out. Only their top brass and political cronies get a ticket on the exodus ships."

"Leaving everyone else to burn," Olivia finished. Her voice hollow as an empty shell.

Nine jumps left. The math didn't work. It would never work.

He studied her face. The shock receded, replaced by a hard set to her jaw. The expression of someone about to dig in for a fight.

"Come with me," he said.

He led her out of the compound, past the noise and the smell of failure. The ten-minute walk to the lake was silent. The water was unnaturally clear, and the rocks at the bottom were visible thirty feet down. They sat on a fallen log as the alien sun bled across the sky, painting it a bruised violet.

"All that tech," Olivia said, skipping a flat stone across the water. It bounced seven times before sinking. "All that work. And we failed. We forgot to factor in the variables."

The ripples disappeared into the dark water. "Can't put greed in an equation."

"No," she said. "You can't."

The silence that followed was heavy, filled with the things they weren't saying.

"What if we just do it all again?" she asked, the words coming out brittle, strained at the edges. "Build all this just to screw it up in the same damn ways."

He turned to look at her. Her face was pale in the strange twilight. Her eyes held the same hollowed-out look he'd seen on a hundred shell-shocked soldiers. The stare. The one you get from counting bodies.

"Oh, we will," he said, the word a rasp in his throat. "Count on it. People are people. Someone will get scared. Someone will get greedy. The screw-up is guaranteed." He paused. "The only thing that matters is who's left standing to clean up the mess after."

A memory flashed. Elena, her face covered in dust, was smiling at him. Gone.

He gestured vaguely at the alien world around them. "This is just... different dirt. Same fight."

Olivia stared out at the water for a long moment, then gave a short, sharp nod. "Yes," she said. "It is."

She stood up and offered him a hand. He took it, her grip surprisingly strong, and hauled his aching body to its feet.

They walked back toward the compound, the only sound the crunch of their boots on the crystalline ground. The impossible weight was still there, settled on their shoulders. Nothing had been solved. Their steps were out of sync.

ONE WAY TRIP

D iego checked his watch. The command center was quiet. Operations lull. Finally. His knee throbbed. Sixty-four years of accumulated damage, all of it screaming at once.

He'd never admit the break felt good.

Luna hunched over her station, recalibrating the portal for afternoon transfers. The orange tabby had claimed its usual spot beside her feet, sprawled on its back and dead to the world despite the steady hum of activity.

His gaze found Olivia absorbed in data streams. The blue glow from her display caught her face just right. That moment at the lake still sat between them, unfinished business that had followed them back to base.

He grabbed two mugs from the coffee station. One got the last of his good beans. Some conversations were worth the sacrifice.

"Coffee?"

Olivia startled, then smiled when she saw the mug. "God, yes. Perfect timing."

Their fingers brushed as she took it. Neither pulled away immediately.

"Portal's down for calibration," Diego said, nodding toward the observation deck. "Ten minutes before Johnson's team starts asking questions we don't have answers for."

"Somewhere quieter sounds good."

The observation deck overlooked the portal chamber through reinforced windows. A wall monitor showed the live feed from Haven, mountains stretching toward an alien sky. They stood at the railing, coffee steam rising between them.

Diego pointed at the screen. "See that inlet? The tall trees near the shore? That's where I'd build."

"I wouldn't have pegged you for lakefront property."

"There's probably a lot you don't know about me."

Olivia raised an eyebrow. "Such as?"

He sipped the coffee, bitter enough to strip paint. "Applied to be a park ranger before the military. Had the paperwork ready and everything."

"Really?" She studied his face. "That makes sense. The way you noticed those flowering patterns yesterday."

"Old habits." Diego shrugged. "Just put them to different use."

"Dr. Choi and I have been analyzing the native flora," Olivia said, turning her mug in both hands. "The cellular structures are completely unlike Earth species. These plants adapted to environmental stressors in ways we've never seen."

Her voice carried that same excitement from the lake. The meticulous Dr. Smith was gone, replaced by a scientist genuinely fascinated by discovery.

"You think we can do it right this time," Diego said.

"We have to." The intensity in her voice surprised him. "It's our chance to learn from the mistakes."

Diego rubbed a coffee stain on his mug with his thumb. "My grandkids would love it here." The words slipped out before he could stop them.

Olivia's hand found his arm. "Your daughter's children?"

"Yeah. Isabella is eight, asks a million questions about everything. Mateo's five watches the world like he's taking notes."

"They deserve better than what Earth became."

"Then we build it for them," Olivia said. "For all of them."

For a second, the image was sharp in his mind: Isabella exploring these forests, Mateo swimming in clean water, and Maria cataloging species that didn't exist in any textbook. A world without surveillance drones, without rationing, without the endless wars that had eaten his life.

The image hit him harder than expected.

"Portal calibration complete," Luna's voice cut through the comm. "Next transport sequence in five minutes. Systems alert in monitoring station two."

The mission crashed back into focus. Diego straightened, professional mask sliding back into place. "Back to work."

Olivia's hand lingered before she let go.

They returned to the command floor as activity picked up for the next transfer. Jack was elbow-deep in equipment near the portal array, his cybernetic leg reflecting the afternoon light.

"Sparky? What the hell are you doing here?"

Jack looked up, grinning. "Power coupling was showing fluctuations. Your Earth team's competent, but they don't speak fluent jury-rigged interdimensional gateway."

"Thought you were setting up the secondary command in Haven."

"I am. But with increased traffic, both sides need maintenance." Jack patted the equipment like a favored pet, then glanced between Diego and Olivia with obvious amusement. "Speaking of maintenance, nice timing on that equipment inspection, boss. Right during calibration downtime."

"Just checking systems, Sparky."

"Oh, I bet you were checking something." Jack's grin turned wicked. "Very thorough inspections, I'm sure. Real hands-on approach to... system diagnostics."

Diego shot him a warning look. "Focus on the actual equipment."

"Right, right. The equipment." Jack winked at Olivia. "Though some systems seem to be running warmer than usual. Might need more frequent monitoring."

Olivia stepped toward her station, but not before giving Diego's arm a gentle squeeze. "Someone has to make sure we don't accidentally tear a hole in reality, Mr. O'Connor. Among other things."

Diego caught Jack's shit-eating grin.

"Not a word."

"Wouldn't dream of it, old man." Jack turned back to his repairs, but his voice carried apparent amusement. "Haven't seen you look that relaxed in months. Good for morale, I'd say. Especially yours."

"What's that supposed to mean?"

"Means you remembered there's more to life than just surviving the next crisis." Jack adjusted something that sparked blue. "About damn time, if you ask me. Which you didn't, but I'm telling you anyway."

Diego grunted and headed toward Captain Johnson, who was studying defensive positions on a holographic display. The familiar weight of command settled back on his shoulders, but it felt different now. Less crushing, maybe.

Three hours since the last crossing. Another group gone. Diego's mind kept pulling him back, observation deck, Olivia's voice, that word. *Them.* Like a vow.

Olivia hunched over her console across the room, hands flying through holographic displays. Her team clustered around her, voices low, focused. She glanced up. Found his eyes. Brief smile before her attention snapped back to the readouts.

His chest tightened. Warmth. Strange after so long. Not unwelcome.

The flow held steady. Each team moved through their sequence, muscle memory from weeks of drilling. No hesitation. No errors.

"Group seven, clear." Emily's voice cut through the comm static. "Landing zone prepped for next group."

Diego thumbed his comm. "Copy. Group eight, standby for sequence initiation."

His gaze drifted. Found Olivia again.

She was already watching.

Something shifted between them. Nothing to do with portals or power consumption or quantum matrices. Just... them.

Neither looked away.

Diego squinted at the numbers on his tablet. The screen flickered once, twice, then held steady. Battery at twelve percent. Another system failing when he needed it most. "Twelve more portal openings with the Tucson materials. Better than I figured."

Dr. Smith nodded, dragging the back of her hand across her forehead. Sweat mixed with the recycled air's chemical tang. "The auto-miners are pulling material faster than we projected. Latest readings suggest we can refine enough stabilizing alloy for two, maybe three transitions daily."

He tucked the tablet under his arm. Hundreds already safe. Hundreds more waiting. Johnson's teams kept the perimeter locked down, a silent, efficient machine. Emily's drones herded the flow of vehicles away from the gateway's rippling mouth like mechanical sheepdogs.

Maria's face flashed through his mind. His daughter. His grandchildren. Their transport was scheduled for the next group.

"Gateway metrics holding steady," Olivia announced. Her voice was sandpaper against glass, worn raw by thirty-six hours without sleep. "Power consumption is exactly where we want it."

Diego grunted. Forty years watching humanity rip itself apart. Forty years of impossible math, counting who lived and who got left behind. This felt different. Not another retreat.

The next group moved toward the portal's edge. Sergeant Lee's wife gripped her daughter's hand. White-knuckle tight. The little girl stared into the rippling vortex, eyes wide with wonder that had no business existing in this shithole of a world. These kids would breathe Haven's clean air. Know full depots. Never taste recycled water with its metallic bite. Never learn to sleep through gunfire.

"Group eight, you're clear." Diego's voice cut through the comm static. "Move out."

A shrill chime sliced through the gateway's hum. His tablet flared. Luna's face filled the screen, the harsh blue light of her workstation carving shadows beneath her eyes.

Emergency alert.

"Boss." A waterfall of data spilled down his screen, peppered with angry red warning symbols. "My APU contact just pushed this. They've moved the Exodus launches. Not three months from now. Next week."

"Next week?" The words scraped like sand between his teeth. Diego's chest tightened, air catching halfway down his throat. "Why the hell would they broadcast that in the clear?"

"That's what snagged my attention. Both sides are doing it. When your enemies stop hiding intel..." She paused, keys clicking in sharp bursts. "Gets worse. Live satellite feeds show multiple Exodus ships already breaking formation. They're not waiting for next week. They're repositioning for immediate launch."

Diego's mind raced through their evacuation manifest. Over a hundred people still waiting on this side. Not counting essential equipment. The throb in his knee sharpened, sending needles of pain up his thigh. "If they're jumping the gun, something spooked them bad. Nobody launches early without a damned good reason."

"Working on that," Luna said, data streams scrolling in the reflection of her electric blue eyes. "But Diego..." The clicking stopped. In the silence, he could hear the hum of her servers, the distant whir of cooling fans. "The transmissions keep mentioning 'environmental acceleration' and 'critical threshold breach.' Tectonic instability is climbing exponentially. Whatever it is, they're treating it like the world is ending tomorrow."

Diego jabbed his comm. "Dr. Smith, we need to talk. Now." He switched channels. "Emily. Get Johnson back here. On the double."

"On it." He saw her break into a sprint, weaving through equipment carts and personnel.

He took the stairs two at a time, his boots ringing against the metal steps. He shoved the control room door open. Olivia looked up from her monitor, the screen's glow turning the hollows under her eyes into bruised shadows.

She grabbed her tablet without a word. "Conference room. The main display can render the satellite feeds."

He nodded. "Luna, get Mia on standby."

"Already on it," came the clipped reply. "She's running preflights on Transport Two."

Diego switched channels again, the plastic earpiece digging into his skin. "Kaito. Drop what you're doing. Conference room. Now."

"I am already on my way." The words came faster than Kaito's usual measured pace. "I have additional intelligence you must see."

The conference room felt like a bunker. Warning colors pulsed across every surface. Orbital displays, environmental readouts, seismic monitors. All bleeding red. Earth's core rotation had spun past another threshold, accelerating beyond the worst-case models. The steady hum of the air filtration system was the only sound cutting through the silence.

Johnson strode through the door. His uniform collar was dark with sweat, but his shoulders stayed square. "What's the situation? Emily mentioned my family."

"They're safe for now," Diego said. The chemical taste of reclaimed water filled his mouth, sharp and bitter. He jerked his chin at Luna, who for once had abandoned her habitual slouch and stood ramrod straight. "Show us."

Luna's hands moved across the interface. The Exodus launch schedule exploded across the main screen, timestamps glowing like fresh blood. "Official broadcasts claim next week. That's a lie." She expanded the visual, and the screen filled with massive vessels breaking orbit. "The elites aren't even pretending to wait. Three months of planning compressed to seven days on paper, but look." Her finger stabbed at the screen. "These bastards are cutting their lines right now."

Olivia stepped forward, her hands moving with unshakable precision over her display despite the exhaustion that made her movements slightly too slow. Seismic data bloomed, fault lines spreading like cracks in glass across a continental map.

"The core rotation data confirms our fears." Olivia's voice was quiet, yet it commanded the room's full attention. "We are looking at days. Not months." She pointed to a specific pattern of rippling fault activity. "This pressure wave is propagating at two hundred thirty kilometers per hour along the continental fault system. It will destabilize the San Andreas and all adjacent lines within forty-eight hours."

The old wound in Diego's forearm flared. Hot. Sharp. Scar tissue grinding against bone.

Ozone. The smell of ozone. Red on gray pavement. A child's scream.

Olivia swiped to Mexico City's live feed. A neighborhood. Just gone. Swallowed by a sinkhole that hadn't existed an hour ago. Buildings tilted at wrong angles, sliding into darkness without sound.

"Twenty minutes ago." Her voice cracked. The clinical mask slipping. "Phoenix. Tucson. The entire Southwest corridor." Her hand shook as she traced the projection. "Seventy-two hours. Then cascade failure across North America."

The air conditioning hummed indifferently. Johnson's knuckles were white where he gripped the table's edge. Red warning lights painted their faces in hellish hues. The numbers on the screen were too large, too final. For a moment that stretched like held breath, no one spoke.

Diego stared at the data. Phoenix. His gaze cut across the table and locked with Kaito's.

Kaito cleared his throat, the sound unnaturally loud in the charged silence. His hand moved to straighten his tie, the motion sharp and reflexive. "Our Southwest corridor projections accounted for forty-three family transits." He paused, his fingers working the silk with mechanical precision. "Those routes are no longer viable."

"Phoenix." Johnson's voice was flat. Empty. "My sister's family. They're right there. Dead center."

The rigid military bearing he'd held just moments before cracked. His shoulders sagged. The memory of his niece's gap-toothed smile on her last birthday. His promise to her of a real celebration once they reached Haven.

"They have two kids," he said, his voice breaking on the words. His gaze locked on Diego, everything professional stripped away. "What are our orders, sir? How do we get them out?"

Silence.

Diego's gaze cut to Johnson. The captain's mask. Gone. Beneath it, just a brother watching his world crumble.

His thoughts circled back. Empty bunkers. Closed caskets. Jakarta. Osaka. All of it.

Luna's voice cut through. "APU brass is running for orbit. Every emergency response system's collapsing." Her hands moved across her screen, fast, precise. "The highways will be death traps by tomorrow. Ground swallows them or the panic does. Either way, they're fucked."

"Martinez-san," Kaito said, his hand finding his tie again. The fabric was already perfectly straight, but his fingers tugged at it anyway, a useless gesture in the face of planetary collapse. "We do not have sufficient pilot resources for an operation of this scale."

Diego paced, his boots striking a harsh rhythm on the floor. Cold coffee from their last planning session sat in mugs on the table, relics of a plan that was now obsolete. Their controlled evacuation had just become a desperate scramble for survival.

"The issue is not just getting those families here," Olivia interjected, her finger highlighting a different projection. "The seismic activity creates a significant tsunami risk for this facility. If the quantum bridge is underwater when it activates…"

"Then those families have nowhere to go, even if they reach us," Johnson finished, his voice straining against control. "So we solve both problems. Or they all die."

Diego stopped pacing. His gaze flickered from Olivia to Kaito, who stood rigid by the far wall. "Can we automate the gateway with monitoring from Haven? Schedule daily openings?"

Automate. The word landed hard.

Diego's hand found the scar on his forearm. Old burn tissue, raised and rough.

He looked across the table at Kaito. That carefully controlled expression cracked. Just for a second.

Thirty years. Gone. Two soldiers standing over a bleeding father. His son screaming for help.

Olivia studied the seismic data, her fingers moving across probability matrices. "Possible. The quantum anchors could maintain position autonomously." She pulled up schematics. "But if that gateway opens underwater, or during a major seismic event…"

Diego's mind supplied the rest. Seawater erupting through an active gateway. The image of Maria clutching her children as a wall of water burst through the portal. Isabella's small hand reaching for him as the torrent swept them away.

He spun to face Luna. "Elevation here?"

Her stylus moved across a topographical map. "Twenty meters above sea level. Projections for a Cascadia-level event show tsunamis reaching thirty meters." She looked up, her face grim. "We would be underwater."

He studied the facility's structural diagrams. The gateway chamber had reinforced walls, but they were designed for hurricanes, not for the weight of an ocean. "What about moving the terminus point? Relocate it to higher ground?"

"Not enough time. But..." Olivia tapped her tablet, her mind already racing through the physics. "I could remain on this side. Monitor the conditions and sever the quantum anchors if it becomes too dangerous. That would prevent the gateway from opening into a disaster."

Diego looked at her. The chemical taste in his mouth sharpened, cutting through the recycled air like acid. "Olivia, you are far too valuable to risk. I have people trained for assignments like that."

Her grip on the tablet tightened. She gave a single, sharp nod, her focus already snapping back to the data.

"We need automated monitoring," Johnson cut in, his voice insistent. "Something that can warn the families in the Southwest and reroute them."

"I can rig it," Luna said, her typing resuming. She cracked her knuckles before diving back into her keyboard. "Satellite links, automated alerts for seismic thresholds."

"Automation." Diego looked at Kaito. The taste of old betrayals filled his mouth. The scent of ozone and burning electronics. A small hand reaching through smoke and debris. The younger man's hand went to his tie again, straightening something, anything, in the sudden chaos.

His palm hit the table. Coffee mugs jumped. The sound cracked through the room.

"All these years. Fighting AI control. Machines making life-or-death calls." The words came out hard, clipped.

His throat closed. The old shrapnel in his ribs burned hot.

"Now I'm trusting one of Luna's algorithms to keep my family safe." He looked at each face around the table. Exhausted. Waiting. No good answers in their eyes. "What's the alternative? Let them burn because I'm too proud to bend?"

He locked eyes with Luna. "You will build in redundancies. Multiple checks. And I want manual overrides on everything. A human hand on every switch."

"I already have the data feeds," Luna replied, her words clipped and precise. "I'm not writing an AI. Just simple logic. If seismic activity exceeds threshold X, or if water levels reach point Y, the gateway locks down. Everything else stays in our hands." She looked up from her screen. "Simple if-then statements. No offense, sir, but even a general should be able to understand them."

Johnson's shoulders squared, the soldier taking over from the brother. "What about transport? Can we get evacuation vehicles to the Southwest faster?"

Diego nodded. The choice settled in his stomach like cold metal. "We redirect every available asset. Priority goes to the critical zones." He leveled a finger at Luna. "Set it up." His gaze cut to Kaito one last time. "But I want a human override on every single decision."

He pushed back from the table. "Alright. We have our work. I want hourly updates on your progress. Dismissed."

The room emptied. Johnson paused at the door, his gaze meeting Diego's. "Thank you, sir." The words carried the weight of a man whose world now rested on their shoulders.

Only Olivia remained, her eyes fixed on the evacuation projections.

"The numbers do not add up," she said, almost to herself. Her finger traced a pulsing fault line. "The accelerated tectonic activity means more than earthquakes. The atmospheric methane releases..." She trailed off, then met his gaze. "You have already calculated the acceptable losses, haven't you?"

Diego didn't answer. Turned to leave.

At the door, she blocked his path. "Diego." Her voice went soft. "We'll make this work. I ran new simulations on the quantum anchors. Might be a way to increase throughput without breaking stability."

He looked down at her. The fierce intelligence that exhaustion couldn't kill. The scientist still there beneath the fighter.

"Together."

Alone now. Red warnings pulsed on every screen. He pulled the tablet from under his arm, battery dead, screen black as void. Not his reflection staring back.

Maria's face.

THE CASCADE

Diego cut straight to it. "Luna's intel confirms it. The APU and EAAU are launching next week instead of next month."

Johnson's coffee mug hit the table too hard. Sarah's tablet screen cracked under her grip.

"We need to move our people now," Diego added.

Kayla pushed back from the table. "The power grid can handle the load, but each crossing will drain us dry. We'll need to cycle generators between portals, no shortcuts."

"We started with twelve crossings," Olivia said. Her hands trembled as she scrolled through data. "But after analyzing the last three operations, I've found our latest batch of stabilization alloys has serious purity issues. We're burning through twice the resources per opening. At this rate, we can only confirm resources for three more guaranteed openings."

"Three?" Emily slammed her stylus down. "That's not even close to..."

"Fifty people per crossing would be ideal," Olivia continued, her voice turning clinical as she retreated into numbers. "But we can push it to seventy-five if they move through one at a time. More granular control to react before quantum destabilization cascades."

Diego looked at Sarah. She was already shaking her head, her mouth set in a grim line.

"We have five hundred and twelve people cleared and ready," Sarah said. Each word came out flat, measured. "All vetted, all with critical skills." Her stylus snapped in half. "Diego, that means leaving the Ramirez family behind. Their kids are five and seven."

Johnson rubbed his jaw, the sound of stubble scraping in the quiet. "What about the receiving end? The main settlement area is secure, but the greenhouse isn't ready yet."

"Two weeks minimum," Ethan said, glancing at Mei.

"Two weeks if you're lucky, farm boy," Jack snorted. "The grid's already redlining."

"We can accelerate with temporary structures," Ethan shot back, his voice rising, "but rush it, and we risk crop failure in an environment where every calorie matters. Plants need time, even in Haven."

Emily's fingers moved across her tablet. "The drone network's operational. We can maintain security, but processing that many people at once through our settlement protocols..."

Three beeps. Rapid.

She stared at the screen.

"Shit."

"Security isn't our problem," Jack interrupted, his metallic leg starting its irregular drumbeat against the floor. "The electrical system is already strained beyond specifications. That's not a population increase, that's a cascading power failure waiting to happen. We'll need two weeks to boost infrastructure." He paused, his grin humorless. "Another Monday morning, huh?"

The server racks whined in response. Three more operations. Diego's chest tightened around the number.

"Jack, break this down for me. How long between portal closings before we can fire it up again?"

Jack poked at the interface. The old tech sputtered, froze, then displayed power curves. "The portal's a power hog. Eight hours minimum to let the reactor cool and the ZPE recharge. Twelve if she decides to be a bitch. No shortcuts."

"And worst-case scenario?"

"Worst case?" Kayla stabbed at the display, highlighting massive crimson energy spikes. "If the ZPE hits a quantum fluctuation or the cooling system runs hot, we're looking at twelve hours between portals, maybe more. And I'd bet my left tit we'll hit at least one bad cycle."

"That's three to five days just for portal operations, assuming nothing goes wrong." Diego's jaw tightened. "And we need everything to go perfectly."

He studied his team. The engineers, the scientists, the soldiers. Maria and his grandkids were safe on the other side, but they were waiting for friends, for neighbors, for the community they'd promised to build together.

"We'll need to prioritize," Diego said. "Break the five hundred down into groups. Critical infrastructure first. Medical, engineering, agriculture. Then families with children."

His eyes locked with Johnson's. Both men had made these kinds of choices before. Both men hated it. "The rest... We'll have to see."

Jack's metallic leg kept its rhythm against the floor. Somewhere in the facility, a generator coughed and steadied.

"Sarah, work with Johnson to prioritize the personnel lists. I want those groups defined yesterday." Diego turned to Jack and Kayla. "You two focus on power efficiency. Each hour we shave off that cycle time saves lives."

Stabilization metals. Another critical failure point burning through their options faster than expected.

"Emily, Olivia, any options to increase mining output?"

Emily scrolled through drone survey data. "The drones have mapped several promising deposits in Haven, but extraction and processing take time. We're weeks away from harvesting those quantities."

"Weeks we don't have," Johnson grunted.

"Speed purification and we risk portal failure," Olivia said, her voice becoming a shield of technical precision. "Last time we rushed, we lost three drones and nearly breached containment."

Diego leaned forward. "Skip to the solutions. What obstacles can we eliminate to accelerate mineral extraction?"

"The refinement stations are our bottleneck," Kayla said. Her eyes lit up. "But I spotted something interesting. Remember the Phoenix plant our recon drones found? Their high-grade purification equipment is exactly what we need."

"What's the quantity?"

"Three machines, each weighing roughly two tons." Kayla's grin turned predatory. "We'd need heavy-lift VTOL planes. And I'd get to blow a wall or two. Win-win."

Food resources. The math was brutal there too.

"How are we on food production?"

"Greenhouse framework is complete," Ethan said. "But we need another week minimum for operational hydroponics. Right now, we support a hundred settlers with fresh vegetables. Five hundred more puts everyone on strict rations until the first harvest."

Kaito's hologram shimmered into existence, the image wavering like heat distortion before solidifying.

"I've secured three months of emergency rations for five hundred people," Kaito stated. "The supplies are already en route to staging areas."

"At what cost?" Diego asked. He'd learned not to trust free lunches from the Nexus Cartel.

"My contacts require something in return," Kaito replied. "Access to Haven's mineral samples from the northeastern quadrant. Exclusive rights to study them."

"No deal," Olivia said immediately. "Those deposits could be critical for our long-term survival."

"So is eating," Diego countered. He faced Kaito's hologram. "How long can we negotiate?"

"Hours, not days," Kaito replied. "They have other interested parties."

Diego's mouth tightened into a line. He turned to Mei. "What about after those rations run out?"

"Initial crop yields should begin within six weeks," Mei said. Her tablet chimed with incoming data. "Growth rates in Haven are thirty percent faster than Earth standard. The soil contains minerals we've never seen before."

"What's the bottleneck for faster hydroponics?"

Ethan leaned forward. "Nutrient calibration takes time. Rush it and we risk losing everything to..."

"Wait," Jack interrupted, staring at his screen like it had personally offended him. "You're telling me the greenhouse needs how much power?"

Ethan blinked. "Fifty kilowatts steady for the grow lights, plus..."

"Fucking hell," Jack growled. "That's competing directly with portal operations. Same power grid."

The power grid. Fourth critical priority. Another way they could all die.

"Options?" he asked. His voice had developed an edge.

Jack scrubbed the back of his neck. "The main issue is capacity. Our infrastructure's barely handling the current load."

"Solar arrays holding at ninety percent," Kayla said. Her fingers moved across the display. "But Haven's sun? Different spectral output. We need quantum mods."

"Three options," Jack said. "First, we salvage the backup fusion generator from the Nevada facility. Gives us fifteen percent more capacity."

"Second option," Kayla jumped in, "retune solar arrays for Haven's frequency. Could squeeze thirty percent more power, but it's delicate work."

"And third?" Diego asked. The two engineers shared a look.

"Strip down the atomic plant here," Kayla said. "Take half the reactor cores and rebuild them in Haven. Risky as hell, would limit our portal operations, but solves power permanently."

"Timeline on the fusion generator?" Diego asked.

"Five days, and we'd need Mia's team for transport," Jack replied. "Four tons, trapped behind Water War-era security."

"The solar modifications?"

"A week of testing here, then gradual implementation. Less risky, slower results."

Diego stared at the power consumption graphs. Usage spikes climbed higher with each system they'd activated in Haven.

"Let's start with solar mods and get the fusion plant moving," Diego decided. "We're struggling for power here already, so we don't touch our plant until we've moved everyone."

He turned to Kaito, whose hologram had stabilized. "Can you source transport for those ore processors?"

"The APU has restricted heavy transport due to exodus preparations," Kaito answered. "However, my contractors can extract the units within thirty-six hours. Another twenty-four to reach you using the southern route through Sonora. The northern corridors are too heavily monitored now."

"The price?" Diego asked. Kaito didn't deal in charity.

"My people will need exclusive transportation rights for their families," Kaito said. "Fifteen slots in the next crossing. Non-negotiable."

"Fifteen slots we don't have," Sarah muttered, glaring at Kaito's hologram.

"The equipment needs to be broken down for portal transport," Kaito continued. "My team can handle disassembly, but we'll need Kayla's expertise for reassembly."

Diego turned to Sarah. "How many people are arriving today?"

"Thirty-two in the next four hours. Johnson's security team, families first, then medical, and Jack's technicians." Sarah's voice stayed professional, but her broken stylus told a different story.

Diego stared at the personnel manifest on the main display. Each name carried skills, families, and hopes. "Have them processed through medical immediately. I want everyone cleared before orientation."

Diego stood up from the command chair. "This is our final gathering on Original Earth." Outside the window, blood-orange sunlight painted the Cozumel facility. "Step outside. Make your farewells. Touch the grass. Feel the wind. Remember it." His voice dropped. "Sarah, give me the list of who stays behind for shutdown procedures."

Sarah's tablet chimed. "Jack, Kayla, and Thompson's demolition crew. Olivia for portal shutdown sequencing. Emily to coordinate final drone sweeps. Johnson and his core team for security until the last transport."

"Timeline?"

"Seventy-two hours after the final crossing," Johnson said. "Longer if we hit complications."

The room emptied slowly. Some lingered, fingers trailing across familiar control surfaces. Others moved quickly, as if staying longer would make leaving harder.

Through the windows, sunlight bled orange and purple across the sky. The same sky that had watched their wars, their failures, their desperate scramble for survival.

As the room cleared, Diego moved to the window. Below, his people scattered across the grounds, some embracing, others standing alone. Dr. Smith paused at the door, met his eyes, and nodded once before leaving.

Diego's reflection stared back from the glass, scarred face, gray threading his hair, eyes that had seen too much. He pressed his palm against the window. The facility's pulse ran through the glass, generators and servers and life support systems working overtime to keep their fragile hope alive.

Tomorrow, they'd tear the universe open to save who they could. Tonight, they said goodbye to the only world they'd ever known.

The Bio-Ag Lab thrummed with electrical noise, sharp chemicals cut through the air, mixing with the earthy smell of soil samples. Diego's boots squeaked against polished floors while environmental systems worked overtime to keep Haven's atmosphere breathable.

Through the observation window, an alien landscape stretched under violet and amber light. Those weird ferns moved without any wind, their iridescent fronds catching light in patterns that made his eyes water if he stared too long.

Mei Choi hunched over a holographic workstation, her usually perfect posture shot to hell. Lines around her eyes that hadn't been there a month ago. Even she looked like she was running on fumes.

Behind her, Ethan paced in his usual pattern. Four steps forward, pivot, four steps back. Diego's gut tightened; the kid only paced like that when the data was bad.

Mei manipulated the projection display, molecular structures rotating as she worked. Blue light flickered across her face, casting shadows that made her look older. "These soil readings show substances we've never encountered. Nothing in our databases matches these mineral profiles."

"What's it doing to our crops?" Diego stepped closer to the display.

A soft ping from one of the incubator screens. The yellow warning light blinked twice, then went green. Diego tracked it. His gut churned. Not random.

Mei gestured toward purple crystal formations scattered through the soil sample. "They're changing our plants at the cellular level." The display zoomed in on plant cells with strange formations clustering around the walls. "We can't verify they're safe for consumption anymore."

Ethan stopped mid-pace, boot scraping tile. "The plants are growing faster than we projected, but they're becoming something else. Something we didn't plan for."

Diego compared the baseline Earth crops with their Haven counterparts on the split screen. The differences jumped out like his uncle Ramón's sixth finger, subtle until you noticed it. "How much faster?"

"Growth rates increased by thirty-seven percent." Mei's voice carried the strain of too many eighteen-hour days. "But edibility? Safety? We're flying blind."

Olivia moved to the readout station, that analytical crease appearing between her brows. Another alert chimed, louder this time. The monitoring station flickered, shadows dancing across the walls.

The purple crystals in the projection triggered Diego's threat assessment protocols. Unknown variables, potential contamination, mission parameters compromised. His hand drifted toward his sidearm, old habits.

"Hold on." Diego looked between their faces. "We've been eating those purple berries for weeks. Same problem?"

Mei's shoulders pulled back slightly. She flicked through images with quick, precise movements. "More complex than that. The berries contain these elements too, but in different arrangements. Native vegetation evolved over millennia to process these minerals safely."

Ethan nodded so hard Diego wondered if his head would snap off. The kid planted his feet like he'd found solid ground in a swamp.

"That's exactly what scares us. Our crops are trying to accomplish in weeks what took native species thousands of generations. Like forcing evolution at gunpoint."

Mei expanded a section showing energy transfers between cells. "These growth patterns indicate rapid genetic adaptation. Fascinating from a research perspective, but potentially catastrophic for ecosystem balance. This rate of change isn't natural, even for an alien environment."

"What's Plan B?" Diego rubbed his temple where a headache was building. "Please tell me there's a fucking Plan B."

Silence except for the environmental systems and another soft alert. The yellow warning light stayed on longer this time before fading. Diego's threat assessment kicked into high gear. The pattern meant something.

Ethan's anxiety smoothed into focus. His eyes locked on his datapad, stylus dancing across the screen with new purpose.

"Hardy strains. Species engineered for mineral stress and extreme conditions." His voice steadied as he brought up crop varieties, each labeled with environmental tolerances. "Plants designed for contaminated environments."

"So we're talking cockroaches after nuclear winter?"

Ethan's mouth twitched upward. "More like desert survivors. Amaranth, quinoa, millet. Tough as your old combat boots, but edible."

The screen shifted to growth projections. Diego recognized several species from Mexico's farming regions during the water wars. Plants that lived when everything else died.

"Japan's vertical farming genetics are still viable too." Ethan's confidence built with each word. "They engineered those for toxic conditions after Osaka. Combine those with desert crops, and we might get plants that adapt without turning into alien monsters."

A knot in Diego's chest loosened slightly, finally, something actionable instead of more problems to juggle.

"Timeline for test beds?"

"With proper help, we plant tomorrow. First data in two weeks, solid results in four." Ethan made notes, his earlier stuttering gone.

The yellow warning light pulsed again from the cryo-storage units. Diego watched the rhythmic pattern, his attention snagging on the timing. Whatever was happening wasn't random equipment failure.

"Good. What about the animal embryos?" He nodded toward the blinking units. "Still in storage until we sort the food situation?"

Ethan and Mei shared one of those looks. The kind that made Diego's spine straighten and his hand check for his sidearm. The same expression officers wore before delivering casualty reports.

"Shit. What happened?" His voice dropped to a commanding tone.

Mei pointed to the yellow indicator Diego had been tracking. "Several embryos required emergency incubation."

"What the hell does that mean?"

Ethan glanced at his datapad. "Storage units malfunctioned during last week's power fluctuations. We either started incubation immediately or lost them completely."

The knot in Diego's chest tightened back up. "How many?"

"Twelve chickens, eight goats, four pigs." Mei pulled up readouts across multiple displays. "Developing normally despite the mineral content in their nutrient solutions."

"The same minerals causing problems with the crops?"

"Yes, though different concentrations. The embryos seem to process them without obvious complications."

Every solution spawned three new problems, like fighting a hydra with a dull knife.

"Status of the remaining embryos?"

Ethan shifted weight between his feet. "Still preserved, but not for long. Other storage units show deterioration patterns. Seven days, maybe fourteen before we face the same decision."

Diego turned toward Olivia. She stood near the displays, scanning data points with that precise focus that usually meant she'd found something useful.

She stepped forward, suddenly animated. "The embryos function as closed biological systems demonstrating successful mineral integration pathways."

Her hands swept through the holographic data with measured precision. "We can quantify exactly how their cellular structures adapt to Haven's environment."

The display shifted to comparative diagrams, cellular structures side by side. "Here." Her lab coat brushed Diego's arm. "This adaptation sequence follows predictable physics principles. The embryonic processing could provide mathematical models for engineering crop solutions."

Diego nodded as connections clicked. In the weeks since arrival, he'd learned to trust Olivia's pattern recognition. When she found mathematical relationships, they led to practical applications.

"So we proceed with embryo development?"

"The probability of success makes it necessary. Both are due to failing storage and the crucial data they provide. The embryos function as living laboratories, demonstrating how Earth organisms successfully integrate with Haven's environment."

"Next step is getting these animals out of the lab once they're developed?"

"Exactly. They'll need proper enclosures, and we'll monitor their continued adaptation to Haven's environment over time."

Diego pulled out his tablet, mentally shuffling personnel assignments. "I'll coordinate teams for livestock enclosures. Jack and Kayla are getting restless working just on portal maintenance."

"We should build three separate areas." Ethan gestured at a hologram he'd created. "Goats in one section, pigs in another, protected pen for birds to keep native predators out."

Diego examined the layout, evaluating sight lines and security factors. The positioning made sense. Close enough to headquarters for safety, far enough to avoid the smell. For a moment, he pictured his grandfather's ranch in Mexico, before the wars turned peaceful farms into strategic targets.

Another alert chimed. The yellow light stayed longer before fading.

Diego made notes. "Thompson's crew can handle main construction. They're rotating guard shifts with Johnson's unit. Good use of downtime."

He looked up at Mei, who was calibrating breeding equipment despite the stress etched in her face.

"When do we need enclosures ready?"

"Poultry first. Just over two weeks. Other livestock several weeks after that."

There's enough time for basic structures if they start soon. Everything on Haven took longer than projected, thanks to the planet's constant middle finger to their best-laid plans.

Mei glanced up from her work. "Have Emily's drones sweep the site first. Avoid those underground fungal colonies you found last week."

"Right. Don't need livestock dropping into sinkholes because alien mushrooms decided to collapse the ground." Diego rubbed his temple where the headache was spreading. "Between crop mutations and storage failures, we need alternatives. Any progress identifying safe native food sources? Things already adapted to this environment?"

Ethan and Mei exchanged another look. The kind that made Diego's trigger finger itch.

"We've identified several promising candidates," Mei began, her tone shifting to something more guarded. "Testing protocols have been challenging without animal models."

Diego's spine went rigid. "What testing methods are you using?"

"Computer simulations, chemical analysis..." Ethan's voice trailed off, his fidgeting with the tablet becoming more pronounced.

"And?" Diego's command voice cut through the lab noise.

Ethan swallowed hard. "Also, direct observations of digestive compatibility."

"Meaning what exactly?" Ice formed in Diego's veins. He knew that tone. Scientists trying to soften bad news.

Ethan brought up an image of an iridescent beetle. "We've confirmed this species is safe for consumption. Exceptional protein content, sustainable harvest rates."

"Confirmed how?" Each word precise as a rifle shot.

Ethan's eyes darted away, shoulders hunched like he was taking incoming fire. "During family visitation day last week, we had an... unexpected test subject."

The lab went silent except for the hum of machines. Diego's world narrowed to Ethan's face.

"Mateo," Ethan whispered.

Everything inside Diego went cold and sharp. His grandson's name. His five-year-old grandson.

"Maria was there, thank God," Ethan continued, words tumbling out faster. "But Isabella dared him, you know how children get, and before anyone could stop him, the little guy just popped it in his mouth."

The image flashed in his mind: Mateo's small fingers. The alien thing disappearing past his lips. Then the nightmare scenarios: rash spreading across small limbs, convulsions wracking his tiny body, respiratory failure, his grandson dying on a lab table while machines beeped helplessly.

His stance shifted without conscious thought. Combat ready. Target acquired.

"His biomarkers remained completely stable," Ethan babbled, oblivious to how close he was to getting his throat crushed. "Protein absorption was remarkably efficient. Digestive enzymes complement human gut flora. Fascinating adaptation potential."

The words hit Diego like shrapnel. *Biomarkers. Protein absorption. Fascinating.*

His grandson reduced to data points.

"And you're telling me this now?" The words came out quietly. Deadly quiet.

Behind him, Olivia tensed. Mei stepped closer, her hands raised slightly in a placating gesture.

Ethan finally registered the danger. His face went pale as he took a step back.

Diego's vision tunneled to Ethan's face. Everything else, the lab, the machines, the alien landscape, disappeared. Only the scientist who'd turned his grandson into an experiment.

"Let me understand this." Diego's voice could have etched steel. "My five-year-old grandson consumed an unknown alien life form. Instead of immediately informing me, you decided to monitor him like a lab rat. And you're sharing this information as if it's a scientific breakthrough rather than criminal negligence?"

Mei moved between them, her composed demeanor cracking. "Diego, I was there too. We monitored him for forty-eight hours, ran comprehensive blood work, neural scans, and enzyme panels. The moment anything seemed wrong..."

"You would have what?" Diego cut her off. "Called me while my grandson was dying? Explained how this amazing scientific opportunity killed him?"

The rage hit him like a physical blow. Hot and consuming. His hands wanted to close around Ethan's throat. Shake him until those clinical observations rattled loose from his skull.

"I... we should have told you immediately." Ethan's scientific detachment crumbled. His tablet slipped from nerveless fingers, clattering against the floor. "You're right. I'm sorry."

Sorry. Like that word could undo the betrayal. Like it could erase the image of Mateo on a lab table.

Diego forced his hands to unclench, leaving crescents of his nails in his palms. Military discipline wrestled with the grandfather's fury.

He closed his eyes. Counted to three. When he opened them, the rage was still there. Coiled. Ready to strike.

"This will never happen again." Each word carved from ice. "Not with Mateo. Not with Isabella. Not with any child in this colony. Clear?"

Both scientists nodded. The weight of their mistake finally landing.

Diego's boots carried him to the observation window. His reflection caught in the reinforced glass. Jaw clenched. Eyes flat. His hands found the frame. Squeezed until bone showed white through skin. Heat radiated from the metal. The facility's steady hum vibrated through his palms. Still working. Still standing. Despite the fractures running through everything.

Haven's violet plains stretched beyond the glass. Somewhere out there, his grandchildren were playing. Exploring. Building memories in a world he'd helped create for them.

Safe.

For now.

He drew breath. Held it. Let it out slow. When he turned back, his face was professional calm. The grandfather locked away. Mission requirements first.

"Native predators." His voice steady now. Empty of heat. "You mentioned them earlier. Status report."

Mei's shoulders dropped. Ethan's rigid posture finally broke. The air between them stayed thick.

"Three distinct groups of those six-legged grazers," Mei said, pulling up aerial surveillance. "Thirty to forty adults each. Emily's monitoring shows breeding follows seasonal cycles, gestation comparable to Earth horses."

Ethan moved cautiously to the projection, his earlier enthusiasm replaced by careful professionalism. "Their young develop faster, though. Full maturity in about six months. Those extra legs help. They're running almost instantly after birth."

Diego watched recordings of the creatures sprinting across Haven's violet plains. Fast. Too fast for easy hunting. He calculated meat yields against capture difficulties.

"Aerial predators take them regularly." Mei displayed footage of something like a giant hawk with a bony crest diving onto one of the six-legged beasts. "They consume the meat without ill effects, though their digestive systems differ significantly from ours."

"Domestication possibilities?" Diego asked, forcing himself to focus on practical solutions.

Ethan consulted his datapad carefully. "If we established a breeding program... some of the incoming colonists have farming experience."

Mei looked up sharply. "The plant specialist from Singapore, was she approved?"

Diego nodded, recalling the impressive qualifications. He'd noticed Mei's unusual interest whenever that candidate came up. "Scheduled for next arrival. Several experienced farmers, too. Couple from upstate New York, another from Malaysia, and one stubborn bastard from Jalisco bringing five hundred agave pups."

Mei's face eased, something like relief flickering across her features. "The forty-five who arrived this morning brought our total to two hundred. Nearly enough for a stable population and sustained growth, if we can feed them all."

Agave. His grandfather's fields stretched endlessly, the sweet earthy scent of roasted piñas, the rhythmic thud of the harvesters. His abuelo would've laughed at tequila production outlasting Earth itself.

"If we incorporate Malaysia's vertical farming with tropical adaptation knowledge..." Mei scrolled through new data displays. "Humidity patterns here could benefit their techniques better than Earth conditions."

"Combine that with drought-resistant strains," Ethan added, his voice carefully neutral, "we could develop hybrids specifically designed to process these mineral compounds safely."

Botanical jargon. Diego lost the thread after thirty seconds. He caught Olivia's eye, nodded toward the exit.

They walked. His boots. Her lighter steps. Falling into rhythm without trying.

Near the command center, Diego stopped. The photograph came out of his pocket before he thought about it. Isabella and Mateo, mid-laugh. One of those rare moments before Earth went to shit completely.

Rage sat in his chest like hot metal. But under it, something else. Heavier.

"We're building something." He shoved the photo back into his pocket. "Something better than what we left. But if we lose ourselves doing it..."

His throat closed. Couldn't finish.

"The children." Olivia's voice went soft. Not her usual clinical precision. "They're why we can't compromise. Why we have to stay human."

Diego's jaw worked. "Yeah."

They moved toward the command center. Behind them, warning lights pulsed from the embryo storage units. Red. Steady. The heartbeat of Haven's future.

Isabella. Mateo. All the kids who'd grow up here, breathing clean air, drinking water that didn't taste like chemicals and failure.

His knee throbbed. The lights kept pulsing.

They had to make this work.

REWRITING THE TEXTBOOKS

T he lights overhead sputtered and died. Three seconds later, they flickered back on. Jack yanked open the junction box panel, metal clanging against the wall.

"The power fluctuations are getting worse," he said.

Acrid burning plastic scraped Diego's throat. Inside the exposed panel, tangled cables and crystalline power nodes pulsed with erratic blue glow. A low-frequency hum vibrated through the deck plates, rising and falling like labored breathing.

"We're pulling more juice than these converters were meant to handle," Jack said, pointing at a blackened connection.

Diego tapped his index finger against his thumb, unconsciously counting failures. Every falter of the lights reminded him how many lives depended on these systems. The familiar knot formed along his neck.

Kayla knelt beside Jack, her maintenance kit open, tools arranged in precise rows. Her blackened fingers traced a dull power node, leaving smudged trails. The circuit pathways sizzled under her touch.

"Those mineral samples we found up north might work as replacements," she said, voice hoarse from three days of continuous work. "They transfer energy better than this Earth junk." She tapped the node with her screwdriver, triggering a spark. "Problem is, we'd have to modify the whole damn grid for their different output. And that's assuming we can even process what we've collected."

"How long?" Diego asked, watching Olivia hunch over her tablet at the viewport. Her fingers moved across the screen in sharp, frustrated jabs.

Jack's cybernetic leg whined as he shifted weight, the servos pitched higher than usual. He'd been favoring it all week.

"Three days minimum, assuming everything goes perfectly." Jack's tone carried zero optimism. "Which it fucking won't. Something always breaks. But the real problem: we'd need to shut down the grid during conversion."

"That's not an option," Olivia said. She set her tablet down hard enough to crack against the console, the sound sharp in the confined space. "Portal stabilization requires continuous power. Even a momentary interruption could destabilize the quantum matrix we've spent months calibrating."

She moved to the junction box, nostrils flared. "We're not maintaining machinery, Jack. We're maintaining the only variable that keeps every colonist on the other side alive."

Another surge ripped through the system. Lights stuttered, consoles beeped warnings, and the life support rhythm faltered. Down the corridor, a transformer squealed like tearing metal.

Diego's fingers found the base of his skull. Muscle knotted there, tight as piano wire. The grid had to hold for the next wave of colonists. But one wrong move with the portal, one power fluctuation at the wrong millisecond, and three hundred people on the other side suffocated in their sleep.

"What about running a parallel system?" Kayla asked, wiping sweat with her wrist and leaving a greasy smudge. "Build a secondary grid with the new minerals, test it, then switch over once stable."

Jack shook his head and kicked the toolbox. Metal tools clattered like dropped ammunition.

"Fantasy talk. We don't have enough components for redundant systems. The last supply run brought half what we requested."

He stared into the junction box, then froze. That look Diego recognized, a solution brewing, probably dangerous.

"Out with it, Sparky," Diego said, shifting weight off his bad knee. "What's cooking in that head of yours?"

Jack drummed his fingers against the metal panel, rhythm accelerating. "The old facility on Earth. We're abandoning it anyway. Those power converters in Security HQ are identical to what we need. Top-line APU tech, barely used." His eyes lit up. "We could salvage them during the next supply run, cannibalize the whole system. Move fast, be in and out before scavengers notice."

Diego glanced at Kayla. Her fingers jabbed at her tablet screen with increasing irritation. The simulation crashed, flashing red.

"The voltage differential is problematic," she muttered. "But if we modify the arrays and recalibrate... no, that wouldn't..." She trailed off, lost in calculations Diego couldn't follow.

"The stabilizers in Admin HQ are complete overkill," Jack continued, words tumbling faster. "Half that equipment is gathering dust while we struggle with basic systems."

The panel clanged shut like a gunshot.

Diego's mind automatically shifted to insertion planning. They'd need Kaito's Nexus operatives for security clearance; the abandoned facility remained under APU surveillance despite decommission orders. Relations with the Cartel ran on mutual necessity, not trust. The components were worth the risk.

"How many people would you need?" Diego asked.

"Just me and Kayla," Jack said. "We know those systems inside out. Two hours tops. Anyone else would slow us down."

"And you're sure these parts will work?" Diego pressed, touching the scar along his temple.

Kayla looked up, exhaustion written in the dark circles beneath her bloodshot eyes. Her uniform bore three days of stains, hair escaping its bun in frustrated wisps. "With modifications, yes. The architecture is compatible. We'd need to adjust for energy density, but the theory's solid."

Diego nodded once. Jack and Kayla always found ways through impossible situations. He'd seen it repeatedly since arriving on Haven.

"Good thinking. Coordinate any cutover with Olivia and Luna. Last thing we need is Luna screaming about her servers losing power during a data migration."

Kayla's tablet pinged with a new warning. She swiped to a different diagnostic, her expression darkening. Red alerts reflected in her irises.

"We've got another problem," she said flatly. "And this one connects directly to our power issues."

Jack groaned. "Of course we do."

"The constant high-voltage surges are overloading the recyclers' filtration membranes," Kayla continued, cutting through his complaint. "Haven's water is shredding our filters. We're burning through DI beds in hours instead of weeks."

The words hit Diego like a punch to the chest. Water shortages. The press of desperate bodies against barricades in Osaka. A child's face, lips cracked, eyes pleading. The dull crack of riot shields. His throat closed, sand between his teeth even here in Haven's filtered air.

"How bad?" he asked, his voice rougher than intended.

"Seventy percent efficiency and dropping," Kayla said, showing performance graphs with jagged red lines trending downward. "We're regenerating them manually for now, but that's just buying time."

She swiped to another screen, blue glow highlighting her exhausted features. "We could switch to electro-deionization, but on the scale we need, the power requirements would cripple our already strained grid."

Olivia gripped the workbench edge, knuckles white against the metal. "So something in Haven's water creates an unusual electrochemical reaction."

Jack ran a hand through his hair, leaving a grease smudge above his ear. He exchanged glances with Kayla, that wordless communication Diego recognized from countless combat partnerships.

"We could redesign the filtration system," Kayla said, pulling up schematics. "Build something calibrated to Haven's specific mineral content."

"Using what?" Jack asked.

His artificial foot went silent against the deck. His mind had locked onto something.

"What about those crystalline formations from the northern caves?" Olivia asked. "I noticed the water runoff there tested at almost zero TDS. If the formation is filtering minerals naturally, its matrix must have an extremely high ion exchange rate."

Kayla's expression brightened, fingers dancing across her tablet with renewed energy. "That could work. Stacking them in dense layers would create a disk filter with high contact time."

"We'd need thorough testing first," Jack added. "Last thing we need is poisoning everyone because some pretty rock had unforeseen properties."

"How long for a prototype?" Olivia asked, tablet ready.

Kayla's tablet clattered against the console. She sucked in air through flared nostrils, then fixed Diego with a stare that cut straight through his tactical planning.

"We could build it in days," she said, voice rising. "But we're drowning here. The power grid is failing. Water recyclers are deteriorating. Environmental controls need recalibration. Half the comms network drops packets when it rains." Her words came faster, sharper. "We're not miracle workers!"

It was there in her eyes, that look from a thousand faces in a hundred firefights. The expression of a soldier who'd run out of ammunition and time. She was right. He'd pushed Jack and Kayla past their breaking point.

Jack's shoulders sagged, all his usual energy drained away. He massaged his thigh where flesh met metal, the connection causing pain.

Diego pulled out his datapad. The passenger manifest loaded.

Names. Too many names. Each one a life he'd chosen. Each one someone else he hadn't. Group Twelve.

The engineers. Bumped off the exodus manifest because some algorithm decided their expertise wasn't worth saving.

"When you head back for those power converters," he told Jack and Kayla, tapping four names on the screen, "grab these engineering specialists from Group Twelve. They were bumped off the APU exodus manifest last week."

"To make room for what?" Jack asked.

"Some bureaucrat's family," Diego said, his voice carrying an edge. "Three power experts and civil engineers were discarded for 'more important people.'"

He scrolled through their qualifications. "Put them to work on the salvage, then bring them back. They'll get hands-on experience with our systems, and we save them from being abandoned on Earth."

Kayla's spine straightened. The rigid set of her shoulders eased, muscle by muscle. "That would solve both problems. Extra hands for salvage, and they'd be up to speed when they arrive."

"And we won't disrupt the transport schedule or anger the agricultural specialists waiting for their turn," Diego added, remembering the tense negotiations over priority listings.

Jack nodded, energy creeping back into his voice. "Smart. We could use help carrying that equipment. Some of those converters are heavy as hell."

Kayla began sketching assignments on her tablet, fingers moving with purpose again. "Anyone specific you want?"

Diego studied his datapad, scanning qualifications and experience. "A team that worked on Exodus ships. They designed power systems for inter-dimensional drives. Should translate well here."

Jack groaned theatrically, some of his spark returning. "Great, more quantum jockeys. People who think everything needs triple redundancy and fourteen approval forms to change a light bulb."

"Those quantum jockeys kept crews alive during inter-dimensional jumps," Kayla replied with a hint of amusement. "We could use that level of documentation. Your notes are diagrams scrawled on whatever's handy, including my maintenance schedule."

"Those diagrams are clear," Jack said, gesturing with a wrench. "And I haven't lost any body parts in three years, so I must be doing something right."

Diego watched them return to work. Heads bent over the tablet. Jack gestured while Kayla typed, their focus carrying the quiet competence that had held Haven through every crisis.

They would hold.

He glanced at his manifest again. Additional names. Relevant backgrounds. Several medical specialists, including Dr. Choi's mother. Expertise in medicinal plants. Valuable, given Haven's unique flora. They'd need her knowledge for those northern crystalline formations.

"We should head to the arrival point." Olivia checked her datapad. Her voice had softened. "First group transitions in twenty minutes."

Diego tapped her shoulder, fell into step beside her toward the portal chamber. Their boots rang against metal flooring. Familiar as any pre-deployment march.

But this was different. Families. Engineers. Doctors. People who'd left everything behind for a chance at something better.

"This is what it's all about," Olivia said quietly, glancing at Diego. Her usual guarded expression opened, revealing something vulnerable underneath. "Not just surviving." She paused, looking at the portal entrance ahead, then back to her tablet displaying the manifest names. "This time we have to do better."

Her quiet intensity hit Diego harder than any speech. He nodded, understanding the weight behind those simple words. The same thought lived in him, driving every crisis, every decision.

The portal chamber's frame vibrated with energy, humming through his boots into his teeth. The equipment stood ready to tear open the fabric between worlds, a bridge from a dying Earth to humanity's fragile new beginning.

He checked his watch: 5:57 AM. Three minutes until activation. Just enough time to wonder if these engineers knew what they were walking into.

Diego's eyes found his grandchildren near the portal area. Mateo bounced like he'd swallowed lightning. Isabella, eight years old, worked hard at looking calm. Failing. The other kids picked up on it, pressing against the safety barrier.

"Abuelo!" Mateo's arm windmilled. "Is it time?"

"Few more minutes, Mijo."

Diego looked at Olivia. She pressed something into Isabella's hand. Small bag. Candied protein from her coffee stash.

He nodded once. Out here, candy counted more than threat assessments.

Sarah worked her datapad three meters away. Refugee manifest. Making sure families stayed together, housing assigned before anyone came through.

"The Richardson twins are coming today," Isabella announced. "They're seven, like Mateo. Their dad can build actual robots!"

"That's right." Diego ruffled her hair, earning a look that sent memories of Elena through his chest. "And their mother is a doctor, which we need."

Mateo pressed his face against the safety barrier. Below, techs made final adjustments. The air hummed with power, rattling loose items. Diagnostic lights strobed across control panels.

Sparky hunched over the main control panel, his cybernetic leg locked in place as he balanced on his good leg to reach an overhead connection.

"Two minutes," Jack said. His hands moved across the panel. Switches flipped. Routine. "Unless this piece of shit decides to blow again." He tapped the console. "Come on, baby. Work for me. Just once."

The children's excitement surged until Sarah silenced them with a look.

Diego crouched beside Mateo. "So, I heard you've been trying the local insects."

Mateo beamed. "They taste like candy! The blue ones are best." He mimed catching something. "They glow at night and make little buzzing sounds!"

Diego's mouth tightened. Mei's team had tested the luminescent arthropods, but he couldn't bring himself to try one. The taste of survival rations lingered on his tongue.

"You're braver than me. Just remember what Dr. Choi said about not eating too many."

"But they're so good! And Isabella won't even try them."

Isabella rolled her eyes. "Because they're gross. They're still bugs."

"Your sister's being sensible," Diego said, winking. "Sometimes new things take getting used to."

"Portal initialization in thirty seconds," Sparky announced. The hum intensified, pressing against eardrums. The smell of ozone prickled Diego's nostrils.

Through the poly-glass, Haven's landscape stretched toward distant purple mountains. The transparent barrier distorted the view slightly, making the amber sky ripple. Large creatures circled high above. A familiar dissonance settled in Diego's gut, the impossible marriage of sterile tech and savage wilderness.

Sarah stepped forward, datapad ready, transforming chaotic transfers into routine.

"Twenty seconds," Sparky announced, wiping sweat from his brow. "Power draw nominal. Flux capacitors..." he winked at a nearby tech, "looking juicy."

Diego guided his grandchildren behind the safety line. The kids kept their distance, having learned after a curious child received a static shock during the first transfer.

"Ten seconds. Power levels are optimal. Containment field..." Olivia frowned, sweat beading on her brow. "Flux variance three percent above normal."

Diego straightened, automatically scanning entry and exit points. "Risk assessment?"

"Minimal. Still within parameters." Olivia's hands worked across controls. "Stabilizing now." Her voice stayed level despite the pressure building around them.

The blue-white glow swelled. Pulsed wrong. Irregular.

Shadows stretched across the walls, alien angles that made his eyes hurt.

Diego scanned the diagnostics. Numbers flickered green. Barely. The portal's hum crawled into his damaged ear, set off that familiar ringing. High-pitched. Constant. Fucking permanent.

His jaw clenched. The vibration lived in his teeth now.

The glow expanded into a shimmering disc. Diego positioned himself centrally and signaled the medical team as figures began materializing. Sarah stepped forward.

"Welcome to Haven. Please follow the yellow line to your right."

The Richardson twins emerged clutching their parents' hands, eyes wide. Their father gripped a tool bag like a shield, while their mother carried a medical kit.

The portal sputtered with an electrical screech. The disc contracted, then expanded erratically.

"What the fuck?" Diego moved toward the control station, knee twinging with each rapid step.

Olivia's face went white. "Seismic activity Earth-side! Magnitude 5.2 and climbing!"

"Well, isn't this just a bucket of sunshine," Sparky growled. His hands working rapidly across the console, "the feedback loop is destabilizing the array!"

A violent shudder ran through the platform, originating from the portal's frame. Warning klaxons blared.

"Portal stability?" Diego barked, motioning security forward.

"Seventy percent and dropping! Earth-side systems are fluctuating!" Olivia slammed her fist onto an emergency sequence.

"I'm rerouting power to the containment field," Sparky shouted over the noise, "but Earth-side anchors are failing faster than I can compensate!"

The portal flashed bright, then dimmed. Through its wavering surface, screams ripped through as equipment crashed to the floor.

"Power grid fluctuations in the staging area!" someone yelled from Earth-side. "Everything's going haywire!"

"Move it, people! This isn't a Sunday stroll!" Sparky bellowed, his voice carrying even over the alarms.

The next group stumbled through at a run, dust-covered and disoriented. A man supported an older woman whose legs buckled.

"Complete chaos back there," he gasped. "Equipment falling everywhere, people scrambling to get through."

"Sarah, expedite processing! Medical team, triage!" Diego commanded. "Olivia, status on the connection?"

"Earth-side technicians reporting major system instabilities. They're scrambling to maintain control." A monitor sparked and went dark. "Their power grid is failing! If it goes, the connection collapses!"

"I need more power to the stabilization field," Sparky barked. "Divert from non-essentials!"

"That includes life support, Sparky!" Olivia protested.

"We can breathe later if this thing collapses!"

People poured through in panicked waves. Parents clutched children, the injured supported each other, all carrying the dusty, desperate remnants of their former lives. The smell of sweat and fear filled the air, mingling with the electric tang of ozone.

"Security team, crowd control! Medical, three units at the entry point!" Diego directed bodies away from the portal, ignoring the stabbing pain in his knee. "Sarah, find those children's parents! Olivia, can you stabilize this?"

"Trying! But the Earth-side systems are failing. The connection is fluctuating!"

Sarah stumbled as a child collided with her legs. She caught the toddler, checked him for injuries, then handed him to a medical aide with crisp instructions. She retrieved her datapad and continued processing without missing a beat.

A teenage boy stumbled through, dragging a younger child. "Mom's still back there! She was right behind us!"

Diego caught him firmly. "You can't go back. The passage only goes one way." The boy's face crumpled. "They'll get her through," he promised, knowing it might be a lie.

A technician's voice crackled, "...losing control systems... primary power fluctuating... The grid's failing!"

"How many more?" Diego asked, turning to Olivia.

"Manifest shows seventeen still on the other side."

"Can the portal hold that long?"

"I don't know. The Earth-side anchors are failing. If their power grid goes, we lose the connection."

A family of four tumbled through, the father carrying twins, the mother limping. Behind them, Diego glimpsed people pushing and shoving, equipment scattered across the floor.

The portal shrieked. Light pulsed erratically across the room.

"I'm losing it!" Sparky shouted, bracing against the console. "Earth-side power is failing! Thirty seconds, maybe less!"

Another group staggered through: five people, then three more. A woman was missing a shoe. A man with a child clinging to his neck.

"Eleven more," Olivia counted down. "Ten."

The portal contracted, then stabilized at half its size.

"Nine. Eight. Seven." With each count, another person emerged.

A technician stumbled through, face streaked with sweat. "Everything's falling over back there. Power's cutting in and out. We're trying to get everyone through!"

"Final power surge detected," Olivia reported. "They're attempting to boost with emergency reserves."

The portal flared once more, allowing a woman and child to tumble through before contracting to dinner-plate size.

"We're losing them," Olivia whispered.

The portal shrank. Edges jagged. Wrong.

Metal screamed. The sound vibrated through Diego's fillings, sharp enough to make his jaw ache.

Flash. White. Blinding.

His eyes watered. Everything went to static and afterimages.

The crack hit like a physical thing. Through his chest. His teeth. The old shrapnel under his ribs gave a hot reply.

Gone.

Just scorched metal and heat shimmer where the portal had been. The smell of ozone and burnt circuits. His knee throbbed in the sudden silence.

Quiet settled, punctuated by sobbing and medical equipment. The smell of electrical burning lingered with sweat and fear.

Diego's gaze fixed on the empty portal frame. His damaged hearing buzzed painfully in the sudden quiet. Seven names he'd recite tonight alongside others: the Tucson researchers, his war squad, Elena, faces that never faded.

The medical team moved efficiently. Sarah coordinated reunifications, her voice steady despite trembling hands.

"Final count?" Diego asked.

Sarah glanced up from her datapad, face grim. "Sixty transfers, Martinez. Seven didn't make it through."

Among the evacuees, Among the evacuees, a familiar face cut through the chaos. Richard Byrne, the SWAT officer from the Tucson mission, guided his dust-covered family toward processing. Their eyes met in silent recognition.

Later, Byrne approached him. "Martinez. Didn't think I'd see you after that warehouse collapse."

"Hard to forget someone who stayed cool during that hellstorm," Diego replied, clasping Byrne's hand. "Your team secured those metal cases. We wouldn't be here without them."

Byrne looked away, swallowing hard. "Not everyone made it." He glanced back at Diego. "That researcher... Carlos and I nearly joined them."

"I know." Diego held his gaze, acknowledging the shared burden. "But your family made it. That matters."

"When I heard you ran this operation," Byrne said, wiping dust from his brow, "I knew it was worth the risk." His voice dropped, eyes darting around. "Tucson's drinking two liters a day, rationing's a joke."

He coughed, the fine dust still coating his throat. "Half the city's dark, rioting every night." Byrne looked back at his wife and children. "People fighting over fucking puddles."

"And the APU patrols?" Diego asked quietly.

Byrne snorted. "Brass keeps saying help's coming." His hands shook. Not from cold. From watching good people get sorted like cargo while Earth burned. "They're picking favorites. Deciding who's worth saving." His jaw worked. "Rest of us just get to watch it all go to shit."

He looked away, composing himself. "Water's brown when it flows. Two men knifed each other over purification tablets last week."

Sarah gently interrupted, "If you'll follow me, we'll get your family processed. Medical checks are mandatory."

"Appreciate it." Byrne guided his family forward, pausing to look back. "Thank you. For remembering us little guys when the brass started saving only their favorites."

Diego's gaze swept the control stations and locked onto Olivia's slumped form at her station, hair plastered with sweat, hands trembling. She had pushed the technology beyond limits to save those waiting.

"Nothing more we can do tonight, Doc," Sparky said softly to Olivia, uncharacteristically gentle as he patted her shoulder. "I'll check the circuit arrays, but that connection's dead as my left leg." He tapped his prosthetic with a hollow sound. "And this thing ain't coming back to life either."

Diego approached the final group. The residual energy hit him like static electricity, raising the hair on his arms. His damaged hearing buzzed. Three families huddled close, clutching meager belongings.

"Welcome to Haven." A young mother cradled a sleeping toddler while her husband held engineering manuals. Others carried medical supplies, technical documents, and tools.

"Major Martinez?" A man stepped forward. "The project coordinator said you would be here, but…"

"Seeing is believing?" Diego nodded. The group reacted to their first breath of Haven's air, inhaling deeply. It carried pine and something like cinnamon, yet alien. The toddler stirred, blinking at the blue-tinted light.

"We've got quarters ready. After medical checks, Sarah will show you your spaces. Rest today, tomorrow you'll start your work assignments." Diego watched them relax at the promise of routine.

The families nodded, some relief visible in their posture.

"What about the others?" a woman asked, voice breaking. Tear tracks cut through the dust on her face. "The ones we left…"

The old ache flared behind Diego's ribs. Each decision carried fragments he'd never dig out.

"We're doing what we can. That's all any of us can do."

The woman nodded once. Her husband wrapped an arm around her. Their teenage son stood rigid, fists clenched, trying to appear strong despite trembling lips.

Diego recognized that look from soldiers too young for battle, from desperate refugees. Someone had to muster the bravery because falling apart wasn't an option.

Sarah moved forward. The group needed processing. Diego stepped back, gave her space.

Olivia shifted closer. Her shoulder almost touched his arm. He didn't move away. The diagnostic screen flickered, amber warnings bleeding into red.

"Feedback cascade should've fried the whole array." Her voice stayed low. "Your protocols held."

Diego's gaze drifted to his grandchildren. Isabella and Mateo chatted excitedly with the Richardson twins, their voices bright against the industrial hum of the facility. They pointed at Haven's strange sky through the viewing ports, already planning adventures among the alien flora.

The ache in his chest sharpened. Seven were lost today. The officers in Tucson. His squad brothers. Elena. Always Elena.

But these children… Earth's children are now playing on Haven's soil, breathing alien air like it was home. Their laughter cut through his guilt like nothing else could.

The familiar weight behind his sternum remained, but something else settled alongside it. Not lighter, maybe heavier. But warmer somehow. As if the ghosts of everyone they couldn't save had found purpose in protecting what they'd managed to build here.

Haven's sun danced across the lake as Diego savored a moment of peace. The water shimmered with iridescent ripples unlike any ocean on Earth. Each breath filled his lungs with a sweet, mentholated scent still foreign after weeks on this new world.

His comm crackled. "Diego, you there?" Dr. Anderson's voice carried an edge of concern, not panic.

Diego pushed himself up from the rock where he'd been watching the alien sunset. "Go ahead."

"Lisa's in Medical. Nothing serious, but we've got a situation. Can you swing by?"

The walk to Medical took five minutes through Haven's orderly paths. Solar collectors hummed overhead, their efficiency dropping as alien pollen coated the panels. Another item for the maintenance list.

Inside, Lisa Choi sat on an examination table, left sleeve rolled up, looking more annoyed than concerned. Her forearm showed patches of reddish discoloration, raised and warm-looking but not angry.

"Started about three hours ago," Dr. Anderson explained, consulting his tablet. "Lisa was doing soil collection near the eastern perimeter. Full protective protocols, gloves, the works."

"I was careful," Lisa said. "Followed every procedure. But around noon I started feeling off. Just queasy, you know? Figured it was something I ate."

Diego examined the rash without touching. The pattern didn't look random. Raised patches followed lines under her skin, like her lymphatic system was lighting up. "This showed up when?"

"After the nausea. Maybe an hour later. Started as a little red spot on my wrist, then spread."

Dr. Anderson tapped his screen. "I've tried standard antihistamines, topical corticosteroids, even broad-spectrum anti-inflammatories. Nothing. The reaction's not getting worse, but it's not improving either."

"Any idea what caused it?"

"That's the problem." Anderson set down his tablet. "Could be soil contact, airborne spores, something in the groundwater she was testing. Hell, could be atmospheric. We don't know."

Lisa shifted on the table. "It's not painful, just weird. Like when your foot falls asleep but warmer. And it's spreading."

The door opened and Olivia entered, tablet in hand. "I came as soon as I heard. How are you feeling, Lisa?"

"Like a lab experiment."

Olivia pulled up environmental data. "Where exactly were you working?"

"Grid reference E-7, then E-4 and E-9. Collected samples from different soil types, different vegetation densities." Lisa recited the locations with the precision of someone who'd repeated this information several times.

"And you were wearing full protective gear?"

"Gloves, boots, long sleeves. I even had my face shield down when I was collecting near those flowering bushes. You know, the ones with the blue petals?"

Olivia's fingers moved across her tablet. "Those are the spiralflowers. We haven't identified any toxic properties, but..." She paused. "Actually, we haven't identified much of anything about them."

Dr. Anderson rubbed his forehead. "That's what's bothering me. Lisa followed protocols, but our protocols are based on Earth biology. What if there's something here that gets through our protective equipment? Something we can't see or smell or detect?"

Diego felt the familiar weight settling in his stomach. The weight of unknown threats, of contingencies he couldn't plan for. "How many others were working in those areas today?"

"Three other soil teams, plus the botanical survey group," Olivia said. "All following the same protocols."

"Get them all checked. Now."

Anderson nodded. "Already sent the message. But Diego, what if this isn't isolated? What if long-term exposure to Haven's environment causes reactions we won't see for days or weeks?"

Lisa looked up from studying her arm. "That's a cheerful thought."

"We need to know what we're dealing with," Diego said. "Olivia, can you correlate Lisa's exposure data with environmental readings from those sectors?"

"Already on it. Atmospheric composition, soil chemistry, biological activity. I'll have a preliminary analysis in an hour."

The door chimed and Mei Choi entered, followed by an older woman with silver-streaked hair pulled back in a neat bun. The woman carried a worn leather case and moved with the purposeful stride of someone accustomed to medical emergencies.

"This is my mother, Dr. Evelyn Choi," Mei said. "I thought her botanical expertise might help."

Evelyn approached Lisa with the calm assessment of an experienced physician. She examined the rash pattern without touching, her dark eyes tracking the raised lines with interest.

"May I see your other arm? And the areas where your protective equipment made contact with your skin?"

Lisa rolled up her right sleeve. No discoloration.

"Interesting. The reaction follows lymphatic pathways but only on the exposed side." Evelyn opened her case and consulted handwritten notes. "I've been cataloging Haven's flora, comparing biochemical properties to Earth species. Some show similarities to plants that cause delayed contact reactions."

"Delayed how?" Dr. Anderson asked.

"On Earth, some fungi release spores so small they penetrate synthetic materials. The immune response doesn't manifest for hours or even days." She indicated Lisa's arm. "This pattern suggests exposure through skin contact, but the affected pathways indicate something more complex than simple irritation."

Mei pulled up Lisa's exposure timeline. "You were in each location for approximately ninety minutes?"

"Yeah, about that. E-7 first, then E-4, then E-9. Took samples, ran field tests, documented everything."

Evelyn nodded. "And the symptoms began approximately three hours after initial exposure?"

"Right. Started feeling sick around noon, rash showed up maybe one o'clock."

"That timing suggests biological interaction rather than chemical irritation," Evelyn said. "Your body needed time to recognize and respond to whatever you encountered."

Dr. Anderson looked at his tablet. "So what are we dealing with? Fungal spores? Bacterial exposure? Some kind of allergen?"

"Possibly all three, possibly none of them." Evelyn's honesty was refreshing after hours of medical uncertainty. "Haven's biological systems don't follow Earth rules. We need to approach this differently."

"Different how?" Diego asked.

"On Earth, I would test for specific pathogens, specific allergens. Here, I think we need to focus on symptom management while we learn Haven's patterns." She consulted her notes again. "I have compounds that might help with the inflammation and the unusual nerve response, but they're supportive treatments, not cures."

Lisa looked at the spreading rash. "How long before we know if this gets worse?"

"Unknown," Dr. Anderson admitted. "Could be hours, could be days. We're monitoring for systemic effects, but honestly, we're in uncharted territory."

The door opened and Sarah Choi entered, moving with the focused energy of a crisis specialist. She surveyed the scene quickly and positioned herself near Lisa.

"What do you need?" she asked Dr. Anderson.

"Help monitoring Lisa and the other teams when they come in for examination. If this spreads to multiple people, we'll need all hands."

Sarah moved to Lisa's side. Fingers on the pulse point. Blood pressure cuff inflating with that familiar hiss. The numbers came quick, automatic, muscle memory from a thousand shifts in worse conditions.

The room's tension loosened. Slightly. Having someone who knew what the hell they were doing helped.

Olivia looked up from her tablet. "Preliminary environmental data shows elevated biological activity in all three locations Lisa visited. Fungal spore counts, airborne particulates, and electromagnetic readings we can't classify yet."

"Electromagnetic?" Diego asked.

"Some of Haven's plants generate weak electrical fields. We don't know why or what effect prolonged exposure might have on human biology."

Dr. Anderson studied his readings. "Lisa, the nerve response you're experiencing, it's not following normal patterns. Almost like your nervous system is being stimulated by an external source."

"You mean the plants are zapping me?"

"Possibly. Or your body is reacting to electromagnetic fields in ways we don't understand."

Evelyn opened several small vials from her case. "I can prepare a compound that should reduce the inflammation and potentially block some of the nerve stimulation. It won't cure anything, but it might make you more comfortable while we figure out what's happening."

"What's in it?" Dr. Anderson asked.

"Extracts from three Haven species I've identified as having anti-inflammatory properties similar to Earth plants I've worked with. Combined with a mild nerve block derived from that purple moss growing near the lake."

Mei looked concerned. "Mother, we don't know the interaction effects of Haven compounds on human physiology."

"We don't know the interaction effects of doing nothing, either," Evelyn replied calmly. "Lisa's reaction isn't life-threatening, but it's progressive. Sometimes traditional approaches work when modern medicine doesn't have answers."

Dr. Anderson considered this. "What are the risks?"

"Minimal, based on my analysis. Worst case, the treatment has no effect. Best case, it provides symptom relief while we develop better protocols."

Lisa shifted on the table. "I'm willing to try it. This tingley feeling is getting annoying, and I can see it spreading."

"All right," Dr. Anderson said. "But we monitor everything. Heart rate, blood pressure, neurological responses."

Evelyn worked quickly, combining compounds with the confidence of decades of experience. She explained each step to Mei and Dr. Anderson, sharing knowledge that might prove crucial for future cases.

"The moss extract contains natural antihistamines, but processed differently than synthetic versions. Rice wine as a solvent preserves the molecular structure." She added drops of clear liquid to a small beaker. "This fungal extract acts as a carrier, helping the active compounds reach affected tissues."

The resulting mixture was pale green and smelled like rain with something sharper underneath, something that didn't exist on Earth.

"This goes on topically," Evelyn explained, applying a small amount to Lisa's wrist. "If you don't react poorly in ten minutes, we'll treat the affected areas."

They waited. Lisa's vital signs remained stable. The test patch showed no additional irritation.

"Okay," Dr. Anderson said. "Let's try it."

Evelyn applied the mixture to Lisa's affected skin. Within minutes, the angry red coloration began to fade slightly. The raised patterns remained but looked less inflamed.

"The tingling's decreasing," Lisa reported. "Still there, but not as intense."

Dr. Anderson checked his readings. "Inflammation markers are dropping. Whatever you're doing, it's helping."

Over the next hour, Lisa's condition stabilized. The rash stopped spreading, the discoloration faded to a dull pink, and the nerve response diminished to barely noticeable levels.

"How do you feel?" Sarah asked.

"Much better. Still aware of it, but not distracted by it." Lisa flexed her fingers. "Range of motion is normal."

Dr. Anderson updated his files. "We need to document everything. Treatment protocols, environmental factors, symptom progression. If this happens again, we'll have a baseline to work from."

"When this happens again," Diego corrected. "We can't assume this is isolated."

The medical teams from the field arrived for examination. Two showed mild skin irritation, one reported intermittent nausea, and one had no symptoms at all. The patterns were inconsistent, which somehow made the situation more unsettling than if everyone had been affected equally.

"Different exposure levels, different individual susceptibility, or different environmental factors in each location," Olivia concluded after reviewing all the data. "We need better protective protocols and regular health monitoring for anyone working outside the settlement perimeter."

Diego studied the team members, noting stress levels and body language. They were handling uncertainty better than most groups would, but the psychological impact was visible. Their beautiful new home had just revealed another layer of potential danger.

"New protocols starting tomorrow," he announced. "Buddy system for all field work. Enhanced protective equipment. Daily health checks for anyone with environmental exposure. And we expand the safe zone around the settlement until we understand Haven's biological patterns better."

"That'll slow down exploration and resource gathering," Mei pointed out.

"Better slow than sorry. We can't protect against what we don't understand, but we can be more careful while we learn."

Dr. Anderson was already updating medical protocols. "I want weekly health screenings for everyone, daily for field teams. Blood work, neurological assessments, the works."

Evelyn packed her case methodically. "I'll continue researching Haven's flora, focusing on species that might cause human reactions. Traditional knowledge combined with modern analysis might give us better tools."

"Mother," Mei said quietly, "thank you."

Evelyn smiled. "This is how knowledge should work. Neither old methods nor new ones alone would have helped Lisa today."

Sarah finished her notes and looked at Lisa. "Any discomfort now?"

"Just tired. And a little paranoid about touching anything."

"That's probably healthy paranoia," Diego said. "Lisa, you're on light duty for a week. Medical monitoring, but no field work until we know more about long-term effects."

"Do you think this will happen again?" Lisa asked.

"Probably," Dr. Anderson said. "Haven's ecosystem is vast and complex. We'll encounter biological interactions we can't predict. The goal is learning to manage them safely."

Diego moved to the window. Haven's settlement spread below.

Security lights sliced through the dark. Harsh. Earth tech forcing itself onto alien ground. The twin moons washed everything purple, and the buildings looked almost right until the shadows fell wrong.

"One day in, and we're already adapting our entire approach to environmental safety," he said. "Makes you wonder what else we don't know."

Olivia joined him at the window. "That's the point, isn't it? Learning to live with uncertainty instead of trying to control everything."

"Earth failed because we thought we could dominate nature rather than understand it," Mei added. "Maybe Haven's teaching us a different relationship."

Diego nodded, but his expression remained troubled. He'd led teams through hostile territory, faced enemies he could identify and outmaneuver. This was different. Haven's dangers were subtle, invisible, potentially everywhere.

His comm buzzed with updates from security teams. Perimeter clear, no unusual activity, all systems nominal. Standard reports that felt less reassuring than usual.

"How's she doing?" Emily's voice crackled through the speaker.

"Stable. Treatment helped, but we're looking at new protocols for field work."

"Copy that. Just finished mapping the areas where she collected samples. Found some interesting electromagnetic readings around those blue flowering bushes. Nothing dangerous, but definitely unusual."

"Send the data to Olivia."

"Already on its way."

Diego looked at the team gathered in Medical. Lisa stable but changed, the medical staff humbled by their limitations, Evelyn's traditional knowledge proving valuable in unexpected ways. Everyone adapting to a reality where their expertise had limits.

"All right, people. Lisa's stable, we have treatment protocols, and we know what to watch for. Tomorrow we implement new safety measures and continue mapping Haven's biological hazards."

"One crisis at a time," Dr. Anderson said, saving his files.

"One adaptation at a time," Diego corrected.

As the team dispersed, Diego remained at the window. Haven's beauty was undeniable, but tonight it felt different. Not hostile exactly, but alien in ways that mattered. They were visitors here, learning the rules of a world that didn't care about human assumptions.

Lisa would recover, probably completely. The team would adapt, develop better protocols, learn to work safely in Haven's environment. But the easy confidence of their first weeks was gone, replaced by something more realistic and more humble.

His comm buzzed with a message from Maria back on Earth. A photo of Isabella and Mateo playing in their backyard, grinning at the camera. The reason he was here, the future he was trying to secure.

Haven offered hope, but not safety. Not yet. Maybe not ever.

That would have to be enough.

STRATEGIC VICTORIES

Luna's voice crackled through the comm system, frustration cutting through static. "Generator's fixed. Gateway's stable. After yesterday's collapse, we couldn't afford another failure. Twelve fucking hours with no backup."

Diego pressed his palms against his eyes. Thirty-plus hours without sleep had left his skull feeling like it was packed with broken glass. He slumped forward in his chair, and sighed.

"Any permanent damage to the equipment?"

"Nothing I can't fix," Luna replied, her tone softer. "But we were completely cut off. No comms, no gateway. If something had happened here..."

The words landed heavy. No comms. No evac. No backup.

No way home.

"Understood. We'll send a tech team once the portal stabilizes." Diego grabbed the tablet, his grip leaving smudges on the plastic. "Martinez out."

The holographic display cast blue light across exhausted faces as Diego dragged himself into the strategy room. Olivia looked like she'd been awake as long as he had, dark circles carved under her eyes. She glanced at Kaito while Diego lowered himself carefully into his chair, fighting a wave of dizziness. Kaito sat motionless, his face giving away nothing.

The eastern deposits had yielded more stabilization metal than expected. Still, Kaito's attention kept drifting to a mountain range northeast of their position.

"That generator failure proves we need redundancy," Kaito said, highlighting the rugged terrain. "In everything."

Diego nodded, the words coming out slightly thick. "We'll put together a contingency. First, more materials."

"Survey shows rich deposits in this sector," Kaito continued, gesturing to the mountains. "Mining bots could extract enough metal to double current capacity."

"Absolutely not." Olivia's hand hit the table with surprising force. She shoved her glasses up her nose. "Those mountains will destroy our equipment. The electromagnetic interference alone..."

Diego blinked hard, trying to focus. Something felt off about this exchange. Olivia never got this heated over preliminary data. Something felt off. Olivia never got this heated over preliminary data, always preferring clinical detachment.

"These metals would let us increase gateway capacity significantly," Kaito pressed. "The eastern deposits won't support Maria's settlement expansion plans."

"The evidence says it's equipment suicide." Olivia pulled up her tablet, fingers moving quickly across the screen. The hologram shifted, showing three flashing red zones. "We've lost three Class-4 drones already. Three! If the mining bots malfunction up there, we lose our only extraction capability."

They kept going back and forth, voices rising slightly. Diego gripped the table edge, watching them. There was something almost choreographed about it. The way Olivia would pause just long enough for Kaito to jump in. The way Kaito would gesture at exactly the right moment.

But maybe his exhaustion was making him paranoid. Perhaps they were just passionate about their positions.

"Western deposits," Diego cut in, his voice hoarse. "Alternatives?"

He zoomed the map with an unsteady hand.

"Insufficient concentration," Kaito replied, straightening his cuff. "We'd burn through reactor capacity for minimal yield. The mountain deposits remain our only viable option for expansion."

Olivia leaned back, crossing her arms. "I won't authorize deployment based on incomplete data. Period."

"Dr. Smith," Kaito said, his fingers drumming against his datapad, "without these resources, your expansion plans remain theoretical. Earth's situation won't wait for our debates."

Diego studied them both. The argument made sense on the surface, but something nagged at him. Olivia never used absolutes like that. And Kaito rarely let emotion creep into his strategic assessments.

"Current resource status?" Diego asked, blinking as the room seemed to tilt slightly.

Olivia's shoulders dropped as she pulled up inventory data. "Eastern site produced 126% above projections. Gives us twelve stable gateway operations with some capacity buffer."

"Twelve operations," Diego repeated slowly. "Enough to maintain the current population and run limited supply chains from Earth. For now."

"Exactly," Olivia said. "For multiple settlements or increased transport frequency, we'd need exponentially more material."

"The mountain deposits show sufficient material for at least fifty additional gateway activations," Kaito added, adjusting the holographic display. "Without access to those resources, Maria's community expansion projects remain on paper."

Olivia didn't argue with the numbers. She tilted her empty coffee cup, frowning at it.

Diego stared at the holographic mountains, their jagged peaks reminding him of operations in rougher terrain. His old knee injury sent up a dull ache. The memories of the Andes came flooding back. Rocky terrain, equipment failures, and casualties from overconfidence.

They needed those resources. But rushing in blind would be suicide for their equipment and maybe their people.

"Survey timeline?"

"Earth's seismic instability is accelerating," Kaito said, displaying a planet-wide map glowing with angry red zones. "Seventeen percent above predictions. We don't have months to debate this."

Diego watched Olivia's hand tremble slightly as she swiped through data. His muscles felt like they'd been worked over with a hammer. Everyone was running on fumes.

"How long for actual survey data?"

"Three days minimum," Olivia said, squinting at drone telemetry. "If we can analyze the electromagnetic fluctuation cycles, we might identify safe windows for mining operations."

"Timeline on expansion needs?" Diego asked, thinking of Maria's blueprints spread across three potential settlement sites.

"With current reserves, we can maintain existing operations indefinitely," Olivia replied. "But significant expansion? Six months before we hit critical shortages."

Diego examined the terrain display again. Those cliffs and valleys would make security a nightmare. And if the electromagnetic interference was strong enough to fry drones, what would it do to people?

The silence stretched. Both Olivia and Kaito watched him, waiting.

"Manual survey team," he said finally. "We send people up there to set up sensor arrays. Get real-time data on these energy fluctuations."

Kaito nodded once. "Equipment can be ready in four hours."

"We'd need three triangulation points minimum." Olivia marked locations on the display. "But that terrain, it's brutal up there."

"I'll lead the team myself," Diego started, then caught himself as his knee sent up a sharp protest and the room swayed. He gripped the table edge harder.

The smart play. The hard play. "No. Jack has the technical expertise for this."

There. The look between Olivia and Kaito. Quick, but Diego caught it. Relief in the way Olivia's shoulders dropped, color rising in her cheeks. Kaito's expression shifted, that controlled mask slipping for half a second.

The passionate argument. The convenient timing. All of it staged.

They'd been working together. Keeping him from going up there himself.

A tired smile tugged at his mouth. "I see."

Olivia suddenly became very interested in her tablet. Kaito's shoulders relaxed slightly.

Diego activated the comm. "Jack, you available?"

The blue light pulsed, and Jack's grease-streaked face appeared, already grinning.

"For you? Always got time, boss," Jack said, wiping his hands on a filthy rag. "Been ass-deep in the environmental controls trying to fix whatever Thompson broke this time."

"Need you for a mountain operation," Diego said. "Three sensor packages. Priority Alpha."

Jack's grin widened. "Mountains? Hell yes. Finally, something more interesting than chasing electrical gremlins through section four."

He leaned closer to the camera. "Please tell me there's a decent chance of something exploding."

"High probability of electromagnetic anomalies frying anything with circuits," Diego replied. "Including that fancy leg of yours."

"Now that sounds like a proper challenge," Jack said, already reaching for his toolkit. "Give me ten minutes to grab my gear. O'Connor out."

The hologram collapsed.

Diego scanned the sensor points. Approach routes. Defensive positions. His brain ran the calculations automatically.

His knuckles cracked. Old habit. Forty years of mission planning lived in his bones.

Then his fingers stopped moving over the display. This wasn't his operation to plan anymore. The realization settled over him like cold water. Hard to swallow, but probably necessary.

"I should verify those sensor calibration parameters," Olivia said, stuffing her tablet into her bag. "Jack's going to have questions about frequency modulation and signal processing."

She headed for the door, that flush still visible on her neck.

Diego grunted. Jack would have questions. Lots of them.

"I'll ensure the equipment manifest is complete," Kaito said, adjusting his cuff. "Though knowing Jack, he's probably already modifying the standard sensor array."

He nodded to Diego before following Olivia out.

"And gather a full security team," Diego called after him. "Thompson, Carter, and four others. I want an overwhelming force for this operation."

Alone in the room, Diego stared at those silent peaks rotating slowly in blue light. He took a deep breath of Haven's air, catching that faint pine scent from the trees outside.

He wasn't just looking at mineral deposits. He was looking at the future. Isabella and Mateo were running through valleys that had never known war, never felt the weight of Earth's failures.

Not just surviving in this place. Building something better. Something worth the fight.

He'd catch an hour of sleep after the mission briefing. Maybe two if he was lucky. The future waiting in those mountains couldn't wait much longer, but it could stay long enough for him to think this through properly.

Olivia stopped in the doorway of the operations center, watching Diego check topographical maps for the third time that morning.

"You're going to wear out those maps," she said, clutching her tablet against her chest.

Diego looked up, blinking away fatigue. "Just confirming elevation changes. These mountains have different magnetic properties than anything we've seen."

"The others are prepped and waiting." Olivia hesitated. "You don't have to check everything yourself."

Diego's fingers tapped against the console, a restless rhythm matching his pulse. "This data is critical for portal stabilization. If we're wrong about these deposits..."

"I lost my father because he couldn't trust his team to handle details," Olivia said quietly. "He was still at his station when the Resource Wars hit our facility."

Diego stopped tapping. Years of ignoring similar warnings from Elena flashed through his mind.

"Jack knows the tech," Olivia continued. "Thompson knows tactics. Let them do their jobs."

Diego studied the mountain terrain one last time. Maybe the real issue wasn't others' competence but his need to control every variable.

"You're right," he said, straightening up. "Time to let someone else take point."

The team was already assembled when Diego entered the briefing room. Jack tapped his datapad, his cybernetic leg jiggling to a rhythm only he heard. Thompson studied equipment specs while Carter arranged medical supplies into color-coded field kits.

Diego cleared his throat. "This mission needs specific technical expertise. Jack, you're taking the lead."

Jack's head snapped up, surprise flashing across his face. "Seriously? About damn time."

Diego rubbed the back of his neck. "Your tech, your mission. I'll advise on security, but operational decisions are yours."

O'Reilly and Thompson exchanged glances. Jack's mouth curved into a satisfied grin.

"Alright, people, gather 'round." Jack activated the holo-map, mountains appearing in 3D. "We've detected magnetic anomalies and mineral signatures, but energy fluctuations are making reliable scans impossible." He tapped three specific formations. "These peaks are our targets."

Diego watched Jack commandeer what felt like his rightful position. The man's casual briefing style grated against decades of military protocol. His hands found his belt, fingers drumming against the leather. One... two... three... He exhaled slowly through his nose.

"Those crystal formations are perfect for the arrays," Jack continued, zooming in. "Based on preliminary data, they're loaded with the neodymium we need for stabilization."

Richard checked weather patterns. "Forty-eight-hour window before that storm system moves in."

"That's cutting it close," Thompson said, studying the approach vector.

"Then we move fast and work smart," Jack replied with a shrug. "O'Reilly, you handle comms. Johnson's team for security. Everyone else, standard loadout but travel light. Questions?"

A dozen tactical adjustments crowded Diego's thoughts. Different approach vectors. Alternative equipment loadouts. Contingency planning that Jack hadn't mentioned.

Thompson tapped her jaw with her index finger. "These energy readings are unusual. What about exposure risks?"

Olivia's voice came through the comm. "The suits have triple-rated shielding. I'll monitor your biometrics throughout."

"Weather window's tight," Thompson noted. "Extraction plan if the storm accelerates?"

"First sign of trouble, we split," Jack said, glancing at Diego. "Equipment can be replaced. People can't."

"Like Kuala Lumpur," Thompson muttered, just loud enough for Diego to catch.

Jack nodded. "Exactly. Not losing anyone to weather again."

Diego blinked in surprise. Jack had been listening to his field stories after all.

Manuel positioned himself where he could see all exits. "Those caves from the initial survey, worth checking for vulnerabilities?"

"Negative," Jack said. "Mission parameters only: sensor deployment. We'll worry about caves later."

Diego's mouth opened. Cave systems could provide natural shelter or concealment for hostiles. Standard reconnaissance protocol. His teeth clicked shut.

O'Reilly ran a final check on comms while Carter knelt beside Jack.

"Your leg's responding to the ambient field," she said, running a scanner over his prosthetic. "Seen it before with Williams. The neural interface gets disrupted by certain frequencies." She adjusted the settings on a small device. "This should filter it."

Jack flexed his artificial leg, surprise flashing across his face. "Damn, Doc. The buzzing stopped."

"Just stay focused on those arrays," she replied, hiding a small smile.

"Bottom line," Jack said, straightening up. "These mountains are weird, the storms are weirder, but we need those minerals. Get in, plant the sensors, get out. Questions?"

Diego's mouth opened again. Jack had covered the essentials, even if his approach lacked the structure Diego would have preferred. Three potential issues with the deployment sequence. Two weather contingencies that needed addressing. One significant gap in their extraction plan.

"One thing," Diego said finally. "The crystals create optical illusions. Trust your instruments, not your eyes."

Jack grinned. "See, folks? Even Martinez contributes when he's not micromanaging. Now gear up. We roll in fifteen."

The team packed efficiently. Diego's hands itched to verify loadouts, check equipment twice, run through contingencies one more time. Instead, he focused on his own gear, checking and rechecking his sidearm until the grip was warm from his touch.

The convoy headed out, kicking up violet dust as they approached the mountains. Crystalline formations jutted from the landscape like frozen lightning, distorting perspective. Static electricity raised the hairs on Diego's arms and tasted like metal on his tongue.

"Whoa, stop!" Jack called out sharply. The convoy lurched to a halt as a deep ravine appeared ahead, edges gleaming with crystals.

Diego leaned forward, muscles tensing. This was Jack's show. He gripped the door handle until his knuckles went white.

Jack approached the edge cautiously. "Well, shit. Unless these vehicles sprouted wings while I wasn't looking, we're not driving across this."

The ravine had been visible on preliminary scans. Diego's jaw worked silently, grinding down the words that wanted to spill out about proper briefing protocols and reconnaissance procedures.

"How wide?" Richard asked, joining Jack.

"Too damn wide," Jack said, squinting through the canyon's optical illusions. The reflections created a dizzying kaleidoscope from the canyon floor.

Diego catalogued potential choke points, escape routes, and defensible positions. His combat instincts refused to shut off despite the absence of threats. Old injury in his shoulder started to ache, stress making itself known through familiar channels.

Jack aimed his scanner at the walls. "Eastern structure looks solid enough. I can clear a path with the resonator. These crystals have an internal structure that amplifies the magnetic field. That's why our instruments are going haywire."

"Olivia, you copy?" Jack asked into his comm.

Her voice crackled through, distorted by interference. "Barely. The energy field affects transmission. The formations act like natural amplifiers for Haven's magnetic field."

The team detoured east. Jack set up his sonic resonator, its weight causing his prosthetic to adjust with a hydraulic hiss.

"Everybody back," he warned, hands moving over controls.

Diego ran the numbers. Safe distances. Blast radius. Jack had positioned everyone right, textbook margins, no gaps. Diego's fingers still tapped his thigh anyway.

The device emitted a high-pitched shriek. Crystal fragments splintered, fracturing light in all directions. Each sonic pulse vibrated up through Diego's boots, rattling his teeth.

"What the hell was that?" Thompson's hand moved to her belt. "Felt that in my fillings."

Jack nodded. "It's almost like it's pushing back. These formations aren't just conducting energy, they're redistributing it somehow."

The air went dead still. Even the constant mountain wind stopped. Diego's neck prickled. No visible threats, but something felt wrong. His hand drifted toward his sidearm before he caught himself.

They drove carefully through crystal-lined passes. Double shadows shifted with each turn, making distance impossible to judge. Thompson gripped the dashboard twice when spatial perception suddenly warped.

At the mountain's base, Jack found a relatively flat area. "Setting up here," he called. The convoy formed a defensive circle as Jack eagerly unloaded equipment.

Orders formed in Diego's throat like a physical obstruction. Positioning adjustments. Security protocols. Weather considerations. He turned away, focusing on unloading his own gear, movements sharp and efficient.

Jack looked around at the waiting team. "Right. Thompson, Carter, power setup. Manuel, get those drones in the air. Johnson, establish a perimeter." He glanced at Diego. "Sound good?"

Diego nodded once, ignoring the casual tone. The assignments were solid, if unconventionally delivered. His shoulder ache spread down his arm.

Jack marked positions on his tablet. "Base station needs a line of sight to all three arrays. These formations are perfect anchors, and they're loaded with neodymium compounds."

"Olivia, confirm visuals," Jack said into his comm.

"Receiving partial data," her voice came through, clearer now. "The mineral composition is exactly what we need."

The team moved. Shelters up. Power lines running.

Click. Snap. Gear finding its place.

Voices low. Clipped. The kind of shorthand you earned after a hundred missions that went sideways.

Against the mountains' hum, they built something that looked like order. Felt like it too, if you didn't look too close at the frayed edges.

O'Reilly swore as his comm unit sparked in his hand. "Shit! Energy field's frying the signal processors." He switched to a backup. "Need to adjust all frequencies."

Jack hunched over his tablet, screen illuminating his face. "Signal strength increases up the slope. Energy patterns follow magnetic lines, with natural amplification through the mineral structure."

Manuel's drone buzzed overhead, the image on his control pad stuttering before stabilizing. "Formations follow identical patterns on all three peaks. Almost looks intentional, like something designed for maximum energy flow."

"Natural formations can follow electromagnetic lines," Diego commented. "Like iron filings around a magnet."

Jack looked up from his readings. "Energy signature's spiking. Strong enough to mess with equipment." His prosthetic leg vibrated in response.

"Might be wise to keep the drones back," Diego suggested. "We don't know what these energy spikes could trigger."

Jack nodded. "Good call. Manuel, maintain a minimum fifty-meter clearance from the formations."

"The interference is worse than I expected," Jack admitted, frowning at his instruments. "Having trouble getting clean data."

Olivia's voice crackled urgently. "Storm's accelerating. Wind speeds are increasing fifteen percent faster than predicted. And it's intensifying the energy fluctuations."

Richard steadied Jack's equipment as a sudden gust hit. "Something's not right with these readings."

The minutes ticked away as clouds gathered faster than predicted. Air pressure dropped, making Diego's ears pop. His headache sharpened, pressure building behind his eyes.

"Talk to me, Jack," Diego said, the words coming out more clipped than intended.

"Five more minutes," Jack replied, bypassing connections with quick movements. "Need to bypass the main coupling and use backup power. The field's screwing with the primary systems."

Diego scanned the darkening sky. Every cell in his body screamed for immediate evacuation. He checked his watch. Checked the storm front. Calculated wind speeds and approach vectors. His promise to let Jack lead felt like a physical weight.

Static electricity crackled across the equipment. A sensor sparked, and O'Reilly jerked his hand back. "Motherfucker!" He sucked a burned finger. "Storm's feeding the field somehow. They're amplifying each other."

The arrays finally hummed online, lights blinking in sequence. "All three transmitting," Olivia's voice broke through the increasing static as clouds rolled in.

The team quickly distributed water and protein bars before Jack confirmed data stability.

Olivia's hologram appeared, flickering unstably. "These energy signatures are unlike anything in our database. The patterns suggest a natural harmonic resonance that could revolutionize our..."

"Save the science for later," Jack interrupted. "How's our data flow?"

"Arrays will run autonomous collection for seventy-two hours. You'll have continuous data back at base." Her image flickered. "But Jack, the storm..."

The first heavy raindrops splattered against equipment. "Pack it up," Jack ordered. "O'Reilly, final systems check. Fifteen minutes."

Diego checked his watch. Storm front accelerating. Pack-up time running out. Jack was cutting it close. Too close. His feet shifted, muscles coiled for action. Issue orders. Take control. Old habits.

The descent was worse than the climb. Each step sent lightning through his knee, loose gravel sliding under his boots. Wind drove dust and rain like needles into exposed skin. The energy field's pulse matched the storm's rhythm, instruments flickering, dying, coming back. Comms cutting to static every third word.

A violent gust nearly knocked Thompson off her feet. O'Reilly grabbed her arm. "This isn't normal. The storm's feeding the energy field!"

Lightning struck a crystal formation ahead, sending electricity arcing between structures. The ground trembled.

Jack raised his hand. "Stop! Path's unstable!"

Crystal fragments began sliding downhill, gaining momentum. "Rock slide!" Manuel shouted.

Diego lunged forward, orders breaking free. "West route! Now!" He caught himself mid-shout, jaw snapping shut so hard his teeth clicked.

Jack shot him a look but didn't challenge the outburst. "West route, now! Manuel, check the drone feed!"

Manuel checked his pad through the rain. "Energy field's weaker toward the western ridge."

The team altered course, picking their way carefully as crystal fragments cascaded around them. Diego noted how quickly Jack had adapted to the crisis, incorporating Diego's instinctive reaction without argument.

O'Reilly's comm unit died with a sharp crack. "Piece of shit!" He switched to an older backup that seemed less affected by the interference.

Olivia's voice broke through in fragments: "...readings show... instability... get out now!"

Rain hammered down in sheets. The ground grew slick with purple mud that clung to their boots. Another crystal formation fractured under lightning, sending dangerous shards skittering down.

"Move your asses!" Jack shouted over the storm's roar.

On level ground, Diego felt some of the tension drain from his muscles, though his shoulder still throbbed. They'd made it through the most dangerous section.

Jack took a headcount, confirming everyone was present and uninjured. "First expedition to probe Haven's mountains without dying! Not bad for a Tuesday."

The rain lessened as they loaded the last of the equipment. Jack grinned, soaked and mud-splattered but triumphant. "Three sensor arrays deployed, mountains survived, and a shitload of data incoming. Anyone want to argue this wasn't a success?"

Diego met Jack's eyes. Something had shifted between them during the crisis. "Mission accomplished," he said. "Good calls up there."

Back at the facility, the team gathered around holographic displays showing their crystal samples rotating in 3D.

"These could revolutionize our power systems," Olivia said, studying the data intently. "They're natural energy conductors, unlike anything on Earth."

Jack nodded enthusiastically. "They follow geological stress lines perfectly. Natural energy conduits. And they're loaded with the neodymium we need for stabilization."

Thompson pointed to a pattern on the display. "Look here. The energy fluctuates in consistent intervals. Almost like it's responding to Haven's magnetic field."

The room went silent. Olivia leaned closer to the display, zooming in on the pattern.

"You're right," she said. "The energy fluctuations follow a consistent pattern that amplifies during storms. Similar to Earth's auroras, but concentrated through these crystal formations."

Thompson shrugged. "When you spend enough time watching through a scope, you learn to spot patterns. The regularity is unusual for natural phenomena, but not impossible."

Manuel's drone footage revealed geometric alignments they'd missed in person. "Could affect our perimeter systems," Richard noted. "These fields might interfere with our sensors."

Jack was already sketching modifications. "We'd need to adjust everything, but imagine the possibilities. With these power sources, we could expand operations tenfold."

Diego surveyed his team, each person having contributed expertise that he couldn't have provided alone. The headache was finally fading. Olivia caught his eye and gave him a subtle nod.

"Good work today, Jack," Diego said, loud enough for everyone to hear. "You got results."

Jack looked up from his tablet. "Did I just get a compliment from Martinez? Someone mark the calendar."

"We're building something here." Diego's voice came out rougher than intended. "Not just surviving. Building."

The team dispersed. Boots on metal. Voices fading down the corridor.

Diego stayed by the displays. His knee throbbed, old shrapnel grinding bone. His shoulder pulled tight, muscles refusing to release hours after the crisis passed.

The mission worked because Jack knew his shit. Not because Diego had micromanaged every detail.

Letting go tasted like copper. Bitter. Wrong.

Sixty years of control habits. They'd kept him breathing through three wars and more failures than he could count. Couldn't just switch them off because Haven's sky was cleaner than Earth's had been.

Some things didn't die. They just learned to live in your chest, heavy and permanent.

Diego's gaze lifted from the mission reports. Behind him, a holographic topo map of the mountains glowed on the tactical display, dotted with newly marked mineral deposits. Olivia entered the briefing room, two glasses and a bottle of Kaito's private red in her hand. The latch clicked shut as she approached.

"You look like shit." Olivia set down the glasses. "Figured you earned a drink after today's climb."

She dropped into the chair beside him. Diego's eyes swept the room. Three exits. Two windows. Clear sight lines. Old habits.

"Jack and Luna think they've cracked it." Olivia leaned forward. "The shielding problem. The mining drones."

"Already?" Diego's shoulder throbbed as he shifted. "We just got back."

"Those two don't waste time."

"Turns out those readings you and Jack hauled your asses up there to get made all the difference." Olivia poured the wine, ruby liquid gleaming. "Luna's recalibrating the drone shields while Jack rebuilds the sensor arrays. Again."

"How soon till we test it?" Diego leaned forward.

"Tonight, if we're lucky. Luna's running simulations now." Olivia settled back in her chair. "If the tests hold up, we could have excavators in the mountains by next cycle."

Diego nodded. "About fucking time."

"If we can keep the alloy production up, we're golden." Olivia swirled her wine. "The commercial ore handlers work, but they weren't built for this kind of volume. Kayla's fix on the refining units was even better than we hoped. The improved alloy purity drastically reduced the material cost for each portal activation. We extracted enough stabilization material for six additional portals with resources we thought would only yield two."

She glanced down at her glass. "That puts us at eight stabilized portal activations, Diego. The current ores should give us enough material for three more when we ship them back to Crucible, but we need to double that if we want to bring more people through."

Diego pushed aside the tablet displaying preliminary sensor data. His shoulders still burned from hauling equipment up sheer rock faces for six hours. Worth every ache, if the early returns held up.

"Another hundred colonists through yesterday." He rubbed the back of his neck. "Just over five hundred mouths to feed, and we need to get more out before it's too late."

"At least the ZPE installation here should be running in a few days," Olivia muttered. "That'll take pressure off the power grid." Dark circles rimmed her eyes. "But we still need those stabilization materials for the portal. The schedule's tight for the return shipment to Crucible."

"Those crystal formations better be worth Jack bitching about his knee the entire ride back." Diego gestured toward the samples between them. "Never met anyone who complained so much about a leg he can swap out for upgrades."

Olivia snorted. "When has Jack ever missed an opportunity to remind us he's suffering for the cause?"

Diego lifted the glass, breathed in the wine's scent before taking a sip. Rich and complex after months of recycled water and protein cubes that tasted like cardboard. The wine spread warmth through him.

"Kaito's gonna notice this missing." Diego took another pull. The taste reminded him of nights in Madrid, before water shortages turned wine into something precious rather than commonplace.

The crystal samples caught the light, throwing off geometric patterns unlike anything he'd seen before. Their structure seemed to violate fundamental laws of geometry, with angles that appeared to change when viewed from different angles.

Diego tapped the rim of his glass. "Jack's been in my ear the whole ride back about these crystals. Says only he can crack the energy signatures."

"I'm considering it." Olivia kept her eyes fixed on the crystals. "He's got the intuition for energy patterns, but I'll need to make it clear that observation comes before experimentation." She glanced up. "We don't need another mess hall incident."

Diego's mouth twitched. "Emily still threatens to shove that modified drone up his ass whenever the cafeteria serves soup." He set his glass down. "But Jack can spot patterns nobody else sees. These formations aren't natural by any standard I know. We might need someone who thinks sideways."

"Just as long as he doesn't plug anything into our power grid before we understand what we're dealing with." Olivia reached to adjust one of the samples. Her sleeve brushed against his forearm as she leaned across the table. "Even without detailed analysis, I can tell these don't match any mineral formation I've ever seen. We'll need a full atomic scan."

The crystal refracted light at impossible angles when her finger touched it. Even after months in Haven, shit like this still brought Diego up short. They weren't just in another place. They were breathing air in a reality with different rules.

Olivia's tablet chimed. She looked down, then went perfectly still.

"What?" Diego tensed, instantly alert.

"Message from Luna." Olivia's voice flattened. "Earth monitoring station data shows a massive earthquake off Turkey's coast three hours ago. Nine point six."

She turned the tablet. The satellite imagery showed a coastline Diego had mapped during three deployments, now completely transformed. Cities were gone, swallowed by dark water.

"Tsunami wiped out everything from Trabzon to Samsun." Her finger scrolled through Luna's report. "It gets worse. A dormant volcano near Sinope erupted simultaneously."

Diego stared at the screen. He'd spent four months in Samsun after the Energy Wars, rebuilding water systems. Walking through the marketplace. Those little cafes where fishermen gathered before dawn. The smell of fresh bread from the bakeries. All of it underwater now.

"Casualties?" His voice came out rough.

Olivia shook her head. "Communications are fried. EAAU emergency response is overwhelmed. Luna's estimate is in the millions. Just preliminary."

The wine turned bitter in his mouth. Diego set the glass down harder than he intended.

The image collided with another: Elena's body broken by falling debris when raiders hit their water treatment plant. Another notification was received too late. Another devastation he couldn't prevent. But this time, he wasn't there to even try.

"We need to push harder on the transfers." Diego's fist closed around the edge of the table. "Figure out a way to get more people through the portal. We're leaving too fucking many behind."

Olivia stared at the devastation on her tablet before setting her glass down. "And we can't save them all." She took a deep breath. "But every additional colonist increases our genetic diversity. If we can get these new deposits processed and back to Crucible fast enough, we might double our transfer capacity."

Diego recognized that burden. He shouldered it every morning when he woke up, responsible for five hundred and twelve souls with no extraction plan.

"We're making this up as we go." He tapped one of the crystals. "These could power the entire settlement for years or blow us all to hell. No manual exists for what we're doing here."

He'd lost people before, seen plans go sideways in seconds. One bad call, one garbled signal, and soldiers died. Here, the stakes were higher with no backup coming if they fucked it up.

"At least we're confronting the unknown with empirical methods." Olivia's voice softened, more personal than her usual scientific tone. "In my APU lab, I worked with theoretical models in isolation. Here, we're testing hypotheses in real time. It's terrifying but honest."

Diego met her eyes, the crystal light casting strange shadows across her face. "Together." The word came out quietly between them.

Elena's memory rose, but without the sharp pain that had been his constant companion for years. The daily fight to keep their settlement functioning, to ensure Maria and the grandchildren would have a real future here, had gradually smoothed grief's jagged edges. He'd loved Elena completely, mourned her appropriately. But he was still alive, still responsible for building something that mattered.

Diego's hand moved across the table, fingertips touching the back of hers where it rested beside her wine glass.

"Olivia," he said finally, "if we figure this out, when we do, and we're not just counting crossings and rationing power..." His thumb traced across her knuckles. "I want something beyond crisis management."

Olivia went still. She turned her hand palm up beneath his, their fingers intertwining. "Diego, I..." Her voice trailed off as she studied their joined hands, then looked up to meet his eyes. "I want that too."

She didn't need to say more. In the dim blue light of the holographic mountains, surrounded by crystal samples that defied physics and reports of Earth's latest catastrophe, they held onto each other and the possibility of something good growing in the ruins of everything they'd lost.

HERDING CATS

E ight crossings left. Diego moved through Haven's warehouse, the clang of hauled crates and shouts of workers rebounding off metal walls. Workers rushed past, their faces blurring as he conducted the cruel mental calculus. One hundred eighty evacuees left on Original Earth, space secured for all, but only if they retrieved those processing units.

His head throbbed after three days of broken sleep. Ten hours until the next portal opening. Eight hours minimum between crossings, or the system would collapse permanently. The processing units stranded in Phoenix weren't just equipment; they represented lives. Sending his son-in-law back to that collapsing hell felt wrong, but the alternative was worse: telling Maria they'd abandoned friends, family, even Johnson's sister and her kids.

He paused, gripping a support beam as workers hurried past. Over five hundred colonists have already come through to Haven. They'd started with plans for just over two hundred, but somehow managed more than double. A small victory now threatened by Phoenix's collapse.

Kaito Nakamura orchestrated the movement of salvaged equipment and supplies across the floor with the precision of a black-market master. His tailored suit stood out against the rust-stained metal and grimy coveralls of the workers.

Morning sun cast harsh shadows through the canopy of salvaged materials overhead, highlighting metal panels patched together from a dozen different sources. The military organization couldn't disguise it: a precision-logistics refugee camp was still a refugee camp. The air hung heavy with machine oil, sweat, and the earthy undertone of repurposed agricultural units.

"Kaito," Diego called, his voice hoarse. He waited as the younger man finished instructing workers, the fluorescent lights sending needle-sharp pains behind his eyes.

"Martinez-san." Kaito bowed slightly, formal but not cold. His hands trembled at his sides.

"Already reviewed it." Diego matched the formality. He fought back a yawn as his vision blurred. "What's the status on those processing units?"

Kaito straightened his tie with precise fingers. Diego had watched him solve daunting logistics problems for months, but this strain was different, not about bribes or black-market routes. Phoenix burning, one hundred eighty lives hanging on equipment he couldn't reach.

"Processing units remain stuck in Phoenix." Kaito's thumb traced the edge of his datapad, his focus momentarily fixed on the screen's glow. "Without them, we can't process Haven's neodymium into portal alloys. Eight crossings now, eleven after processing. Then it's over."

Diego stepped closer, the floor tilting beneath him. He blinked hard, trying to focus. "What's the complication?"

Kaito checked his high-tech watch, then pulled out his datapad. "Three VTOL units attacked during riots. Pilots escaped, but..." He turned the screen to show footage of crowds overwhelming a landing pad, people clawing at rising aircraft.

Diego stared at the screen. The scene burned, familiar. The desperate eyes, the primal need driving violence. Flashes of Osaka superimposed over Phoenix: children screaming, gunfire, that taste of copper and fear filling his mouth. The same desperation, different continent.

"The remaining units?" Diego asked, mentally mapping alternatives through the fog settling in his thoughts.

"Grounded. Phoenix PD's shooting civilian aircraft, thinking they're all raiders." Kaito smoothed the lapel of his suit. "The city's collapsing faster than our timeline. Need to move before warehouse defenses fail."

"And the processing units?"

"Secured in a warehouse outside Phoenix. My people are protecting them, but..." Kaito paused. "The situation deteriorates hourly."

Diego glanced toward the families sorting supplies, unaware their rescuers faced another unwinnable choice. He'd started the mental calculations already: kids first, essential personnel, then what? The processing units were designed to avoid that choice. Every delay meant fewer people were saved.

"What other transport options?"

"Negotiating with private contractors, but with current conditions..." Kaito showed his datapad's map dotted with riot hotspots. "Many refuse to fly, regardless of payment."

Diego pulled out his holo-comm, the device strangely heavy. As he turned away to make the call, Kaito remained nearby, watching. Diego called Mia, whose face materialized in the air, immediately reading the tension in his expression.

"Hey boss, perfect timing. Just finished tweaking the big VTOL's stabilizers." Mia wiped grease from her hands with a rag.

"How fast can you ready the bird for emergency pickup outside Phoenix?" Diego kept his voice low, though Kaito stepped away to give him privacy.

"For you? Two hours if I skip a few safety protocols. The risk feels worth it." Her voice carried a grin. "Lucky, I enjoy insurmountable challenges."

"Processing units. Heavy load." Diego memorized the coordinates, the numbers blurring before his eyes. "Might need to thread through hot zones."

Mia moved toward her aircraft, tools clinking against her belt. "Riots again? Must be Tuesday. You riding shotgun?"

Diego shook his head, the motion sending a wave of dizziness through him. "Can't this time. Sending my son-in-law instead."

"Manuel? Didn't think you'd let a tactical cop near this operation."

Kaito watched from meters away, head tilted slightly, face blank.

"Manuel knows Phoenix better than anyone. His background in crisis response helps with civilians in distress." Diego straightened his spine against the pain radiating down his back. "I need to stay for the next crossing."

"Fair enough." Mia climbed into her cockpit. "Tell him to pack light, be ready in two hours. I'll strip non-essential safety protocols to speed cargo modifications."

Diego ended the call and turned. Kaito had moved closer; workers still bustled around them.

"Manuel Rodriguez is an interesting choice," Kaito said. "Though his law enforcement experience could prove valuable if things deteriorate further."

Diego watched Kaito's perfectly controlled posture. The scared kid he'd dragged from Osaka's rubble still lived somewhere beneath that businessman's composure. "Sometimes direct action works best. Manuel handles himself well, and knows when not to."

Kaito nodded. "I'll have my people brief him on warehouse security." His mouth twitched. "And warn them about his action movie quotes during operations."

Diego almost smiled. In this moment, they were just two men trying to save what remained.

Diego hesitated before calling Manuel. Sending him back to Earth threatened his family's unity on Haven. Without those units, they'd lose everything they'd built. He steadied his hand and made the call.

Maria's face appeared instead; the momentary resemblance to Elena was so striking that Diego's breath hitched. The greenhouse behind her represented everything they were building, everything at stake.

"Papa! Perfect timing. I was reviewing soil composition data." Maria smiled warmly, her eyes focused like someone solving complex equations. "Manuel's helping Jack with irrigation. Want me to get him?"

"Please, Mija. It's important." Diego watched her brow furrow, then smooth in understanding.

"Everything okay?" Maria stepped away, her hologram walking alongside Diego toward a quiet corner.

"Supply run complications. Nothing critical yet, but I need Manuel's help."

Maria nodded. "He mentioned his team's been restless, wanting to help more." She called offscreen, "Manuel! Papa needs to talk to you!"

The hologram shifted as Manuel appeared, his hands and face smudged with dirt from irrigation work. "Diego? What's happening?"

"Phoenix run. Those processing units determine if our remaining evacuees get left behind. Johnson's sister and her kids are in Phoenix too, get them on the return flight if possible, but the units have absolute priority." Diego kept his voice level while the pressure in his temples built. "Maria's safe on Haven, but we need those units to ensure everyone makes it across."

Manuel's spine snapped straight. Dirt-covered hands found a rag. Wiped clean. "When?"

Diego's knuckles went white against the crate edge. The room tilted. His knee throbbed. "1400 hours. Portal opens at 0600 tomorrow. Eight hours to secure the units and get back." He checked the monitor. Seismic readings climbing. "Weather's holding. But those tremors..."

"I'll gather my team. Standing by to transfer to Original Earth at 1400."

Diego noted Manuel's adoption of "Original Earth," a term that had spread through Haven in recent weeks. The distinction seemed important, separating the world they'd left from the one they built.

Behind Manuel, Maria stepped into frame. Her mouth tightened slightly, shoulders squaring the way Elena's had when family was threatened.

"Team ready in ninety minutes. Final checks during transport," Manuel confirmed, his voice steady with confidence. "Bring modified riot gear? Might help at police cordons."

Diego weighed options against mission failures. His concentration slipped, the room going momentarily dark before snapping back into focus. Too much firepower would make them look like raiders. Too little might cost his son-in-law's life. Another impossible choice where failure meant watching his family's world collapse.

"Minimal gear, but pack tear gas and non-lethal rounds as backup." Diego watched Manuel nod. "Don't look like we expect trouble, but keep options for problems."

The memory of Phoenix flashed in his mind: desperate civilians clawing at water center gates, AI deploying sonic deterrents. He'd seen how ordinary people turned violent when desperate.

"Manuel, those people aren't the enemy. They're just surviving."

Manuel's expression softened slightly. Diego recognized that look from Manuel's stories about the water riots he'd faced during his tactical response days.

"Copy that. Non-lethal only, minimal profile, respect civilians." Manuel straightened. "I'll get it done, Diego. For all of us."

The simple addition carried weight. Not just a mission acknowledgment but a promise to his family. To return.

As Diego ended the call, his comm suddenly vibrated against his palm. The device illuminated with Olivia's ID just as a worker approached, seeking approval on a distribution problem. Diego motioned for the worker to wait, his finger hovering over the reject button. Manuel's mission needed focus, but the comm persisted.

Sighing, Diego accepted the call while signaling the waiting worker forward. He scanned the inventory manifest with his left hand while Olivia appeared disheveled on screen, her lab coat stained with mineral deposits. Her eyes shone with dangerous excitement.

"Diego, you need to see this." Her enthusiasm cut through his exhaustion. "We might have caught a break. Get to the filtration plant. You won't believe what they've done. It could change everything about our capacity to support the remaining evacuees."

"They?" Diego approved the manifest with a thumbprint. "Who, Olivia?"

"Jack used his demolitions background, and Kayla's combat engineering kicked in." Olivia laughed. "They've either solved our water problem or created an expensive bomb. If it works, we could potentially support all one hundred eighty remaining evacuees, even if the Phoenix units fail."

Diego's attention sharpened through the pain. "Even without the processors? You're sure?"

"Not yet, but preliminary tests..." Olivia grinned. "Just come. I need your assessment before we tell Kaito. This could be our backup plan if the Phoenix retrieval fails."

"On my way. Bring emergency containment gear?"

"Just hurry. Time's burning. And try not to shoot anything when you see it."

The call ended. Workers continued around them, oblivious to the razor's edge they all walked. Diego forced himself forward despite the thundering in his skull and the heaviness in his limbs. If they'd improved filtration capacity to support all one hundred eighty evacuees, it would transform their operation. No more choosing who lives, if either Manuel retrieved those units or Olivia's backup plan worked.

Maybe this time they'd made something useful.

Diego trudged into the water treatment facility. Each step sent the room tilting sideways. Industrial pumps vibrated through the concrete, rattling his teeth. The acrid smell of mineral deposits burned his nostrils, churning his already sour stomach.

His comm unit buzzed against his hip. Manuel's name flashed on screen. Diego squint-ed at the message about team assembly, but the letters refused to hold still. Sixty-two hours since his last real sleep. Or seventy-two? The numbers slipped away like water.

Jack O'Connor balanced on a massive crystalline disk over the main filtration tank. His cybernetic leg caught the harsh overhead lights as he adjusted something at the core of the contraption. The safety harness around his waist looked like a child's toy, frayed rope threatening to snap.

"Before you start lecturing us about proper safety protocols," Kayla called from below, noticing Diego's narrowed eyes on Jack's harness, "I should mention we actually tested this system on a smaller scale first. Jack wanted to skip straight to full-size implementation."

Jack didn't look up from the exposed wiring. "Because smaller versions are for cowards. Some things you gotta commit to all the way."

Diego squinted at the network of crystalline formations arranged in concentric circles. Crystalline dust crunched under his boots while the pumps' thrum dug into his skull.

The design reminded him of ancient water wheels, but these crystals pulsed with inner light synchronized to the water flow. Haven's minerals transformed into a self-sustaining filtration system.

"It works." Olivia approached with a tablet. She glanced at Diego's face, hesitating briefly before handing him water quality readings. "The results are extraordinary."

She stepped closer. "This system could significantly increase our clean water supply. Enough for all three hundred evacuees instead of just the hundred and eighty we planned for, if Manuel secures those additional processing units."

Diego's chest loosened for a moment. Three hundred. No more heartbreaking choices. No more deciding who lives and who stays behind.

"The crystals attract and bind the problematic minerals." Olivia's words tumbled faster. "Jack discovered it completely by accident."

Jack's prosthetic whirred as he climbed down. "Sample jumped. Did its own thing." He wiped crystal residue on his pants. "These bastards have properties that make no goddamn sense. Almost like they're alive."

His grin was all wrong angles. "Perfect for making shit explode, though."

Kayla rolled her eyes, wiping residue from her hands. "What Jack means is we've built something sustainable here, unlike his usual 'blow it up first, ask questions later' approach."

"In plain English," Diego said. He swayed as purified water flowed into the collection tank. Water ran clearer than anything their previous systems produced.

"We built a filter that cleans itself," Jack said, tapping the structure. "No clogged filters, no daily maintenance, no more water rationing."

Diego moved closer, ignoring how the room tilted with each step. The engineering was raw ingenuity, slapped together but effective. The hum of the pumps vibrated up his arm from the tank's railing. "How stable is it?"

Kayla flipped through notes on her tablet. "Six hours running without problems. I've been monitoring hourly. The crystals adapt to different contaminants. More efficient over time."

Diego's eyes followed the power supply line. His jaw tensed. Exposed copper. Cables, spliced together with electrical tape, hung inches above the water's surface. A bare connector swayed on its cord, each oscillation bringing it closer to the tank.

He pointed at the wiring. "You have live electrical running over an open water tank." His finger shifted to the makeshift harness. "That safety line would snap if you sneezed."

"That's exactly what I said." Kayla shot Jack a pointed look. "Some of us care about safety protocols."

Jack opened his mouth, but Diego raised his hand. "I know it really works. But this facility needs to function long after we're gone. Three hundred lives depend on this system not failing when no one's around to fix it."

"Three hundred," Olivia repeated quietly. "All of them. No one will be left behind if Manuel succeeds."

Diego nodded. The possibility settled somewhere deep, past muscle, into bone.

Three safety violations. His eyes caught them automatically, trained response he couldn't shut off. Halfway around the tank and already counting.

The array was brilliant. Exactly what Haven needed. But the implementation?

Shit.

"How will you prevent this from becoming my next emergency, Jack?" Diego asked. He gripped the tank as the floor seemed to shift beneath him.

Jack's gaze flickered from the wiring to Diego's white-knuckled grip on the tank. His cybernetic leg whirred softly as he shifted his weight. "Already working on proper safety measures." He pulled out schematics with confidence. "We can route power through proper conduits with shutoffs. Kayla found sealant on the last run."

"I've mapped all the safety upgrades while he was playing with explosives." Kayla wiped more mineral dust from her hands. "We're constructing a proper platform with guard rails that fold down for maintenance."

Jack nodded. "Also adding backup filters in case we need to take parts offline. No more scrambling when something fails." He grinned. "These crystals can take punishment, though. Yesterday I dropped one from the top catwalk and it barely..."

"Save the demolition stories for poker night." Diego fought both a smile and the dizziness.

Diego's comm vibrated again. The text blurred into meaningless shapes.

Kayla wiped sweat from her forehead. "The exodus ship engineers have proven invaluable. They completely redesigned our power distribution grid to handle the increased load from this water system without blowing every fuse in Haven."

The mention jolted Diego's attention. The exodus program rejects, had brought unexpected skills to Haven. The ship captain they'd pulled from the rejection pile had decades of experience maintaining life support systems. The lead engineer had designed habitat domes before the APU deemed her "non-essential."

"What about the new generator?" Kayla asked. "When will it arrive? The foundation sits ready."

Diego pressed his palms against his temples. The room blurred into smears of color. His damaged knee throbbed with each heartbeat. Jack's voice faded as something sharp twisted behind his eyes.

Olivia stepped closer. "Diego? You don't look good."

"Just tired." The facility's humming intensified, drilling into his skull. Since the exodus announcement, he'd barely managed more than an hour of broken sleep, coordinating Security, cataloging resources, solving crisis after crisis.

Jack and Kayla continued discussing power distribution grids and system redundancies, their voices merging into incomprehensible noise. Technical terms slipped past Diego's comprehension.

Olivia's hand on his arm felt surprisingly warm. "When did you last sleep properly?"

Diego stared at the pulsing crystal array, its blue-white light turning his stomach. Three days ago, he'd nodded off during a security briefing, jerking awake when his tablet clattered to the floor. Before that, maybe four hours reviewing agricultural reports. Everything since had blurred into a haze of caffeine and stimulants.

Olivia's eyes narrowed, taking in details he couldn't hide.

"Can't stop now," Diego mumbled. His words slurred together. "The water system, Manuel's mission, security protocols..."

"You're lecturing them about safety violations while running yourself into the ground." Olivia's grip tightened as he swayed. "That's the real violation here. Their creation works, but safety protocols can wait four hours."

Diego grimaced but nodded. The room spun. "Next security rotation starts in..." He tried to calculate. "Four hours. I need to brief the team on the new perimeter protocols and Manuel's mission status."

Olivia gripped his wrist. "Look at me, Diego." He focused on her face. "Manuel has his mission. Jack and Kayla have their upgrades. I've got the calculations. What we need is a clear head when decisions matter."

Diego leaned against her, surprised by the steadying comfort.

Olivia pulled him toward the exit. "The generator arrives before tonight's portal closes, or tomorrow at the latest. And if either of you wakes him before he's had four solid hours of sleep, there will be consequences."

Diego tried to protest but yawned instead. The last of his adrenaline abandoned him.

"Four hours," he reluctantly agreed as Olivia guided him out. Behind them, Jack whistled. Kayla muttered something that sounded like "finally someone he listens to."

Diego's comm vibrated with another message. Olivia took it before he could reach for it.

"Manuel says they're assembled and ready, ahead of schedule. Everything's proceeding exactly as planned."

Diego's shoulders unlocked.

"Wake me in three hours. Manuel needs confirmation of the latest intelligence before heading into APU territory."

"Four hours," Olivia said firmly. "I'll handle the intelligence confirmation with Security. You've trained Manuel well."

As they walked through Haven's corridors, Diego noticed how Olivia moved with quiet authority, how she positioned herself to catch him if he stumbled, how her clinical mask had slipped just enough to show genuine concern.

"The water filter," he mumbled as they reached his quarters. "It works? All three hundred?"

Olivia smiled, and her whole face changed. "Yes. If Manuel gets those processing units, we bring everyone through. No one gets left behind."

For the first time in days, Diego's shoulders dropped. He allowed Olivia to guide him to his bunk, too exhausted to maintain his independence. As sleep pulled him under, her hand briefly touched his shoulder.

"Rest," she said. "We've got this. For once, let someone else carry the weight."

Diego's breathing evened out as exhaustion finally claimed him. Perhaps in this new world, built together, he didn't have to carry everything alone.

EVERYTHING'S FINE!

Raised voices penetrated the door as people argued with Olivia. Her sharp tone cut through the others.

Diego woke in Olivia's office, the scent of her lavender diffuser mingling with Haven's fresh, clean air. The constant low hum of technology vibrated through the walls. His face itched with three days of stubble as he sat up, at least grateful his knee wasn't throbbing yet.

"I don't care what the priority level is," Olivia's voice carried through the door. "He needs rest, and you need to wait."

Diego swung his legs off the couch. His vertebrae cracked in rapid succession as he straightened, each pop a small reminder that sixty-four wasn't young anymore. His boots sat beside the sofa, arranged with military precision, laces tucked neatly inside. Olivia's doing. A flicker of warmth surprised him, quickly followed by the familiar weight of responsibility settling across his shoulders like lead.

The argument beyond the door escalated. Kaito's clipped tones. Dr. Choi's insistent cadence. Words broke through the fog. "Critical." "Immediate attention." Diego's pulse jumped. Double-time.

A half-empty coffee mug sat abandoned on Olivia's desk, lipstick smudged on the rim, offering a glimpse into the woman behind the physicist's stern exterior.

"If you don't back off," Olivia's tone hardened to steel, "I will personally ensure you're assigned as Jack's target for the next month."

Diego stood, a small smile tugging at the corner of his mouth. Anyone who had experienced Jack's pranks knew better than to risk that particular punishment. He briefly remembered Emily's hair being bright blue last month. His amusement vanished as his eyes caught the timestamp on his datapad.

"Six hours?" he demanded, his voice a raw rasp. Twenty-two days into establishing Haven, and I'm unconscious for six hours? My team made dozens of decisions without me. The perimeter security remains incomplete. Water filtration is still showing contaminants. The thoughts hammered against his skull. Catastrophic failure. Perimeter breach. Water contaminated. A dozen ways to die before sunrise.

Diego yanked the door open. Olivia stood squarely between Kaito and Mei in the narrow hallway. All three heads swiveled toward him.

He ran a hand over his face. "You needed it," Olivia said, crossing her arms. "You've been surviving on stims and sheer willpower since we arrived."

"We have critical..."

"Everything's handled," she cut him off, her tone softening. "Jack and Kayla finished the filtration system while arguing about torque settings. Sarah coordinated arrivals without making anyone cry. And yes, Kaito secured the generator transport route, though he refused to smile about it."

His shoulders sagged against the doorframe. Half a second. The knots in his muscles loosened, then locked up again. They didn't need me. The thought cut both ways, settling somewhere between his ribs like shrapnel.

"The world didn't end because you slept." Olivia's mouth twitched. Almost a smile. "Though these two seem hell-bent on waking you for whatever crisis they've decided can't wait."

Diego stretched. His spine cracked. Years of working with Kaito and Mei made their body language easier to read than any report.

Kaito stood frozen, datapad at regulation angle. But the tells were there. That muscle jumping in his jaw. The skin tight around his eyes. A wrinkle near his collar where his suit should have been perfect. Resource problems. Had to be.

Mei practically vibrated on her toes, soil sample containers clutched between white knuckles. Her eyes were bright with barely contained excitement, words visibly backing up behind her pressed lips, too numerous to organize.

"Alright," Diego swiped a hand across gritty eyes. "What couldn't..."

"The embryo tests!" Mei burst out. "They're viable, mostly, but..."

"Generator route's compromised," Kaito interjected, his voice low and tight. "APU increased patrols unexpectedly."

Diego's stomach clenched. "Mei first. Define 'mostly viable.'"

"Minor mutations in genetic sequences," Mei tumbled over her words, "but nothing life-threatening. Unusual protein markers integrating with Haven's mineral structure at cellular levels."

Radiation protocols blazed through his mind like warning flares. "How minor?"

Olivia's slight nod acknowledged the unspoken: every animal and crop represented survival, not science. If Haven altered embryonic DNA, what might it do to human genetics? To Isabella and Mateo's developing bodies?

"Cosmetic variations in coloration and pattern," Mei clarified. "But the good news..."

"Chicken eggs hatched." Kaito's interruption broke through Mei's excitement, his gaze fixed on Diego. "One rooster, the rest hens."

"All healthy," Mei insisted. "Despite unusual feather patterns."

The rigid set of Diego's shoulders eased slightly. Chickens were their test case; successful breeding would validate plans for larger livestock. Healthy chicks, even with variations, marked their first real win in weeks. Still, the mutation question lingered in his mind, a worry to revisit once more urgent matters were addressed.

"Show me the genetic analysis," Olivia stepped forward.

Mei handed her tablet to Olivia. The screen displayed complex sequences Diego couldn't begin to decipher. The women huddled over data, exchanging technical terms that might as well have been a foreign language.

Kaito cleared his throat, still standing rigidly, waiting for his turn.

"Let them work," Diego said quietly, stepping aside. "Generator situation. Details."

"APU increased patrols along our planned route," Kaito lowered his voice. "Added unexpected surveillance coverage. Window for moving the generator shrunk to twelve hours, maximum."

The weight of hundreds of lives pressed down on Diego's shoulders like a physical thing. Two days without generator power, and life support systems would begin to fail, freezing out half their remaining launch window. "How long?"

"Twelve hours at most," Kaito displayed patrol patterns on his pad. "After that, risk becomes unacceptable."

Behind them, Olivia whispered, "These protein markers are incorporating Haven's mineral structure at a cellular level."

"Yes!" Mei's enthusiasm carried through the hall. "The embryos are adapting to Haven even before birth!"

Diego turned back to Kaito's map, compartmentalizing to focus on one crisis. The patrol routes formed a complex web across the screen, but there was always a weak point. He had promised Maria he would make this work, create a safe future for her children. Failure wasn't an option.

"Here," he pointed to the coastline. "The drones adjust for magnetic interference from these cliffs. That's our window."

Diego retraced patrol routes, his mind shifting to aggressive options. Last week, Emily's combat drones had proven effective against that massive bird-creature. Could their stealth handle the APU's monitoring drones?

"Drone inventory?"

"Emily has three full swarm units prepped. New quantum shielding makes them virtually invisible to standard detection."

The approach took shape: remove their surveillance, create a blind spot, and slip the generator through before the APU response. Simple. Clean. Effective.

But the risks... If APU forces caught them sabotaging equipment, it would draw unwanted attention. Investigation meant scrutiny. Scrutiny meant discovery. Discovery meant failure.

Behind him, Mei and Olivia's excited chatter continued. Everything they'd built, everything they protected, all hanging on the edge with each decision.

Diego's fingers tapped against his thigh. Three exits from the valley. Two choke points where they'd be exposed. The ridge line offered cover but limited their retreat options.

Emily's drones could map it in six hours. Thermal imaging, motion detection, the works. Standard reconnaissance.

Isabella asking about the purple grass yesterday. Why it grew in spirals. Mateo's laugh when the alien bird had landed on their roof, its six-foot wingspan casting shadows. Maria at breakfast, jaw set exactly like Elena's used to when she'd made up her mind about something.

The drones could do it. Question was whether they'd come back.

Diego pulled up his holo-comm. "Emily. Luna. Priority channel, now."

Two translucent figures materialized. Emily sat at her drone station, multiple screens glowing behind her. Luna perched cross-legged amid floating data streams, one hand absently stroking the fluffy orange cat purring contentedly in her lap.

"Need options for APU drones," Diego angled his comm to include Kaito. "Increased patrol coverage on generator transport route."

Emily's eyes lit up. "Q-shielding renders them ghosts. We could..."

"No direct engagement," Diego cut her off. "Need something subtle. Equipment failure, not sabotage."

Luna's fingers moved through data streams, a 3D coastline materializing beside Professor Whiskers, who batted lazily at the holographic projection. "These cliffs?" A grin tugged at her mouth. "APU drones recalibrate when passing this zone. Natural electromagnetic interference. Nav systems compensate automatically."

"And?" Diego prompted.

"Can amplify interference. Trigger emergency protocols." Luna's eyes sparked with the challenge, popping her gum as Professor Whiskers nuzzled against her neck. "Temporary offline for diagnostics. Standard procedure. Seen it during thunderstorms near these mineral deposits."

Diego frowned. "If they've upgraded since Climate Conflicts? If they detect artificial enhancement?"

"Their tech security? Pathetic." Luna countered, fingers still flying through data.

Emily's face remained pure focus, but Diego caught her slight eye roll at Luna's dismissal of APU systems. Professional rivalry hummed between them.

"Can make this look natural," Luna continued. "Zero digital prints. A ghost in their logs."

"How long?"

"Twenty minutes minimum before diagnostic cycle completes. Longer during shift change."

Diego nodded. "Clean operation. No footprint. Just a 'natural' electromagnetic anomaly causing system reset."

"Right," Luna grinned, absently scratching behind Professor Whiskers' remaining ear. "Got the frequency. APU cybersecurity's gotten sloppy since the war."

"Emily, position drone swarm for backup. No engagement unless necessary."

Emily nodded sharply. "Three Mark-VIIs staged within five klicks. Quantum shielding is invisible to APU sensors. Thermal dampening is active. Weapons primed but dormant till authorization delta-six-nine."

"Luna, you're running point. Make the call if Emily needs to go aggressive."

Luna's moved through data streams. The orange tabby pressed warm against her ribs. "Copy that. Syncing the pulse with their patrol rotation." Her gum snapped. "Surveillance is plan Z. We do this clean or we don't do it at all."

"One thing," Emily spoke up before he could continue, her military posture contrasting sharply with Luna's casual sprawl. "If we go hot, APU sees our tech. Even if we destroy them all, they'll know someone's operating beyond their level."

Diego inhaled, the sweet alien air filling his lungs with its strange mix of cinnamon and something floral he couldn't identify. She was right; engagement would reveal their capabilities and raise dangerous questions that could lead back to Haven, to his family.

"Will make sure we don't need that option," Luna countered. The cat stretched on her lap, batting at a holographic drone. "APU techs won't know what hit them. Running diagnostics while we slip through."

"Good. Updates every five minutes once in position."

Diego ended the call and turned to find Olivia watching him. Her gaze lingered on his face, something unspoken passing between them, recognition of the burden they shared before he shifted to Kaito.

"Your people can handle the generator transport once we create the window?" Diego kept his voice low.

"Already staged and waiting," Kaito displayed the transport plan on his pad. "Convoy prepared with clearances and cover documentation. Escort teams in position. Generator moving within three minutes of Luna's opening."

Diego reviewed the details. Kaito's thoroughness hadn't changed since he was a kid during the Osaka evacuation. Every contingency covered, every angle considered. It had saved both their lives more than once.

"Good. Keep me updated on..."

Olivia approached, her focus shifting from genetic analysis to their conversation.

"We need to talk about what happens if we can't get the generator," she said quietly.

The responsibility wrapped around his chest like a steel band, making each breath a conscious effort. "Four portal openings left. If we lose the generator, we condemn people we promised to save." The words came out strained. Isabella's hopeful eyes and Mateo's innocent questions about their new home haunted him.

"We prioritize people over equipment," Olivia finished. "But that means abandoning most infrastructure plans."

Diego stepped closer. "I promised these people a future, Olivia. Not just survival."

"I know." Her hand found his arm. Warmth through the fabric. Through the skin.

They'd figure it out. Maybe. They always had before.

Her words, so much like Elena's, weren't a memory that cut but a lifeline he hadn't realized he was missing. The room closed in around him. His throat tightened. The walls seemed to pulse with Haven's alien rhythm. Twenty years of keeping everyone at arm's length, of carrying every burden alone, pressed against his ribs like a weight he could no longer hold. The need for something solid, someone real, overwhelmed his usual discipline.

Diego pulled her into a tight embrace.

She stiffened for a heartbeat, then gradually relaxed, her arms encircling him. Her hair brushed against his cheek, carrying a scent that triggered a cascade of memory. Elena. For a moment, the similarity was so sharp it stopped his breath, a physical ache spreading beneath his ribs.

But instead of the crushing grief that usually followed Elena's memory, something else came. A loosening in his chest, as if twenty years of holding his breath had finally ended. He could almost hear Elena's voice, not the screaming from his nightmares but the gentle way she used to talk him through his worst moments after missions. You're allowed to let someone help, Diego. You don't have to carry everything alone. The guilt that had always followed her memory was absent, replaced by a feeling of permission. Permission to be here, now, with someone else who understood the weight of impossible choices.

His arms loosened slowly, reluctantly. Olivia's eyes met his, wide with surprise, a question forming there that neither was ready to ask. Color spread across her cheeks as she stepped back slightly.

"Thank you," he said, voice rougher than intended. "For believing when the rest of us doubt."

Olivia adjusted her lab coat, smoothing invisible wrinkles, her eyes darting away and back.

Kaito remained outwardly impassive, though Diego caught the slight crinkle at the corners of his eyes, the closest to approval the man would allow himself.

"Kaito," Diego called as the younger man turned to leave. "If Luna's plan fails, we move to contingency beta. Have Johnson's team ready."

Kaito paused, his shoulders stiffening. "Direct confrontation with APU forces."

"I know," Diego whispered. "But we're running out of time. Four more portal openings. That's all we have to complete the evacuation and retrieve our teams."

For a moment, Kaito's rigid composure slipped, revealing their shared burden. Behind the cartel's power and efficiency, Kaito carried the same weight Diego did, protecting his people however necessary. "Johnson will be ready. Discreetly."

Diego nodded, watching Kaito disappear down the corridor.

The silence left him alone with Haven's strange sounds filtering through the temporary walls. Wind whispered through triple-lobed vegetation, rustling with a papery quality unlike anything on Earth. The air carried a faint sweetness, reminiscent of cinnamon mixed with copper, making his tongue tingle with each breath.

Distant trilling of unknown creatures echoed across the valley. Underneath it all, a cloying scent of decaying vegetation, rich and slightly nauseating, reminded him of the alien biochemistry surrounding them.

This wasn't home. Could never be home. But it remained their only chance.

The floor beneath him pulsed, Jack's temporary power conduits struggling under the load. Lights dimmed momentarily, shadows deepening across Olivia's face. Haven's fragility couldn't be more obvious.

The tremor hit. His body jerked.

Osaka. Buildings folded in on themselves. Voices screaming through dust. Throat coated thick, bitter, choking.

He blinked hard. The present stuttered. Came back.

People had died in Osaka because he couldn't move fast enough. Not this time.

Eight days. Diego counted them like he counted everything else now, bodies, resources, time running out.

Hundreds of lives. All of them waiting on choices he'd make.

Olivia hunched over the data streams, jaw tight. Numbers cascaded across her screen. All red.

"Twelve hours," she said quietly, not looking up. "That's not much margin for error."

"Never is." He watched her fingers trace calculations across the display. "You think we're crazy for trying this?"

Olivia finally looked at him, something soft flickering behind her analytical mask. "I think we're crazy for not trying it sooner." A pause. "Though I suppose saving the world requires a certain level of professional insanity."

The corner of his mouth twitched upward. When was the last time someone had made him almost smile?

Glass shattered down the hallway, followed by Jack's cackle and a string of obscenities that would make a drill sergeant proud. Boots thundered against flooring.

Diego's almost-smile died. "What the hell?"

Emily's voice echoed through the corridor. "Jack O'Connor, I swear if that drone comes near me again..."

Another crash. More laughter. The sound of something electronic shorting out with a spectacular pop.

Olivia's mouth quirked upward, watching Diego's expression shift from resignation to weary annoyance. "Brilliant minds," she murmured.

"With the impulse control of caffeinated teenagers." Diego shook his head. "Should we intervene?"

Before Olivia could answer, wet paint splattered against the wall outside their makeshift command center, followed by Emily's furious roar of indignation.

"Your engineers," Olivia said, unable to suppress her grin now, "your problem."

Diego pressed his fingertips against his temples, but found himself fighting his own smile. "Tomorrow, we're saving humanity. Today, I'm apparently running a daycare for overgrown children with engineering degrees."

Olivia's laugh surprised him. Rich and genuine, it cut through the constant tension that had been his only companion for weeks. For a moment, the weight pressing down on his chest lightened.

When their eyes met, he saw the same exhausted relief there, the same desperate need for just five minutes where the fate of the world wasn't balanced on their shoulders.

A high-pitched whine built up from down the hall. Emily's combat drone spun to life.

"Shit." The moment shattered. Diego glanced back at the transport route still glowing on Kaito's datapad. Twelve hours. Manuel's life hangs in the balance.

Time to save his engineers from themselves before they destroyed their only chance at salvation.

One catastrophe at a time.

A projectile screamed past Diego's head. Duck. Assess. Cover. The corridor spun as he dropped, knees hitting concrete, hands searching for weapons that weren't there. Blue paint splattered the wall behind where his head had been a second before.

"Stand down!" The command burst from him with battlefield authority, the kind that had halted charging soldiers mid-stride during the Hydration War. The hover-drone stuttered to a halt, its GridSense Network rotors whirring to silence.

Combat chemicals flooded Diego's system, the same cold clarity that had kept him alive through three resource wars. His tongue curled at the back of his throat, the corridor's blend of ozone and chemical paint triggering memories of Osaka: the acrid scent of short-circuited WaterSecurity Network systems and desperate graffiti warnings marking safe water zones. Forty years later, his body still knew exactly what to do with fear.

The ARIA-modified drone's targeting system swiveled and locked onto Emily at the corridor's far end. She stood at parade rest despite her ruined uniform, now transformed into an abstract expressionist canvas of neon green splotches.

The repurposed CrisisPredict water gun in her hands remained at shoulder height, her trigger finger relaxed but ready, identical to her stance when piloting million-dollar BattlefieldAwareness drones into contested airspace.

Behind an overturned equipment cart, Jack and Kayla peered over the edge with the mischievous satisfaction of engineers whose chaos had worked perfectly. Jack's cybernetic leg stuck out awkwardly, the customized wooden peg he'd installed that morning now dripping with blue paint.

"Target acquisition complete," Emily reported with pilot precision, her voice carrying the clipped tone of someone who'd spent too many hours monitoring drone feeds. "Subject identified via thermal signature despite suboptimal corridor lighting. Hostile's mobility algorithms failed to compensate for uneven weight distribution in that ridiculous wooden appendage."

From behind the cart, Jack emerged with blue paint cascading from his beard like melting wax. His wooden prosthetic thumped against the floor with each step.

"This beautiful piece of craftsmanship wasn't built for stealth ops," he growled. "Besides, I was just running a field calibration test on my new dampening circuits. Not my damn fault, Emily's wearing that radioactive puke-green monstrosity you call a uniform."

"Holy shit, that splatter pattern is gorgeous," Kayla said, studying the paint with the gleeful focus she usually reserved for high explosives. She ran her hands through her short-cropped hair, leaving blue streaks that matched the tattoos running up her arms.

"Spread radius is only about three-quarters what I'd get with a proper explosive package, but the color distribution is surprisingly uniform. Next time, we should rig it with a micro-charge detonator. Just enough kick to make the colors fly."

Diego pressed his tongue against his teeth until he tasted copper. Combat stress, he understood. This was chaos masquerading as teamwork. Paint fights six hours before the inter-dimensional generator transport. His grandchildren's future hangs on whether these people can focus when it matters. Adrenaline coursed through him with nowhere to go, leaving his muscles coiled, fingers twitching from the neurochemical surge and crash.

"Knock it off." The quiet command cut through the corridor.

Jack immediately stopped tapping his prosthetic. Emily lowered her weapon. Kayla's excited smile faded as she stuffed her hands in her pockets.

"ZPE generator transport begins in six. Everything runs perfectly, or we're screwed. That thing weighs twelve tons and draws enough power to run Mexico City. One mistake and we lose our window to Haven."

Emily's gaze tracked across the corridor as she mentally mapped extraction routes. "Sir, drone swarm is already programmed for pattern-CyberShield-7, with redundancy protocols if the main sequence fails." Her fingers twitched slightly, muscle memory from thousands of hours at drone controls.

Jack switched from prankster to technician, his expression shifting to the focused intensity of a man mentally reviewing complex wiring diagrams.

"Power conduits are triple-checked. Had Luna run an AI diagnostic sweep too, though I don't trust those silicon-brained bastards since what happened in Osaka." He rapped his knuckles against his prosthetic. "Not after what they did to your people."

Kayla's knuckles popped in sequence. "Structural supports are reinforced along the transfer path," she said. "Set micro-charges at junction points if we need an emergency reroute. Non-lethal, obviously." She flashed a smile that wasn't entirely reassuring. "Well, mostly non-lethal."

"Jack, Kayla," Diego said, his voice cutting through their lingering amusement. "Run diagnostics on all power conduits again. I want transmission efficiency at ninety-nine percent minimum. No room for error tonight."

He fixed Emily with the stare that had intimidated both recruits and generals. "Recalibrate that swarm. Zero delay tolerance between units. We get one shot at inter-dimensional transport."

The engineers scattered, but not before Jack snapped a mock salute with his paint-covered hand. "Aye aye, Captain Hook. My circuits are yours to command. Just remember, if we screw this up, we're only destroying a twelve-ton experimental power source that could theoretically crater half the Yucatán Peninsula."

The distinctive sound of keyboard clicks from an adjacent lab drew Diego's attention. He turned to find Olivia leaning against her lab's doorframe, observing the aftermath with quiet amusement. She'd clearly been monitoring their antics through the security feed while working on final calculations.

Shadows under her eyes spoke of too many nights calculating quantum fields while running on coffee and determination. Yet her expression held the understanding of someone who recognized the utility in controlled chaos.

Olivia glanced at the retreating engineers, then back to her tablet. With a swipe, she closed the intricate quantum formula filling the screen. "Sometimes I feel like I'm herding cats, brilliant, heavily armed cats," she said. "Don't worry, I made Jack disable any actual weapons in those drones. They shoot nothing deadlier than paint and embarrassment." She gestured toward the massive equipment dominating the lab. "The team needs to blow off steam before we attempt whatever madness this is."

Diego watched Olivia coordinate their chaos. Elena had managed civilian evacuations during the Hydration Crisis with the same instinctive balance, knowing when to enforce discipline and when to release pressure. The parallel hit him sideways. He waited for the familiar ache, the guilt that always followed thoughts of Elena. Instead, something unfamiliar stirred in his chest. Not the crushing weight of loss, but something lighter. Possibility.

"Six hours until transport." The statement hung between them, weighted with significance beyond its simplicity.

"Portal calculations are holding steady," Olivia replied, brushing a strand of hair behind her ear. "The quantum alignment matrices I've been modeling show a ninety-seven percent probability of successful transport. Luna verified the math twice."

Her words carried weight beyond physics, settling into the future itself. Tonight would determine whether Haven remained a theoretical model built on quantum algorithms or became humanity's second chance.

Diego checked his watch, the digital numbers counting down to everything that mattered. Six hours. Enough time for the adrenaline to dissipate, for his team to remember what they were really here for.

He'd inspect the engineers' work in an hour, verify their antics hadn't compromised anything critical. The same instincts that had triggered his combat response to a paint projectile would keep them all alive tonight.

Paint wars were fine, maybe even necessary for morale. But tonight every circuit needed to function flawlessly, every connection to hold, because Isabella and Mateo's future depended on hardware and quantum calculations that couldn't tolerate even microscopic failures.

BREEDING QUOTAS

Diego found Olivia outside the medical center. She paced the same strip of dirt, data tablet pressed against her chest. Her long fingers tapped a frantic, silent rhythm against its metal edge.

"I was waiting for Dr. Thompson to finish the inventory," she said, her eyes fixed on the entrance. "This can't wait."

He recognized the look. It belonged on the faces of recon scouts just back from seeing something they shouldn't have. "What happened?"

"The embryo project. There are anomalies."

Shit. Even with Haven's population over five hundred, long-term survival was a numbers game. The artificial gestation program was their insurance policy, a way to build numbers and keep the gene pool from becoming a puddle.

"How bad?"

"Bad enough I'm pulling her out of whatever she's doing."

Diego followed Olivia inside. The sharp tang of antiseptic burned his nostrils, a sudden transport to field hospitals and the stench of hasty surgeries during the Water Wars. Dr. Thompson stood in the middle of the supply room, directing the cataloging with brisk efficiency. Her pen made sharp, distinct taps against her tablet with each confirmed item.

"Batch 17-C verified," she said to Sarah Choi, who was sorting sealed packages of surgical gear. "Trauma kits?"

"Another wave of supplies just came through the portal," Sarah reported. Sweat beaded on her hairline despite the cool air. "High priority antibiotics for the respiratory cases, surgical equipment for the expanded OR, and the emergency trauma kits you wanted after the mining incident."

"Good." Dr. Thompson nodded, her eyes glued to the screen. "Catalog it all. Priority items stay. The rest goes to secure storage." She looked up, squinting against the fluorescent glare. "Split the trauma kits between here and the mining operation. We had two close calls last week when a tunnel support failed."

Her gaze fell on Diego and Olivia. "Martinez. Dr. Smith. What's wrong?"

Olivia stepped forward. She squared her shoulders, a familiar motion. The kind soldiers made before delivering a casualty report.

"We have anomalies in the lab embryos," she said. Her voice was steady, but her hand gripped the tablet so hard her knuckles were white. "It's specific to the artificial gestation units, not the natural pregnancies. Our theory is the mother's body acts as a filter, a buffer against Haven's mineral load. The AG units don't have that. The embryos are getting a direct, raw dose. Mei's team documented every stage."

The pen in Thompson's hand stopped moving. A dead stop. She set it down, the click loud in the quiet room.

"What kind of adaptations?" she asked, setting the pen down with deliberate care. "How many are affected?"

"Minor, so far," Olivia replied. "Cellular structure changes. Enhanced mineral absorption."

Thompson's spine straightened. The air in the room changed. She was already two steps ahead, reordering triage in her head. He'd seen the same shift in medics under fire.

"How many embryos are we monitoring?"

"Three livestock embryos in gestation, two more in vitro," Diego answered. "All five are showing it. The natural pregnancies, all twenty-seven women, are clean. Scans are normal."

Dr. Thompson snatched her tablet from the counter, her fingers flying across the screen, pulling up files. "Why the hell wasn't I informed immediately? If something like this crossed over to human development, we'd be looking at a divergence event." Her grip on the tablet tightened.

"We confirmed the pattern three hours ago," Olivia said. "Mei saw odd mineral uptake in some seedlings and suggested we cross-reference the embryos. That's when we saw it."

Dr. Thompson began to pace the narrow aisle between shelves, eyes locked on her tablet. "Look at this," she said, stopping to point a shaky finger at the screen for Olivia. "Abnormal cellular mitosis." She resumed pacing. "Non-standard mineral integration... possible nucleotide substitution..."

Sarah caught Diego's eye for a fraction of a second, a silent question he didn't answer. She quietly stacked her supplies, and the door clicked shut behind her.

"The implications..." Thompson stopped again, leaning a hand against a supply shelf for support. "If this is what happens to livestock without a maternal buffer, we need to know why. The natural pregnancies are fine now, but what if we ever need to use artificial gestation for humans? We'd be creating a subspecies, with no idea what the long-term effects would be."

Diego had seen this before. The moment the map proved useless and soldiers realized they were deep in uncharted territory. He knew the only way forward was to focus on the next step, the ground right in front of your boots.

"First things first, Doc," he said. His voice was the same one he used for mission briefings, calm and practical.

Thompson's eyes locked on his.

"We have five embryos adapting," Diego continued. "Not mutating. Not damaged. Adapting. It's what life does here. It finds a way."

The rigid line of her shoulders lost some of its tension. Her breathing was still too fast.

"You don't have the training for this," Diego said, "because nobody does. This is new ground. One problem at a time."

Olivia stepped in. "We still have options, Emily," she said, her tone softer than Diego's hard pragmatism. "We could try to modify the gestation units, create a filtration system that mimics a mother's body. Or, we could see if these adaptations are actually beneficial for survival on Haven."

Thompson took a deep, shuddering breath, held it, and let it out slow. A combat breathing technique. He'd probably taught it to her himself.

"You're both right." She placed her tablet on the counter, her movements measured. "Step one is documentation. Monitoring. We need to know exactly what these changes are before we react."

She picked up the tablet again, her fingers steadier this time. "We'll need more equipment. Specialized monitors. For mineral absorption rates, genetic expression."

"Already on the next supply list," Olivia said. "The Auckland connection delivered."

The initial shock was burning off, replaced by the cold fire of her training. It was like watching a good soldier get their bearings after an ambush.

"If I look at this from an evolutionary standpoint." Thompson's voice came out stronger now. "These might be beneficial precursors. The mother's body acts as a buffer, sure. But maybe that buffer also prevents advantageous adaptations."

Her fingers moved across the tablet. Fast. Purposeful. "We need to understand the maternal filtering mechanism. If we could replicate it artificially..."

She stopped. Her gaze drifted to the sample storage unit in the corner. Cold metal. Waiting. "But we also have to consider these changes might be good. If Haven is causing this, maybe it's helping the next generation prepare to live here."

"That's why we need you," Olivia said. "Your medical knowledge, Mei's botanical data. Together you might see the whole picture."

Diego took a step back, a silent retreat. They were past the breaking point. The low hum of the air recyclers and the soft beeping of monitors filled the space his voice had occupied.

Thompson tapped her screen, a new file appearing. "I'll need to coordinate with Mei. Analyze how natural pregnancies filter these minerals. And we need to increase monitoring on the expectant mothers, with their consent."

Her panic was gone, replaced by a scientist's focus. "These adaptations might be our first real glimpse of humanity's future here. We need to understand them, not run from them."

Diego caught Olivia's eye. She gave him a slight, almost imperceptible nod. Crisis contained. Situation stable. He returned the gesture.

Every problem was the first of its kind. Every solution had to be built from scratch.

Diego's comm crackled to life as he checked the morning security reports. Mei's voice cut through the static, with controlled urgency.

"Diego, get to Bio-Ag. We have a cascading failure in the first-batch cryo-storage."

He was moving before she finished speaking. The livestock area hit him with chaos instead of the usual calm hum of machinery. An alarm shrieked from the lab section. Workers clustered around a massive cryo-unit covered in frost, its display flashing critical red warnings. But past the crisis, in the central area, twelve fluffy chicks huddled under heat lamps. Their peeping mixed with the mechanical alarms, a counterpoint of life against failure.

The talk with Dr. Thompson still nagged at him. Human embryos adapting to Haven? What kind of world was he building for Isabella and Mateo? The chicks behind their glass barrier seemed to have found answers he was still searching for.

"Status report," Diego said, his voice cutting through the noise.

"Primary storage unit for the first embryo shipment," Mei said without looking up from her control panel. "Coolant system failed twenty minutes ago. We've lost power to three chambers already."

Diego scanned the failing equipment, automatically checking for vulnerabilities and escape routes. The unit looked like it was hemorrhaging cold, vapor streaming from multiple vents. One of the chicks pecked at its barrier, oblivious to the crisis just meters away. Heat from their lamps hit his face. Sharp. Wrong against the cold pouring off the failing cryo-unit.

"What have we lost?"

"Twenty-eight chicken embryos in chamber one. Thirty-five pigs in chamber two." Ethan's voice was strained as he fought with a manual release valve. "Thirty goats in chamber three just went critical."

Three hundred embryos. Gone. But the living chicks proved the concept worked. These failures hurt, but they weren't fatal. Diego's shoulders relaxed a fraction. "What's left?"

"Chambers four through eight are still stable, but the cascade is accelerating." Mei pulled up a schematic showing the unit's internal layout. "Each failure puts more strain on the remaining systems."

Diego moved to the display, studying the chamber configuration. Military logistics training kicked in. Triage. Save what you could. The chicks' peeping grew louder behind him, as if sensing the tension. They were adapting to Haven better than anyone had hoped. Increased bone density, faster metabolism. Nature solves problems it hadn't even identified yet.

"What's in the endangered chambers?"

"Chamber four holds the rabbits," Mei said, then caught herself as she read the fluctuating readings. "Diego, the stasis field is failing. We have maybe five minutes before it goes critical."

Rabbits.

His mother's kitchen in Tucson. The rich smell of conejo en chile colorado filling the tiny house. His abuela's recipe was perfected over decades. Meat falling off bones, soaked in deep red sauce she'd spent all morning making. The family is fighting over the last pieces, using fresh tortillas to mop up every drop. Full bellies, safe family. Everything that mattered.

His voice came out rough with memory. "Forget stasis. Get them out. Prep them for incubation. Now."

"But the incubators aren't configured for mammals," Mei protested, her hands already moving toward the emergency release protocols.

"Figure it out. I'm not losing them."

Ethan abandoned the valve and sprinted toward the incubation units. "I can modify the temperature controls, but we'll need synthetic amniotic fluid."

"We've got synthetic colostrum formula," Mei called back, opening chamber four manually. Vapor poured out as she carefully extracted sealed containers. "The base proteins should work for embryonic suspension. Our medical team helped design it for Haven's mineral composition."

Her hands moved with precision. The rabbits were more than protein. During the Resource Wars, rabbit colonies kept entire neighborhoods from starving. Fast breeding, efficient feed conversion, minimal space requirements. Isabella and Mateo might grow up knowing the taste of real meat instead of protein paste.

"What else is at risk?" he asked, studying the remaining chamber readings.

"Cattle embryos in chamber five. Dual-purpose breeds for meat and milk. Angus, Simmental." Mei handed the rabbit containers to Ethan, who disappeared into the lab section with them. "Duck and turkey in six. The newer sheep varieties are seven and eight. Hair breeds that don't need shearing."

Smart selections. He remembered how water-intensive wool sheep became during Earth's droughts. "Priority order if this keeps cascading?"

Mei hesitated, running calculations. "The sheep. They'll handle Haven's climate better than anything else we've got."

"And if we lose the cattle?"

"We have backup embryos in the newer units." She gestured toward the sleek cylinders humming along the far wall. "These older transport containers were always a risk. After this failure, we'll transfer everything to the upgraded systems."

The alarm finally cut off, leaving them with the gentler sounds of successful life. The chicks had settled back to contented peeping. Ethan stepped through the lab doors. Determination cut through exhaustion like a blade through flesh. The alarm shrieked, then died. Silence. Then the chicks. Just peeping now. Content.

Ethan came through the lab door. His jaw was set. Grim. But his shoulders squared. Ready.

"Rabbit embryos are in emergency incubation. Rigged the system with modified colostrum base. Should hold them stable while we sort out proper gestation protocols."

Diego nodded. Crisis managed, but barely. "Timeline if they're viable?"

"Gestation periods still match Earth standards," Mei said, pulling up projections on her tablet. "The faster cellular growth only happens early on. But if this works, we could have our first Haven-born rabbits in four months instead of waiting for the full livestock program."

Four months. The enhanced metabolism also meant faster reproduction. A single doe could produce twelve kits per litter instead of eight. Within a year, they could have a steady protein supply that didn't depend on shipments from Earth.

"Space requirements?"

"That storage area," Mei pointed toward the facility's far end, "could become a rabbitry. Ventilation's already installed."

Diego walked over, boots echoing on concrete. Perfect defensive position. Elevated, clear sightlines, single access point. Just like the community shelters they'd fortified in Phoenix. He ran his hand along the wall, checking structural integrity. The space had good bones: solid floor, proper drainage, and air circulation already in place.

California Whites made good mothers. During the Famine Wars, their colony had produced steady litters even on limited feed. Haven's native grasses would provide even better nutrition.

"Get Sarah's schematics for the Arizona agri-domes," he said, turning back to Mei. "She'll know exactly what this retrofit needs."

"I can send her the emergency protocols and space requirements," Mei replied. "Those agricultural engineers who arrived yesterday, the Patel brothers, could handle the construction. Their urban farms kept entire districts fed when supply chains collapsed."

"Do it. Today." Diego looked at the failing cryo-unit, then at the newer storage systems humming with preserved potential. "And transfer everything else out of these old containers. We're not gambling with Earth's genetic legacy on outdated equipment."

Mei nodded, already composing messages on her tablet. "Should I include the metabolism enhancement data? The way these embryos are adapting to Haven?"

"Everything," Diego said. "Sarah needs the complete picture." He paused at the emergency incubation units where Earth's last rabbits fought for survival in Haven's alien environment, then looked toward the successful chicks under their warming lamps. "Three months until rabbit stew. Six months until fresh milk from those cattle embryos." The corner of his mouth twitched upward. "We're not just surviving anymore, Mei. We're building something that'll last."

And one day, he'd teach Isabella his abuela's recipe. Something his grandmother had taught him, passed down through generations. A real connection to Earth, to family. To home.

That, he swore.

Diego left the Bio-Ag facility. Haven's afternoon heat pressed down, making his knee throb with each step. The settlement had changed. Shelters gone. Real buildings now. Workers hauled construction materials from the warehouse, some to the new hydroponics dome, others toward residential expansion.

Kids darted between buildings. Isabella and Mateo's age. Playing tag. His grandchildren among them, Isabella's dark hair streaming as she chased some boy in a red shirt.

Mexico City. Before the wars. Children in the plaza.

His hand moved to his hip. Empty. No tablet. Jack had it, fixing the screen after Diego dropped the fucking thing during water filtration inspection. Messages piling up somewhere. Olivia's updates among them.

His chest went hollow, like all the air had been sucked out through his ribs. Hours without contact. The silence scraped raw.

Diego cut across the central plaza. Sarah Choi directing medical supply teams. He nodded. The children's game spilled across his path. Mateo and two kids sprinted past, squeals bouncing off metal walls. Too loud. Too carefree for borrowed time.

The engineering bay. Jack's voice carried through the open door, giving someone grief about maintenance procedures. Standard Jack.

Diego entered. Boots rang against metal. The smell hit: solder and machine oil, nothing like Olivia's clean soap scent. Jack hunched over his workbench. Components scattered. Tools everywhere. Half-eaten sandwich going stale.

"About time you showed up." Jack looked up, grin splitting his grease-smudged face. "Thought you might've forgotten about this." He grabbed the device.

The toss came without warning. Combat instinct kicked in. Diego's hand snapped up, caught it mid-flight. Cool metal. Familiar weight.

"Nice catch, old man. Fixed the screen and upgraded the processing core. Should run faster now." Jack leaned against his workbench. His cybernetic leg squeaked. Always that fucking squeak. "Unless it decides to explode. Which is always possible."

Diego checked the first message. "What's this about you being my executive assistant?"

Jack's eyebrows shot up. "Oh yeah, Kaito called." His prosthetic clicked. Weight shift. "Emergency food supplies arriving before the portal closes. Guess I'm supposed to track your schedule now." The wink came next. "Should I pencil in your 'meetings' with Dr. Smith?"

Diego's jaw clenched. "Watch it, Jack."

"Hey, just saying, check your collar for lipstick next time." The grin widened. "What would Maria think about her old man getting..."

"Luna blow up any more drones?"

"Nah, Emily radioed in. Her team's heading back, should make it before portal closure." Jack adjusted something on his leg. Click-whir-click. "Speaking of explosions, you might want to tell your girlfriend to stop leaving such obvious evidence..."

"That's enough." The command voice. Decades of making lieutenants jump.

Jack raised his hands. Mock surrender. That smirk still there. "Yes, sir, Mr. Smoochie face, sir."

Diego turned. Left. Jack's jokes hitting closer than comfortable.

The path to Maria's house wound past the hydroponics dome. Workers installed UV-filtered panels. Careful movements. Precise. Diego had insisted on proper safety protocols. No more Jack and Kayla's "creative" solutions that nearly killed three people last month.

The prefab house. Pristine white. Recent construction. Diego stopped at the steps. His knee screamed.

Children's laughter from the plaza. Isabella's voice among them.

Facing rogue AI felt easier than this conversation.

The door opened before his knuckles met wood. Maria. Dark eyes like his. Cargo pants, tank top, hair pulled back. Working clothes.

"Papa." The hug came fast. Her shampoo hit him.

Teaching her to ride a bike. Tucson. Before everything went to shit.

"I saw you coming. That leg's giving you trouble."

Her arms felt stronger now. The soft teenager gone. Muscle earned through survival. The girl who'd hidden behind his shoulder had become someone who faced supply shortages without flinching.

"Just needs rest."

"Jack fixed my tablet. Apparently appointed himself my executive assistant."

Maria's eyebrows rose. "Executive assistant? That explains his message about your 'important meetings.'" Her mouth curved. "Pretty sure he spelled executive with three X's."

Heat climbed Diego's neck. Damn Jack. "About that..."

"Papa, you don't have to explain." Her expression softened. "We've all lost too much to waste time worrying about what makes us happy. Now come inside before your leg gives out."

Inside. Cool air. Relief from Haven's heat that made breathing work. Children's artwork on walls. Isabella's careful Earth animals. Mateo's abstract Haven creatures.

The living room showed roots taking hold. Earth photos mixed with Haven specimens in jars. A tablet on the coffee table. Mateo's toy truck. Coffee scent from the kitchen.

Sunday mornings. Tucson. Elena humming.

Maria gestured at the couch. One of the few pieces they'd brought through. "Coffee?"

"Black."

Diego eased down. Stretched the leg. Lightning up his thigh.

The photo caught him: Maria and Manuel's wedding. Young. Hopeful. Before Resource Wars. Before impossible choices.

Maria returned with mugs. Settled across from him, feet tucked under. Teenager gesture. His chest tightened.

The coffee burned going down. Mission briefings. Planning sessions. This required different courage.

"Olivia and I..." His thumb traced the mug's rim. "Started during portal preparations. Long nights. Planning. She cuts through bullshit. Sees the heart of things."

Maria's silence. Afternoon light through windows. Patterns like the quantum gateway's shimmer.

"Remember when water filtration failed?" The ache radiated from old bone. "Thirty-six hours straight. Found her passed out over calculations. Brought coffee when she woke." Another sip. Liquid heat. "That's when things changed."

Her fingers had brushed his taking the mug. Her eyes lighting up at real coffee.

"She doesn't hide behind credentials. Gets dirty with us. Fights."

The Richardson twins. Numbers said no room. Olivia found a way.

"I wasn't looking for this, Mija." The mug felt heavy. Elena's smile surfaced. Tucson. Before Water Wars destroyed everything.

Maria leaned forward. "Papa, you've spent your life taking care of others. Military. Protecting us during the wars. Now Haven." A gesture around them. "When did you last do something for yourself?"

The question stung. Through the window, Isabella's laughter mixed with construction sounds.

"Your mother…" His throat closed.

Elena humming. Coffee. Sunday mornings.

"Would want you happy," Maria finished. Her hand squeezed his. Strong. Callused from construction. "We all do."

"Papa." Maria set down her mug. Click against table. "When Mama died, I waited for you to cry."

The words hit like sniper fire. Unexpected. Precise.

"I was twelve. Thought after the funeral, when we got home, you'd finally let it out." Her voice stayed level. Fingers twisting. "Instead, you unpacked your service pistol. Started checking windows."

The memory came unwanted. Maria curled on Elena's side of the bed. Clutching the pillow. Radio crackling. Riots spreading north. The neighborhood needed organizing. Supply runs required coordination.

"There wasn't time. Water riots spreading. You needed protection. The neighborhood…"

"Papa." Her hand covered his. "I used to lie awake. Listening to you walk circles. Every night. Checking locks. Cleaning weapons. Making lists. Never just… sitting with it. With her being gone."

Diego's vision blurred. Coffee carried Elena now. Her laugh dodging his attempts at fresh tortillas. The fierce arguments about deployments. Her touch when nightmares woke him.

"I couldn't..." Voice cracking. "If I started grieving, who protects you? Keeps lights on? Water running? If I fell apart..."

"You were afraid you'd never put yourself back together."

The diagnosis hung between them. Outside, children's voices. All he heard: his boots on hardwood. Night after night. Walking circles around loss he couldn't afford.

Maria leaned forward. Elena's determined expression. "Papa, know what I see when you look at Olivia?"

His throat worked. Nothing came.

"You remembering how to hope. Want something for yourself instead of just surviving." Elena's steel in her voice now. "But also pulling back when you get close. Like loving her betrays Mama."

The mug trembled. "What if I can't protect her either? What if..."

"What if you waste time together being afraid of losing it?"

Physical blow. Olivia's quiet strength. Her brilliant mind. How she looked at him. How many moments already lost?

"She doesn't need perfect, Papa. She needs present. All of you. Including the part that hurts for Mama."

Something broke loose in his chest. Elena's face. Not just final moments. Small moments locked away. Humming while folding laundry. Teaching Maria to read. Cupping his face after deployment nightmares.

"Elena." The name escaped. Confession. "Couldn't save her. Was deployed. Couldn't get back..."

Words dissolved. Raw. Broken. Military discipline crumbled. Static-filled communication. Desperate transport attempts. Arriving to find a grave. A daughter who'd learned the world took everything.

Maria's arms wrapped around him before the first sob finished. Diego didn't try for strong. Let himself be held. Years of grief poured out. Ragged gasps. The mug slipped. Maria caught it. Set it aside without breaking embrace.

Through tears, Olivia surfaced. Her hand during the water crisis. Warmth in her eyes. The fear keeping him from opening. Terrified loss would destroy him completely this time.

"So tired," he whispered. Voice rough. "So damn tired of carrying this alone."

Afternoon light painted floor patterns. Father and daughter held each other. First time since Elena's death without building walls. Grief still there. Would always be. Maybe Maria was right. Maybe he could carry it differently. Learn to love without forgetting.

The Last Door Slams Shut

D iego pushed through the conference room door. Coffee-stale air hit like a fist.

Haven's sun carved harsh angles through reinforced windows. Light and shadow. Chessboard patterns across metal.

The portable table groaned under computers and coffee mugs. One leaked. Steady drip onto the floor.

Mei hunched over her tablet, genetic sequences scrolling past too fast for anyone else to track. Olivia sat close enough their shoulders almost touched, pulling up the same data.

Kaito claimed the back wall. Arms crossed. Dark eyes moving. Always moving. Old habits.

Sarah Choi's hands sorted personnel files into stacks. Each one exactly aligned. The precision of someone who'd learned control through repetition.

Johnson positioned himself by the door. His palm rested on his sidearm. Not gripping. Just... there.

Jack had taken two chairs. His prosthetic leg stretched across the gap between them, metal catching the overhead lights. The whir when he shifted was barely audible over the facility's hum.

Everyone looked up when Diego entered. Normal meeting energy. Good.

"Where are we?" he asked, settling into his chair. The familiar ache in his shoulder flared as he leaned back.

Mei activated the central display with a soft chime. Charts materialized above the table, casting blue light across their faces. Tissue samples from their vat-grown livestock floated in the holographic space, cellular structures highlighted with phosphorescent markers that pulsed like tiny heartbeats.

"The vat-grown animals are showing unexpected genetic modifications," Mei said, her voice tight with concern. "Chickens, rabbits, even the early calf batches. We're seeing consistent cellular modifications across all vat-grown animals."

Diego studied the rotating samples, watching protein chains twist into configurations he didn't recognize. The display hummed softly, processing terabytes of genetic data. "How modified?"

"Every batch from the vats shows the same pattern," Olivia said, adjusting her glasses. "The changes appear stable and the meat tests safe for consumption. But it comes with a cost."

"Which is?" Jack said, metal fingers drumming against his thigh.

"Accelerated life cycles," Mei continued, manipulating the display to zoom in on cellular structures. "They reach maturity about seventeen percent faster, breed more frequently, and unfortunately, age faster. What should be an eight-year lifespan for rabbits becomes closer to six and a half years, based on our models."

The room went quiet except for the steady drip from the coffee mug and the low hum of the holographic display. Diego rubbed the scar on his temple, the familiar throb that came with bad news.

"Every batch is the same?" Sarah asked, leaning forward.

"Identical genetic modifications," Mei said. "Something in our vat systems is causing this. We're using local water, local nutrients, even filtered air from Haven's atmosphere. Despite decontamination protocols, some form of contamination is getting through and modifying the embryos during development."

"What about breeding them naturally?" Diego asked.

"That's where genetics gets interesting," Olivia said, pulling up reproduction charts. "The modifications appear to be dominant traits. If two modified animals breed, most offspring will be modified. But we'll get some normal Earth animals occasionally, depending on the genetic combinations."

Jack's cybernetic leg whirred as he shifted position. "So we get mostly fast-breeding, short-lived animals, with some normal ones mixed in?"

"Exactly. The enhanced animals breed faster but our models project shorter lives. The occasional normal offspring should live standard lifespans and breed at normal rates."

Mei's scientific detachment was slipping. "We can't predict the ratios or maintain stable population levels with that kind of genetic lottery."

The math hit him square in the chest, driving the air from his lungs. His shoulders ached under the sudden weight. Food shortage. Rationing. Someone would have to decide who got enough protein and who didn't.

"What about the larger animals?" Sarah asked. "Cattle, sheep?"

"First calf batch shows identical cellular patterns based on our analysis," Mei said. "Same seventeen percent acceleration across all metabolic processes. We're projecting similar shortened lifespans scaled to their size."

"Could we keep using the vats? Skip natural breeding entirely?" Diego asked.

Olivia shook her head. "Limited genetic material. We can't run vat production indefinitely without breeding programs to expand the genetic base. But natural breeding gives us unpredictable ratios of modified versus normal animals."

"And even if we could," Mei added, "the modified animals' accelerated reproductive cycles make planning impossible. One season we'll have surplus protein, the next we'll face serious shortages."

The conference room door burst open. Dr. Anderson hurried in, his usually neat appearance disheveled, short blonde hair mussed like he'd been running his hands through it.

"Michael?" Diego stood. "What's wrong?"

"I just finished running genetic stability tests on the pregnant colonists," Anderson said, catching his breath. "Maria Santos at sixteen weeks. The Chen family at twelve weeks. I was terrified after seeing Mei's animal data."

"Problems?" Diego's chest tightened.

Anderson shook his head quickly. "No changes. None. Clean genetic scans, normal fetal development." He activated his datapad, showing stable human fetal development patterns. "Human maternal biology is filtering out whatever's contaminating the vats. Liver, kidneys, spleen, placental barriers, they're all working together to protect developing humans entirely."

Relief flooded through him, followed immediately by a deeper dread settling in his gut like cold lead. No genetic changes in humans meant they remained unmodified. But it also meant no adaptation to Haven's environment. No enhanced reproduction to offset the unstable food supply.

"So humans reproduce at normal Earth rates," Sarah said, "while our food animals cycle through unpredictable genetic combinations."

"We'll have protein surpluses followed by severe shortages," Jack added. "No way to predict the timing."

The weight settled deeper into Diego's chest. Someone would have to decide who got fed during the shortages and who didn't.

"What do we need for long-term sustainability?" he asked, his voice rougher than intended.

Mei brought up population models. Numbers cascaded through the air like falling rain: caloric requirements, production rates, sustainability projections. "Without predictable livestock yields, we need agricultural expansion and significantly larger human populations to maintain genetic diversity and labor capacity. Three hundred more people from Earth minimum. And much larger families to build sustainable population levels before the protein volatility destabilizes everything."

"How many children?" Sarah asked, though her tone suggested she already knew.

"Three to four per couple. Starting immediately. We need to establish breeding populations large enough to weather the food instability."

The words settled over the room, heavy and inescapable. Diego's vision blurred for a moment as old memories clawed their way to the surface. Food allocation boards. Medical treatment rationed according to reproductive potential. Elena's file stamped DECLINED in red letters because her cancer treatment wouldn't yield sufficient population benefits.

His throat constricted. "You're talking about breeding quotas."

"We're talking about survival," Olivia replied, but her voice lacked conviction. "Colony-level genetic sustainability."

The recycled air pressed against his lungs. Diego loosened his collar, but it didn't help. The conference room walls seemed closer than they had a minute ago.

"People won't accept reproductive mandates," Sarah said, her fingers unconsciously tapping against her tablet.

"They'll have to understand the biological necessity," Mei said, her scientific detachment slipping. "The greater good requires sacrifice."

Greater good. The phrase landed like a gut punch. He'd heard it before, in different rooms, from different mouths wearing the same expressions of clinical determination. Always followed by decisions that destroyed individual lives for statistical outcomes.

Jack shifted in his chair, cybernetic leg whirring softly. "Sounds familiar."

"It's not the same thing," Olivia said, but her voice cracked slightly.

Diego walked to the window, needing distance from the population data floating behind him like ghosts. Outside, Haven stretched endlessly under its alien sun, the landscape they'd fought to claim and build with their own hands. They'd built this place to be free from the tyranny of algorithms and efficiency calculations. Or so they'd told themselves.

"Elena died because of the greater good," he said without turning around, his breath fogging the reinforced glass.

The room fell silent behind him. Even the holographic display seemed to dim.

"That was different," Mei said quietly.

"Was it?" Diego faced the group again, the familiar rage building in his chest. "We're looking at data that tells us people need to have a specific number of children. For colony survival. How exactly is that different?"

Anderson opened his mouth, then closed it, his medical training warring with his conscience.

"The science is clear," Mei said, but she'd closed her datapad.

"Science was clear then too," Diego said, his voice cold and steady, the tone that ended arguments. "Elena's reproductive potential was calculated at point-four children due to her age and medical history. The AI decided that wasn't efficient enough. So they let her die."

Sarah set down her personnel files with deliberate care. "Information is different from mandates."

"Is it?" Diego asked, touching the scar on his temple where the shrapnel had torn through. "When we tell people their reproductive choices determine colony survival? When we hand them data that says they're not having enough children fast enough?"

The population models still glowed in the air above them, unchanged by moral arguments or personal trauma. The food crisis remained real regardless of their discomfort with the solutions. Math didn't care about ethics.

"So what do we do?" Jack asked, his question cutting through the tension.

Diego rubbed his temples, the familiar ache building behind his eyes. The same headache he'd gotten reading Elena's medical files, watching her hope die one bureaucratic decision at a time.

"We give them the information. All of it. Then we let them choose."

"That's unpredictable," Mei said, scientific precision clashing with uncertainty.

"Yeah," Diego said. "It is."

Kaito straightened against the wall, speaking for the first time since the meeting began. "Predictable usually means someone else is making the choices."

The conference room went quiet. The population data spun slow on the holo-display, red projections catching light like blood on steel. Through the window, Haven's landscape ran to the horizon. Beautiful. Dangerous. Both.

"We provide support," Diego said, though he wasn't sure what that would look like yet. "Medical care, resources, education about what we're facing. But no mandates. No quotas. No algorithms deciding who lives and who doesn't."

"And if people choose not to have enough children?" Olivia asked, her voice thin with worry.

Diego stared at the sustainability projections floating between them, watching the colony's future balanced on a knife's edge. He thought of Elena, of all the people who'd died for someone else's calculations of the greater good.

"Then we figure something else out," he said. "Because the moment we start making those decisions for people, we become exactly what we left behind."

They nodded. They pushed back from the table, movements deliberate despite the exhaustion etched in their faces.

Diego checked his watch. "Before we wrap up, we have another situation. Admiral Wilkins stuck his neck out for us, and now his family's at risk."

The ventilation system's hum filled the quiet room. Diego tasted metal on his tongue from the recycled air.

"Wilkins redirected three corvettes today. APU patrols closing in on our position." Diego's jaw tightened. "He's kept us ahead of them so far."

Kaito's eyebrows lifted. Sarah's lips parted in a silent "wow." Olivia's datapad dimmed as she looked up, eyes wide.

"If anyone discovers what he did, he'll face court-martial at best. At worst," Diego paused, letting them fill in the blanks, "you know how the APU handles traitors."

Sarah's pen stopped moving across her notepad. The silence stretched out, broken only by the soft cycling of the air system.

"I offered him and his family sanctuary here," Diego continued. "They're heading to Playa now, but the APU will connect him to these events soon."

Mei frowned. "Can we accommodate them with our resources?"

Diego nodded. "We'll stretch things, but it's doable. The Admiral's expertise would be invaluable, strategically and operationally."

Kaito leaned forward. "We owe him that much. Without his intervention, we wouldn't be having this meeting."

Olivia glanced at her display, blue light washing across her face. "We can make it work with careful planning."

Something loosened in Diego's chest. One crisis was addressed, though it connected to everything else they faced.

"We're running critically low on stabilization resources," he said, leaning forward. "Three days, maybe less." No point in sugar-coating it. "After that, anyone still on Earth stays there permanently."

He fixed his gaze on Kaito. "What are our chances of securing more metals quickly? Be straight with me."

Kaito's fingers steepled. His pulse hammered against his ribs.

Jack cleared his throat. "About that meeting you missed, boss. Manuel got back with the equipment last night. We've been running diagnostics since dawn." He nodded to Kaito. "Tell him about those additional mining bots we tested."

Kaito paused, measuring his words carefully. "The acquisition included additional mining bots. Manuel was persuasive in negotiating for them as part of the package."

Diego narrowed his eyes. "And I'm just hearing about this now because...?"

"You missed our meeting this morning," Kaito replied smoothly, adjusting his tie. "I thought it best to wait until I had your full attention."

The genetic crisis had pushed the entire meeting from Diego's mind. Diego's eyes stayed locked on Kaito for three long seconds before he looked away.

Diego fixed Jack with a stare that could strip paint. "Run that by me again?"

Jack shifted uncomfortably. "Boss, we weren't just moving equipment. Manuel also managed to snag your annual supply of smile vitamins. Though I see you haven't taken any yet."

Olivia ducked behind her datapad. Diego caught the corner of her mouth twitching.

"Since you've got energy for jokes," Diego said with dangerous quietness, "you can test those bots personally. I hear the northern range is lovely this time of year."

Jack's grin faltered. "Come on, boss. Someone's gotta break the tension around here. We've been drowning in bad news all morning."

Diego maintained his stern look before releasing a short laugh. "Next time, try coffee instead of smart-ass comments. Now tell me about these bots before I reconsider the caves."

"Same specs as our current units," Kaito explained. "But now we can run multiple extraction sites simultaneously."

Diego caught Olivia's eye. She gave him the slightest nod.

Diego scanned the readouts. His knee throbbed. "If these work." His index finger tapped against his thumb. Counting. Always counting. "Two more openings. Maybe three if we push it."

Dozens more families. More genetic diversity. More people who might actually survive what came next.

His chest loosened. Slightly.

"Time's against us," he said, pushing back from the table. "Let's get to work."

Mei's head came up. "One more trip. Maybe. Who goes?"

The question sat between them, sharp-edged and unavoidable. Who gets a new life in Haven, and who faces Earth's collapse?

Diego dragged his fingers through his hair. "Families with young children first, then critical skills. We need as much diversity of DNA as possible now."

Sarah nodded, making notes. "I'll compile a list with those criteria."

"Admiral Wilkins' family must be included," Olivia added. "He's risking everything."

Diego nodded, feeling the weight of that decision. "They'll be on the list."

"Mei and I will expand agricultural capacity," Ethan said. "We'll adjust crop plans based on the genetic data and monitor food safety."

Sarah spoke next. "I'll compile priority lists for crossings so everyone's ready when needed."

"I'll get those mining bots running," Jack added, grinning. "I promise they won't explode. Mostly."

Olivia's eyes went skyward, but she smiled. "I'll recalibrate portal systems for maximum efficiency. Every crossing must count."

Kaito leaned forward. "I'll pursue additional stabilization metals through my contacts."

Diego scanned the faces. Exhaustion carved into every line. But their spines stayed straight.

This. This was why they kept going. Why the math didn't matter when it said they'd fail.

"Makes me wonder why you keep me around," he said, allowing himself a small smile.

"Someone's gotta keep your ego in check," Jack replied with renewed energy.

Laughter cut through the weight pressing down on them.

"Let's get to work before I start believing you," Diego said, shaking his head.

The team dispersed, movements quick and purposeful. As they left, Diego felt something he hadn't experienced in days: genuine hope. Not desperation masquerading as optimism, but the real thing. Seventy-two hours to prove they could beat these odds, too.

Olivia lingered behind. Diego turned to her, seeing his own determination reflected in her green eyes.

"Thank you," he said, the words carrying more weight than a simple expression of gratitude.

She met his gaze, nodding once. "This is what we came here for, Diego. To build something better."

He nodded, and as she passed, her fingers briefly touched his.

Tonight they would begin mining. Tomorrow, Wilkins' family will arrive. And in seventy-two hours, they'd either find enough materials to save dozens more families or face the permanent reality of separation from Earth, with all the genetic consequences that entailed.

The holo-comm's urgent chirp cut through the silence. Diego rolled upright, the motion automatic after decades of training. Twelve hours of sleep, the first real rest in weeks. Olivia's warmth pressed against his side, her breathing unchanged.

He reached for the device without disturbing her.

Squinting at the screen in his quarters on Haven, Luna's name pulsed in pale blue letters.

"Luna? What's going on?" Sleep roughened his voice.

Luna's image flickered from Earth-side, punk-red hair wild around her face. Server racks and blinking lights filled the background. Warning klaxons wailed behind her. "Diego, we've got multiple inbounds. Mia's eight minutes out with Admiral Wilkins' family, but we have a problem. James was supposed to bring thirty-five people. He's got six hundred refugees crammed in there instead. And the seismic activity is screwing with our portal..."

Static burst across the connection. The image dissolved into pixels.

"Luna?" Diego's chest tightened. The smell of overheating electronics drifted from the comm unit.

The signal snapped back. "Stabilization is failing. We've got a situation here on Earth." Luna's hands flew across controls beyond the camera's view. Behind her, technicians rushed between stations, voices sharp with panic. Someone shouted about power fluctuations.

Diego stood and stretched, working the stiffness from his shoulders. The old shrapnel wound in his left shoulder flared. He brushed a strand of hair from Olivia's face, the gesture automatic now.

"Luna, talk to me." He paced the narrow space between wall and bed, bare feet silent on cold metal. "What's the..."

"Six hundred?" Olivia sat up, hair catching light from the screens. Sleep still fogged her eyes.

"James is inbound. Too many people." Luna's voice cut through static, sharp edges on every word. "Mia's fighting the storm. Admiral's family with her."

More alarms shrieked. The sound vibrated through Diego's fillings.

"Storm front's accelerating," Luna said. Her gum popped. "Seismic alerts spiking. Shit. Hold on."

Another alarm joined the chorus.

The connection struggled. Background chaos bled through. Shouting voices. Equipment failure alarms. The harsh buzz of overloaded circuits.

"Mia reports she's got enough fuel to make it back, but with these conditions..." Luna's voice cut out. Another alarm shrieked. "Shit, the weather system's..."

"She knows what she's doing." The words came out harder than intended. Diego's chest tightened. Thomas's family. Up there. In that storm.

Olivia swung her legs over the side of the bed. Grabbed her tablet from the nightstand. Her fingers moved across the screen.

On the holo-comm, Luna dragged her hand down her face. That gesture always preceded bad news.

"James just radioed..." Luna's voice cut out as alarms blared. "Loading his scheduled thirty-five when... shit, we're losing the connection... everything went to hell."

The image flickered, dissolved, came back. James's panicked voice bled through the static: "Hundreds of people charging the gates. They stormed..."

Diego's hand found the scar on his temple. The familiar groove under his fingertips.

"Six hundred people?" His throat tightened. "Forced their way aboard?"

Christ.

"He doesn't know exact numbers but estimates..." The transmission broke up. "APU security forces showed up, weapons ready. James had to choose: take off or watch people get gunned down..."

Static consumed the connection. The lights in Diego's quarters flickered.

"Luna?"

The signal snapped back. "Wouldn't abandon civilians. APU authorities started evacuating terminals. The public is panicking, screaming, rushing..." Another equipment failure alarm shrieked. "Most are parents with children."

Diego caught Olivia's gaze. She gripped her datapad, knuckles showing white. "Portal's redlining," she said, studying her readings through the flickering display. "Field collapse risk if we push..."

"Six hundred people scattered across dimensions." The words came out flat. His chest felt hollow. Kids who didn't understand what was happening. Parents just trying to...

"We need options." His voice carried the edge of command. "Luna, what's James's..."

"Fifteen minutes to arrival, assuming the weather..." Luna's face had gone pale on the comm screen. Earth's facility lights flickered behind her. Warning klaxons competed with human voices. "Weather holds."

Diego pressed his fingers against his forehead. The weight of six hundred lives pressed down. Olivia's hand touched his arm, warm and steady against the chaos.

"Luna." His voice carried across the dimensions. "Get James on the line. We transport fifty at a time, no..."

"Already connecting..." Static burst. "Working on more resources, but they'll be processed after..."

"James," Luna's voice came through static and crowd noise, "Diego needs..."

James's face filled the screen. Exhaustion. Deep lines. Behind him, bodies packed the cabin too tight. Children screaming. Engine roar. Adults shouting over both.

"Situation?" His voice cracked through the static.

Background noise from the jet exploded: crying, shouting, someone screaming about their child. James turned away from the camera. "Everyone, calm down! We're going to..."

"Hell of a thing," James said, turning back. "Six hundred desperate people crammed in here. A bunch are kids. When I tell them only fifty can go through..."

"Keep them calm as long..."

The connection died. Emergency lighting kicked in throughout Diego's quarters, bathing everything in red.

"Luna?"

"Still here. James is..." Her transmission fluctuated. "Addressing the crowd over the planes overhead speakers."

Diego cut the connection. Olivia was staring at her screen, color draining from her face. Her hands shook as she magnified something. Warning alerts pulsed across her display.

"What is it?" He moved closer, looking over her shoulder.

"Seven-point-oh earthquake." Her voice came out barely controlled. Red warning indicators pulsed across her map overlay like a heartbeat. "Eighty miles from Isla Mujeres. Twenty minutes ago."

The familiar weight settled in his chest. Heavier now. Personal. "How long do we..."

"Eighteen minutes." Olivia's hand trembled against the desk edge. "Tsunami projection. Direct hit on Cancún."

Diego's mind flashed to the hundreds of desperate people trying to rush into the crucible facility.

"Get me Luna again," he ordered, grabbing his boots and yanking them on while Olivia connected the call.

Luna's face appeared on the comm, more worried than before, the Earth facility behind her now in even greater chaos. "Diego, the seismic..."

"I know. How many people are still at the shore facilities on your side?"

"Over four hundred."

Diego cursed under his breath. The same story everywhere. Panic makes people stupid.

"Tell security teams to evacuate those people. Anyone who doesn't move gets marked off the list completely." Diego said. "And Luna, get me Mia."

The holo-comm crackled, and Mia's face appeared, standing in what seemed to be an Earth-side command center. "Martinez, I assume you're tracking this?"

"Mia, you're cleared for immediate landing. Get those people through the portal."

"Descending now through some nasty weather. Diego, I've got thirty-eight passengers back here, including the Admiral's family. We're way over safe capacity, but what's the alternative?"

"No alternative. Just get them through." Another tremor registered on Olivia's data-pad. Diego's left knee throbbed. "The tsunami's coming. Clock's running."

"Roger that." Rotors whined through the connection. "Touching down in two minutes."

Diego turned to Olivia. "How long until the wave hits the facility?"

"Fourteen minutes, maybe less." She pulled up satellite feed. The water offshore had pulled back, leaving a massive depression that was already beginning to surge back toward the coast. "Quake was shallow. Wave formation is accelerating."

Through the comm, Mia barked orders at her passengers.

"Wheels down," Mia reported. "Moving people to the portal now."

"Good. Get through fast, Mia. Anyone who hesitates gets left behind." Diego's said. "Once you're through, we're shutting it down until this passes."

"Understood. First group entering the portal now."

Diego gripped Olivia's shoulder. "If you see any signs of pre-collapse, shut it down. I don't care who's still waiting. We can't risk losing everyone."

Olivia nodded. Her tablet showed readings fluctuating with each group passing through. Numbers are hovering just below critical thresholds.

Diego switched channels. "Luna, get your people through now. That's an order."

"But the quantum field stability requires constant monitoring, and if I leave the controls..."

"Luna." Diego's voice dropped. "Move. Now."

"Teams Two and Three are heading to the portal," Luna reported, her hands moving across her workstation in rapid keystrokes.

"What about you?"

"Someone needs to monitor these systems until the last possible moment. I'll be right behind the final group. Promise."

Luna stared at her screens for a moment, then began typing with renewed intensity.

"Wait. I can route the exterior cameras through the communications array," Luna announced.

"Do it."

The display screens in his quarters flickered, shifting to live feeds from exterior cameras around the Earth facility. The coastline stretched out before them, water retreating further into the ocean.

"Olivia, you see this?"

Olivia nodded, syncing her datapad with Luna's feed while monitoring portal status.

"Perfect. I can monitor the wave's progress and shut down the portal."

Diego continued issuing commands through his holo-comm. Every team member is accounted for and moving.

The live feed showed the wave building offshore.

"Mia," he called through comms, "status report."

"Queued up for the portal," Mia replied. "Just a few more people."

Diego's attention was split between Olivia's wave monitoring and Luna's real-time adjustments.

"Good work. Now get yourself to that portal."

Diego stared at the video feed. The wave offshore had grown massive. "Portal's redlining!" Warning alarms blared through their facility.

"Shit." Diego gripped the console edge until his joints ached. "Olivia, tell me you saw that."

The seismic disruption registered on Olivia's monitors as the Earth-side quantum field destabilized. Diego watched the readouts spike into critical ranges.

"Luna, get to that portal right now!" He barked into the comm. "That aftershock, it's destabilizing our connection."

The feed showed the wave cresting against the shoreline. Water moving with the inevitability of a landslide.

"Diego, the portal's stability is dropping fast!" Olivia worked frantically. "The quantum field is destabilizing. We're losing connection with the control panel. We need the manual shutoff!"

Through the comm, Luna's voice crackled with static. "Moving now, Diego! But we've still got families here. I can't just abandon..."

"Luna, there's no time! Get through that portal now, or get clear!" Diego watched the portal's energy readings spike beyond safe parameters. "That's an order!"

Diego burst through the courtyard entrance. Time splintered.

The portal's quantum field rippled. Mercury disturbed, spreading wrong. That steady hum gone. Now a warble that set his teeth on edge.

Dark water gushed through from Earth. Crushing force. Already ankle-deep around his boots, rising fast. The smell hit him—bitter, chemical, Earth's dying oceans concentrated into liquid despair. Cold bit through his pants. His knee screamed.

People stumbled. Fell. Picked themselves up from mud that hadn't been there thirty seconds ago. Panicked shouts bounced off walls, fighting with the roar of rushing water.

"Luna! Mia! Report!" Diego's voice cut through. He was already moving, sprinting toward the portal frame. "Status!"

Silence.

Wrong. All of it wrong.

Static crackled through his comm. Rushing water underneath. Distant screams from Earth, faint but there. Always fucking there.

He ran for the manual shutoff panel. Boots sloshing through mud. The portal's field convulsed, edges bleeding purple that had no business existing in nature.

His datapad's monitor feed showed it. A wall of water. Massive. Bearing down on the Earth-side facility.

Through the portal itself, seawater sprayed. Hit Haven's packed dirt. Wrong place. Wrong world.

"No, no, no..." The tsunami was about to breach the gateway.

More water surged through. A familiar figure burst through the portal's surface: Mia, her flight suit soaked and hair plastered to her face, flung forward onto Haven's ground by the rushing water.

Just as he reached for the emergency shutoff, a small carrier case tumbled through the portal from Earth, sliding across the wet ground. An angry yowl emerged from inside as it skidded to a stop.

His fist slammed the shutoff. The portal collapsed, the quantum field imploded with a deafening crack, energy crackling across his skin as it collapsed into nothingness. The sound was deafening, and then silence. All that remained were stunned people strewn about the courtyard and the water rushing down the hill away from the encampment, leaving only an empty frame where their connection to Earth had been.

Keying his comm with shaking fingers, Diego called out. "Luna! Luna, come in! Luna, respond! Please..." His voice echoed across Haven's flooded courtyard. Static crackled back at him.

Mia stumbled forward, covered with mud. Her hands shook so hard she tucked them under her arms. Her eyes were wild, face drained of color, bearing that hollow look of someone who'd just survived when she shouldn't have.

"She was right behind me, Diego. Luna was helping people through. She tossed that cat carrier through first, then she turned back. Said something about a kid. They were right there. Right there."

Before him, this woman who'd faced down gunfire without flinching started to break apart. She pressed her hands against her mouth, shoulders shuddering as she fought to contain what was clawing up from inside her.

"Oh god, they were right behind me. I heard Luna calling out orders to close the security door. I should have reached back, I should have..."

"Luna!" The shout into his comm was pointless, he knew. The quantum field had collapsed. Anyone still on the other side when that wave hit...

A strangled sob escaped Mia's throat. "I should have... God, I should have waited. Should have grabbed her arm, pulled her through. I should have made sure she was..."

Dead air crackled from his comm. The device dropped from numb fingers. The brilliant hacker who'd saved their asses more times than he could count. The woman who never took shit from anyone but would walk through fire for a friend.

His knees hit the wet ground. The impact was nothing compared to the crushing weight in his chest. Luna was gone.

The reality tore through him like shrapnel, each breath a struggle as the cold mud soaked into his clothes. His mind tried to reject what he knew was true. Luna, who'd cracked through APU firewalls with that cocky smile. Her take-charge attitude during their darkest moments. Her fierce loyalty that never wavered, not once.

The tears came hot and fast, streaking down his weathered face as memories crashed over him. Luna, breaking into secured networks while humming punk rock under her breath. Luna, staying up all night to trace a security breach. Luna, making coffee at four in the morning and cursing at malfunctioning hardware with vocabulary that would make a drill sergeant blush.

Gone. All of those people are gone.

The world went quiet around him. Someone crying nearby. Everything else felt muffled, distant. In that moment of utter stillness, the finality crashed down on him. Earth was gone. Luna was gone. The billions they'd left behind might as well be in another universe now.

Kneeling there in the cold mud, sixty-four years old and broken, every mission he'd led, every soldier he'd lost, every choice that had brought them to this moment pressed down upon him. He'd failed to protect her when she'd always been there for the mission.

Olivia's hand found his shoulder, steady and grounding. She held him for a moment, her own grief a quiet presence beside his. Then she rose, her voice cutting through the chaos with quiet authority.

"Sarah." The word came out steady. Had to. "Full headcount. Now. Processing stations in the main hall." Olivia's hand cut toward the medical building. "Medical emergencies east. Engineering teams, get pumps on that water before it hits the electrical systems."

People moved. Following her voice through the smoke.

Diego's vision swam. Couldn't track the motion. Sarah's crew scattered with their datapads, the screens casting sick blue light through the haze. Bodies to count. Living ones first. The dead weren't going anywhere.

"Move!" Sarah barked at someone frozen in the mud. "If you can walk, you can help."

The water kept rising. Black with Earth's poison. Two inches. Three. Creeping toward the junction boxes like it had all the time in the world.

Diego tried to stand straight. The ground tilted. Or maybe that was him.

Through the smoke, Olivia's voice cut clear. Giving orders. Making sense of chaos. Christ, when had she gotten so good at this? When had he gotten so old?

His comm buzzed. Priority alert from the settlement. He couldn't read it. Letters swimming. Hand shaking too hard to hold the device steady.

The counting continued. Each number another person who'd made it through. Each gap in the sequence someone who hadn't.

Diego blinked. Tried to focus. Dust. Exhaustion. His vision wouldn't clear.

Sarah's team spread out, tablets glowing through smoke. Counting. Living first. The dead could wait.

The dead could wait.

They needed a leader. He knelt in the mud, useless, while Olivia did what he couldn't. What he should be doing.

"Get those children inside," she ordered, pointing toward the main hall. As the survivors moved with new purpose.

Pushing himself to his feet, muscles aching from cold and the weight of loss, Diego stood. Haven remained. They would survive. Luna's sacrifice wouldn't be meaningless if they built something worth her life.

But right now, in this moment, with mud sliding from his boots and Luna's angry cat yowling from its carrier, Diego bore every one of his sixty-four years and the crushing weight of everyone he'd failed to bring home.

THE WORK OF GRIEF

Diego stood before the portal frame, its metal edges still radiating heat from the energy discharge. Where the shimmering barrier had been moments before, only empty air remained.

Nothing. Just the hollow arch of titanium against Haven's bruised sky.

Luna's voice echoed in his memory. Clear. Determined. Then the comm crackled with static and the sound of rushing water before cutting to silence. Logically, she was 'Missing in Action'. But that final, empty crackle of the comm hadn't felt like a question; it had felt like a verdict.

A soft meow drifted from the platform's edge. Professor Whiskers sat in his carrier, yellow eyes reflecting the harsh work lights. The metal handle was still warm from Luna's grip three minutes ago. Diego's fingers traced the exact spot where hers had been.

"She got you out, didn't she?"

The cat pressed against the mesh, purring. Diego remembered Luna arguing with him three days ago about power distribution, her hair still damp from working in the coolant tunnels. She'd called him an "overgrown boy scout" when he'd insisted on safety protocols. He'd never hear her voice again.

Wind stirred the alien vegetation growing along the platform's edges. The air here was too clean, too pure. It made his lungs work harder, like breathing mountain air after decades of recycled atmosphere. Haven's air. Home now, whether they liked it or not.

Diego straightened. Sixty-three people needed him to be functional.

"Move!" Diego's voice cut through the ambient noise. "Jack, I need those generators online. Sarah, count every soul. We're not losing anyone else."

The team scattered. Boots rang against the metal grating as people hurried to follow orders. Equipment clanged. Someone shouted a status report about power fluctuations.

In the middle of the controlled chaos, Olivia appeared at his elbow. Her t-shirt clung to her shoulders, soaked through, and mud streaked her arms. She stared at the empty portal frame, tears cutting tracks through the grime on her face.

"The field matrix is gone," she said. "I know you're thinking about forcing it back online. But the quantum substrate collapsed completely. Any attempt to reopen it would create a cascade failure. We'd lose everyone here."

Diego sighed. "Copy that." The words came out rougher than intended.

Olivia stayed beside him, close enough that her shoulder almost touched his arm. Neither spoke. The dead portal frame stood between them and everything they'd left behind.

Diego turned to face the scattered survivors. Work lights cast harsh shadows across their faces. Haven's alien landscape stretched beyond the platform, all twisted trees and glowing undergrowth. The air shimmered with humidity and carried scents he couldn't identify.

Jack attacked the primary generator housing with a crowbar, his movements sharp and violent. His cybernetic leg whirred with each pivot. Sparks flew as he pried open an access panel.

"Quantum stabilizers are shot, but if I reroute through the auxiliary coupling..." He yanked components free and tossed them aside. "Son of a bitch. Just need to recalibrate the dimensional frequency matrix."

"Jack." Olivia stepped toward him.

He ignored her, his hands moving frantically across control surfaces. Sweat beaded on his forehead despite the cool air. "I can fix this. I've rebuilt worse systems from scrap."

"Jack, listen to me."

"No." He slammed his palm against the generator housing. The metal dented. "I'm not listening to anything until I get this goddamn portal working again."

Olivia moved closer. Her voice dropped. "The quantum substrate is gone. Even you can't fix physics. It will take years to mine and process the resources to rebuild it."

Jack's hands stopped moving. He stared at the exposed circuitry for a long moment. Then he picked up a wrench and hurled it across the platform. It clanged off the portal frame and skittered into the darkness.

"Fucking quantum mechanics."

Admiral Wilkins stood near the equipment staging area. His uniform was soaked through, but his spine remained straight. His hands were clasped behind his back in perfect military posture. A muscle jumped in his cheek like a timer counting down to something breaking.

His children huddled against his legs. Emily's face was streaked with tears, and Michael clutched a stuffed animal to his chest. Both stared at their father with wide, frightened eyes.

"Dr. Smith." The Admiral's voice carried military precision. "What's the status on portal restoration?"

Olivia approached slowly, her expression careful. "The portal is gone, Thomas. The quantum field collapsed when the connection was severed. If we tried to force it open now, the energy backlash would kill everyone on this platform."

The Admiral's rigid composure shattered. His legs simply ceased to hold him. He sank to the muddy ground and crushed his children against his chest, the sound from his throat a ragged, guttural keen.

Sarah crossed the platform toward them, her boots moving carefully through the puddles. Her boots moved carefully through the puddles. She crouched beside the Admiral and placed her hand on his shoulder.

"Come on," she said, her voice barely audible over the generator noise. "There's space in the medical bay. You can sit with them somewhere dry."

The Admiral let her help him to his feet. Water dripped from his uniform. His children pressed close to his sides, small hands gripping his pants.

They walked toward the medical station, leaving dark footprints on the concrete.

The emergency was over. The crisis was just beginning.

Diego turned back to the dead portal. The metal reflected Haven's strange light, casting broken shadows across the platform. Sixty-three more souls under his protection now. Luna had made sure they got this far.

Diego picked up Professor Whiskers' carrier and headed toward the others.

Cold seeped through Diego's wet clothes.

People moved around, checking equipment, whispering medical updates. Boots splashed through puddles.

Diego forced himself to move, each step deliberate. Movement helped when thinking hurt too much. Children moved through the shellshocked crowd with purpose that stopped him cold.

Isabella guided a small boy clutching a worn stuffed rabbit. Tear tracks cut clean lines through the dirt on his face. She spoke quietly, her voice steady despite the chaos.

"Dr. Choi is growing rabbits right now," he heard her say. "Maybe tomorrow we could visit them."

The boy's grip on his stuffed animal loosened. Nearby, Mateo helped a girl his age with her backpack, his small hands methodical as he checked each zipper and strap.

These kids moved differently than normal children. No games. No chatter. Their voices mixed with equipment noise and status reports like they were part of the operation.

Similar scenes played out across the platform. Children who'd been on Haven for weeks now guided newcomers through processing lines, leading families toward stations.

A small hand tugged Diego's sleeve. He looked down to find Mateo grinning up at him, the expression jarring against the grief hanging over the platform.

"Abuelo, can I show Amy where the glowing flowers are? She doesn't believe they change colors."

Diego knelt, wet ground soaked through his pants, Mateo's eyes held something too old for five years.

"That's a wonderful idea, mijo." Diego ruffled Mateo's hair. "But we need to wait. Amy's parents need to know where she is right now."

Mateo's brow furrowed with real concentration. "Why are they crying so much? Haven is safe."

Diego chose his words carefully. "Remember the big storms in Tucson? The ones that flooded streets?"

Mateo nodded.

"On the other side of the portal, there was a wave bigger than any storm we've ever seen. It was very scary for Amy and her family." Diego glanced at the dead portal frame, twisted metal still radiating heat. "That's why we closed it."

"Like when the door goes SLAM for the scary dust! Right, Abuelo?" Mateo's face turned serious.

Diego nodded, his weathered hand ruffling the boy's hair. "Just like that, mijo."

"So Amy needs to stay with her parents for now. Later, when they feel better, you can show her all the amazing things about Haven."

Mateo considered this with the gravity of someone weighing important decisions, then nodded. "I'll tell her about the flowers now so she has something good to think about."

Diego looked at the small girl standing beside Mateo. Brown eyes wide but not panicked. Her clothes still carried Earth's acrid dust, marking her as one of the last evacuees.

"Where are your parents, Amy?" Diego softened his tone, knees protesting as he knelt beside her.

Amy pointed toward Sarah's station, where a couple were finishing paperwork. The woman's dark hair escaped a messy bun in weather-beaten strands, and the man's security uniform bore O'Reilly's unit patches.

"Let's make our way over there." Diego stood, offering his hand. Amy hesitated before taking it, small fingers ice-cold against his calloused palm. Mateo bounced alongside as they walked, his energy the only normal thing left in the world.

"Mama, Papa!" Amy called out. Her parents turned, and Diego watched years of held breath finally release.

"Diego Martinez, head of operations." He extended his free hand to Amy's father. "Your daughter's already friends with my grandson."

"Jared Vaulker." The man's handshake was firm despite exhaustion that went bone-deep. "This is my wife, Zoey. We were with O'Reilly's security detail in Tucson."

"Can I show Amy the glowing flowers?" Mateo bounced on his toes, five years old breaking through the serious act. "Please?"

Diego smiled at his grandson's energy. Even here, even now, the boy found wonder worth sharing.

"Mijo, how about we give Amy's family a day to settle in?" Diego squeezed Mateo's shoulder. "Tomorrow you can show her the baby chickens. Dr. Choi says they're peeping like crazy now."

Mateo's eyes lit up. "The yellow fluffy ones? Can I show her how they eat the special food?"

"If Dr. Choi approves." Diego's eyes moved to the Vaulkers. They leaned into this. Small thing. Normal thing. "The chickens are part of our agricultural program. First livestock born in Haven."

Zoey managed a smile that reached her eyes. "That sounds wonderful. Amy loves animals." She brushed her daughter's hair back. "But your abuelo is right, cariño. We need to get settled."

Amy's face brightened at the prospect of seeing chicks, fear receding beneath the promise of small, living things that weren't afraid.

"The chickens make funny noises," Mateo whispered, leaning close to Amy. "And they run really fast when you give them treats."

Diego excused himself, watching as Mateo launched into another excited description. The boy's enthusiasm carved a small space of light in the darkness before the weight of their losses resettled on Diego's shoulders.

Across the platform, Olivia, Emily, and Sarah huddled near the medical station, voices low but urgent. As he approached, Emily's words reached him.

"We should set up a memorial service tomorrow for everyone we lost."

The words found their mark. An image of Luna chomping on bubble gum, that choppy red hair falling into her eyes, flashed through his mind. Professional loss was one thing. Losing a friend cut deeper.

He approached with the measured stride that came automatically after decades of command. Sarah clutched her datapad. Names of the dead already compiled, no doubt. Categorized. Timestamped. Olivia met his gaze, and he saw his own hollow exhaustion reflected there.

"A memorial service would help everyone process what happened," Olivia said, her voice carrying careful control. "Not just to mourn, but to acknowledge what we've accomplished. Every person here represents someone saved."

She turned to Emily and Sarah. "Could you two gather volunteers to help set it up for tomorrow night? Something honoring both our losses and our future."

Emily nodded. 'I've got some ideas. Maria does too, let's bring her in on this.

"I'll create a complete list of those we lost," Sarah said, fingers already moving across her tablet. "And make sure every family can contribute something meaningful. Their stories deserve telling."

As Diego listened to them plan, soft pressure against his leg made him look down. Professor Whiskers had escaped his carrier and wound between Diego's ankles, purring despite the chaos around them. The cat looked up at him with amber eyes, completely unbothered by the grief hanging over the platform.

"Luna's cat should be at the memorial too," Diego said, reaching down to stroke the orange fur. "She gave her life making sure others made it through, including this little guy."

The cat's relentless purr cut through the heavy quiet. Across the platform, Mateo was still describing Haven's wonders to Amy, his small hands gesturing excitedly as her parents listened with the desperate attention of people grabbing onto hope. Isabella guided another lost child toward the processing stations, her young voice calm and sure.

Professor Whiskers bumped his head against Diego's palm, demanding more attention. The memorial would happen tomorrow. The dead would be honored. And these children would keep doing what they'd learned to do: show newcomers that even after everything, there were still small miracles to discover.

Diego perched on a rock at the lake's edge, the alien sun sinking below the horizon. Orange light scattered across the water in copper reflections, painting everything in dusky purples. Emily's drones circled overhead, their antigrav units creating that high-pitched whine that never sounded right in Haven's atmosphere.

Sarah directed volunteers as they placed Echo Blooms around the gathering. The bioluminescent flowers cast a gentle glow in the fading light, their faint cinnamon scent cutting through the fresh smell of Haven's clean air.

His gaze fixed on the flowers. The muscle along his jaw bunched. Luna would never see another sunset. James would never retrofit another piece of Earth tech. Chloe Wilkins wouldn't save another goddamn life.

Water hit the shore in that too-quick rhythm that still felt wrong after months here. Diego had stood through memorials on three continents and two wars, but this wasn't the same. These weren't soldiers who'd signed the same dotted line. These were civilians. Science team. Support staff. On his watch.

"Should've triple-checked those fucking seismic readings," Diego muttered. His fingers found the stone's rough edge, pressing until the burn in his tendons was sharp, real. Better than the hollow ache in his gut.

He scanned the faces huddled in the alien twilight. One hundred and eighty. A miracle they'd saved so many. A fucking tragedy, it was all that was left of humanity.

Across the gathering, Mateo giggled as he chased Isabella between groups of colonists. The sound jolted through Diego's chest, sudden and brutal. His breath caught, held. The kids sounded exactly like Maria at that age, racing around his legs after deployment. Luna would've enjoyed watching the kids play. James would've been rewiring Emily's drone lights for efficiency while bitching about power draw.

Another mission, another cluster of graves. Was he leading these people down the same road to oblivion that Earth faced?

Behind him, Sarah arranged photographs, each placement deliberate. Photo corners aligned. Equal spacing maintained. Her hands moved without hesitation as she positioned Luna's photo. Jack tinkered with memorial banners, his mechanical leg making that rhythmic click-whir, while Emily secured the display against Haven's unpredictable winds.

Gravel scuffed nearby. Olivia dropped onto the rock beside him, shoulder pressed against his. The contact anchored him.

"Luna spent three days arguing with me about load distribution specs for the north valley grid," Olivia said. The words came out rougher than usual, catching on something. "She'd already mapped integration points for quantum storage utilizing Haven's crystal matrices." She squeezed his arm. "We need to finish what she started."

Diego swallowed. There was nothing to swallow. Just a dry, tight knot of muscle where his voice used to be. "I keep getting people killed. Luna. James. Chloe." He couldn't push out more words.

"We'll honor them by building what they came here to create," Olivia said firmly. "Together."

The night air cooled rapidly, carrying that weird electrical smell preceding Haven's magnetic storms. Diego laced his fingers through Olivia's.

"We'll make it count," he said. "For them. For us."

Manuel approached the memorial path, each step measured with tactical precision. Eyes scanning perimeters, body positioned between threats and his children. Isabella arranged glowing blooms in patterns while Mateo rearranged colors into geometric shapes resembling circuit diagrams.

"Luna said Mateo had an engineer's brain," Olivia murmured. "Said he processed spatial relationships like someone three times his age."

Jack limped over with more Echo Blooms. "Remember when Luna hacked my leg's neural interface? Rewired it to play 'Another One Bites the Dust' whenever I walked past med bay." His laugh sounded genuine. "Took me half a day to figure out she'd piggybacked the signal through my diagnostic port."

A voice cut through the murmurs, and Emily stepped forward from the engineering group, a sad smile on her face. "Worse than what she did to my security drones. Programmed them to dance to 'Stayin' Alive' during Johnson's briefing. She had targeting sensors synchronized with the bass line."

Quiet chuckles moved through the crowd like an electric current.

Diego remembered Luna's fierce grin when she'd cracked the colony's communication problems. Forty hours hunched over equipment, surviving on caffeine tabs and protein bars, until she'd recalibrated their systems to compensate for Haven's electromagnetic field. "Frequency doesn't matter," she'd told him, eyes bloodshot but triumphant. "It's the pattern disruption that's key."

By the water, Maria and Manuel gathered more blooms. Maria handled the alien plants with a biologist's care, showing Manuel exactly how much pressure the stalks could withstand before their bioluminescence faltered. They worked in silence, sharing loss that drew them closer.

Mei Choi coordinated the agricultural team, creating memorial wreaths that combined Earth's circular patterns with Haven's asymmetrical aesthetics. Their designs looked disjointed but revealed complex patterns from different angles, much like Haven itself.

Diego squeezed Olivia's hand before standing. His boots crunched against shore rock as he moved to the center of their memorial circle. The colonists quieted.

Professor Whiskers wound between Diego's ankles, the orange tabby's one good ear twitching as he settled beside Luna's memorial photo, a living remnant of her final act of preservation.

"Luna told Mateo something last week about code," Diego said. The words scraped out of him, rough and uneven. "Said every line matters, even after it's overwritten. What we say about Luna, James, and Chloe tonight becomes part of Haven's foundational history."

Sarah stepped forward, arms crossed tightly. "James retrofitted my sister's medical scanners before evacuation. Said practical skills transfer between worlds." Her composure fractured. The words came out rough, jagged. "Those updates saved people when the tsunami hit Crucible."

"Luna hacked my prosthetic's neural interface," Jack said, tapping his leg. "Said my cursing needed musical accompaniment." The laughter that followed was raw but genuine.

With every story, the group drew closer, collective memory creating connections stronger than grief alone.

Diego watched Manuel place a protective hand on Mateo's shoulder. The gesture was automatic. Familiar. The weight of command pressed against his ribs, familiar and unwelcome.

Stay functional, Martinez.

Wilkins' voice. Sharp. Clear. Cutting through the memory fog like it had that day in the Admiral's office. The brass fixtures. The smell of gun oil. The weight of Elena's loss crushing his chest.

Diego blinked hard, forcing himself back to Haven's purple twilight. This wasn't Elena's memorial. This was here. Now. His people.

Diego looked at Jack. The man was in pain, his leg's servo whining with each adjustment. But he kept working. Arranging lights. Telling stories. Using the hurt to honor the dead.

Emily's fingers never stopped moving across her control pad. Tears tracked down her face, but the security sweep continued. Grief and duty running parallel tracks.

Sarah, who'd buried more people than anyone should have to, methodically preserved memories while building protocols to protect the living. She'd lost her sister months before Earth's collapse, but she was still here. Still fighting.

Pain. Everyone here felt it. But they weren't just feeling it. They were using it. Jack wasn't ignoring his mechanical leg's discomfort, he was standing on it anyway. Emily wasn't setting aside her tears, she was crying while she worked. Sarah wasn't forgetting her losses, she was turning them into shields for others.

Something shifted in his chest. Not the hollow ache, but something harder. More focused.

"I see something," he said, his voice steadying. "Look around. Really look."

The colonists turned to each other, confused.

"Jack's prosthetic is giving him hell, but he's still here, making sure we remember Luna properly. Emily's running security protocols while she grieves. Sarah's planning protection for families she's never met." Diego's gaze swept the circle. "You're not setting the pain aside. You're putting it to work."

The crowd fell silent except for the alien rhythm of waves and the distant whine of drones.

"The people we lost, they're still on the team. Luna's quantum theories. James's practical solutions. Chloe's determination to save lives." Diego looked at Mateo, then Isabella. Two kids who would grow up in this strange new world. "We carry their work forward. Not in spite of losing them. Because we lost them."

Manuel nodded once. A soldier's understanding.

"Our strength isn't about forgetting the pain," Diego continued. "It's about making the pain count for something. Building Haven into the place they would've wanted to see."

Professor Whiskers mewed once, as if agreeing, then settled more firmly against Luna's photo.

The memorial continued as Haven's stars emerged overhead, but something had shifted. The grief remained, but it had found a purpose. The colonists shared more stories, made more plans, wove the memory of the dead into the fabric of the living.

Diego stood with his people, watching them transform loss into determination. No borrowed wisdom. No echoes of past conversations. Just what he could see with his own eyes, in this moment, on this alien shore.

They would make it count.

LETTING GO

It had been three days since the memorial. Thomas hadn't left his quarters. Meals sat untouched outside his door, growing cold like everything else in his world. He recognized that hollow stare from his own mirrors after Elena. The man was drowning in plain sight. Time to throw him a rope, whether he wanted it or not.

Diego found Olivia hunched over her workstation, data streams cascading around her like digital rain. Haven's settlement sprawled beyond the window, morning light catching the metal frames of half-finished buildings. Kids chased each other between the water purifiers while their parents hauled supplies, voices carrying through the recycled air. The sound of people building something that might last.

Olivia glanced up as he entered, dark circles shadowing her eyes. "Thomas should be here soon. I pulled together those apprentice files you wanted." She gestured at the floating displays. "We're down to thirty-seven candidates. Lost another machinist yesterday, complete burnout."

Diego eased into the chair, his knee grinding like old machinery that needed oil it would never get. Real coffee waited on the desk, steam curling upward. One of their few luxuries, rationed like everything else that mattered. "How many specialists can we afford to lose?"

Heavy footsteps echoed in the corridor, but slower than usual, like someone carrying invisible weight. Thomas appeared in the doorway, uniform wrinkled, sleeves twisted at odd angles. The man looked like he'd been sleeping in his clothes, if he'd been sleeping at all. His eyes were bloodshot, unfocused.

"Admiral."

"Just Thomas." His voice came out rough, hoarse. "No navy left."

Olivia nodded toward an empty chair. Thomas sat heavily, hands folded in his lap, staring at them like they belonged to someone else. He blinked slowly, as if trying to remember where he was.

Diego had pushed grieving soldiers before. Sometimes they needed the shove. Sometimes it broke them worse. But Haven couldn't afford to lose Thomas now, not when they were hanging by threads already.

"We need your help with the apprentice program. Kids with potential but no direction. Medical staff burning out because they're working sixteen-hour shifts. Engineers making mistakes because they haven't slept in a week."

Thomas lifted his head slowly. "What exactly..." He paused, rubbed his forehead. Stared at his hands for several seconds. "What are you asking me to do?"

"Training program. Real one, not committee bullshit." Diego leaned forward. "Thirty-seven candidates between fourteen and twenty-two. Medicine, engineering, agriculture. They need someone who knows how to build leaders."

Thomas reached for his notebook, leather worn smooth from years of handling. His fingers traced the cover for a moment, trembling slightly, before opening it. The pen moved across the page in careful strokes. Stopped. Started again. The lines wavered.

Olivia moved closer. "When we lose a specialist here, decades of knowledge dies with them. We're one accident, one heart attack, one critical mistake away from skill gaps we can't fill." She gestured at the holographic displays floating between them, casting prismatic light across Thomas's notebook. "This isn't about buildings or equipment. It's about preserving what we know before it disappears forever."

Thomas's spine straightened, vertebra by vertebra. His gaze lifted from his hands to meet Diego's. The pen dropped from his fingers, clattered on the desk.

"The future depends on passing on knowledge," Diego continued. "From crop rotation techniques to surgical procedures to reactor maintenance protocols. Someone needs to coordinate between departments, make sure these kids actually learn what they need to survive out here."

"Your experience with officer training," Olivia said. "That structure, that systematic approach. That's exactly what we need."

Diego's thumb found the scar on his palm. Those endless meetings where nothing got decided while people died waiting. Promotions based on connections instead of competence. Good soldiers passed over while some admiral's useless nephew got fast-tracked to command positions that got better men killed. "We keep the discipline, the standards that actually matter. But the political horseshit ends here."

Thomas picked up his pen again. His hand shook as he gripped it. "I led a combat drop on Titan where the only thing that kept us from getting wiped out was chain of command. When comms go down, protocol is all you have, Martinez."

Diego's voice went flat. "Jakarta flooded while APU commanders followed evacuation protocols that led straight into deeper water. Clear alternate paths available, but standing orders prevented adaptation."

Thomas's pen stopped moving. He set it down carefully, precisely. "I've seen entire units dissolve into chaos because some hotshot decided to 'adapt' on his own. We lost twelve good people in the orbital riots because of that kind of thinking."

Diego had seen communities tear themselves apart over leadership disputes and resource allocation arguments. Watched good people die because nobody could agree on who was in charge when decisions mattered. "I've seen what happens when nobody's in charge too."

"The APU separated families with algorithms," Diego said. "Parents classified non-essential, kids sent to state facilities. All for maximum efficiency." He met Thomas's gaze, held it. "Here, families train together. The engineer's daughter learns medicine. The farmer's son studies mechanics."

Thomas picked up his pen again, tapped it against the notebook in steady rhythm. His next words came out clear, without the hoarseness from before. "A community that can defend itself. One that knows how to build, heal, and survive whatever comes next." He looked back at the holographic displays. "What's the timeline?"

"First group starts next week," Olivia said, highlighting training schedules with quick gestures. "Fifteen apprentices, hands-on work in the fab bay and medical center."

Thomas nodded. His pen started moving again, faster now. The shaky lines from moments before gave way to firm, controlled script. "I'll need complete personnel files. Current training protocols and resource limitations." He paused, stared at the page. "What was I saying?"

"Personnel files," Olivia prompted gently.

"Right." Thomas shook his head, refocused. "Already compiled." Olivia transferred the files to Thomas's tablet. "Luna had everything organized before..." Her voice trailed off.

Thomas's expression softened for a moment. "She did good work."

Diego watched Thomas scroll through the information. The man was asking questions now, making notes. But his movements were still unsteady, like someone operating on muscle memory alone.

"Thomas." Diego moved closer. "We're not building a military here."

Thomas looked up from the files, pen poised over his notebook. "Structure is what keeps people alive in crises. Without clear authority and defined responsibilities, you get chaos."

"And bureaucracy killed people too." Diego thought of Jakarta again, of authorized evacuation routes that led straight into deeper water while safer paths remained blocked by red tape and rigid thinking. "Systems that couldn't adapt just broke when the world changed faster than protocols could keep up."

Thomas was quiet for a long moment, pen tapping against paper in steady rhythm. Outside the window, children's laughter echoed off the settlement walls.

"Balance," he said finally. "Structure with flexibility. Training with judgment calls." He straightened in his chair. "What resources do I have?"

Olivia smiled for the first time since Diego had entered the room. "Whatever you need. This is priority one."

Thomas flipped to a fresh page in his notebook. Started to write, then stopped. Rubbed his eyes. Started again. "Department head interviews first. Individual skills assessments for all candidates. Then we design practical training scenarios based on real problems." His pen moved across the paper, steady now. "They need to learn to think, not just follow procedures."

"The outlying homesteads too," Olivia added. "Some families have been establishing farms further out, beyond the main settlement."

Diego rubbed his jaw, stubble scratching against his palm like sandpaper. The thought of reconnecting with Earth still twisted his stomach. Hope and terror in equal measure.

"What about contact protocols?" Thomas asked, not looking up from his notes. "If we reestablish communication with Earth?"

Diego paused. Everyone they'd left behind. Everyone still fighting over scraps while Haven grew stronger. "We focus on Haven first. Get our people settled, our systems stable, our community secure." He met Olivia's gaze, caught the flicker of disappointment there. "Can't save anyone else if we don't survive ourselves."

Olivia nodded reluctantly. "Which means we need to do this right the first time."

Thomas stood abruptly, walked to the window. Below, a group of children had organized some kind of game around the water purifiers, their shouts mixing with the steady hum of machinery. Adults moved between the buildings with purpose, carrying tools and materials.

He stayed there for a long moment, hands clasped behind his back. His shoulders went rigid. When he spoke, his voice came out quiet, raw.

"What's the goddamn point?" His voice caught. He took a shuddering breath. "The one person who made any of this matter is gone. Everything we built, everything we..." He stopped. His hands dropped to his sides.

Diego started to respond, but Thomas held up a hand, still staring out the window. A child's bright laugh carried up from below. Thomas flinched like he'd been struck.

"But Chloe would have been first in line to help build something better. She always said I cared more about protocols than people, about following rules instead of doing what's right." He turned back to them. His face was composed again, but his hands shook slightly. "Maybe it's time to prove her right about something."

Diego gripped Thomas's shoulder. "Your experience, your standards, but with room to build something better than what we left behind."

Thomas nodded slowly, returning to his chair and notebook. When he picked up his pen again, his handwriting was steady. "When do we start?"

Diego sat on a weathered boulder, scanning the valley where Haven's grasses swayed in the breeze, three weeks since the portal's collapse. Below, the growing community buzzed with activity. The familiar routine of threat assessment kept his mind occupied, away from the ghosts that crowded the quiet moments.

The mountain wind whipped his jacket. He inhaled Haven's sweet, spicy scent, tasting mineral richness that Earth's dust-choked air had forgotten. His fingers scraped against rough stone, cataloging wind direction and thermal patterns while his knee twinged from old shrapnel. Small actions. Measurable data. Things he could control.

Movement in the valley perimeter. His muscles tensed. Just springers. Two adults, one juvenile. Movement patterns indicated play, not distress. Their wing membranes caught

Haven's amber light as they glided between rock outcroppings. Elena would have loved watching them, would have sketched their flight patterns in that worn journal of hers. The thought hit sideways, sharp and sudden.

The valley stretched before him, tall blades transforming the hillside. No longer strange. Home. The word still felt foreign in his mouth.

A flock of diamond-winged creatures rode thermal currents overhead. Emily called them "kites." Their aerial dance reminded him of hawks circling his childhood home in Mexico City, before water wars turned the sky toxic. These creatures moved with purpose, understanding something his people were still learning.

The sensor array pinged softly: scans complete. Mineral deposits, enough for decades of settlement needs. Luna's work, still keeping them safe. Her ghost in the machine, calculating threat matrices with the same cynical precision she'd brought to everything else. But his attention kept returning to the valley's edges, scanning for threats that weren't there.

Gravel crunched behind him. The cadence was instantly familiar.

"Let me guess, tactical assessment of the local flora?" Olivia settled beside him on the boulder. Glass clinked as she pulled out a squat bottle and two sturdy cups. "Kaito's private reserve." Her eyes held mischief, but something deeper lurked underneath. Recognition.

"Liberated?" The corner of Diego's mouth twitched upward. "That's what we're calling theft these days?"

"Tactically acquired." She poured rich red wine into both cups. The liquid caught Haven's sunlight like blood. "Actually, he left it with a note about celebrating strategic victories. Though I suspect he just wanted to avoid Jack asking about his fancy booze."

Diego accepted the cup, arching a single eyebrow at her in playful judgment. Their fingers brushed. "Maria's gotten good at that look," he said, his jaw tightening slightly, the muscles working beneath his scar. "Reminds me of her mother."

"Speaking of looks." Olivia's voice carried gentle concern beneath the teasing. "You're running diagnostics on the horizon again. Jack swears you practice it in mirrors. Says it's more intimidating than his arc welder."

"I do not brood." Diego fought for dignity through his chuckle. "I assess. Strategize. Two completely different things."

"And I suppose you just happened to pick the highest, most scenic spot for your 'strategic assessment'?"

"Routine perimeter sweep." His shoulders relaxed despite himself. She read him too well.

Wine slid across his tongue, complex and rich. "Jack cornered me this morning, grinning about the crystal formations. Says we can expand the arrays by thirty percent within two months. Power increase means sensor range to the eastern ridge. Those cat things came from that direction last time. Early warning could give us three, maybe four minutes."

"The increased power output makes the hydroponics facility viable. We could achieve true food security." Olivia leaned forward, her voice gaining momentum. "Mei's already mapping cultivation zones."

"The children would appreciate that. Isabella's been asking for tomatoes, though she seems more interested in those luminescent fruits Mei discovered."

"She's not the only one. The whole Bio Ag team is fascinated by their properties." Olivia shifted closer, her shoulder brushing against his. "I've been running development projections. The biodiversity here exceeds our Earth databases by forty percent. In twenty years, we could have a civilization that works in harmony with its environment."

Diego nodded. Haven's sunlight danced across her features, highlighting the fine lines around her eyes. Lines earned through years of focus, of carrying impossible burdens. "We're not just surviving anymore. Isabella's asking when she can plant a garden."

Olivia's expression softened, her eyes growing distant with possibilities. The unspoken realization hung between them. Not survival. Home.

Isabella's future. Mateo growing up in a world with clean air and abundant resources. The fierce need to protect them had expanded, encompassing more than just family now.

"And I wouldn't want to build this with anyone else," he said, the words surprising him with their honesty.

Olivia studied him, something vulnerable shifting across her features. "Even when I steal Kaito's wine?"

The weight of it all felt different now. No longer the crushing burden of abstract duty, but the solid anchor of specific faces: Maria, the kids, Olivia. Promises etched into his bones, worth every sacrifice they'd made to claw their way here.

"Especially then." Diego's hand started toward hers, hesitated for a heartbeat, then committed. His thumb traced patterns across her knuckles. "Three weeks ago, all I knew was the objective. Survive. Secure. Report." He paused, his voice roughening. "I don't know the protocol for... quiet."

Olivia's fingers trembled slightly against his. "After Aiden died, I found refuge in research. Data was a fortress. Numbers don't grieve." She swallowed hard, meeting his gaze. "I never expected to find someone who understands that particular kind of armor."

Diego shifted on the boulder, turning to face her fully. The familiar scent of Earth-made shampoo now mingled with Haven's flowers. "Every time I look at what we've built here, I see your work, your courage." His hand trembled as he brushed a strand of hair from her face, the gesture carrying the weight of a man unused to gentleness. "Your refusal to let us just survive when we could thrive."

Olivia leaned into his touch, holding his gaze. Her eyes, wide and searching, mirrored his own careful hope.

Her hand, warm and calloused from lab work, anchored him. This emotional terrain was far more dangerous than any battlefield he'd ever faced. His pulse hammered against his ribs, a frantic cadence he hadn't felt since his twenty-fourth birthday, since before the wars taught him that hope was a luxury.

As dusk approached, Diego stood, automatically scanning the darkening tree line. His right knee protested with a sharp jolt. Twilight softened edges, blurred outlines, transformed every shadow into a potential threat. He offered his hand to Olivia, feeling her familiar warmth as she rose beside him.

Gravel crunched beneath their boots as they descended toward the settlement, hands linked. The setting sun painted the valley in deep purples and blues. At a bend, Diego paused, glancing back at the lake. Its surface rippled, native fish breaching, sending rings across the water.

Below them, the settlement glowed with purpose: the soft blue light from Mei's hydroponics bay, the section of land Maria had marked for Isabella's school garden, the steady hum of Jack's expanded power array. Their contributions. Their future.

The weight of it all felt different now. No longer the crushing burden of abstract duty, but the solid anchor of specific faces: Maria, the kids, Olivia. Promises etched into his bones, worth every sacrifice they'd made to claw their way here.

Diego's tablet buzzed against his hip. Thomas would be at tomorrow's briefing, no doubt bringing new complications. But for now, under Haven's first stars, Olivia at his side, the future wasn't just possible. It was tangible, breathing, alive in the woman whose hand fit perfectly in his.

EPILOGUE

Diego sank into the weathered porch chair. Six years on Haven, and the creak still marked each evening. His knee throbbed, warning him the temperature would drop soon. Old shrapnel. Never stopped complaining.

Isabella sat cross-legged on the porch steps, braiding native fibers. Some collection she kept. Purple strands that smelled like cinnamon and copper. Her dark eyes found his face. That look. Pure Maria. Pure Elena before her.

"You really shut down the gateway?" Isabella's voice went quiet. Hair fell forward as she dropped the braids. "Even with Luna still on Earth?"

Diego's chest went hollow. The shriek of twisting metal. The smell of ozone. Luna's the final look, "I understand, Diego," played in his skull. No accusation, no plea. Just acceptance.

"Some choices stay with you," he finally managed. "Some ghosts never leave."

Professor Whiskers leapt silently onto Diego's lap, the cat's amber eyes holding his gaze for a long moment before settling into a familiar circle. Diego's fingers found the soft spot behind the cat's ears, earning a deep rumble of approval. The purr vibrated against his thigh.

Nearby, Mateo crouched at the shoreline, examining rocks with his digital tablet beside him. His systematic approach to categorizing minerals had become his latest obsession. When he finally selected a stone and threw it, bioluminescent fish scattered beneath the surface, their blue-green light fragmenting like underwater stars.

"Fourteen skips!" Mateo called out, documenting the result on his tablet. "That's a new record." His eyes widened as he remembered their conversation. "But why did they let computers pick who got saved? That's stupid."

He dropped onto the bottom step, still focused on his tablet. "My teacher said her uncle's family got rejected because they scored too low. But her uncle fixed machines with like, nothing. How's that not important?"

Isabella gave her brother a patient look. "It wasn't that simple, Mateo."

"But it is simple," Mateo insisted, gesturing with his stylus. "People aren't numbers. You can't just add them up."

The screen door whined open behind them. He didn't turn but smiled. Olivia's steady tread on the planks was as familiar as his own.

"And most of it actually happened," Olivia said, catching Isabella's eye with a gentle smile. She perched on the wide arm of Diego's chair.

Diego feigned offense, hand clapped to his chest. "Every word was accurate, Dr. Smith." He gave Isabella his most serious expression. "Military precision."

Isabella and Mateo exchanged amused glances. Olivia's laugh joined theirs, bright and clear against the evening air.

"Don't encourage him," Olivia said to them, her eyes dancing. "Your grandfather has been embellishing stories since before we met."

"Not embellishing," Diego corrected, catching her hand. He pressed a quick kiss to her palm. "Strategically enhancing."

Professor Whiskers stretched across his lap, a languid, unimpressed weight. The cat had survived the journey between worlds with a soldier's stoicism. Luna's cat. The one small piece of her he'd managed to save.

Isabella straightened from her spot on the steps and moved to the porch railing. She drummed her fingers against the wood in a rhythm Diego recognized. Maria used the same unconscious pattern when thinking deeply.

"But those exodus ships," Isabella began, her voice careful but determined. "The way you described them, they really separated families because a computer decided someone wasn't worth saving?"

Diego exchanged a glance with Olivia. They'd agreed the children needed to understand Earth's collapse, but moments like this still cut deep.

Olivia spoke first, leaning forward, her hands clasping and unclasping.

"I remember working with a system that was supposed to distribute water fairly during the first shortages," she said, voice dropping lower. "We thought we were helping, creating something fair and logical. But I watched my colleague's neighborhood get their rations cut in half while mine stayed the same." She shook her head, eyes distant. "When I questioned it, they showed me calculations I couldn't argue with, numbers that somehow made sense on paper but felt wrong."

Diego's hand stilled on Professor Whiskers' fur. The ache in his knee sharpened, a phantom echo of kneeling in the dust beside Kaito's father. "I saw it happening in Osaka, back in '61. Water rationing systems that suddenly favored certain neighborhoods. Made sense, at first. Until they locked down water access panels in poor districts without warning. Mothers scanning identity cards while their children cried from thirst."

The taste of tear gas. The weight of a child's body against his chest.

"Soon every decision got filtered through the systems. Who deserved medicine, who deserved education slots, who deserved passage on the exodus ships." The words came out harder than he'd intended. "Your efficiency rating, that's what mattered. Water rations. Whether your family stayed together during evacuations. All of it, reduced to a number."

And Luna chose to stay. Luna's face on the facility monitors as the tsunami approached. She could have evacuated with the others, but someone had to keep the gateway stable for the final transfers. Her last words, through static: "The cat, Diego. Don't forget the fucking cat."

Then her laugh, sudden and bright even in that moment. "Sorry, language. But seriously, save Professor Whiskers. He's smarter than most of the people you're evacuating anyway."

"Abuelo?" Isabella's voice cut through the memory of static and rushing water. "You're making that face again. The one Mom says means you're thinking about the before times."

Diego blinked, the porch coming back into focus. He found Isabella watching him, her dark eyes studying his face. Professor Whiskers headbutted his hand gently, demanding the attention that had momentarily lapsed.

"Your mother knows me too well," he admitted. Something in Isabella's expression, that stubborn tilt of her chin, so much like Maria, made his chest tighten. He stood abruptly, needing to move, and pulled her into a hug.

He pulled her into a gentle hug, dislodging the cat who gave an indignant meow before settling on the vacant chair. Isabella went rigid with surprise, a teenager unused to this sudden, overt affection from her stoic grandfather, before she melted into the embrace. She smelled of the botanical lab where she'd been volunteering and the native flowers she'd been studying. His arms tightened briefly around her shoulders, recognizing the newly angular frame that reminded him she was no longer a little girl.

"And you're just like your mother," he murmured against her hair. "Too smart for your own good."

When he released her, Isabella stared up at him, mouth slightly open. She blinked rapidly before a small smile tugged at her lips.

"Think that's enough history for one night," he said. "You both have early starts tomorrow."

"Fine," Isabella conceded with a small smile. "But I expect the full account of the first exploration team tomorrow. The historical archive needs accurate firsthand accounts." She nodded to Mateo. "Come on, geology wizard. Don't you have a presentation to finish for tomorrow?"

Mateo clutched his tablet to his chest. "But I just need a few more specimens."

"You can collect them tomorrow," she promised. "I'll help you organize your data before breakfast."

"You will?" Mateo asked, his resistance fading. "Could you help me with those graphs? The ones you showed me last week made the temperature stuff way clearer."

Their footsteps clattered across the porch and through the screen door, leaving a sudden quiet behind them. Professor Whiskers immediately reclaimed Diego's lap as he sat back down, turning three precise circles before settling with a contented rumble.

Olivia shifted from the arm of the chair onto the wide seat beside Diego, her weight warm against his side. One hand came to rest on her rounded belly, the curve still a wonder to him after all they'd been through.

"You're doing it, you know," she said softly. "What you promised Maria when we first arrived. Creating a world where her children could live without fear of being assigned a value by an algorithm."

Diego covered her hand with his own. "We're doing it," he corrected.

They'd been married four years now, a partnership built in the desperate final days on Earth and strengthened through Haven's early struggles. Her brilliant mind and his tactical experience had kept their small colony alive through those first precarious years.

Olivia guided his hand to where their baby drummed a steady rhythm beneath her skin. The tiny foot or elbow pushed against Diego's palm through the fabric of her shirt.

"I never thought I'd have this," she whispered, eyes wide with wonder as another forceful kick pulsed against his fingers.

"A second chance," he agreed, spreading his fingers to cover more of the rounded curve. Their child, already strong and active, would join Haven's first generation of native-born citizens.

"Not just for humanity," Olivia clarified, turning to face him fully. Her blue eyes held his. "For myself. A family. A home that isn't defined by efficiency metrics or resource allocation algorithms." Her voice caught. "A child who will never know what it means to be assigned a value."

Her words landed, and for a second, all the air left his lungs. He had to look away, his gaze falling from her eyes to the gentle curve of her stomach. This new life, weighed against the millions tallied and discarded.

"Our child will know what matters," Diego promised, his palm still resting against her belly. "How to value what can't be measured."

Professor Whiskers stretched across both their laps, paws kneading against Diego's thigh while his orange fur caught the last rays of sunlight. The cat's purr rumbled against Olivia's rounded belly, a sound that seemed to calm the restless movements beneath her skin. His amber eyes, half-closed in contentment, reflected the alien sunset streaming through their window.

The battle-scarred tabby had claimed this exact spot every evening since their arrival in Haven, as if establishing some vital territorial boundary between past and present. His missing ear twitched at distant sounds only he could hear, while his remaining whiskers tested the air for scents that belonged to neither Earth nor this new world, but to the spaces between.

The sun finally slipped below the horizon, painting the sky with vibrant purples and deep oranges unlike any sunset on Earth. As twilight settled, two moons traced paths across the sky, a sight so alien yet so familiar it still stole the air from his lungs.

Bioluminescent fish began their nightly dance beneath the water's surface, their lights growing brighter as darkness fell. In the distance, Haven's small settlement glowed with warm light, windows illuminated not by AI-optimized power grids but by simple solar cells that residents installed themselves in community work parties.

Diego's hand found Olivia's. Darkness settled across their new world. The memories were still there, would always be there. Luna's sacrifice. Earth's final desperate days. The millions left behind.

Professor Whiskers rose, stretched in an elaborate arch, and dropped silently from their laps. The cat paused to look back at them, silhouetted against the last light of day, before padding silently into the house, a small ghost moving between worlds, carrying its own quiet memories.

Whatever challenges might come, they'd face them as humans always had, making their own choices: messy, imperfect, and real.

About the Author

Heath A. Barker is an author who bridges the worlds of logic and heart. For thirty years, his professional life was dedicated to the precision of systems, security, and technology, where he managed the networks and defended the data of the digital age. This world of calculated planning was irrevocably changed in 2017 by the profound loss of his wife to cancer.

In the aftermath, he found an unexpected refuge in writing, first through the healing power of poetry and later in building entire fictional worlds. This journey through grief ultimately led him to find love again, and he is now married to a wonderful partner who serves as his biggest cheerleader, bravely reading through the messiest of first drafts.

Drawing from his unique background, his stories are deeply infused with the themes that drive him: the unbreakable bonds of family, the challenges of leadership, and the critical question of what it means to be human in a world increasingly dominated by technology. As a father to two daughters and three sons, these are more than just fictional concepts, they are the legacy he contemplates daily.

He is currently developing several long-form fiction projects, including the three-book dystopian military sci-fi series, *Fleeing Oblivion: A Journey to Haven*; a cyberpunk romantic thriller; and a new venture into Romantasy and Urban Fantasy. Heath lives in Bullhead City, Arizona with his wife and family.

Acknowledgements

To **Amber**, my steadfast companion through countless drafts and revisions. Your willingness to read the same passages as they transformed beneath my struggling pen showed me what unconditional support truly means. This book exists because you believed it could, even when I didn't.

To **Erik and Gary** without whom I would have found another squirrel to chase! Your encouragement and accountability kept me on track when I needed it most.

To **Hylie**, whose honest feedback and sharp eye helped me see the forest for the trees. You asked the hard questions that made this story stronger, clearer, and truer. Thank you for not letting me take the easy way out.

To **Cassi at Draft Doctor Editing**, for bravely wading into this beast of a manuscript and helping me find the story within. Your keen eye and insightful guidance turned a tangled narrative into something I am proud to share.

Cover and Artwork by **D'Arte Oriel**, the incredible artist behind the cover. You created the perfect gateway into this story, giving it a visual identity that is as powerful as the words inside. Thank you for sharing your immense talent with me.

Edge design by **Painted Wings Publishing** For holding my hand and guiding me thorugh the Edge artwork process. What you do is so freaking awesome!

Portal Founder

To my sister **Cherie**, whose success as an author has been both inspiration and guiding light. Your words gave me courage to place mine on the page, even after doubt made me want to delete everything I'd written.

To **Josh,** I am so humbled by your creative talents and your support of this project! You sir should find time and write for yourself not just for work!

www.ingramcontent.com/pod-product-compliance
Lightning Source LLC
Chambersburg PA
CBHW030636110726
47901CB00002B/466